Praise for the *New York Times* bestselling
Royal Spyness Mysteries

"Wonderful characters . . . [A] delight."
—Charlaine Harris, #1 *New York Times* bestselling author

"[A] showcase for the series' many strengths . . . Fans of
P. G. Wodehouse looking for laughs mingled with some ama-
teur sleuthing will be quite pleased."
—*Publishers Weekly* (starred review)

"The perfect fix between seasons for *Downton Abbey* addicts."
—Deborah Crombie, *New York Times* bestselling author

"A smashing romp."   —*Booklist* (starred review)

"Brilliant . . . This is so much more than a murder mystery.
It's part love story, part social commentary, part fun and
part downright terrifying. And completely riveting."
—Louise Penny, #1 *New York Times* bestselling author

"An insightful blend of old-fashioned whodunit, clever satire
and drawing-room comedy of errors . . . A feisty new heroine
to delight a legion of Anglophile readers."
—Jacqueline Winspear, *New York Times* bestselling author

"As usual, Georgie's high spirits and the author's frothy
prose are utterly captivating."   —*The Denver Post*

"As Bowen spins her yarn, she supplies plenty of suspects,
an amusing blend of British and Hollywood royalty and a
web of betrayal. The author's fans will savor every detail."
—*Richmond Times-Dispatch*

"Charming and quite smart, Georgie is a breath of fresh air."
—*Library Journal*

P9-DWO-874

Berkley Prime Crime titles by Rhys Bowen

Royal Spyness Mysteries

HER ROYAL SPYNESS
A ROYAL PAIN
ROYAL FLUSH
ROYAL BLOOD
NAUGHTY IN NICE
THE TWELVE CLUES OF CHRISTMAS
HEIRS AND GRACES
QUEEN OF HEARTS
MALICE AT THE PALACE
CROWNED AND DANGEROUS
ON HER MAJESTY'S FRIGHTFULLY SECRET SERVICE

Constable Evans Mysteries

EVANS ABOVE
EVAN HELP US
EVANLY CHOIRS
EVAN AND ELLE
EVAN CAN WAIT
EVANS TO BETSY
EVAN ONLY KNOWS
EVAN'S GATE
EVAN BLESSED

Anthologies

A ROYAL THREESOME

Specials

MASKED BALL AT BROXLEY MANOR

Crowned and Dangerous

RHYS BOWEN

BERKLEY PRIME CRIME
New York

BERKLEY PRIME CRIME
Published by Berkley
An imprint of Penguin Random House LLC
375 Hudson Street, New York, New York 10014

Copyright © 2016 by Janet Quin-Harkin
Excerpt from *On Her Majesty's Frightfully Secret Service* by Rhys Bowen
copyright © 2017 by Janet Quin-Harkin
Penguin Random House supports copyright. Copyright fuels creativity, encourages
diverse voices, promotes free speech, and creates a vibrant culture. Thank you for buying
an authorized edition of this book and for complying with copyright laws by not
reproducing, scanning, or distributing any part of it in any form without permission.
You are supporting writers and allowing Penguin Random House to continue to
publish books for every reader.

BERKLEY is a registered trademark and BERKLEY PRIME CRIME and the B colophon
are trademarks of Penguin Random House LLC.

The Edgar® name is a registered service mark of Mystery Writers of America, Inc.

ISBN: 9780425283493

Berkley Prime Crime hardcover edition / August 2016
Berkley Prime Crime mass-market edition / August 2017

Printed in the United States of America
1 3 5 7 9 10 8 6 4 2

Cover illustration by John Mattos
Cover design by Rita Frangie

*This book is dedicated to my dear friend
Barbara Peters, owner of the Poisoned Pen bookstore
in Scottsdale and champion of all things mystery.
Thank you, Barbara, for your help, encouragement,
friendship and lunches at the wine bar!*

*Thanks also to my wonderful team of agents,
Meg Ruley and Christina Hogrebe, and to Jackie Cantor
and Danielle Dill and all at Berkley and Penguin.
You are the best.*

As always, thank you to John for his brutal editing!

Chapter 1

DARKEST NIGHT, THURSDAY, NOVEMBER 29, 1934

In an Armstrong Siddeley motorcar with the Honorable Darcy O'Mara, heading northward.

No idea where we are going, but Darcy is beside me so that's all right.

I was in a motorcar, sitting beside Darcy, and we were driving northward, out of London. He had whisked me away earlier that day, after we had both attended Princess Marina's wedding to the Duke of Kent. I first thought I was being taken for a romantic dinner. Then, as we left the streets of London behind, I began to suspect it may not be a dinner we were going to but a hotel in a naughty place like Brighton. But we were heading north, not south, and I couldn't think of any naughty places to the north of London. Surely nobody goes to the industrial grime of the Midlands to be naughty? I suppose in a way I was relieved. Much as I wanted to spend the night with Darcy, and heaven knows we had waited long enough, there was also that element of worry about the consequences.

Darcy was being enigmatic, driving with a rather smug grin on his face and not answering my questions. Eventually I told myself that we were probably going to a house party somewhere in the country, given by one of his numerous friends, which would be quite an acceptable thing to do, if not as exciting as a night at a hotel in Brighton, signed in as Mr. and Mrs. Smith. But as the lights of London vanished and we were driving into complete darkness I couldn't stand it a minute longer.

"Darcy, where on earth are we going?" I demanded.

He was still staring straight ahead of him into the night. "Gretna Green," he replied.

"Gretna Green? Are you serious?" The words came out as squeaks. "But that's in Scotland. And it's where people go when—"

"When they elope to get married. Quite right."

I glanced at his profile. He still had that satisfied smile on his face. "I know you too well, Georgie," he replied. "You're altogether too respectable. You've inherited too much from your great-grandmother." (Who, in case you don't know, was Queen Victoria.) "You don't want to take that next step with me until there is a ring on your finger, and I respect that. So I aim to remedy the situation. If we drive all night then by tomorrow you will be Mrs. Darcy O'Mara and I can take you to bed with a clear conscience."

"Golly," I replied. Not exactly the most sophisticated of answers, I know, but I was taken by surprise. I found myself grinning too. Mrs. Darcy O'Mara. Not quite as lofty as Lady Georgiana Rannoch, but infinitely more satisfying. I couldn't wait to see my sister-in-law Fig's face when I returned to London and waved my ringed finger at her. The thought of Fig led me to a more practical consideration. Darcy was a young man of no fixed abode. He had an impeccable pedigree. He had grown up, like me, in a castle. He would inherit a title one day. But, also like me, he was penniless. He lived by his wits and accepted clandestine assignments he wouldn't talk about. He slept on friends' couches or looked after their

London houses while they were away on their yachts or on the Riviera. That sort of life was fine for a single man, but I could hardly share a couch at a bachelor friend's establishment, could I?

Tentatively I broached this matter. "So, Darcy, if I'm not being too inquisitive, where had you planned for us to live?"

"I hadn't," he said. "You'll go back to your brother and I'll go wherever I am offered an assignment. I'm saving any money I earn and when I have enough to establish us in a suitably proper form of residence, then we'll announce our marriage. Gretna Green is just to make sure that if anything untoward happened and you found yourself"—he paused and coughed—"in the family way, we could then wave our marriage certificate at them and all would be well and your honor would be intact."

I had to laugh at this. Actually I think I giggled, nervously, but these were such heady topics to be talking about with a man.

"So how long do you think it might take, until we can afford a place of our own?" I asked.

"Not too long, I hope." He sighed. "If only my father hadn't lost all his money and had to sell the castle and the racing stable, we could have moved into my ancestral home. You would have liked Kilhenny Castle. It's less wild and remote than Castle Rannoch. Quite civilized, in fact."

"Your father still lives in the lodge, doesn't he?"

"Yes, and he's paid to run the racing stable by the American who bought the whole shebang. He's now the hired help on an estate our family has owned for centuries. I can't go near the place. Too painful." He paused again. "Not that my father would want to see me anyway. He doesn't like me very much."

"He doesn't approve of your lifestyle?"

Darcy snorted. "He's hardly in a position not to approve, is he? I wasn't the one who sold the family heritage. No, it's simpler than that. He has never forgiven me for staying alive."

"What?" I looked up at him sharply. His mouth was set in a hard line.

"When the Spanish flu reached us in 1920 I was away at prep school in England. My mother and my two little brothers caught it and died. My school was so freezing cold and miserable that not even the flu could survive there, so I survived. My father once said, when he was in his cups, that whenever he looks at me he is reminded that my mother died and I lived."

"Hardly your fault," I said angrily.

"My father never was the most rational of men. Always had a terrible temper and always carried grudges. But let's not talk about him. We're about to embark upon an adventure and to hell with our families."

"That's right," I said, covering his hand on the steering wheel with my own. "Since they don't support us, then it's none of their business whether we get married or not."

Lights sped by us from the other direction, illuminating the interior of our car for an instant before plunging us into darkness again. I was picturing telling my family that Darcy and I had married. My brother, Binky, would be happy for me. Fig would not approve because Darcy was penniless and also a Roman Catholic and . . .

"Golly!" I said again, sitting bolt upright in my seat. Darcy turned to look at me. "I can't marry you, Darcy," I said. "I'd completely forgotten, but I'm not allowed to. I'm still in the line of succession to the throne and we're not allowed to marry a Catholic."

"I thought we agreed you could just renounce your claim to the throne and then all would be well," he said. He looked at me with a half smile on his face. "Unless, of course, you'd rather give up the chance to marry me just in case you become queen someday."

I chuckled. "Since I'm currently thirty-fifth in line it would have to be another visit of the Black Death to wipe out those between me and the throne," I said. "And who would ever want to be queen? Of course I want to marry you, but I think it has to be done officially. I have to petition the king and I believe it has to go through Parliament. So we'd better turn around and go back before we go too far."

Darcy shook his head. "I'm not turning around. We're going to Scotland and we're going to get married. We won't tell anybody, and in due course you can approach your royal kin and ask permission to marry me. Then we can have a proper wedding at a suitable church with veil and bridesmaids and nobody but us need ever know that we were married already."

"Can one do that?" I asked.

"Who is to know?"

"What if the king and queen refuse my request?"

"Why would they? And if they did, then I'd renounce my religion if it was the only way to marry you."

A lump came into my throat. "Darcy, I'd never ask you to do that. Your religion means a lot to you."

"I agree that my family did fight for it for many hundreds of years, but as I say, if it's the only way to marry you, then so be it. Becoming an Anglican wouldn't be so bad . . . just a watered-down form of being a Catholic."

I laughed now, with relief. Darcy loved me so much that he was willing to give up anything for me. I can't tell you how wonderful that felt.

WE DROVE ON. It was becoming really cold. I found a rug on the backseat and tucked it around my knees. Then it started to rain, a hard-driving sleety sort of rain that peppered the windscreen. Darcy swore under his breath as he peered closer, trying to see where we were going.

"We could find somewhere to spend the night if this is going to continue," I said. "It's no fun for you driving in these conditions."

"No, we'll keep going," he said. "It will pass."

But it didn't. One by one, signposts to the Midland cities came and went. We stopped for a meat pie and beer at a pub in the middle of nowhere. A big fire roared in the grate and I looked at it longingly as we rushed through the rain back to our motorcar.

By the time we reached Yorkshire the rain had turned to snow—a heavy wet snow that stuck to the windscreen wipers and started to pile up as it was pushed from side to side. No other traffic seemed to be crazy enough to be on the road.

"We should stop," I said. "This is becoming dangerous."

"It's a good solid motor," Darcy replied. "It should handle the conditions all right."

"I don't want to skid and find myself upside down in a ditch," I said.

We passed by roads leading to the cities of Leeds, then York, although no sign of them could be seen. We seemed to be driving through bleak hills with little sign of human habitation. We might have been in the middle of nowhere. Suddenly Darcy jammed on the brakes and I felt the rear of the motor sliding sideways. I think I screamed. Darcy fought to right us. We spun around. Headlights flashed crazily onto trees and snow. Then, miraculously, we stopped sliding. I opened my eyes to find us facing the wrong way.

Chapter 2

"What was that?" I asked, my voice horribly shaky.

"A bit of a wild ride for a moment there." Darcy sounded almost as if he'd enjoyed it.

I glared at him, fear giving way to anger. "You didn't do that on purpose, did you?"

"Of course I didn't. Do you take me for an idiot?"

"Then why did you brake suddenly like that?"

"Because there is a damned-fool lorry blocking the road ahead." Even he sounded tense now. He opened the door, letting in a freezing draft and swirling snow, then stepped out into the blizzard. I wrapped the rug more firmly around me, trying to peer out through the snow to see what was happening. Darcy had vanished into the swirling whiteness. I held my breath until he returned, looking grim.

"Well, that's that for tonight," he said. "The road ahead is blocked by snow. I asked if there was another route we could take but the chap said that if the Great North Road was blocked then the smaller roads would be hopeless. His very words were, 'If it's snowing like this down here, then a right bugger of a blizzard would be howling up on the moors.'" He sighed impatiently. "We'll have to wait until someone comes to clear it tomorrow. Or the day after. . . . The chaps there didn't seem to know much, just that we can't go any farther. So I'm afraid we'll have to take your suggestion and find a place to spend the night."

"We passed a pub a mile or so back," I said.

"Then we'll try that." Darcy scraped the coating of snow away from the windscreen, then dusted himself down before he climbed back in and carefully turned the motor around. "I hope they'll have some kind of accommodation. I don't want to have to go back too far." He slapped his palms against the steering wheel. "Oh, this is too frustrating, isn't it? Just when I thought I had planned everything perfectly. When I'd persuaded that hopeless maid of yours to pack a case for you. When I'd managed to borrow a suitable motorcar. And now this."

I laid my hand on his sleeve. "It's only a delay, Darcy. They'll have to clear this road pretty quickly, won't they? It's the main artery to Scotland and the north of England. What is a day or so more?"

He nodded. "You're right. Just a delay. We've waited three years. What's one more night?"

"I remember when you first met me you made a bet with my friend Belinda that you'd get me into bed within the week, or was it a month?" I gave him a quizzical stare.

He grinned. "I can't remember, but clearly I lost the bet and should pay up. I hadn't banked on your stern willpower and royal sense of propriety."

"And circumstances conspiring against us, as they are now," I said. "My mother could never believe we were taking so long about it."

Darcy gave a half laugh, half snort. "Well, your mother is hardly a good role model for chaste living, is she? How many times has she been married? Or not married, as the case may be?"

My mother had in fact bolted from my father, the Duke of Rannoch, when I was two, and since then had been a great many things to a great many men on six of the seven continents. Antarctica had only escaped as it was too bloody cold! At this moment I could appreciate her reasoning, as my feet had turned to blocks of ice.

※

WE STARTED RETRACING our route southward. The pub I had remembered seeing was called the Pig and Whistle. It looked inviting in a quaint countrified sort of way, but the front door was, alas, locked and no lights shone. Darcy got out, shook and rattled the front door, then came back to the motorcar in disgust, brushing the snow from his jacket.

"Stupid licensing hours," Darcy muttered as he put the motor into gear again. "Why can't we be like France and Italy and let everyone drink all night if they want to?"

"Because we don't want half the population blind drunk and unable to work, I suppose."

He snorted at this. "Do you see them all blind drunk on the Continent?"

"I suppose they grow up used to it. And they drink wine rather than beer and whiskey. Wine is supposed to be good for you. And they don't work as hard as we do. Drive past any café in France and you'll see men sitting around with glasses of wine in the middle of the morning. They just don't take life seriously."

"How come you're always so damned rational and composed?" he snapped. "Anyone would think you didn't want to elope with me." He stopped and turned sharply to look at me. "You do want to, don't you? I never actually asked you."

The question caught me by surprise. Did I want to? Wasn't I worried about what my royal relatives would say? Hadn't I looked forward to the long white dress and veil all my life? Then I looked at Darcy. Even in the darkness of the motorcar he was so handsome, and I loved him so much. "Of course I do," I said.

"You hesitated before you answered me," he replied.

"Only because I'm too cold to make my mouth move."

"I could warm it up for you," he said. He reached behind my head and drew me toward him, kissing me long and hard. "Right," he said when we broke apart a little breathlessly. "Let's find somewhere to spend the night before we both end up frozen to death."

We drove on, hoping to see at least a village close to the road. I think we must have been almost back as far as York when we finally found any sign of human habitation, at least humans who might be still awake. This was also a pub, a little off the road and by a railway crossing. The sign, swinging in the blizzardlike wind, said *The Drowning Man* and showed a hand coming out of a pond.

"Hardly encouraging," Darcy said dryly. "But at least a light is still burning and hopefully someone is still awake."

He opened the driver's side door, letting in a great flurry of snow, then wrestled the wind to close it hurriedly before running across to the pub. I peered through the snow-clad windscreen, watching him. He knocked, waited, and to my relief the door finally opened, letting out a band of light across the snow. Darcy seemed to be having a prolonged conversation during which the other person could be seen peering at me, then he marched back to the car. For a horrible moment I thought he was going to say that they had nothing available and that we'd have to drive on. But instead he came around to my door and opened it for me.

"They appear to have rooms. Hardly the most welcoming of places, from what I can see, but it's really a case of any port in a storm." He took my hand and led me through the snow to the building. I was going to say the warmth of the building, but in truth it wasn't much warmer than the motorcar had been. One naked bulb hung in a hallway and an uncarpeted stair disappeared into darkness.

"Caught in the storm, were you?" the innkeeper asked. Now that we could see her, I noticed that she was a big-boned cart horse of a woman with little darting eyes in a pudgy, heavy-jowled face.

I shot a swift glance at Darcy, praying he wouldn't make a facetious comment along the lines that we were actually heading for the Riviera and took a wrong turn.

"We were heading for Scotland but the road is closed," I said before he could answer.

"Aye. We heard that on the wireless," she said. "Reckon it will take days, don't they? So you'll be wanting a room, then?"

"We will," Darcy said.

"I've just the one room," she said. "The others are occupied. You are a married couple, I take it?" And she gave us a hard stare, trying to see a wedding ring through my gloves, I suspected.

"Of course," Darcy said briskly. "Mr. and Mrs. Chomondley-Fanshaw. That's spelled 'Featherstonehaugh,' by the way."

I fought back a desire to giggle. She was still eyeing us suspiciously. "I don't care how it's spelled," she said. "We don't go for airs and graces in this part of the country. As long as good honest folk have the brass to pay, we don't care how many hyphens they have in their names."

"Right, then," Darcy said. "If you'd be good enough to show us the room?"

She didn't budge but pointed. "Turn right at the top of the stairs and it's at the end of the hall. Number thirteen."

Then she reached into a cubby and handed us a key. "Breakfast from seven to nine in the dining room. Breakfast is extra. Oh, and if you want a bath you'll have to wait till morning. Hot water is turned off between ten and six. And the bath's extra too."

Darcy gave me a look but said nothing. "I'll take you up first then go and get the bags," he said. "Come on."

I followed him up the narrow stair. An icy draft blew down at us.

"Are there fires in the rooms?" Darcy turned back to ask the landlady, who was still standing there watching us.

"No fireplace in that room," she said.

"And I suppose a cup of hot chocolate is out of the question?" There wasn't much hope in his voice.

"Kitchen closed at eight." She turned her back and walked into the darkness of the hallway.

"We don't have to stay here," Darcy whispered to me. "There must be proper hotels in York. It's not that far now."

"It's still miles away. And we've no guarantee anyone else has a room," I said. "If all the roads northward are closed . . ." In truth I felt close to tears. It had been a long day, starting with helping to dress the bride at Kensington Palace, then the ceremony for Marina and Prince George at St. Margaret's Westminster, then the reception at Buckingham Palace and the long, cold, snowy drive. All I wanted to do was curl up into a little ball and go to sleep.

The floorboards creaked horribly as we tiptoed down the hall. Number thirteen was about the gloomiest room I had ever seen—and I had grown up in a Scottish castle noted for its gloominess. It was small, crowded with mismatched furniture and dominated by an enormous carved wardrobe that took up the one wall where the ceiling didn't slope. In the midst of this clutter was a narrow brass bed with a patchwork quilt on it. A naked bulb gave just enough anemic light to reveal sagging and stained curtains at the window and a small braided rug on the bare floor.

"Golly!" I let out the childish exclamation before I remembered that I had resolved to be sophisticated from now on. "It is pretty grim, isn't it?"

"It's bloody awful," Darcy said. "Sorry for swearing, but if ever a room deserved the word 'bloody,' this is it. Let's just get out of here while we can. I wouldn't be surprised if the landlady didn't kill off the guests during the night and make them into pies."

I started laughing at the thought. "Oh, Darcy. What are we doing here?"

"My lovely surprise," he said, shaking his head, but smiling too. "Oh well, if we start off life together in these surroundings it can only get better, can't it?"

I nodded. "Do you suppose there is an indoor loo or will it be at the bottom of the garden?"

We explored the hall and were relieved to find a lavatory and bathroom of sorts at the far end.

"I'll go and get the bags," Darcy said. "If you're really sure you want to stay."

"I'm not sure that I want to undress. I'd freeze." I reconsidered. "But I suppose I shouldn't crease my good outfit any more. Do you have any idea what Queenie packed for me?"

"I told her sensible outfits to travel in. And your nightclothes."

"Knowing Queenie, that will mean a dinner dress and riding boots."

However, when he returned with the bags I was pleasantly surprised to find that she had packed my sponge bag, a warm flannel nightdress and dressing gown, and my tweed suit. She rose considerably in my estimation. In fact I felt quite warmly toward her. She'd be asleep right now in Kensington Palace, with fires in the rooms and hot chocolate whenever one rang a bell, while her mistress . . . I looked around the room again but words failed me. Darcy had undressed rapidly and looked ridiculously rakish in maroon silk pajamas. I felt shy about undressing in front of him, then reminded myself we were about to become Mr. and Mrs.

I turned away and unbuttoned my jacket. Then I remembered the dress had hooks down the back. I reached around but clearly they were impossible. Then a voice said, "Here, let me," and he was unhooking them for me. I was horribly conscious of his hands touching my skin. He helped me out of the dress, then put his hands on my shoulders and kissed the bare back of my neck. It was an incredibly sexy gesture and on any other occasion I would have responded. But at this moment I was cold and tired and a little frightened. I turned to him and buried my head on his shoulder.

"Oh, Darcy, what are we doing here?" I asked, half laughing, half crying.

His arms came around me. "I wanted our first night together to be very different from this," he said.

"We've spent nights together before," I reminded him. "At least parts of nights."

"I meant our first real night together," he said. "You know what I meant. And we will certainly save that sort of thing for a better time. I bet that old bat will be listening for any creaks in the bedsprings."

That made me laugh. I finished undressing, put my robe on over my nightclothes, then climbed into bed. The sheets were stiff and icy.

"It's freezing," I said through chattering teeth.

Darcy tiptoed around to turn off the light, and when he climbed into bed beside me the springs did indeed give an ominous twang that set both of us giggling like schoolchildren.

"That certainly rules out hanky-panky of any sort," he said, still chuckling. He wrapped me in his arms. "Still freezing?" he asked.

"Better now," I whispered. "Much better."

Chapter 3

Friday, November 30

Snowed in somewhere in the wilds of Yorkshire, on our way to elope to Gretna Green.

Golly, life is quite exciting these days!

The next morning we were woken by creaks and footsteps in the hallway, doors slamming and the sound of a motor starting up in the yard below. I was still lying in Darcy's arms, his face a few inches from mine and his warm breath on my cheek. Darcy's eyes opened; he looked at me and smiled. "Good morning, Mrs. Chomondley-Fanshaw," he said.

"Spelled 'Featherstonehaugh,' don't forget," I reminded him. A pale and watery sun shone in through a dirty window, then a train tooted and rattled over the level crossing.

Darcy sat up, shaking out his hands. "My arm has gone to sleep," he said. "But you know what—if trains are running, maybe we can leave the car at York Station and catch a train northward."

"Oh yes, let's do that," I said. "And let's not wait here for breakfast. I bet it will be ghastly."

"Good idea. Let's just get dressed and go. At least in York there will be news about the state of the roads there, and whether trains are running."

Filled with renewed optimism we dressed hurriedly. Darcy didn't even bother to shave and the stubble made him look more roguish. "They won't believe you're Mr. Chomondley-Fanshaw at the next place, looking like that," I said, stroking the roughness of his cheek. "They'll think you're a pirate carrying me off."

"You like the thought of that, I can tell," he teased, raising an eyebrow and making me blush.

He carried the suitcases downstairs and put them in the car boot, before returning to settle up the bill.

"You'll not be wanting breakfast?" the landlady demanded. "After I've gone to the trouble of heating up the black pudding?"

"We have an appointment in Scotland," Darcy said tactfully. "We have to change our plans and see if we can catch a train from York."

"I shouldn't think so with all this snow," the woman said with obvious relish. "On the wireless they said it might all be shut down for days. Trains, roads, the lot."

On that encouraging note, we left. The motor started, to my relief, and we drove back southward until we came to the signpost to York.

"It says fourteen miles," I said, fighting back disappointment. "That's a long way."

"York is on the main train line to Scotland. Let's just hope these side roads aren't blocked. The snow doesn't seem so bad here."

We turned off the highway onto a smaller road. Darcy seemed to be right and the snow here was already melting a little in the morning sunshine.

"I hope we come to somewhere soon," he said. "I'm starving. How about you?"

"Absolutely ravenous," I agreed.

At a crossroads we found a transport café, with lorries parked outside. Darcy pulled up beside a laundry van with no complaint from me. Inside it was warm and smoky and noisy but we were treated to enormous mugs of coffee and equally large plates of bacon, eggs, sausage, fried bread, baked beans and black pudding. And I have to confess that we ate it all. We emerged in a much more cheerful mood, in time to see another van unloading the morning newspapers.

"Perhaps the paper will have up-to-date news about the state of the roads and railways," Darcy said, and he went to get one from the delivery boy. He came back to me.

Blizzard Halts Traffic on Great North Road, said the headline. He scanned on down the column. "They don't seem to know much more than we do," he grunted. "Or at least they didn't when this paper went to press. In fact, if you ask me . . ."

There was a long pause.

"If I ask you what?" I demanded. Then I saw his face.

He was staring at the front page as if he were having a vision. He had gone deathly white.

"Darcy, what's wrong?" I leaned in to see what he was looking at. The main headline and lead article were about the storm but right below that, in big black letters, a headline read, IRISH PEER ARRESTED FOR MURDER.

Darcy's hand was shaking and I held the paper with him to try to read the small print.

Thaddeus Alexander O'Mara, Sixteenth Baron Kilhenny in County Kildare, Ireland, was arrested yesterday, charged with the murder of Mr. Timothy Roach. Mr. Roach, an American from Chicago, purchased Kilhenny Castle and the adjacent horse racing stable from Lord Kilhenny several years ago. Lord Kilhenny had still acted as manager and trainer of the racing stable until a doping scandal earlier this year. Mr. Roach was found inside the library at Kilhenny Castle, having been struck violently on the head by an ancient battle club belonging to the O'Mara family.

"Oh, Darcy." The words came out as a whisper and my breath hung in the still, cold air, like smoke.

Darcy looked up at me with hopelessness in his eyes. "I must go to him right away," he said. "You're a good driver, aren't you? This car isn't hard to drive. It has preselected gears."

He saw my blank stare and added, "You only have to move the little lever on the panel, then press the accelerator. Easy. I can't take it across to Ireland. I only borrowed it from a friend for a couple of days. If you can drive it back to London, I'll take a train from York."

I hesitated, considering my limited driving experience and whether I could handle a big powerful motorcar like this. Having never owned a motorcar, my driving had been limited to the estate wagon on the grounds of Castle Rannoch or into the nearest villages, where the only traffic on the road would be an occasional Highland cow or sheep. I'd taken out our ancient Rolls a few times but usually it was the chauffeur who drove while I sat in the backseat. But I pushed these thoughts hurriedly from my mind, trying to come to terms with everything. One thought, more than others, shouted in my head and I blurted out, "Why would you go to him? You told me what he thinks of you. Would he even want to see you?"

Darcy gave a hopeless little chuckle. "Probably not. In fact almost definitely not. He'll probably tell me to go to hell, but someone has to be there for him. He's his own worst enemy, Georgie. He'll lose his temper and say stupid things he doesn't mean and alienate the jury. Someone has to stick up for him and there's nobody else."

"What about your sisters?"

"He doesn't like them any better than he does me. And besides, one is in India and they are both busy with their own families. They've little children and husbands. They just can't drop everything and rush over to Ireland. And they don't know anything about courts and legal procedure and how to investigate a crime."

I didn't want to ask whether he thought his father was

innocent. A man with a violent temper who hated his own son and who had had everything he loved taken from him might well have been tempted to commit murder.

"I've no idea how one gets from York to Holyhead and the ferry." He was already walking ahead of me back to the motorcar, talking more to himself than me. "Change in Manchester?" He turned back to me. "You'll be all right driving back to London? I don't think there should be snow on the roads south of here. I'll write down the address for you. It's Eaton Square. You know it, of course. It's just around the corner from your place. Explain what happened. . . ."

The words were just coming out of his mouth, as if he couldn't control them. I caught up with him and put a hand on his arm. "Darcy, calm down. I'll come with you."

He shook his head violently. "No. Absolutely not. I don't want you there."

I suppose he must have noticed the hurt look on my face. "You don't understand," he said hastily. "I was waiting for the right moment for you to meet my father and to tell him about us. This would be a disaster. He'd resent your being there, seeing him in a position of weakness, and he'd take an instant dislike to you. And I'm afraid he's like my namesake, Darcy in *Pride and Prejudice*: his 'good opinion once lost is lost forever.' He is famous for harboring grudges."

"How did such a disagreeable person manage to produce such a wonderful son?" I said, gazing up at him with love in my eyes.

"My mother, I suppose. She was a lovely person in all ways, inside and out. She made my father behave himself and she turned him into a better person when she was with him. And then she died. And he lost hope, I suppose, and reverted to his former crotchety self. I wish you could have met her, Georgie."

"I wish that too. But we have to accept things as they are, don't we? My father died, as did your mother, and we've both been left to fend for ourselves. But the good thing is that we have each other. I'll do what you want, Darcy. Whatever makes it easier for you. Why don't we drive together to Holyhead and I'll see you onto the ferry and then take the car back to London if that's what you want."

He touched my cheek. "You're a wonderful girl, Georgie. I'm so sorry it all went wrong and my lovely surprise didn't work out and we never got to Gretna Green. But I'll make it up to you, I promise."

"Don't worry about it. We'll get married soon, when this horrid business is all sorted out. We'll have a big fancy wedding. And we'll invite your father."

He nodded. "Yes." As if he was trying to believe it.

"So we should get going. It's a long drive to Holyhead."

"I don't want to put you through all that, Georgie. The train is much simpler and probably much faster. There is bound to be snow on the moors between Yorkshire and Lancashire and the roads could be closed there too. No, we'll drive together into York. I'll take the train and you've got a straight shot into London down the Great North Road. Knowing you are home safely will give me one less thing to worry about."

"All right. If that's what you want," I said flatly.

"I do. I really do." He opened the driver's door to the motorcar for me. "You drive. Get some practice while I'm with you." I took my place behind the wheel and tentatively drove off. The roads were empty with only a dusting of snow. We drove in silence past snowy hedgerows and dry stone walls. Sheep huddled together in snowy fields. Smoke curled up from cottage chimneys. It would have been a charming scene straight from a Christmas card if I had been able to enjoy it. Instead my stomach was clenched into a tight knot. I tried to think positive thoughts, tried to come up with something encouraging to say to Darcy, but I couldn't think of a single thing.

He, on the other hand, was trying valiantly. "Do you know the Princess Zamanska?"

I wondered if he had cracked up. "Zamanska? Never heard of her."

"Oh, I thought you might, seeing that you are practically neighbors. But now I come to think about it, your family wouldn't move in the same circles. They wouldn't approve of her lifestyle and she'd find them too staid and boring."

My nerves were at snapping point. "Why are we talking about some foreign princess?"

"Because she's the one who lent me the car. You'll like her. She's a funny old thing. Quite eccentric. Lives life on the edge. Motor racing, balloon riding, dog sledding . . . she's done it all. Number sixteen Eaton Square."

"Is there a Prince Zamanska?"

"Zamanski," he corrected. "He's male. Or rather was, until he was assassinated by angry peasants for riding his hunt over their cabbage fields. The princess had to flee for her life. Came here with little more than the clothes on her back."

"And enough money to live in Eaton Square and own an Armstrong Siddeley," I pointed out.

"Well, yes. She's not exactly starving. The prince might have had failings in many ways but he was shrewd enough to keep all his money in a Swiss bank account. His widow lives quite well."

We were coming to the outskirts of York. And then, all too soon, we arrived outside the railway station. I don't know whether it was fear or the big greasy breakfast I'd eaten, but I was now feeling positively sick. I had no idea how long it would be before I saw Darcy again. I had grown used to him flitting off to far-flung corners of the world, but this was different.

"You'll write to me or telephone me, won't you?" I said in a small voice. "You will let me know how things are going, and if there is anything I can do."

"Of course I will. Will you be staying with your brother at Rannoch House?"

"I suppose so. Now that the wedding is over I don't expect they'll want us to stay on indefinitely at the apartment in Kensington Palace, and Binky did say I was welcome to stay with them, whatever dear Fig thinks."

He took my hands in his, looking at me with concern and longing in his eyes. "Drive carefully."

"Of course I will." I gave him a smile, hoping to look more confident than I felt.

"And take care of yourself."

"You too."

We stood there looking at each other, with so many things hanging unsaid.

Then he managed a smile. "I love you, Mrs. Chomondley-Fanshaw, spelled Featherstonehaugh."

"I love you too."

He gave me a chaste little kiss, then he turned and walked away, swallowed up into the noise and bustle of York Station.

Chapter 4

FRIDAY, NOVEMBER 30

**Driving back to London alone. My poor Darcy on his
way to Ireland. I just pray things turn out all right
for all our sakes!**

My drive south went quite smoothly. The snow had vanished
by the time I drove out of Yorkshire and a wintery sun shone,
drying up wet roadway. The motorcar handled easily
enough, but I found myself gripping the steering wheel
tightly, all the tension in my body transferring itself into my
fingers. There had been a horrible mistake, I told myself.
Darcy would find out the truth quickly and his father would
be released and thank Darcy for coming to his aid and all
would be well. I said this out loud to myself over and over
as if speaking the words would make them come true. I did
not allow my thoughts to move into the realm of *what if?*

Twilight was settling over the city by the time I drove
into London. I don't think I had ever had to drive through
city traffic before. Maybe once into a town near Castle Rannoch but not even into Edinburgh, which was a good deal

more staid than London. Lights flashed in my face, horns
honked, double-decker buses pulled out in front of me. And
I had little knowledge of the roads in this northern part of
the city. So I followed the main stream of traffic and prayed.
More by luck than anything else I found myself at Baker
Street Station. This was now more familiar territory. It was
quite dark by the time I reached Oxford Street, then down
Park Lane to Knightsbridge. I finally turned into Kensington Gardens with the solid brick shape of the palace ahead
of me.

I opened the front door expecting to be greeted by
warmth and a maid rushing to take my coat and bag. Instead
I stood in a completely deserted hallway and felt a cold draft
swirling around my legs. It was reminiscent of my first arrival at Kensington Palace, when it had been equally cold
and unwelcoming. A strange feeling came over me, a sense
of unreality, that perhaps the last weeks had never happened
except in my dreams or imagination. Any minute now a
ghostly white figure would waft past me down that hallway,
just as it had when I first visited, and I would be back where
I started. I stared at the dark hallway and my heart jumped
when I really did see a figure coming down the stairs toward
me. But she was not white and ethereal. In fact she was all
too solid and she didn't float. She clomped.

"You have returned?" the figure demanded as she came
toward me. I sighed. Marina might have left but her cousin,
the dreaded Countess Irmtraut von Dinkelfingen-Hackensack,
was still in residence. The last person I wanted to see at this
moment.

She was regarding me with that critical, haughty stare.
"They tell me you have already departed."

"I only went away for a little while. Not for good," I said.

She frowned. "What was not good about it? Was it for
bad, then? Why would you go away for something bad?"

The countess's English was annoyingly literal.

"No, I meant I only intended to be away for a couple of
days, but unfortunately the road north was closed by a blizzard and I had to return."

"A blizzard? What is this?"

"A snowstorm."

She made a disparaging hmmph noise. "I do not think in England you know what a blizzard is. In Russia we have blizzards. In Germany we have blizzards. Real blizzards. Powerful blizzards."

"It was enough of a blizzard to close a major road," I said. I tried to think of a way to change the subject. "So how long will you be staying?"

"I had intended to remain a few more days in England to visit places of culture before I departed for my parents' *Schloss* outside Berlin. But now a military man comes and tells me the apartment is to be closed up and I must leave. He is even more unpleasant than the first military man. He talks as if he is giving orders to me. And I am a countess, related to royal families. This is not right, is it?"

"Absolutely not," I agreed. I felt a sinking feeling in my stomach. "So when do we have to move out?"

"Tomorrow. He tells me he sends away the last of the servants and closes this apartment in the morning."

"Oh golly." On the drive down, I had hoped for a few days to catch my breath before I had to face Fig. Surely Darcy would telephone me with news at the palace. If he rang my brother's house then Fig was likely to instruct the butler to say that I was not there. She had done it before.

"Have most of the servants left, then?" I asked.

She nodded. "Most inconvenient. I had to ring for a maid to bring up more coal for my bedroom fire."

"And what about meals?" I had not stopped for food on the way down and was now feeling decidedly peckish.

"I send my maid to collect a tray for me. But it is cold meat and pickles for my luncheon. This is a meal for peasants, not for aristocrats." She turned to glare in the direction of the kitchen. "And do you know what they sent up for my breakfast? A kipper. Do you know this fish called a kipper? It is most disagreeable. Full of little bones. Where are the eggs and kidneys and bacon, I ask, but I am told this is what Cook prepared for me. I think they wish to drive me out by serving unpleasant food. It will be the frog in the cave for dinner, you see."

I had to smile. "You mean toad in the hole? I quite like that. It reminds me of nursery food."

"I find this place most disagreeable," she said.

"But Marina's wedding was lovely, wasn't it?" I looked back at the stairway, picturing her coming down the stairs with her sisters holding her train and fussing over her head-dress. Was that only yesterday? It felt like a lifetime away.

"Yes, it was a fine wedding," Irmtraut agreed. "But I am not sure she will be happy with this bridegroom. This English prince, there are bad stories about him, I think."

"He has sown a few wild oats, I agree," I said and instantly regretted it.

"He has been a farmer? He worked in fields?"

I tried not to laugh. "No, it's an English expression. It means he has led a wild life in some ways."

"The English language is ridiculous," she grunted. "I will never understand it."

"If you were here long enough you'd get the hang of it," I replied, again not pausing to consider my use of words.

"What would I wish to hang?" she asked. Then she sniffed. "Another stupid English expression, I suppose."

"I'm afraid so. But I think that Prince George seems genuinely fond of Marina and I hope he will try to make her happy."

Irmtraut sighed. "It is the duty of royal persons to accept their marriage, no matter how disagreeable. She will do her duty, I know." She looked up at me sharply. "But you—you will not do your duty, I think. You will try to marry this man who is a Catholic and thus forbidden to you."

"I'm only thirty-fifth in line to the throne," I said. "I hardly think it will matter to the crowned heads of Europe who I marry. But yes, I do plan to marry for love."

I don't know where this conversation would have gone but a door opened behind us and a maid came into the hall. She stopped in surprise seeing me there.

"Your ladyship." She curtsied. "We didn't expect you. We were told you had already departed and would send for your maid and your things."

"I had to return unexpectedly," I said. "I have to deliver the motorcar back to its owner but then I would like something to eat. Can you tell Cook that I would like some dinner sent up to my room when I return, please. Something warm and nourishing. I have been traveling all day."

She squirmed in embarrassment. "I'm afraid it's only leftovers, my lady. We were instructed to clean out the kitchen. They're shutting up the whole apartment, you know. There was enough stew for the countess here, but . . ."

I hesitated. I was tired. I was emotionally exhausted and I really didn't want to go out looking for food. I knew that other apartments in the palace were occupied by my royal great-aunts; in fact the Prince of Wales referred to them as the "Aunt Heap." They would undoubtedly be sitting down to good meals tonight. But I also knew that those royal ladies were hot on protocol and one did not visit uninvited.

"I'm sure Cook will do her best and find something for me when I return," I said. I was going to ask her to send for my maid to have my suitcase carried up to my room, but in the current circumstances it seemed easier to carry it myself. Heaven knew what Queenie had been up to while I had been away. Two days would have been long enough for a few disasters. I went up the two flights of stairs and opened the door to my room. I didn't really expect to find Queenie there. But I did expect to find a fire burning in the grate. Instead my trunk was sitting on top of my bed, the curtains were closed and the room was freezing. Hardly a warm welcome home.

I went over to the wall and tugged on the bellpull, feeling decidedly irritated now. It was the maid who had spoken to me in the front hall who appeared long before Queenie—naturally.

"My lady?" she asked. Then she went on before I had a chance to say anything. "Oh dear. You'll want your fire, of course. I'll send someone up to lay it for you. And your bed needs to be made up again." She gave me a bright smile. "Don't worry. It will all be done by the time you come back."

I deposited my suitcase on the floor and turned to leave again. There was no point in lingering. It was too depressing for words. To have gone from the high excitement of a royal wedding followed by an elopement to Gretna Green to this cold and lonely room almost brought me to tears. Just as I opened my door I heard the sound of feet approaching. Not the gentle tap of feet but full-blown gallumphing. I think the pictures on the walls shook a little as Queenie appeared at the top of the stairs, panting as she attempted to run. She was a big girl and not what one would describe as light on her feet.

"What the blooming heck are you doing back here?" she demanded. "That Mr. O'Mara told me you'd be gone and I should go back to your brother's place to wait for you."

"I had to return unexpectedly," I said.

She put her hands on her broad hips and sighed. "Now I suppose you'll want your bags unpacked again?"

"It is your job, Queenie," I pointed out. "Where were you when I rang for you?"

"Down in the kitchen having a late cup of tea," she said, "and finishing the seedy cake."

"It's a good thing we are leaving," I commented. "Your uniform is about to burst at the seams."

"I needed to eat to keep up me strength," she said defiantly. "All these ruddy stairs to go up and down. But what are you doing back here? I thought from what Mr. O'Mara said that you'd be in a nice hotel somewhere having a bit of the old how's yer father." And she accompanied these last words with a knowing wink.

"Certainly not," I replied haughtily, although I think I might have blushed. "Besides, what I do is none of your business, Queenie. I told you many times a good lady's maid never questions her mistress or her mistress's behavior." I looked at her, standing there with her blouse buttons bursting, hair frizzing out from under her cap, traces of past meals streaked liberally down her front and her usual vacant and cowlike expression on her face, and I sighed. "I had hoped you might have learned a thing or two from the other maids here."

"I have," she said, still defiant. "Didn't you notice I said 'bloomin' heck' instead of 'bloody hell'? One of the other maids said that swearing wasn't proper and she'd be fired if she ever said a swearword. So I thought I'd better watch me language a bit."

"Quite right," I said. "You know I've been far too lenient with you. I let you take too many liberties, but I expect you to shape up from now on or I really won't be able to keep you. I have to return the motorcar to its owner now but I expect my room to be warm and comfortable by the time I get back."

"Bob's yer uncle, miss," she said, never having learned after two years to address me by my proper title. Then she added, "So what happened, then? You and Mr. Darcy didn't have a falling-out, did you? He didn't jilt you, did he?"

"Certainly not. Mr. O'Mara had a family emergency and had to return home to Ireland unexpectedly."

"Oh, does that mean we might be going to Ireland? I'd rather do that than go back to your right cow of a sister-in-law."

I was about to tell her, for the hundredth time, that it was not her place to criticize her betters, but it never seemed to sink in. "We will not be going to Ireland. Mr. O'Mara does not want me there at the present."

Then I walked away, afraid that she might spot the despair on my face.

Chapter 5

FRIDAY, NOVEMBER 30

Back in London and my last night at Kensington Palace.

**Feeling really unsettled. I have no idea what tomorrow
   might bring.**

It was becoming decidedly foggy by the time I turned the
motorcar into Eaton Square and found number sixteen. The
spiky silhouettes of trees in the middle of the square loomed
eerie and indistinct in the mist and the air smelled smoky,
making it hard to breathe. This might turn into a real pea-
souper by the middle of the night. I was glad it wasn't far
from Kensington Palace. I managed to park the motor without scraping anything and went under the portico to the front
door. It was opened by a maid. I would dearly have liked to
just hand her the keys and ask her to tell her mistress that I
had returned the motorcar, but I realized she'd probably
want an explanation of why the motor had been returned so
quickly. So I told her who I was. She admitted me, took my
coat, hat and gloves, then showed me through into a delightful sitting room. Before I could take in more than the roaring

fire in the grate with a polar-bear-skin rug on the floor in front of it a woman rose up from the Queen Anne chair by the fire where she had been sitting.

Darcy's description of "a funny old thing" had made me expect someone quite different from the person standing before me. I couldn't say how old she was—maybe forty, or a little older, but she was dressed in black silk pajamas and in her hand was the longest ebony cigarette holder I had ever seen, in which a black Russian cigarette was burning. Dark hair cascaded over her shoulders in luxurious waves. Her face was exquisitely made up with pouting red lips and she batted impossibly long black eyelashes at me a couple of times. The word "sultry" formed itself in my brain as she held out a long slender hand to me.

"Come. Let me look at you."

I approached cautiously.

She was examining me critically and I was horribly conscious of my creased suit and hair that had been squashed under a hat. "So you are the one," she said at last. "Interesting. I wouldn't have said you were at all his type. But where is the dear boy, and what are you doing back here? I thought Darcy said you would be away for some days." Her voice was deep and throaty, her English with just enough hint of precision and perfection to show she wasn't a native speaker.

"I'm afraid Darcy had a family emergency and had to return unexpectedly to Ireland," I said. "He asked me to bring the motorcar back to you with his thanks."

"Nothing too serious, I hope?" she said.

"I hope so too."

She took my hand in hers. "But you are freezing. Sit down. Here by the fire. Will you take sherry or brandy?"

"I shouldn't disturb you any longer, Your Highness," I said.

She laughed. She had a deep, throaty laugh that matched her voice. "You must call me Alexandra, or Zou Zou. All my friends do. Now sit. I insist."

I did as I was told while she crossed the room to where a silver drinks tray stood on a low Chinese cabinet. Then she poured me a generous glass of sherry. As she poured I had time to look at my surroundings. The furniture was an interesting and eclectic mix of antique, exotic and modern. On the walls were paintings that even I, not extremely well versed in art, recognized. Surely that was a Monet? And a Chagall? And a Turner over the fireplace? And a virgin by some Italian master? Darcy was right when he said she was not exactly penniless.

"It was very good of you to lend Darcy your motorcar," I said.

She laughed again. "I did still have the Rolls to get around in, and my little Lagonda sports car. And I was delighted to help out. I am very fond of him, you know. I would do anything for him."

The way she said those words shot a dagger of warning through my heart. I tried not to think what Darcy's relationship had been with her, or still was. Was this one of the friends' couches he claimed he slept on when he was in London? If so, then I didn't think that he actually slept on the couch. The princess handed me my sherry.

"Drink up," she said. "Get that down you and you'll feel better. I always do. I find sherry so much more comforting than gin when I need bucking up. And you clearly need bucking up at the moment." She resumed her position in the chair across the fire from me. "So tell me, what's wrong?" she asked. "Tell Auntie Zou Zou everything. Maybe I can help."

"I don't think so," I said. "I don't think there is anything any of us can do." But I found myself telling her what I knew. She was a good listener. She nodded when I had finished. "My goodness. I had no idea. I never read newspapers apart from the social column. Too depressing for words. Poor boy. I understood that his father was a difficult man and their relationship was fractious, but this—this is terrible. So why did you not go with him? Does he not need the support of a loving woman at this difficult hour?"

"He didn't want me there," I said, and I heard the tremble

in my voice. "He said this wasn't the time to introduce me to his father."

"I suppose not. A proud man does not like to be seen in such circumstances. So where are you staying in London?"

"I've been at Kensington Palace, helping Princess Marina before her wedding."

"Oh, of course. The famous wedding. I wasn't invited, of course." She paused and a frown crossed that perfect face, then she grinned. "Probably because I knew the groom a little too well." And she laughed again. "So will you stay at the palace and join the Aunt Heap?"

"Oh no. The apartment is being closed up and I'll go back to my brother at Rannoch House."

"Oh, of course. You're Binky's sister. How thick of me. One hasn't seen anything of him since he married that dreadful woman. Is she really as poisonous as one hears?"

"She really is," I said and we shared a smile.

"Then I don't envy you." She waved her cigarette holder in my direction. "You must stay for dinner tonight. I have a fun crowd coming. People you might know."

"Oh, I couldn't possibly," I began but she waved the cigarette holder again.

"I absolutely insist. You look tired and worried and I'm sure the food at Kensington Palace won't be up to snuff. Royal food is always so stodgy and boring, I have found. Their chefs have no imagination. Mine, on the other hand, was lured from Paris."

"I'm not dressed for dinner," I said.

"One can see that. But we're about the same size, aren't we? Clotilde can find something of mine for you, I am sure."

"I couldn't possibly—" I began again, as I entertained visions of my spilling something down a Parisian silk gown.

"Now you are being difficult," she said. "Darcy will tell you that I like to get my own way. As does he, does he not? Such a forceful young man." And she gave me a self-satisfied smile. Then she glanced at her wristwatch and said, "I tell you what. My guests will not arrive for an hour. I'll have my chauffeur run you back to the palace, you go and change into something more suitable and he'll bring you back in time for dinner. Surely you can't say no to that?"

"Thank you. I accept most gratefully."

"Good," she said. "I shall question you mercilessly, you know. I want to find out every detail about you and Darcy. How you met. How long you've known each other. Your plans for the future. I find it all so fascinating that he wants to settle down and give up such a pleasant and fancy-free lifestyle. Will you retire to the country and grow potatoes, do you think?"

"I have no idea what he has in mind," I said, "but I can't imagine Darcy settling down anywhere, can you?"

"Oh yes. I think I can see him as lord of the manor with ten children around him, being blissfully happy, much to the chagrin of all the young women in London."

She rang the bell then. I was driven back to the palace in the same Armstrong Siddeley by an extremely good-looking German chauffeur whom the princess addressed as Fritzi. As we drove at a snail's pace through the fog I kept wanting to tell Fritzi that I had changed my mind and would not be returning to dinner after all. The thought of facing a dinner party with the princess and her smart friends was overwhelming at this moment. They would all be dressed in the height of fashion. I'd feel like a fish out of water, terrified that I'd knock over a glass or spill the soup. And I would feel the princess's eyes on me with that quizzical stare, wondering whatever Darcy could see in me. And what if he telephoned the palace while I was away, expecting to find me there? Would the servants hear the telephone in the front hall? Would they take a message properly?

A PATHETIC ATTEMPT at a fire had been started in my bedroom but it still felt icy after the intoxicating warmth of the princess's sitting room. Queenie had my trunk open and items of clothing strewn over the bed.

"I can't find your slippers," she said, looking up at me. "I know I put them in here somewhere."

"Never mind the slippers now," I said. "I'm going out to dinner. I need my smartest evening gown, my black pumps and my jewel case."

She sighed. "You would, wouldn't you, right after I stuffed them shoes with newspaper and all, right at the bottom." She flung out items of clothing with gay abandon.

"I think the burgundy velvet is the best we can do," I said. "And the rubies to go with it."

"Bob's yer uncle," she said. "Here you are." And a dark red missile was hurled in my direction. I took it and stared at it in horror. It was obvious it had been crammed into a trunk any which way and was now awfully creased.

"It will need ironing, Queenie," I said. "But remember it's velvet. You iron it on the wrong side, with a cool iron or you will melt it."

"I know," she said huffily. "I'll have to see if there's still an ironing board in the place."

I was going to ask her to run a bath but Queenie didn't handle multiple commands well. Instead I went down the hall and turned on the taps myself.

Feeling quite revived after my bath I waited for her to return, half in dread about what she might have done to my dress. She had certainly ruined enough items of clothing. But miraculously she returned with the dress looking quite respectable, then helped me into it. It wasn't exactly fashionable but it was presentable. I nodded as I looked at myself.

"And the evening shoes, Queenie?"

I sat down at the dressing table and held out my feet.

"Here's the right one," she said and put it on.

"And the left?" I asked as a sinking feeling formed in my stomach.

"I can't seem to find the left one," she said. "I'm pretty sure I put both of them in the trunk, but it ain't here now."

"Queenie, I can't go to dinner with one shoe on," I said.

"You've got other shoes," she said.

"Daytime shoes, not evening pumps. I can't go to a dinner in brogues!"

"It's a long dress. Bend yer knees a bit and no one will see."

If I hadn't been so angry it would have been funny. "I took them both off in this room, Queenie. Keep looking until you find it. Go on."

"I already looked once," she said.

"Try under the bed," I suggested.

She sighed and got down on her hands and knees. "Only a chamber pot under there," she said.

"Try the wardrobe."

"I already looked there," she said, opening the door defiantly. She disappeared inside, leaving only a large rear end facing me. Then she said, "Well, blow me down. Here it is, in the back corner." She produced my pump. "My old dad said I'd forget my head if it wasn't on my shoulders." She laughed and slipped the shoe onto my other foot.

"You can thank your lucky stars that I had to go out to dinner tonight," I said. "Otherwise we'd have been miles away and never found it. And I'd have to buy a new pair of shoes out of your wages."

She chuckled at this. "Go on. You don't pay me enough to buy a pair of good shoes."

This, of course, was true and the only reason that I kept her on. I had no money. She took almost no wages while supposedly I was training her. The training had been going on for two years now and she was no nearer to being employable. She would probably never be employable, which meant I was stuck with her. I sighed.

"My jewel case and my fox fur stole, if you don't mind. I don't want to keep the princess waiting."

"Dining with a princess, are we?" she said, as she fastened the rubies around my neck. "Coming up in the world since you took on this job at the palace."

"Actually she is a friend of Mr. Darcy's," I said and wished I hadn't uttered the words out loud. The phrase "we are just good friends" flashed through my mind. I wrapped the stole around me.

"I don't know when I'll be back, Queenie," I said. "You don't have to wait up. Just make sure my nightclothes are laid out. You know—nightclothes, not my bathing suit and my ski jumper."

"I know. I ain't completely daft," she said. "And I'll tell them in the kitchen that you ain't taking your dinner here, okay?"

"Yes, please do." I started down the hallway.

"One more thing," she called after me. "Can I have your helping of stew, then?"

I sighed again as I walked down the stairs.

Chapter 6

FRIDAY, NOVEMBER 30

**Chez Princess Zamanska. Dreading this! Why did I
agree to it? Because she is not the sort of person one
says no to, I suppose.**

I heard the sound of laughter as the maid admitted me to 16
Eaton Square.

"The company is in the sitting room," she said unneces-
sarily. Then she opened the door and said, in dramatic fashion, "Lady Georgiana Rannoch, Your Highness."

Heads turned in my direction. Princess Zamanska had
been standing with her back to me, wearing a black backless
evening gown. Her hair was now piled in curls on her head,
held in place with a black ostrich feather. There were diamonds at her throat. The cigarette holder was still in her
hand.

"Dear little Georgiana," she said, coming to me. "How
charming you look. Come and meet everybody."

She led me into the group of people standing with glasses

in their hands, around the fire. "I don't know if you've met Georgiana Rannoch," she said. "Bertie Rannoch's daughter, you know."

"Poor old Bertie. Such a shame," someone muttered. For a second I misinterpreted this as such a shame he'd had a daughter like me, but then the person added, "Dying so young like that."

"My sentiments exactly," Princess Zamanska said. "The Riviera feels positively dull and lifeless without him, doesn't it? But you'll never guess what—this sweet young thing has now captured the heart of our dear Darcy."

They were all looking at me, and I could feel them sizing up my old-fashioned and well-worn dress. Some stares were amused, some intrigued.

The princess took my arm. "Let me introduce you. My countrymen the Count and Countess Rostoff," she said. "And perhaps you know Dicky Altringham? And Bubbles Cantrell-Smythe?" I did, but only by name and by pictures in the *Tatler*, not by moving in such fashionable circles. Then there was a Sir James and Lady Something-or-other—"He's big in banking, you know. A good man to know if you want a loan." Much laughter at this. She moved on to a dashing Frenchman whom she introduced as Le Marquis de Chambourie. Another person I had heard of but never met. He was already eyeing me with interest. *"Enchanté,"* he said and kissed my hand, his lips lingering a little too long on my skin.

"Behave yourself, Jean-Claude," she said. "You are not allowed to devour her before dinner." She turned to me. "And we are still waiting for our most distinguished guests. She always likes to be fashionably late."

The doorbell sounded.

"Ah, here they are now," she said.

We stood, listening expectantly as there was a low murmur of voices in the hallway. Then the maid appeared, looking a little flustered. "The Prince of Wales and Mrs. Ernest Simpson."

OH CRIKEY. I stared in dismay as my cousin David and his poisonous lady friend came into the room. He looked dashing in white tie. She, I was amused to see, was wearing a black beaded evening gown quite similar to that of the Princess Zamanska. The princess must have noticed this too as I saw a flash of amusement cross her face.

"How good of you to come, sir," she said, going over to meet them.

"Wouldn't miss it for the world, would we, Wallis?" the prince said.

"And Mrs. Simpson. How lovely to see you again. It's been ages. Not since Bender's yacht that time."

"How are you, my dear?" Mrs. Simpson said. "Such a lovely dress. Paris, I think."

"What, this old thing?" the princess said and gave a deep chuckle. "I'd almost forgotten I had it but Clotilde fished it out from the back of one of the wardrobes and reminded me I hadn't worn it for ages."

I glanced at her with admiration. In one sentence she had managed to put Mrs. Simpson in her place without seeming to do so. By running down her own dress she had also insulted Mrs. Simpson's. I decided I might like her after all. One could not tell from Mrs. Simpson's perfect face whether she minded or not.

The company was presented, one by one, to the prince and his lady companion. I noted there was no longer a Mr. Ernest Simpson in tow. Rumors were that she was trying to initiate divorce proceedings. About time too. I don't know how the poor man agreed to play gooseberry for so long. But what Mrs. Simpson thought would happen next I could not imagine. Of course the prince could never marry her. She was a twice-divorced woman. He would be head of the Church of England one day and the church did not sanction divorce.

The introductions came around to me. My cousin's face lit up in a warm smile. "Hello, Georgie. Didn't expect to find you here. Have you recovered from yesterday? Dashed freezing in the church, but all in all a splendid wedding, wouldn't you say? Too good for my brother."

I wasn't sure if he meant the wedding or the bride. "It was lovely, sir," I said, addressing him correctly even if he was my cousin. Protocol demanded it. "The reception at Buckingham Palace was particularly nice."

I gave Mrs. Simpson a gracious little nod because she had not been invited, and saw a look of vexation cross that perfectly made-up face. Enjoying my rare moment I went on, "And I thought your speech at the reception was brilliant, sir. Very funny, and you said all the right things."

"Well, one could hardly let Bertie do it, could one?" he said with a chuckle.

"Can you imagine it?" Mrs. Simpson chimed in, looking around the company with a malicious gleam in her eye. "D-d-d-dear f-f-f-friends and f-f-f-family. The man is hopelessly embarrassing, isn't he?"

"He's a very nice person," I said. "He just gets flustered when he has to speak in public."

"Or to our father," the prince said. "He never can speak to the king without stuttering."

"That's because His Majesty gets so impatient with him and snaps at him. When he talks to people like me and his daughters he never stutters."

"That's because you're so nonthreatening, honey," Mrs. Simpson said, giving me one of those condescending smiles she was so good at. "How are you, Georgiana? I haven't seen you since we were on the same boat going to America. Did your mama get her divorce? I gather that was the reason for her trip."

"She did, thank you," I said. "And I hope you managed to conclude your . . . spot of business properly." Since the rumor was that she also wanted to set divorce proceedings in motion, she understood what I was hinting at.

"Quite satisfactorily, thank you," she replied, her face a mask of composure. "In fact I think I can say that everything is proceeding smoothly." She looked around, then went on, an edge now to her voice. "Except for the fact that I don't have a drink in my hand. David—find me a gin and tonic."

There was the slightest of gasps from the rest of the party. Only his family addressed him as David, within the confines of their palaces, and even a close friend like Mrs. Simpson should have addressed him as "sir" in public. And certainly not ordered him to fetch her a drink.

"Allow me," Princess Zamanska said hurriedly. "Pierre— a gin and tonic for Mrs. Simpson. And you, sir?"

"I'll have the same. Thanks awfully," he said. "So what have you been up to, Zou Zou? Any motor racing recently?"

"The weather has been too beastly, hasn't it?" she said. "But I do have a new toy. I have just bought an aeroplane. A dinky little two-seater. I thought flying was the next obvious thing to do."

"Good show!" The prince nodded enthusiastically. "We can go up together sometime. I enjoy flying planes myself, although Wallis hates going up with me, don't you, old thing?"

"Terrified he's going to kill us both," Mrs. Simpson replied.

"Then you and I shall see if we can loop the loop together," the princess said.

"You're both crazy, do you know that?" Mrs. Simpson said, raising her eyes in despair. "Actually we were just over in Germany. That country is doing so splendidly now, isn't it, David? Herr Hitler has really got them back on their feet. So proud and prosperous and well organized. I was saying to David I wouldn't even mind living there. A little house up in the mountains like Hitler's. So charming."

"You would not find it so charming if you had to live there for long," Princess Zamanska said. "Wild horses would not drag me to Germany again, and as a Polish woman I fear for my country."

The gong sounded and we went in to dinner. The Marquis de Chambourie was assigned to escort me. He tucked my arm through his a little too firmly for my taste.

"So where have you been hiding until now, you delectable

I was driven back to the palace and found that the fire in my room had not succeeded in making it much warmer. There was no sign of Queenie. I struggled with the hooks on my dress and climbed into a cold bed. Then I curled into a tight little ball and tried to sleep. But sleep wouldn't come. Had Darcy telephoned? I pictured him also lying alone in a cold bed, worrying and thinking of me.

In the morning a hard-boiled egg and toast were brought up to my room. Queenie finished repacking my things and I went downstairs to send someone to find a cab for me. I looked up when I heard the brisk tap of feet and for a moment I thought I was seeing yet another ghost. Then I saw that this man was very much alive. He just bore a remarkable resemblance to the major who had been his predecessor at the palace and who had died in a tragic fall.

"Lady Georgiana," he said, in his fruity military tones, "I can't apologize enough. I had no idea, you see. I understood from the servants that you had already departed and left your maid to have your belongings sent on. If I'd known you were still to be in residence I would have made sure that you were properly fed and looked after."

"It's quite all right, Major . . . ?"

"Halliburton," he said. "Grenadier Guards."

"Major Halliburton," I said. "Please don't apologize. I had intended to be gone but I had to return unexpectedly. I'll be moving to my brother's house this morning, so I'll be departing in a few minutes."

"No, no. Please feel free to stay as long as you want," he said.

"But I understood the place was to be closed up and the servants sent elsewhere today," I said.

He glanced around before lowering his voice. "That was to make sure a certain other lady went home to wherever she came from," he said, giving me a conspiratorial grin. "I understand that she expressed an interest in staying on indefinitely, and as she was not the easiest of guests . . ." He didn't have to finish the sentence. "But with you it is quite different. That lady invited herself, so I am told. She wasn't even supposed to be here. Everyone was surprised when she showed up on the doorstep."

"Don't worry. We'll both be out of your hair today, I promise," I said.

"What does this major have in his hair?" a voice behind us demanded, and there was Irmtraut, dressed for travel in a green Austrian cape. "I hope it is not fleas or lice. I do not think this place is cleaned very well."

"It is merely an expression, Countess," the major said. "An English idiom."

"I am glad that I return to a country where people say what they mean. And no silly expressions like 'toads in the cave' and 'raining cats and dogs.'"

Then she swept past us and out the front door.

The major and I exchanged a smile.

❧

A TAXI WAS summoned, and the luggage was piled in for the short trip to Belgrave Square. It was still horribly foggy and we crept through Kensington Gardens, seeing only a few feet in front of us.

"Blimey, if it gets much worse I'm going 'ome," the driver muttered as he pulled up outside Rannoch House. Our butler, Hamilton, opened the front door.

"Why, Lady Georgiana, what a pleasant surprise," he said. "I was not informed that you were expected. Let me take your coat, then go and make sure that your room is ready for you." He peered out into the street where Queenie was wrestling with the bags. "I'll send a footman to help with your luggage."

"Is His Grace at home, Hamilton?" I asked.

"At his club, I believe, my lady. But Her Grace is here."

He had only just said the words when Her Grace came down the staircase toward us.

"Georgiana!" she exclaimed, a look of surprise on her face. "What are you doing here? We understood that you had moved into Kensington Palace."

"Only until the wedding," I said. "I was invited to keep Princess Marina company and now she and the Duke of Kent are on their honeymoon, so the apartment is being closed up and I have returned here for a little while, if that's all right with you."

Her eyes darted nervously. "Why yes, of course. Binky will be pleased to see you. He's off at his club as usual. Goes there every morning to read the papers. Seems to prefer reading them there, which is silly because we have the very same newspapers here." Turning, she said, "We'll have coffee in the morning room, Hamilton." She went through ahead of me and took up position in the best armchair beside the fire. I went over to the window seat, suitably far away from her.

"How are the children?" I asked. "Both well?"

"Podge has had a cold. I don't think the London air agrees with his chest. I suggested to Nanny that she not open his windows at night, but she is of the old school. All children should sleep with windows open, no matter what."

"That's how I was brought up," I said. "As you know only too well, all the bedroom windows at Castle Rannoch are always kept open."

"Things may improve now that the new central heating is being installed," she said. "You must come and visit sometime next summer. So where are you off to now? Another royal residence?"

Fig deeply resented that I was royal by birth and she only tenuously by marriage. She resented even more that I had quite a chummy relationship with Queen Mary. Also that I had a rich mother. "Or perhaps it's back to America with Mummy? You seem to lead an exciting sort of life."

"I'm not sure of my plans, Fig. For the moment I'd like to stay in London." I heard the sound of luggage being dragged upstairs. "But don't let me keep you from what you were doing. I should probably go up and supervise Queenie unpacking my things."

Fig sighed. "I can't understand why you still have that

dreadful creature as your maid. She simply isn't up to snuff, Georgiana. She discredits the whole family."

"You know why, Fig," I replied. "I have no money. No allowance. Nothing. I cannot employ a decent maid. Queenie works pretty much for her room and board."

Fig scowled. "I don't know why you are telling me this. It is not your brother's duty to support a spinster female sister. The family paid for your season. You turned twenty-one. All our obligations ended there. It is not our fault that you have failed to make a suitable marriage. Heaven knows the family has tried hard enough on your behalf."

"Nobody that I would describe as suitable, Fig, as I told you once before." I was referring to Prince Siegfried (usually known to my friends as Fishface), who'd made it clear to me that if I produced an heir he'd never bother me again.

She sighed. "You didn't happen to meet any good prospects at the wedding, did you? There were quite a few young Continental chaps in evidence from what I could see. Of course, we were not invited to the reception at the palace, but I understand that you were." Another withering look.

"I am capable of finding my own chap, thank you, Fig."

"You mean that O'Mara person? I hope his name will not be mentioned again in this house. You do know that his father is a murderer? A common criminal, Georgiana. You must put all thoughts of him aside."

"His father is accused of murder," I said. "Innocent until proven guilty."

"You know what they always say: Like father, like son." She nodded as if she had scored a point.

"I think I'll go up and see the children in the nursery," I said.

"So how long do you think you will be staying?" she asked as I stood up.

"I'm not sure," I said. "My plans are a little up in the air, as usual."

"Only we won't be here much longer ourselves," Fig said with something close to a smirk on her face.

"I thought you were having central heating put in at

Castle Rannoch and you were going to spend Christmas in London."

"That was the original plan," she said. "But now my sister, Ducky—you remember Ducky, don't you?"

"Very well," I said, trying not to shudder. Fig's family all seemed to be as unpleasant as she was.

"Well, Ducky also received her share of the inheritance from our aunt and she has bought a small villa in Nice. Not as grand as your mother's, of course. But somewhere to go in the winter. And they have asked us to join them. We'll be going out there at the end of the week."

"Oh, I see," I replied. "And I suppose there's no chance of my staying on here alone for a while?"

She shook her head. "I'm afraid not. Just won't be possible. We'll be closing up the place, you see. Sending the servants back to Scotland. We simply can't afford to keep two houses open."

"I'm able to survive quite well on my own now," I said.

"But it's the added expense, isn't it? Money is horribly tight, Georgiana. And one understands that the price of coal has shot up." She was staring into a fire that was glowing most healthily. Then she turned back, waving a bony finger at me. "You know what you should do? You should talk to the queen, as you seem to be quite chummy with her. Surely one of your aged royal aunts can use you as a companion. I understand that Kensington Palace is full of them. Isn't it known as the Aunt Heap?"

"Don't worry about me. I'm sure there are plenty of places I can go," I said brightly. "My grandfather has always told me I'm welcome to stay with him."

Fig blinked rapidly, something she did when nervous. "You mean your mother's father? The one who was a policeman? Who lives in Essex?"

"It would hardly be the old Duke of Rannoch. He's been dead for thirty years."

"Georgiana, it simply isn't done. Someone of your social standing cannot stay with a retired Cockney policeman in Essex!"

"The king and queen go to Sandringham," I pointed out. "That's only one county away."

"You know what I mean," she snapped. "One does have the honor of the family to uphold."

"The family gives me no money to uphold their honor," I pointed out. "But don't worry. I expect the Princess Zamanska can find me somewhere."

"Who?" she asked. "Zamanska? Not that dreadful woman one reads about jumping out of planes?"

All in all I was holding my own rather well. I should have enjoyed needling her. Heaven knows she had said enough hateful things to me over the years. But the thought running through my head all the time was that I had to be where Darcy could find me. He would telephone as soon as he had any news. Hopefully that would be before the end of the week. And then he'd ask me to go to him.

HAMILTON HAD JUST brought in a tray of coffee when we heard the sound of the front door slamming and footsteps in the hall. My brother, Binky, appeared, his face half hidden under a big red scarf. "Beastly day out there, Fig. The air positively tastes like soot. I don't think Nanny should take the children out into the gardens."

"You know how hot she is on fresh air and exercise," Fig said.

"That's the point. The air isn't fresh." He unwound the layers of scarf, then looked up and saw me sitting on the window seat. "Why, Georgie, old bean. How splendid. Have you returned home after the wedding?"

I noticed that he still thought of Rannoch House as my home whereas his wife saw me as an unwanted visitor.

"Hello, Binky," I said. "Yes, I got booted out of Kensington Palace this morning so I thought I'd come here to catch my breath before I go off somewhere else."

"Jolly good," he said. "Lovely to have you, isn't it, Fig?"

"What? Oh yes. Yes, of course." And she hurriedly took another sip of coffee.

"By the way, Georgie," Binky said, "you're not still keen on that O'Mara chap, are you? I've just come from the club and all the chaps were talking about his father. I don't know if you've heard, but he's been arrested for murder. Apparently he bashed some American chappie over the head with one of the family weapons. I don't know if there is a hint of insanity there, but the man sounds to be an out-and-out bounder." He perched on the sofa, facing me. "Apparently he's been running this very successful racing stable for the American millionaire who bought his estate when he went bankrupt. They had a string of successes . . . gold cups, you name it. And then it turns out that it was all because he was doping the horses. Injecting them with some concoction of drugs to make them run faster. Absolute blighter. And of course it all came to light when a horse that was leading in a big race dropped dead before the finish and the drugs were found in its system." He leaned toward me. "They never did prosecute but the American sacked him right away. Didn't want him anywhere near his horses. So I suppose Lord Kilhenny was angry and got his revenge."

"Absolutely barbaric," Fig said. "Binky, you are to tell Georgiana that we never want to hear that name mentioned again and she is forbidden any contact with this Darcy person."

"Just a minute," I said, feeling my face flushing red. "We don't even know that Darcy's father is guilty yet, and whatever he might have done, you can't tar Darcy with the same brush."

"I'm afraid Fig's right this time, old bean," Binky said. "Your chap might be true-blue as they come, but the scandal will hover over him just the same. Blight him for the rest of his life, I shouldn't wonder."

"Then he will need friends to stick by him," I retorted. "And fortunately Darcy seems to have plenty of friends, including me."

"If it comes out that you are in any way connected to him, it would be all over the newspapers," Fig said. Clearly she was enjoying this. "The family would be mortified."

"You need to get right away for a bit," Binky said. His face lit up. "I'll tell you what—Fig may have mentioned that we're off to the south of France next week. Ducky and Foggy have bought a villa. Actually 'villa' is rather a grand description of what seems to be a rather poky little house . . ."

"When one buys an ordinary little house in Nice one refers to it as a villa, Binky," Fig corrected.

"Very well." Binky shrugged. "Anyway, as I was saying, we're off to this so-called villa and perhaps you should come with us."

"Oh golly," I said at the same time as Fig said, "Oh no, Binky!"

"But, Fig. This is my sister," he said. "If she's in a spot of bother, it's up to us to rescue her."

Fig's eyes were darting nervously now. "You just said yourself it was a poky little house, Binky. 'Little' being the operative word. There would be no room for Georgiana."

"She could share a bedroom with Maude," Binky said. "They got along so splendidly last time, didn't they?"

Which shows you how sweet but utterly clueless my brother was. I was still speechless. I was still remembering the last disastrous stay at a villa in Nice, when I had to share with Ducky's daughter there too. Actually Maude and I had loathed each other at first sight. Ducky had been so stingy with the food that it was almost one lettuce leaf each, and Ducky's husband, Foggy, had made advances to me when he caught me alone in the hall. There was absolutely no way I was going with them to the Riviera.

"How kind of you," I said, "but I really couldn't inconvenience you like that. As I told Fig, there are plenty of places I can go. My mother has said she'd love to have me with them in Berlin, and they now have a villa on Lake Lugano."

"She's still with that German chap?" Binky asked.

"Yes. In fact they plan to marry," I said.

"You know, that might not be a bad idea for Georgiana," Fig said, waving a finger at Binky now. "There are still plenty of young German counts and barons and I gather life in Berlin is an absolute social whirl. I wouldn't know, of course, not having the means to travel. But you should consider it, Georgiana. Your mother's beau is stinking rich, so one hears. You'd have a lovely time. And you might finally meet someone. Someone rich and suitable."

"But I don't want to meet someone, Fig. And please don't worry about me. I'm sure I can take care of myself. You go and have a lovely time with Ducky and Foggy. Just take care you don't put on too much weight."

That last remark was naughty of me, but I felt the need to strike back. I was overwrought and angry at the way the whole world seemed to have condemned Darcy along with his father. And at the back of my mind was the worry that everything they had been saying was true. What if his father was found guilty? What if Darcy was shunned from polite society? Then I realized that none of that mattered. If he was shunned, I'd go and live with him in a little house like my grandfather's. Nothing would matter as long as we were together.

Chapter 8

Having come to this conclusion, I went up to see what awful torture Queenie was putting my clothes through. I found she was sitting on my bed, mopping a very red face.

"Blimey, miss," she said. "I'm bushed. I had to drag all this stuff up these ruddy stairs."

"Did Hamilton not send the footman to help you?"

"Yeah, but by the time he arrived I'd been up and down twice."

"Well, you'll be pleased to know that it doesn't all need to be unpacked," I said. "We shall not be staying long. So maybe only a couple of day outfits and one dinner dress should suffice."

"So where are we off to this time?" she asked. "Somewhere nice and warm?"

I hesitated. Where would I go when Binky and Fig set off for Nice? I could write to my mother to ask if I could stay with her. I could, indeed, go to the queen and see if she had any little job she'd like me to do. These had certainly proved interesting in the past. Then I remembered that the Dowager Duchess of Eynsford had told me I was always welcome at Kingsdowne. And Lady Hawse-Gorzley would also welcome me in Devon. And my former stepfather, Sir Hubert Anstruther, might even be in England, back from his latest mountaineering trip. He had always been fond of me and at one time had tried to adopt me. So I did have places where I was welcome. No need to panic yet. It was just that none of them was in London, and I had to stay in touch with Darcy. I had to know what was happening and what he wanted me to do.

That was when I thought of Belinda. She had been my best friend in school. She had led a very wild and naughty life that had finally caught up with her. She now found herself in trouble, as they say, and at her wits' end. I had written to my mother to see if she might let Belinda hide out at one of her villas until the blessed event was over. Since Belinda and my mother were kindred spirits and had led similarly naughty lives, I was sure that Mummy would take pity on her and whisk her off to Lugano or Nice. And if Belinda was abroad, then her little mews cottage might be the perfect place for me.

"I'll be back in time for luncheon," I said to Queenie, then I bundled myself into my coat and scarf and headed out into the murk. Belinda lived not too far away in a delightful mews cottage in Knightsbridge. I didn't think she'd be likely to be out on a filthy morning like this so I tapped on her door and heard footsteps coming down the stairs. Belinda opened it, wearing silk pajamas and looking glamorous as usual, if decidedly frail. The image of Camille flashed through my mind.

"Georgie!" she said, her face lighting up. "How lovely. I thought for some reason that you had gone away, now that the wedding is over. Come in, do." She almost dragged me into the house before more of the fog could curl its way in with me.

"I was away," I said, "but Darcy had to rush off to Ireland unexpectedly, as I'm sure you now know."

She looked around in surprise. "No. Why?"

"You don't read the newspapers?"

"Never. It's all bad news, isn't it?" She had gone ahead of me into her cozy sitting room and draped herself on the sofa. I headed for the chair near the gas fire.

"Well, I'm sure you'll hear soon enough when you are out in society. His father has been arrested and Darcy rushed to his side."

"Darcy would." She nodded. "But how horrid for you both."

"We'll come through it, don't worry," I said. "But how about you? You don't exactly look in the pink."

"No, I've had some terrible bouts of sickness. They call it morning sickness but I've been vomiting into the afternoon and evening. No food seems to appeal to me. I gather it should stop soon. God, I hope so. I don't know why women ever have children from choice. It's beastly."

"Have you heard from my mother yet?"

"Not yet. But it doesn't matter anymore, Georgie. I don't need her."

I was confused. She couldn't have lost the baby, or she wouldn't be feeling so sick. I wondered if the baby's father had changed his mind and come to seek her out and marry her, but I didn't think it would be wise to ask. So I waited.

"I've just had a piece of good news," she said, staring out past me to the swirling fog beyond the window. She hesitated, infuriatingly. I was itching to tell her to get on with it, but one doesn't. "Well, I suppose in a way it's bad news. But good for me."

Finally I could stand it no longer. "For heaven's sake, tell me," I insisted.

"My grandmother died," she said.

"I'm sorry."

She grimaced. "I suppose I should be too, but I'm not, really. She was never the warmest of women. Always telling one to sit up straight; and why wasn't I married? Very narrow. Very judgmental. If she'd found out about the baby, I'd have been cut off without a penny." A big smile spread over her face. "Well, as it happens she died at the right moment, and left me quite a lot of money. It seems she disliked my stepmother as much as I do, so she only left a token amount to my father and the rest to me. I'm quite a wealthy woman, Georgie."

"I'm so glad for you. So what will you do?"

"I understand it will take ages for the will to be settled, but the solicitor is willing to give me an advance, which means I can go to the Continent and rent a small place where nobody knows me. Not the Riviera, of course. Too many people I know there. I'm thinking Italy. Somewhere the English don't go."

"Not Positano, then. Or Florence."

"Absolutely not. One of the lakes, maybe? Or a little seaside village? I'll stay there until the baby is due, then go to Switzerland and have it at a good clinic, arrange for the adoption and come home."

"You make it all sound so simple," I said. "What if you look at the baby and fall hopelessly in love and can't give it up?"

She smiled as she shook her head. "I really don't see myself as the motherly type. But we'll face that hurdle when we come to it. The point is that as of this moment I don't have to worry. I'm free. I'll find a little villa, hire a local woman to cook me divine Italian food and fatten me up, and while I'm there I'll work on designing a new collection, then come back here and open my own salon."

"I'm happy for you, Belinda," I said.

She nodded. She didn't look terribly happy. "In the circumstances it's the best that can be hoped for, I suppose."

I realized then that she had really loved the man who'd betrayed her. It's hard for us women to get a man out of our minds and hearts.

"So when will you go, do you think?"

"Before Christmas, I hope. Christmas alone in London would be too utterly bloody, and of course I can't go home. The wicked stepmother would notice, I'm sure. I couldn't do up my trousers yesterday. I can't tell you what a shock that was. Made it all so real suddenly. So I'm aiming for Christmas in Italy." She reached across to me. "Why don't you come with me? We'd have fun together. It would be like the old days."

"We certainly would," I agreed, "but I can't leave London in case Darcy needs me."

"Why didn't you go to Ireland with him?"

I stared into the glowing bars of the fire. "He said he didn't want me there. Or at least that his father wouldn't want me there at such a terrible time."

"Poor Darcy, having to face such an unpleasant matter all alone. What was his father arrested for?"

"Murder," I said.

"Crikey. No, you're probably wise to keep well away. There's nothing you could do and the newspapers will be waiting like hawks. Your family would probably be furious."

"I don't see why. Darcy has done nothing wrong. He is not responsible for his father's behavior."

"But you know what newspapers are like. King's cousin linked to murder?"

"Darcy is clever. I'm sure he'll find out it was all a mistake." I said this to convince myself as much as her. "So what is going to happen to this place when you go?"

She smiled then, the first time I'd seen a real, happy smile. "Brilliant. I've managed to let it for a really good amount. An American professor teaching at LSE. So what with the money from Grandmama and the rental I'll be living rather nicely for once. Not having to worry where the next penny is coming from." She broke off and looked up at me. "Sorry, that was rather thoughtless, wasn't it? You're obviously still worrying where the next penny is coming from."

"I do happen to have a little stashed away at the moment. Besides, money isn't everything," I said, then wished I hadn't.

"No," she said. "Money isn't everything."

I stood up. "I should be getting back. I just stopped by to see if you were all right."

"Are you staying with your brother?"

"That's right," I said. "With my brother."

We hugged. "Write to me when you have an address," I told her. "I have no idea where I'll be going after this, but if you send it to Castle Rannoch I'll get it eventually."

"I will. And maybe you can come out and see me when all this awful business with Darcy's father is cleared up." From the way she was looking at me I could tell that she was feeling more apprehensive than she appeared and needed a friend.

"I will if I possibly can," I said.

"I'll send you the money for the ticket. It will be lovely."

"Yes." We stood looking at each other. I was remembering my first day at Les Oiseaux, my first day at any kind of school. I was socially inept, having never mixed with other girls, naïve and clueless. Belinda wore silk stockings and smoked in the bathroom. She seemed hopelessly out of my league until we had to share a bedroom with an utterly awful German girl who was horribly hot on the rules and told tales. Then we had to gang up against her and became fast friends.

"Take care of yourself," I said. "I'll see you soon."

"You too."

I glanced back as I walked down the mews and saw the curtain twitch. Belinda was watching me go. I felt horribly torn. Of course I wanted to be available for Darcy. And we had been about to get married, hadn't we? If all went well I could still hope to be Mrs. O'Mara by the new year. We might even be living together in a flat somewhere. Or in an Irish cottage. But that would mean that I couldn't go to Belinda when she needed me. "Oh bugger," I muttered. Why did life always have to be so complicated?

❦

I PASSED THE rest of the day pacing around, unable to settle or to push back the worry. Why hadn't Darcy given me a telephone number where I could reach him? Why hadn't he telephoned me with the news? I realized, of course, that he had only been there one day. He probably had no real news as yet. He was probably feeling as wretched as I was. I went down to Binky's desk and took out writing paper only to realize that I didn't know where to address a letter. "Kilhenny Castle Lodge, Ireland," might not be enough for the postman. How little I knew about Darcy's home and background!

I went down to Binky's study and found an atlas, poring over the map of Ireland until I gave a squeak of excitement. Stately homes and castles were shown in small red letters and there, not too far from Dublin, close to the town of Kildare, I saw the words *Kilhenny Castle*.

At least I could now write to him. A letter from me would make him feel better. I took up my pen and wrote, telling him how smoothly I had driven to London. How much I had enjoyed meeting the princess. I even described the dinner party, Mrs. Simpson, the French marquis pawing my thigh and the incident with the fork. I could see him laughing at that, with those adorable crinkles at the sides of his eyes. And of course I told him how much I loved him and that I would come as soon as he wanted me there. I gave the Rannoch House telephone number, just in case he had forgotten it or didn't have it with him. I didn't even put the letter on the salver in the front hall for the servants to hand to the postman. I went out again myself and found a postbox.

I felt a little more cheerful as I came home to find tea had been served and the children had been brought down from the nursery for the daily ritual of interacting with their parents. Podge was telling his father a complicated story and Fig looked most uncomfortable holding baby Adelaide on her knee. Adelaide looked equally uncomfortable, but she waved her arms excitedly when she saw me. Podge rushed to me, wrapping his arms around my legs. "Auntie Georgie, you came back!" he said. "Are you going to stay a long time? Can we go to the park and feed the ducks?"

"I think you're all heading off for France again next week," I said, kneeling on the rug and taking Adelaide from Fig. Addy came willingly with a smile of relief on her face.

"You can come with us," Podge said. "Can't she come with us, Daddy?"

"There isn't enough room for me," I said hurriedly, before one of them had to answer. "Nowhere for me to sleep."

"You can share my room," he said.

"You'll already have Addy and Nanny in your room." I smiled at his earnest little face. "And I have important things I have to do here in England. But you'll have a lovely time playing on the beach."

"The beach is all stones," he said bluntly.

"I think it's about time Nanny took you back upstairs," Fig said. "You have crumbs all over your jumper. And Adelaide needs changing. She'll make your skirt wet, Georgiana."

Nanny stepped forward instantly and whisked Adelaide away from me.

"I want to stay and talk to Auntie Georgie," Podge wailed, but Nanny took him firmly by the hand.

"She'll come up to the nursery tomorrow," she said.

"He is becoming very whiny," Fig commented. "Help yourself to tea, Georgiana. Mrs. McPherson baked gingerbread today."

I needed no urging to try some. I was just finishing a second slice when I heard the telephone ringing in the hallway, then Hamilton's soft Scottish voice. "Rannoch House. The butler speaking." Then I heard him say, "I will fetch her right away, sir."

I was on my feet as he came into the room. "A telephone call for you, my lady," he said.

I tried to walk in a civilized manner, rather than sprint to the telephone. My hand was shaking as I picked up the mouthpiece. "Hello?"

"Georgie, it's me," he said.

"Darcy? I'm so glad to hear your voice. I've been waiting and worrying. What news? What have you found out? Is it going to be all right?"

"Georgie, be quiet and listen to me," Darcy said. "I'm

afraid all the news is bad. It is quite obvious to me that my father is guilty. There will be an awful trial and he'll probably be hanged."

"Darcy, how terrible for you," I started to say but he interrupted me.

"I've thought long and hard about this, but I've come to the painful conclusion that you and I should have no more to do with each other. I will not have your life blighted the way mine will be. So I'm breaking our engagement, Georgie. I will not be contacting you again, and you should not try to contact me."

"No!" I shouted and the word echoed up the high stairwell. "I don't accept that. I love you, Darcy. For better or worse, remember? I'll stick with you, no matter what."

His voice still sounded completely calm, as if he was talking to me about the weather. "It's because I love you that I'm doing this. Luckily we are not already married so I don't have to weigh up the better-or-worse aspect. I only want the better for you. I will not put you through hell and that is final. Good-bye, my darling. I wish you only happiness."

"No, Darcy. Don't go. This is stupid. I love you. I won't let you go." I was shouting now, which a lady is not supposed to do. And crying too.

"Good-bye, Georgie." There was a click and the telephone line went dead.

Chapter 9

SATURDAY, DECEMBER 1
RANNOCH HOUSE, LONDON.

The worst day of my whole life.

I stood there in the cold hallway with tears trickling down my cheeks.

"No," I said again, to nobody this time.

I couldn't bear to face Binky and Fig. Binky would try to be kind and say platitudes about it all being for the best and at least the chap had done the right thing. Fig would have a malicious gleam in her eye and say that everything she had heard about that family was that they were no good and this proved it. I looked around me like a trapped animal. I had to escape. I had to talk to somebody, but who? Belinda hadn't had too much success with men herself. And she would probably say the same kind of thing as Binky. Given the circumstances, it was all for the best. That left me with two choices: my grandfather or the Princess Zamanska. I realized that I hardly knew her but I had seen that she didn't care a hoot for the rules of society. And she did care about Darcy.

Then I decided that I needed to be hugged and comforted.
The princess could come later. Right now I knew who I
needed to be with. I put on my coat and hat hurriedly, before
anyone could come out into the hall, and fled through the
deserted smoggy streets to the nearest Underground station.
When I disembarked an hour later at the quiet little stop at
Upminster Bridge, the smoky London fog had turned to
estuary mist, damp and curling about me. My footsteps
echoed as I walked up the slope to my grandfather's street.
It felt as if I was the only person alive in the world.

Granddad lived in a pleasant little semidetached on a
quiet back street. It boasted a pocket-handkerchief-sized
lawn on which stood three serious-looking gnomes. The
rosebushes, so pretty in summer, stuck out dead bare
branches, but a light shone through the leaded panes of the
front door and I heard voices coming from inside. He was
home but he had company. That was the last thing I needed
right now, especially if it was his neighbor Mrs. Huggins,
who was sweet on him and trying to lure him into matri-
mony. She was nosy and gossipy and I could say nothing in
front of her. But I wasn't going all the way back to Belgravia
now. I rapped on the knocker and I heard my grandfather's
wheezing cough and a voice said, "Hold on. Hold on, I'm
coming." Then the front door opened.

He peered out, frowned, then raised his eyebrows in surprise. "Blimey, love, you're the last person I expected to see.
Well, ain't you a sight for sore eyes. Come on in, do. I was
just about to have me tea."

"You've got guests?" I asked as I stepped into the narrow
hallway and he shut the door behind me. "Because I don't
have to stay. . . ."

"What? Oh, that. No, ducks, that's just the wireless.
Keeps me company. I'll turn it off." I hung my hat and coat
on the pegs of the hall stand, then followed him to the
kitchen. The voices were suddenly silenced. A steaming
plate piled with what looked like steak and kidney pudding
sat on the table.

"Oh, you're having your supper," I said, never having got the terminology for meals of the lower classes quite right. Dinner at lunchtime and apparently tea at what would be for us an early dinner. "Sit down and eat it. Don't let it get cold."

"Her next door brought it round for me," he said. "Steak and kidney pud. My favorite. There's plenty here. Can I get you some?"

I shook my head. "I'm really not hungry, but I'll have a cup of tea if there is one in the pot." Another thing I had learned about people like my grandfather was that there was always a cup of tea in the pot. They drank it by the gallon and the kettle was always ready and hot in case a neighbor came to visit.

"Of course there is," he said. "Help yourself. The milk jug's in the larder."

I poured a cup of tea then came to sit opposite him as he tucked into the pudding.

"I'm glad you've still got a good appetite," I said.

He nodded. "She may be a bit of a nuisance but she certainly can cook. How's that relative of hers getting along with you, then?" Mrs. Huggins was Queenie's great-aunt.

"Between the two of us she's as hopeless as always," I said and managed a smile. "I don't think she'll ever improve, but I need a maid, she needs a job. We probably suit each other."

He looked up, a kidney poised on his fork. "I saw your picture at that royal wedding. You looked very smart. Was it as lovely as they said?"

"It was very nice," I agreed. "Princess Marina looked beautiful."

"And what's she like, then? Foreign?"

"Her English is perfect and she was delightful," I said. "I really enjoyed my time with her." Apart from the murder, I thought. That was rather unsettling. It seemed that my life moved from one worrying incident to the next, each striking closer and closer to home.

"So where are you off to now?" he asked. "And what brings you to my neck of the woods? I don't suppose you came all this way just to say hello to your old granddad."

"I love seeing you at any time," I said. "You know that. But you're right. I'm afraid I bolted. I had some bad news and I ran out of the house and came straight to you, because you're the only person I can talk to."

"Bad news?"

"You might have read about it in the papers," I said. "Darcy's father has been arrested for murder."

"Blimey. So that was the Irish aristocrat they mentioned. Hit someone over the head with a battle-ax, didn't he?"

"A battle club." I took a deep breath. "Darcy just telephoned me to tell me that he wants us to break all ties. He doesn't want me linked to him in any way."

Granddad nodded. "He always struck me as a thoughtful young man. He thinks he's doing the right thing."

I looked up, as shocked as if he had slapped me across the face. "I thought at least you would understand," I said angrily. "I love him, Granddad. We were going to sneak up to Gretna Green to get married, when we learned about this. I don't want to live without him."

"But you can see his point of view, can't you?" he asked calmly. "He's looking out for you. He knows what it will be like with the reporters hovering like vultures. He knows that the gossip will follow him for the rest of his life. People will nudge each other and say, 'He's the one whose father was a murderer.' Then they'll nod and move away from him."

"That's so unfair. Remember Binky was wrongly arrested once. It hasn't blighted him. And Darcy is a wonderful person, Granddad, and he must be hurting terribly. I want to be with him. I want to help him get through this."

"And how do you think you could help him, ducks?" he asked gently. "Don't you think you'll give him even more to worry about, trying to protect you from the press?"

This made me hesitate and consider. Did I really think I could be of help to him? Would seeing me there, knowing I was on his side no matter what, make him feel better? Then

I thought if someone in my family was arrested for a crime, I'd want Darcy there with me. And if there was the slightest hope, the slightest chance that his father was innocent, then two heads would be better than one.

"If the situation was reversed then I'd want Darcy there," I said.

"If that's how you feel, what's stopping you?" he asked.

"What?"

"Go over to him. If he tries to send you away say you're not leaving him in the lurch whatever happens." He wagged a finger at me. "But you have to be sure that you're up to it. It won't be easy. Those reporters, they'll be hanging round like a pack of wolves, everywhere you go. And your family might not like having you mixed up with a murder trial."

"Bugger my family," I said, making him burst out laughing so that I had to smile too.

"I never thought I'd hear that word coming from your lips," he said. "I bet your governess didn't teach it to you. And that sister-in-law of yours would swoon if you ever used it in front of her."

"It's not a word I use often," I said, "but in the circumstances it seems quite appropriate. I mean, it's not as if I'm anybody important, is it? The Prince of Wales sneaks off with Mrs. Simpson. The Duke of Kent has the shadiest of pasts. I really don't think the newspapers will find me very interesting."

"You know what they're like with anything to do with the royal family," he said. "The public laps it up. Especially when it's something shady, some kind of scandal."

"So you really think I shouldn't go?" I said. "What would you have done if my grandmother's family had been in some kind of trouble?"

This made him laugh, a low, wheezing kind of chuckle that shook his body. "That's how I met her, love. I'd arrested her brother for being drunk and disorderly outside the Nag's Head. He was only a young kid, so I marched him home and it was his sister who opened the door. Blimey, she looked a right corker. Smashing, she was."

"I wish I'd met her," I said.

"Yer mum got her looks from her," he said. "Luckily she didn't take after my side of the family or she wouldn't have earned tuppence on the stage. Have you heard from her recently?"

"Not since she went back to Germany."

"I hope she's not going to marry that German bloke," Granddad said.

"I rather think she intends to."

"No good will come of that. Those Germans, they'll start to build up for another war, you mark my words. They were humiliated after the last one and they're a proud lot. They'll want revenge. And your mum will find herself on the wrong side."

"Golly, I hope not," I said. "But you never answered my question. If you were in the same predicament, would you go?"

He stared down at his plate for a moment, then looked me in the eye. "Yes, I believe I'd go. After all, what have you got to lose? If you get there and he won't see you and he demands that you turn around and go straight home, then at least you tried. At least he knows how much you care about him."

"You're perfectly right, as always," I said. "I always get good advice from you. I'm so glad I came. I'll pack a small bag and take the Irish Mail train in the morning." Then I broke off as a thought occurred to me. "Oh crikey. Queenie. What am I going to do with her? I can't take her with me to Ireland. Things will be complicated enough without having her with me. And I can't leave her at Rannoch House. Fig would go mad and turn her out and besides, they are off to the Continent in a week. Do you think her family would take her back for a short while?"

"For a very short while," he said. "They weren't half glad to get rid of her last time after she set fire to their kitchen. But I'll have a word with her great-aunt next door. I'll explain things and I'm sure she'll take her in. Just don't make it too long, will you?"

"I've no idea how long I'll be away. We'll just have to

see, won't we? But it will be one less thing to worry about if Queenie is safe and sound back here."

"Don't give it another thought, love. You send her in this direction and we'll make sure she's all right."

I came around the table and kissed the top of his bald head. "You really are my favorite person in the whole world, apart from Darcy," I said. "When I'm married one day and I am mistress of a castle or stately home I'll bring you to live at the lodge and we can visit each other every day."

"Now, wouldn't that be nice," he said, giving me a wistful smile. "Let's just hope it all turns out all right."

Chapter 10

December 1 and then Sunday, December 2

**I make a big decision. I do hope it's the right one. I just
wish I knew.**

I arrived back to find Fig and Binky dressed and drinking
sherry before dinner. Fig glared at me in annoyance. "Where
have you been, Georgiana? You didn't let anyone know you
were going out, and we're ready to go in to dinner at any
moment."

"I'm sorry," I said. "I went to see my grandfather and the
train back took longer than I anticipated."

"You went to see your grandfather?" She sounded exactly
like Lady Bracknell in *The Importance of Being Earnest*
when she uttered those famous words "A handbag?"

"Do I need to have your permission before I go to visit
my relatives?" I said, the tension of the day making it harder
for me to control my annoyance.

"No, of course not, but you are a guest in this house and
it is only common courtesy that you let your hosts know
when you might be late for a meal."

"Please feel free to dine without me," I said. "I'm not very hungry."

Binky came over to me then. "You're obviously upset, old bean," he said. "One can understand that. Why don't you go and have a nice long bath and then Mrs. McPherson can make you something simple like an omelet."

"I don't see why we should impose on Mrs. McPherson . . ." Fig began, but Binky cut her off. "Mrs. McPherson is dashed fond of Georgie. I'm sure she'll be delighted to help her to feel better."

"You're very kind," I said to Binky. Then I pressed my lips together. I had a horrible feeling that I might burst into tears at any moment.

"I sincerely hope you did not ask your grandfather whether you could stay with him, after our little discussion, Georgiana," Fig said.

Binky looked at her in surprise. "Why would she want to stay with her grandfather? Dashed inconvenient that far out of London." He looked at me long and hard. "Are you not happy here, Georgie?"

"Binky, you are so dense sometimes," Fig said, before I could reply. "She'll obviously need somewhere to stay when we go to France."

"Why can't she stay on here?" Binky asked.

Fig glared at him. "Because we are going to close up the house and send the servants back to Scotland," she said.

"Georgie lived here quite successfully without servants once before, I seem to remember. She cooked me a boiled egg for breakfast."

"When you were falsely accused and arrested for murder, if I remember correctly," I said.

"Quite right. You were splendid. Solved the whole thing." Binky nodded to Fig.

"In exactly the same predicament as Darcy's father finds himself right now." I drove home the point in case they hadn't picked up on it.

"Not exactly the same," Fig said. "Binky was innocent and everybody knew it."

I was about to say that Darcy's father might be innocent too until I remembered that Darcy himself believed his father to be guilty. A wave of despair swept over me as Binky went on cheerfully,

"And Georgie did look after me jolly well, Fig. She was an absolute brick the whole time. I owe her my life, Fig, so I don't see why we can't let her stay on here."

"Binky, my dear, I must protest . . ." Fig began to say, but I cut in.

"No, please don't worry about me. I'm leaving in the morning. I'm going to stay with friends. It's all arranged."

With that I made my way swiftly to my room. I had Queenie run me a bath and then she brought me a lovely tray of soup and an omelet. In spite of not wanting to eat, I managed to finish both and felt decidedly better. Tomorrow I'd be going to Darcy. And I was going to be firm and strong and not take no for an answer.

"Blimey, up and down these ruddy stairs," Queenie complained when she had taken my tray down again.

"Yes, I realize you've had to work too hard recently," I said. "So I'm giving you a break."

"We're going somewhere nice and warm?" She looked hopeful.

"I'm going somewhere horrible, but you don't have to come," I said. "You can go home to your family."

"Not to them, miss. Lord love a duck." She grimaced.

"Are you not fond of your family?"

"Well, yeah, in a way, I suppose. But they won't want me there. Not after last time. They'll be afraid I'll blow up the stove again. And my old dad spends his life telling me how useless I am and I'd forget my own head if it wasn't attached to my body."

"I can see their point, Queenie," I said. "You are hopeless, but your great-aunt, Mrs. Huggins, has said that you are welcome to come and stay with her until I get back. You can have a nice rest."

She didn't look particularly grateful. "But my place is with you, miss," she said.

"I'm afraid I am going where there will be no room for a maid. And I don't even know how long I'll be away. Maybe only a few days, maybe longer. I'd be happier knowing you were safely with relatives."

"All right. If you say so." The fact that she didn't say "Bob's yer uncle" underscored her reluctance to go home. I suspected that Mrs. Huggins made her work harder than I did.

"If you could make sure I have sufficient clothes to last me for a week or so—my tartan skirt, my good cashmere sweater—and I'll wear my tweed suit. And don't forget my underwear and nightclothes."

"No evening dresses?"

I shook my head. "I don't think they will dress for dinner where I'll be."

"At least I won't have to bother about finding any bleeding tissue paper," she grunted as she went to start packing.

MY JOURNEY TO Ireland did not start particularly auspiciously. When I came to get dressed I found that Queenie had packed all the items I wanted to wear, except for one stocking that couldn't be found. This involved opening my big trunk and taking out most of my clothing, leaving us both feeling frustrated and annoyed. I was more cross with her than usual because my own nerves were at snapping point. In the light of day, with the journey a reality, I questioned whether I was doing the right thing. If Darcy really didn't want me there, if my appearance only complicated the situation for him, he would not be pleased. I suppose I was hoping that he'd run toward me with his arms open, saying, "I couldn't bear to live without you either." But whatever the outcome I was determined to go through with it.

The next complication came when I was preparing to leave. Queenie had become quite weepy, convinced that something terrible was going to happen to me and she'd never see me again. She had produced a large red and white handkerchief and traipsed around behind me blowing her nose at intervals like a foghorn. I had Binky's permission to leave my excess luggage in my room to be collected either when I returned or when I knew where I would be staying. I had just seen a still-tearful Queenie off into a cab (a final treat from me) when Binky came out of his study.

"You're off, then? Are you sure you'll be all right?"

I nodded, feeling a bit tearful myself. "I'll be fine, thank you. And thank you for letting me leave my luggage here. That's one less thing to worry about."

He looked at me long and hard. "You're going to that chap O'Mara, aren't you?"

"I'm afraid I am. He shouldn't be all alone at this time."

"I'd imagine it will be pretty beastly."

"I expect it will, but I won't give up on him because of something his father has done. Remember when you were accused of murder, Binky? Remember how horrid it was?"

"And you stuck by me and got me out of prison. Brilliant, Georgie. I've been grateful ever since."

"I want to help Darcy in any way I can."

He put an arm around my shoulder. "You're a splendid girl, Georgie. An absolute brick. True-blue. I hope O'Mara appreciates you."

"I hope so too," I said.

Binky rummaged inside his pocket. "I know that funds are tight, Georgie. I thought this might help a little." He handed me what looked like several folded five-pound notes.

"Oh no, Binky. I couldn't take your money," I said. "I do have a little to get by on at the moment."

"No, I insist, Georgie." He thrust the notes into my hand. "Take it. It's the least I can do."

"Golly, Binky, are you sure you can afford it? Fig is always saying how hard up you are and I don't want to deprive your family."

"Between you, me and the gatepost, that money from Fig's aunt is going to come in jolly useful. I'm buying a new stock of Angus cattle for the estate. I want to make it profitable."

"Good for you, Binky. Good luck. I hope you have a lovely time in France."

"That is a matter of question," he said. "But I must say I enjoy spending time with Podge on the beach. He's a splendid little chap, isn't he?"

"Yes, he is. I'm very fond of him." I looked around. "I should be going, then. Good-bye and thank you for having me."

"Anytime. Always a pleasure." He gave me an awkward hug. We did not go in for physical affection in our family. "And I'll have Hamilton find you a spare door key so that you can come and claim your luggage."

"You'll do what?" a sharp voice behind me asked.

"Getting a front door key for Georgie so that she can collect her luggage when she returns."

"You're giving her a key to our front door? So that she can come and go as she pleases?"

"I don't see why not."

"That's because you don't think, Binky," she said. And she tried to give him a knowing look—the type of look that parents give each other when they don't want to say something in front of the children.

I had had enough of my sister-in-law. "Honestly, Fig. What on earth do you suspect? That I'll hold orgies on the drawing room floor the moment your back is turned? Or do you really think I would sneak in and sell the silver spoons, or steal your precious coal? Maybe, God forbid, help myself to some tea from the caddy?"

"Really, Georgiana, you go too far. Speak to her, Binky. She is insulting your wife."

She glared at him. Binky went rather red. "Dash it all, Fig. This is frightfully bad form, you know. It's Georgie's house as much as it is ours. I happened to inherit because I'm a chap, but this is the Rannoch family home and Georgie is welcome to come and go as she pleases. Furthermore it's my home, and Georgie's my sister, and it's about time you try to get along with her. After all, I make a big effort to get along with your dismal crowd, don't I?"

"My dismal crowd?" There was a sharpness to her voice that would have cut glass.

Binky, to my amazement, continued. "Come off it, Fig, you have to admit that your sister and brother-in-law are about as boring as they come, and yet I, being an easygoing kind of chap, have agreed to spend a whole winter cooped up with them. So if you want us to go to France, you'd bally well better learn to be a bit more civil to my sister, or there will be no more trips."

There was a stunned silence. I had to refrain from applauding. Binky's face was now bright red, but he flashed me a triumphant grin. I rather suspect it was the first time he had ever stood up to her.

"Well!" Fig said, her own face ashen white. "Well!" There was another long pause. "I'll be going to the morning room if you need me." And she stalked off, her grand exit spoiled only by the banging of her bony hip into the corner of a side table. She pretended it didn't hurt.

Binky and I stared at each other. "Well done, old bean," I said.

He looked sheepish. "There will probably be hell to pay later, but I must say it was worth it."

"You should have put your foot down long ago," I said. "If she tries to start bossing you around, just put her over your knee and give her a spanking with the hairbrush."

He let out a delighted chuckle. "You know, I think I will. Damned good idea."

The fog had melted away to be replaced by drizzle as I came down the steps into Belgrave Square. I hailed a taxicab and was taken to Euston Station to catch the Irish Mail. But when I went up to the ticket counter I found out that the Irish Mail train did not leave until eight forty-five at night. How stupid of me not to have checked first. I certainly didn't want to return to Rannoch House. But I didn't want to sit in a station all that time either. I supposed I could deposit my suitcase at the left luggage and explore London a little, but I was in no mood to go exploring, and the weather certainly wasn't inviting. I wanted to get the journey over and done with.

"That is the only train to Ireland?" I asked. "I'm in an awful hurry to get there."

"It's the only through train that goes right to the ferry," the man at the ticket counter said. "But you can take a train to Chester and then change to the North Wales line that will take you to Holyhead, where you may be able to find an earlier ferry. I'm not sure how often they run in winter."

"I think I'll try it anyway," I said. "Better than waiting around here."

"That's as may be." He didn't look convinced.

"How long does the journey take?" I asked.

"The Mail does it in twelve hours, but your way could take a lot longer, especially if you have to wait a while for a ferry."

"And this is definitely the quickest route?" I asked.

"It's the only route," he said. "Unless you want to go up to Liverpool and across from there to Belfast, which takes a lot longer still."

Of course Belfast was no use to me. So I was forced to book a ticket on the next train heading for Liverpool and to change trains at Chester. I found the right platform and off we went. Four hours later we arrived at Chester. It was an hour before the next train on the North Wales line to Holyhead. I saw instantly why the journey took so long. We stopped at every little town along the Welsh coast. Darkness had fallen before we reached Chester. As we went deeper into Wales the rain intensified so that by the time we arrived at the dock in Holyhead it was bucketing down. That was when I realized that I had forgotten to bring a brolly. Not that it would have done much good at that moment. The wind would have turned it inside out in seconds. So I got absolutely drenched walking from the station to the quayside to find out about a ferry. Then it turned out I'd have a two-hour wait. I sat alone in a cold and miserable waiting room, wishing I was back in my grandfather's warm kitchen, back at Kensington Palace, even back at Rannoch House with Binky and Fig, which shows you how low I was feeling.

By nine o'clock, when we had to board the ship, the wind was howling and even in the darkness I could see the white-caps on the Irish Sea. I decided I wouldn't be able to sleep in that kind of weather so I didn't take a berth. Instead I found a quiet corner in a lounge and tried to make myself comfortable. This wasn't easy. As soon as we left port the boat bucked and rolled like a wild thing. Anything that wasn't bolted down slid and rolled and crashed. There were almost no other passengers and I began to regret bitterly that I hadn't waited for the Irish Mail and the daytime ferry. At least I would have had a good chance of arriving safely. After an hour I wasn't sure we'd ever make it to Dublin and sat there, holding on for dear life and asking myself what use I'd be to Darcy if I perished at sea.

When a large man wearing a sou'wester came up to me I was sure it was to instruct me to abandon ship. Instead of that he asked to see my ticket. He took one look at my face, which was by now positively green.

"You want to get some food and hot drink in your stomach," he said. "Best way to combat feeling seasick."

The notion that I should go to a restaurant and not to a lifeboat almost made me laugh with relief. I couldn't stand the thought of food, but I did slither, stumble and grab my way to a snack bar and managed to drink hot cocoa without spilling too much.

"Ah, but it's a wild night, that's for sure," said the soft-voiced Irishwoman behind the counter. She didn't look at all worried about this.

"I'm surprised that ferries actually sail in such bad weather," I said.

This made her laugh. "Lord love you. If we stayed in port when there was bad weather, we'd never leave. I take it you've never crossed the Irish Sea before?"

"Never," I said.

"So your first time in Ireland, then?"

I nodded.

"It's a pity you're not seeing it in spring the first time. At this time of year it can look rather bleak. Will you be staying in Dublin, then?"

"Near Dublin. With friends," I said, not wanting to give her more information than that.

"And you'll be with them for Christmas, I've no doubt." She gave me an encouraging smile. "Lovely. That will be lovely. We celebrate a grand Christmas in Ireland."

The hot chocolate had started to spread warmth through my body and I found, as the seaman had predicted, that I was feeling better. Well enough, in fact, to have a toasted tea cake. Then I staggered my way to the nearest warm corner and miraculously nodded off.

Chapter 11

MONDAY, DECEMBER 3

**Arrived in Ireland early this morning. Golly, I'm
terrified but no going back now. Courage, Georgie.
Rannochs never give up in the face of adversity!**

I dozed fitfully and awoke to deep rumbles and crashes. For
a second I couldn't remember where I was, then my stiff
neck reminded me that I had been lying against the hard
wall of a ship's lounge. I sat up, alarmed by the noises. Had
we hit something? Was the boat breaking up? Then I realized that we were not being tossed around anymore. I got
up and went over to a window. It was still quite dark but
through the rain-streaked glass I thought I could make out
occasional lights. Thank heavens. That meant we had come
into harbor and those noises I had heard were the sounds of
gangplanks being pushed up onto the boat. I peered at my
watch. Four o'clock in the morning. An announcement
crackled, telling passengers that the gangway was midships.
I gathered my belongings and joined the hearty few who
had braved the crossing with me, disembarking onto a wind-

swept and rainy dock, apparently in the middle of nowhere. There were no signs of a city, no signs of civilization at all, and the wind was still driving the rain almost horizontally. If I hadn't been raised at Castle Rannoch, where this weather counted as normal, I might have turned around on the spot and fled back to England. Except that I didn't want to face that crossing again!

"Is this Dublin?" I asked a man who was striding out confidently as if he knew where he was going. I had a horrible sinking feeling that I might have taken the wrong boat.

"Dun Leary," the man replied. I had no idea what this meant but I wasn't going to show my ignorance. So I followed the other passengers to a bleak railway platform. I waited with the others and then boarded a small train that chuffed through the night. Eventually I could make out city streets and bigger buildings and soon we pulled into Dublin's main station. It was still only five o'clock in the morning, much too early to show up at Kilhenny. What was more, the station was still deserted and the restaurant still closed. I sat on a bench, feeling wet, cold, miserable and far from home.

At six o'clock the station started to come to life and the café opened. I was starving by this time and treated myself to a proper breakfast. Thus fortified, I went to find out which train would take me to Kilhenny Castle. It seemed I'd have to get out at Kildare and find other means of transportation from there.

"You wouldn't be the first person who wanted to get to Kilhenny Castle this week," the ticket clerk said, grinning as he handed me my ticket. "I'd never even heard of it a few days ago. Now it seems the whole world wants to go there."

I said nothing as I handed him the money then headed for the platforms. By now my suitcase was feeling remarkably heavy and I felt sick, tired and scared. If the whole world was heading to Kilhenny Castle then everyone had been quite right about warning me to stay away. Someone in the press would indeed recognize me. I still had time to turn around and go back to England. But then I told myself that nobody knew of my relationship with Darcy. I'd say I was merely visiting friends nearby and came to see the castle for myself. Pure curiosity, that's all. I felt somewhat reassured as we chugged out of the station. It was still dark but a gray dawn gradually appeared, revealing a green and rain-streaked countryside. We were passing through a gentle land of rolling hills and green fields. And many of the fields had horses in them—fine Thoroughbred horses that tossed their heads and galloped away at the toot of the train's whistle.

After several stops we came to the town of Kildare. The rain had subsided to a gentle drizzle. It was still early in the morning. I expected the town to be awaking gently from sleep, but quite a few people got out of the train with me and the town beyond was all hustle and bustle. Then I saw that it was market day. Stalls were being set up, cattle were being led to pens and people from the country were unloading their produce. It seemed a pleasant enough little market town, almost identical to such towns in England, and it was strange to think I was in another country. Apart from the gentle Irish lilt to the voices I could have been anywhere. I was met with a smile when I asked a man if a bus went near Kilhenny Castle.

"Only if you don't mind a two-mile walk in the rain," the man replied. "If you want to get there you'd better find Barney's taxi. He'll be happy to take you if he's out of bed yet."

So it seemed it was a taxi or nothing. Barney was eventually found and the clock on the town hall chimed nine as we set off. Barney was a big, florid man who liked to chat.

"You'll be another of those reporters, I don't doubt," he said. "But I warn you, you can't get near the actual castle. The police are making sure of that. Of course, that American gentleman didn't want visitors, did he? Put up big iron gates where there had been none in his lordship's time. Not at all what you'd call the friendly sort. They say his man-servant shot at a trespasser once."

There was a long pause and then he went on, "Of course, his lordship wasn't exactly beloved either in these parts. Had a terrible temper on him, even before he lost his wife in the Spanish flu. But after that, well, it was hard to get a civil word out of him. Bite your head off if he was in a bad mood, so they say. I never met him myself. I don't exactly hobnob with the gentry." And he laughed at his own joke.

Again I said nothing.

"You're not thinking of staying in the village, I hope? Both the pubs are full and I doubt you'd even find a spare bed in Kildare or Newbridge. There are even reporters over here from America. I drove some American woman to Kilhenny a week or so ago and she gave me a pound as a tip. A pound! Imagine that! Well, I thought perhaps she wasn't familiar with our money, but I certainly wasn't about to point out her mistake to her."

And he chuckled again. We were driving between hedgerows that would have been leafy in the summer, but were now a mass of twisted and bare twigs. Beyond them were rain-soaked fields with puddles in them and depressed-looking cows or horses standing stoically. There were patches of bare woodland, gently rising hills, a stream gushing under a stone bridge. Now and then we passed a stone farmhouse, or a row of cottages, and then we came to a small village with a row of shops, a pub called the Harp and a church, surrounded by tombstones. Rooks flew from a yew tree, cawing. But apart from that there was no sign of life.

"This is where you'll want to be dropped off," Barney said.

"Where's the castle itself?" I asked, realizing as I said it that it was still far too early to call upon anyone. "Is it far to walk?"

"Not unless you're one of those lady reporters with high-heeled shoes," he replied, chuckling. "About a quarter of a mile down that lane to the entrance. You'll come to the wall around the castle grounds just after you leave the village but the gate's a good way beyond."

"Can you drive me there?" I asked. "I'd like to see for myself."

"It's your money," he said. "I've got nothing but time."

He let the clutch out and we nosed into a narrow lane. We hadn't gone far before we came upon a high brick wall on our right. On our left was an open field with some kind of excavation work clearly in progress—mounds of earth and tarps covering some areas.

"Are they building something there?" I asked.

"No, it's those archeologists. Apparently it's a prehistoric site and they are digging up an ancient burial chamber or something. I can't understand this sudden interest in digging up old remains. If it was a palace or a treasure trove of gold, well, that's one thing. But they find an old broken piece of pottery and they act as if it's wonderful. Waste of time and money, if you ask me."

"How long have they been working on this site?" I asked.

"A couple of months now, it would be. Stupid time of year to start, if you want my opinion. Too cold and rainy."

"Are they staying nearby?"

"Apparently they asked if they could stay at the castle but the American told them to go and jump in the nearest lake. I told you he wasn't the most hospitable of men. So they're at the O'Mara Arms in the next village. Ah, here we are now."

I found that my heart was racing. To our right was a gateway, with ancient stone gateposts on either side, each one topped by a crumbling stone lion. A new metal gate, tipped with what looked like spears, now barred the entrance. Beyond it the driveway ran straight between borders of yew trees and in the distance I caught a glimpse of the castle itself, an imposing building of gray stone rising above the trees with a turret at one corner. It reminded me of my home at Castle Rannoch. I thought of Darcy, running through those grounds as a little boy. A happy little boy until his mother and brothers died and his father became so bitter.

"So the American man lived in the castle. Where exactly did Lord Kilhenny live after he moved out?" I asked, wanting to know where the lodge was but not wanting the taxi driver to know how much I already knew.

"I know nothing about it, me darlin'. Just what I've read in the papers like everyone else. So where to now?"

"I suppose you'd better drop me off in the village," I said.

"You're planning to stay, are you? I don't think you've a chance of finding out much here or getting an interview with any of the family. But it's not for me to say." He turned the motor toward those tall gates then reversed. At the sound of our engine a policeman appeared from among the trees and stood watching us as we drove away.

"I see that the Garda is still keeping an eye on the place," Barney commented.

"Guards? I thought he was a policeman."

"The Garda are what we call our police force. I take it it's your first time in Ireland, then."

"That's right," I said. I glanced back and saw the policeman still staring after us. It appeared that getting in to find Darcy would not be easy. There were a few signs of life as we came back into the village street. A milk cart, drawn by a tired old horse, was delivering bottles to doorsteps. The newsagent was opening up, setting out morning papers. The greengrocer was arranging cabbages under a canopy from which rain dripped. Barney stopped the taxi outside the Harp.

"I'll leave you here, then. They have a telephone at the pub. They can get a message to me if you want to be picked up later."

"Thank you." I climbed out, retrieved my suitcase and paid him. He asked what seemed rather a large amount but I suspected his rates had shot up in the last week when reporters paid without quibbling. The taxi drove off and I stood alone in the village of Kilhenny, not sure what I should do next. Rain dripped off the brim of my hat. I looked around, wondering how I could ask about finding the lodge without word going all over the village, and whether I would have to walk back that half mile lugging my suitcase. And it occurred to me that Darcy might not even be at the lodge. If his father was still being held in prison somewhere, maybe even in Dublin, would he not want to be close by? I could see now that this quest of mine had not been well thought-out. I should have stayed in Dublin and asked my first questions there rather than rushing into the middle of nowhere.

But I was here now, and unless I could persuade Barney to come back for me, I was stuck here. The frosted glass door of the pub was firmly locked but as I was standing there the milkman came toward me with two bottles. He nodded a good morning to me then went around the side of the pub to put the bottles outside another door.

"Were you waiting for someone, miss?" he asked as he returned.

"No, I just got here," I said. "And I'm not sure what to do next."

He grinned. "Another of those lady reporters, I suppose. Well, you're out of luck if you're looking for a room here. There's already two of them staying at the pub. And Mrs. O'Shea has taken in two more as paying guests. I don't know what they think they are going to report on. The trial will be in Dublin, won't it?"

I nodded, then took a deep breath. "Lord Kilhenny's son. I understand he came back here to be with his father."

"He might have done."

"And Lord Kilhenny was living at the lodge when this happened?"

"I only know what I've been told, like everyone else. But yes, his lordship had been living at the old gamekeeper's lodge since that American bought the castle. He'd no business to go and sell it if you ask me. The O'Mara family had owned that place since the twelve hundreds. I knew no good would come of selling it to an American, even if he did claim Irish ancestry. And no good has come, has it. That man got rid of all the servants and he'd been living there like a hermit ever since. Didn't mix with anyone. If he went out, it was in one of those big black motorcars, driven by his man. And now this."

"I think I'd like to take a look at the lodge for myself," I said. "Is it on the castle grounds?"

"Not exactly. It's off to one side, on the road where the home farm and the stables are. It used to be the old entrance to the castle until they had the present driveway built in the last century."

"So it's past the new gates?"

"It is not. It's before them. You turn down that little lane when you come to the castle wall. Keep following the wall and then you'll see the roof of the stables ahead of you and you'll find the lodge in a little spinney, off to the left all on its own."

"Thank you," I said. "I wonder if there's anywhere I might leave my suitcase for the moment?"

"I don't suppose Mrs. Murphy at the pub would mind. Knock on the door there and see what she says."

With that he went back to the milk cart, empty bottles jingling. I tapped on the door and was greeted by a pleasant-looking woman in a flowery pinny. Of course she'd be glad to look after my suitcase, she said. She was only sorry she couldn't offer me a place to stay, but she was bursting at the seams. She must have taken pity on my drowned-rat appearance because she poured me a cup of tea and said she'd be glad to feed me my midday meal if I was still in the village.

I had just spruced myself up in her ladies' room and was about to face the rain again when I heard footsteps coming downstairs and a woman came toward me. One look at her and I knew she was American. She was wearing a purple scarf over very blond hair set in tight little waves, and her mouth was a bright red gash of lipstick. She eyed me with interest.

"Don't tell me you're another one of the fraternity," she said. "Which paper do you work for, honey?" The accent confirmed my suspicion.

"I don't work for any paper," I said. "I'm just staying in Dublin and popping over to visit a friend here." Then I decided attack was the best form of defense. "How about you? Presumably you're from an American newspaper?"

"Magazine, honey. Ladies' magazine. Our readers love tales about dukes and earls and things. Especially bad ones. I've been trying to get some dirt from the locals. So which of them is your friend? Maybe I could come along with you."

"I don't think so," I said hastily. "My friend hasn't been

well. I plan to keep things really quiet and simple, if you don't mind."

As I went to leave she called after me, "I didn't get your name, honey."

I said the first thing that came into my head. "It's Pauncefoot-Smith. Belinda Pauncefoot-Smith."

She laughed. "You English with your snooty names. You crack me up."

"And your name?" I asked.

"Connie," she said. "Connie Wright."

"Nice to meet you, Miss Wright," I said. "Now I fear I must brave the elements. My friend lives a long way out of town."

"There's some guy with a taxi around sometimes," she said. "You could have the innkeeper call him."

"Oh, I don't mind walking, thank you," I said. I left the pub and set off in the wrong direction, just in case she had decided to follow me. Then I slipped between houses and managed to cut back along a footpath between allotments. The rain had now subsided to a gentle drizzle. I followed the lane back to the castle wall, then saw an even narrower lane going off to the right. At first I walked gently uphill, then the land dipped ahead of me and I saw the red roofs of the stables among green fields. There was a flash of movement and color coming over the rise and I realized, with something of a thrill, that the horses were being put through their morning paces. They came toward me until the ground echoed with the thud of their hooves. Then they rounded a corner and were gone. So life at the stables was going on, even without an owner or trainer. Unless the American had hired a new trainer after he sacked Darcy's father.

I had been so intent on watching the horses that I hadn't been paying attention to what was happening on the other side of the lane. I turned and saw that the high wall had disappeared to the left. There was now a dense stand of woodland beside the road and among the trees I spotted a house, or rather cottage. It too was built of gray stone but had a depressing look to it, with small windows and overhanging eaves. Witch's house from the Brothers Grimm came into my mind. I would not have wanted to live there. But smoke was coming from the chimney, which must mean someone was living there now. I took a deep breath and followed the flagstone path that wound between the trees to the front door.

I had rehearsed my speech so many times during the past twenty-four hours. "Hello, Darcy. I'm here and I love you and I'm not leaving so don't try to make me. I want to do anything I can to help you."

I repeated it once more as I approached the front door. I lifted the big black knocker and brought it down with a resounding crash. At the sound, rooks rose cawing from nearby trees. The front door opened and I found myself staring not at Darcy but at an older version of himself. The dark curls were tinged with gray, the face had deep frown lines etched onto the brow, and the mouth turned down at the corners. Those lines turned to a scowl when he saw me.

"What the devil do you think you're doing here?" he demanded. "How did you even know that I'd come home? Damn and curse you blasted reporters. If you don't get out of my sight this very minute I might well consider committing a second murder. After all, you can only hang once."

Any sensible speech had deserted me. He looked truly frightening, his eyes blazing with anger, and I well believed that he could kill without thinking twice about it.

"You don't understand, Lord Kilhenny," I stammered, because my heart was still beating really fast. "I'm not a reporter. I didn't even know you would be here. I came to see your son."

"Darcy?" he demanded. "And what might you want with my son?"

What should I say now? Obviously not that Darcy and I had been about to get married. I tried to think of something reasonable but my brain still refused to work. Then the need to come up with a reply was taken from me. There were footsteps in the dark hallway beyond and a voice demanded, "Georgie? What are you doing here?"

Chapter 12

Darcy and I stood there, staring at each other. I couldn't tell what emotion lay behind those alarming dark blue eyes. Not anger, surely. But fear? I mustered every ounce of self-control and put on a bright smile.

"Hello, Darcy! So my friends were right. They said they'd seen you in Ireland. I'm staying with pals in Dublin and I thought I couldn't possibly be so close without looking you up. The gang in London all send their love." I could hear that I was babbling but I couldn't stop.

I thought a flicker of amusement lit his eyes for a fraction of a second.

"Good to see you, old thing," he replied in similar tones. "I had no idea you were visiting Dublin. I'd ask you in, but it's not exactly convenient."

"Not exactly convenient?" Darcy's father thundered at him. "It's bad enough you turning up here out of the blue and foisting yourself upon me. The last thing I need at the

moment is your absurd London crowd bursting in on us."
He turned back to me with a scowl. "And who might you
be, young lady?"

"Oh, just one of Darcy's many London friends," I said.
"We're all so frightfully fond of him, you know."

Before Darcy's father could explode or lunge at me,
Darcy edged past him and grabbed my arm. "Calm down,
Father. She meant well. Go back inside."

He forced me away from the doorstep. "Good of you to
come, old thing, but in the circumstances I'll walk you back
to the village and see if we can find some means of transportation for you. I presume you didn't drive yourself?"

"No, I came by taxi. A nice man called Barney." I turned
back to Darcy's father, who was still glaring at us. "I'm so
frightfully sorry to have disturbed you, Lord Kilhenny.
Please forgive me."

Lord Kilhenny shot me a final angry look then turned his
back on me, disappearing into the darkness of the hallway.
Darcy still had a firm hold on my forearm and propelled me
up the flagstone path. We walked fast, without saying a word
until we were back on the lane and out of sight of the lodge.
Then Darcy turned to face me. His eyes were blazing. "Why
did you do this, Georgie? I told you not to come. I told you
that you and I must sever all ties. I thought I made that quite
clear. Are you out of your mind coming here?" He was still
gripping my arm so firmly that it hurt.

"Let go; you're hurting me!" I exclaimed. "I came because I love you, and I'm not going to let you go through
this alone." I stared at him defiantly. It had begun to rain
more heavily again and he was wearing an old jumper and
corduroy trousers that would soon be soaked. His dark curls
were already plastered to his forehead and rain streamed
down his face like tears. He didn't appear to notice.

"But it's all over between us. It has to be, don't you see?"
He had been shouting. Now I heard the hopelessness in his
voice. "You must take the next train back to Dublin and go
home. I insist."

"You can't force me. It's a free country. I can come and

go as I please. And I choose to stay near you, whether you want it or not." I heard the wobble in my voice as I said this.

He sighed. "Don't be a fool. The place is crawling with reporters. Someone is going to recognize you."

"And if they do, so what? I'll say what I said to your father: that I'm staying with friends in Dublin and thought I'd come out to show support for my pal Darcy. What's so worrying about that? Nobody knows that we're engaged."

"But we're not engaged anymore." There was now desperation in his voice. "We can't be. You have to see that. We can never marry. I won't put you through this. I won't have your life blighted the way mine will be. As soon as this business is over I'm going far away—Australia, maybe, or South America."

"Then I'm coming with you. I'll start learning to throw the boomerang or brush up on my Spanish."

He gave a brittle laugh and gripped my shoulders. "God, Georgie, do you think I don't want you with me? Of course I do. I can't bear the thought of being parted from you. But everywhere I go I'll be known as the son of a murderer. I can't allow that to happen to you. I won't allow it."

"You really believe that your father is guilty, do you?" I asked. "Has he confessed to the crime?"

He released me and turned away. "Not exactly. But the evidence is overwhelming."

"Have you asked him outright if he did it?"

He was frowning at me. "He won't talk to me, but as I said, the evidence is overwhelming. He and Mr. Roach had a loud argument and my father was heard to tell Roach that he'd kill him one day."

"Lots of people threaten to kill each other," I said. "So what other evidence is there?"

Darcy shook his head, staring out past me. "Plenty. There were no visitors that evening and nobody in the castle except Mr. Roach's manservant. Mrs. McNalley, who comes in to cook and clean, had already gone home for the night. Mr. Roach's man went into the library to see if his master needed anything before he went to bed, saw signs of a struggle, and found Roach lying there with the back of his head stove in and an ancient battle club that had hung on the wall lying nearby, covered with blood. And when the Garda tested the club my father's fingerprints were on it. Nobody else's. Rather conclusive, wouldn't you say?"

"But what does your father say?"

Darcy sighed. "The trouble is he can't remember anything. I should have told you before, but after my mother died, my father took to the bottle. That evening he drank himself into oblivion, judging by the empty Jameson bottle that was found on his kitchen table next morning. He remembered the argument earlier and even remembered telling Roach that one day he'd push my father too far. But the evening is a blank. He has no recollection of going to the castle and certainly not of killing Roach."

"So he might not be guilty."

Darcy gave a short and bitter laugh. "Do you think any jury would take drunkenness or amnesia as an excuse? His fingerprints were on the club. Nobody else's."

"Was there any blood on his clothing?" I asked.

"I have no idea."

"Because if this Mr. Roach was hit with considerable force then it's highly likely that at least one drop of blood spattered in the killer's direction."

Darcy looked at me and shook his head in disbelief. "Your royal relatives would swoon on the spot if they heard you saying that."

"I'm trying to be helpful, Darcy. I'm trying to see if there is any remote possibility that your father was framed."

"Framed? How could he have been framed?" He was shouting now and rooks rose cawing again.

"He would be the ideal person to pin this on, wouldn't he? Turned out of his ancestral home. Accused of horse doping. Sacked from his position as trainer at the stables. And the recent argument when he threatened to kill this Mr. Roach. Such a strong motive for wanting Mr. Roach dead."

"Exactly," Darcy snapped. "So many reasons that any jury would find him guilty."

"But if he wasn't guilty?" I asked quietly.

He stared out past me, to where the distant shapes of horses galloped across the landscape. For a long while he said nothing. I could hear the far-off thud of hoofbeats that faded away to silence.

"Do you believe with all your heart that he is guilty?" I asked. "From all that you know of your father?"

"Of course I don't want to," he said. "And the truth is that I know little of my father. I was away at school from the age of seven. He always had a fiery temper, I know that. But I don't ever remember him beating me or my brothers. He'd explode in anger, yell a bit, and then it would all be over and forgotten. But that was before he took to drink. Alcohol robs a man of reason, doesn't it?"

"It also robs a man of balance," I said. "If he was blind drunk, wouldn't it have been easy to push your father over? To disarm him if he was swinging a club?"

"So you think he could be innocent, do you?" he asked.

"I don't know him," I said. "But I think he deserves to have someone on his side. And for selfish reasons of course I want him to be innocent, for your sake. For both our sakes."

"My darling Georgie," he said and wrapped me in his arms. "I didn't want you to have anything to do with this sordid business, but now that you're here, I'm awfully glad."

I rested my head against his shoulder, feeling a brief moment of perfect peace.

"I'm sorry I barged in on your father like that," I said as he released me. "I didn't realize he'd be there. I thought he'd still be locked away in prison."

"He was released on bail yesterday," Darcy said. "At least his useless solicitor managed that much. The family having been a backbone of the community for a thousand years. Not a flight risk. All that sort of stuff. Apparently the judge agreed, although my father can't leave the immediate area without a police or legal escort. But better than Dublin jail."

"You're soaking wet," I said, as I became conscious of the wet wool against my cheek and the smell of wet sheep. "You'd better go back and change before you catch a cold."

"I think a cold is the least of my worries right now," he said, managing a smile. He released me from his arms. "We have to decide what to do with you first. There really is nowhere for you to stay here. Even if my father were not in his current state, the lodge is too small. I'll take you back to the village and the wisest thing would be for you to take a train back to Dublin." He corrected that. "Actually the wisest thing would be for you to go back to London."

"Which you know I'm not going to do. I want to be with you here. I want to help. If nobody is working on your father's behalf then we have to. Two heads are better than one, Darcy."

He sighed. "I don't know, Georgie. I don't know anything anymore. How can I do my best for my father if I'm constantly worrying about protecting you?"

"You don't have to protect me. I'm a big girl. And if this whole thing had happened a day later, if there hadn't been a snowstorm in Yorkshire, then I'd have been your wife by now and of course my place would be at your side. So let's have no more talk about sending me back to London, all right?"

"I can see you're going to be stubborn about this."

"Absolutely right. I am. You can't get rid of me that easily, Darcy O'Mara. I've wanted to marry you since the moment we first met. When you picked me up in a London café and told me to put on my posh frock because we were going to crash a wedding."

"You should have refused me then. It would have saved you a lot of trouble."

"What, and ended up married to Prince Fishface instead? That would have been a better option?"

We looked at each other and had to laugh.

"God, Georgie. What a mess."

"We'll get through it." I took his hand and we walked on.

"So where do we start?" I asked after we had walked for a while in silence.

"I suppose the question would be who else might have a motive for wanting a reclusive American dead," he said.

"His manservant?"

"Hired in America. Seemed intensely loyal. Quite broken up about his employer's death."

"What do we know about this Mr. Roach?" I asked.

"Not very much," Darcy said. "I wasn't around when my father declared bankruptcy and the castle and stables had to be sold to pay his debts. An American millionaire, I was told."

"That's all?"

"Apparently a reclusive type who had inherited money and wanted to go back to his Irish roots. Books and horses, those were his interests, so I heard. One of the reasons he bought this particular castle was that it came with both."

"And his money came from where?"

"Family money. They built property in Chicago at the beginning of the century. He was the last survivor and inherited it all, I'm told."

"Are there any valuable objects in the castle?" I asked.

Darcy frowned. "Apparently the rare books in the library are worth something. Maybe some of the portraits. But it's not as if we had a Frans Hals or a Gainsborough."

"And nothing was stolen? I was wondering if Mr. Roach interrupted a burglary in progress."

"I don't think anything was taken. The Garda nosed around a bit and found nothing suspicious."

"The manservant heard nothing?"

"He says he was in the kitchen, washing up Roach's late supper. That's down two floors from the library and the walls are rather solid. He didn't know that anyone else was in the house. He came up and stumbled upon the body."

"Has your father engaged a good lawyer?" I asked.

This made Darcy laugh again. "He's using the family solicitors, Leach and Leach. They've been our family lawyers since seventeen hundred and something. Old Mr. Leach must be eighty and his son approaching sixty."

"Then you must persuade them to hire a top-notch barrister."

"Top-notch barristers cost money and we have none. Besides, what would be the point? The prosecutor would show the jury the weapon with my father's fingerprints on it and they'd all find him guilty."

I stopped and swung to face him. "You really believe he's guilty, don't you? Your own father. You don't even want to save him from the noose."

"Of course I want to save him," Darcy retorted angrily. "But I have to face facts. You have to face facts. And the big question is, who else could have done it?"

"That's what we have to find out," I said.

Chapter 13

As we approached the village Darcy released his hand from mine.

"We can't be too careful," he said. "There are news reporters staying at the Harp, just hoping for the odd juicy detail for their readers. Star-crossed lovers would be just what they are looking for. Especially if one of them is almost royal. Can't you see the headline?"

I nodded. The high street had now come to life. A wagon loaded high with peat was wending its way slowly past. Two housewives had just come out of the baker's shop. The enticing aroma of freshly baked bread wafted toward us. A farmer walked past, a sheepdog at his heels. He nodded curtly to Darcy but said nothing.

"We must keep an eye out for an American reporter," I muttered to Darcy. "She tried to weasel out of me who I was visiting and why I was here. I lied and said I was Miss Pauncefoot-Smith, visiting a sick friend."

"Not Chomondley-Fanshaw?" Darcy grinned. It was the

first time his face had relaxed since he appeared at the open door.

"It was the first thing that came into my head," I said.

"But all the more reason to get you away from here rapidly," he whispered. "These press people are not stupid. It won't take them long to find out who you really are, and then they'll never leave you alone."

"I'm not going back to England," I whispered back. "I suppose I could find somewhere to stay in Dublin and still be able to help. I presume that's where the detectives are situated, isn't it? I might be able to find out something useful for you."

"I don't think that would be wise." He looked alarmed. "The Garda detective who seems to be handling the case is an Inspector Callahan. He clearly thinks he's Ireland's answer to Sherlock Holmes. He is also not prepared to look beyond my father as the one and only suspect. And he's fiercely republican. Fought for Ireland's freedom. So if he found out that a member of England's ruling family was trying to get herself involved, he'd probably hang my father on the spot."

"Point taken," I said. "Shall I see if there is somewhere to stay in Kildare, then?"

Darcy frowned, thinking. "I'm sorry," he said. "This has all been a bit overwhelming. It's hard to remember that three days ago we were on our way to Scotland without a care in the world."

"I know," I said. "But it will all come right in the end, Darcy. We just have to get through a tough time ahead. And if it's bad for us, think how your father must feel."

"I wonder," he said. "Last night, when he'd had a couple of whiskeys, he said it might be better all around if he put a gun to his head and blew his brains out. Fortunately he doesn't own a gun. But he may not be much help in his own cause."

I saw the pain on his face. "I should retrieve my suitcase from the pub," I said. "The landlady was nice enough to look after it for me."

Darcy nodded. "She's a good sort. Her son and I were great pals when we were young. In fact—" He broke off as we neared the pub. "Well, talk of the devil."

A young man had just come out of that side door. A strapping chap, well muscled and red faced from spending his life outdoors. He wore a tweed jacket and a tweed cap on his head and his face lit up when he saw Darcy.

"They said you'd come back, Mr. Darcy," he said, striding up to take Darcy's hand.

Darcy clapped him on the shoulder. "None of this 'Mr. Darcy' nonsense, Paddy. You're my oldest friend." He turned back to me. "This is Miss Georgie, a friend of mine from London. And this is my old pal Paddy Murphy. Paddy and I got up to some rare old high jinks together, didn't we?"

"We did that." Paddy was still beaming, then his smile faded. "I'm terrible sorry to hear what's happened to your dad," he said. "Most around here think it's a terrible shame." He looked around. "There's not a person here who wanted to see the castle go out of O'Mara hands in the first place, and that American man was never welcome here. Never wanted to have anything to do with the local community. All his food was shipped in from Dublin. Never so much as bought a loaf of bread here. And never showed his face in the village. It was said he wanted to come back to his Irish roots, but not once did he come down to the Harp and meet the local men."

Darcy nodded, then he said, "Paddy, you wouldn't happen to know where there might be a vehicle I could borrow? My father's estate car is locked away in the garage at the big house and the Garda won't let anyone in or out."

Paddy frowned. "I'd let you borrow mine but I have urgent need of it myself right now. My wife, Maureen, is about to give birth to our third child any day now. And she didn't have an easy time of it with the last one. So I'm thinking we might be dashing for the hospital in Kildare."

"Of course. I quite understand," Darcy said. "Three children already. Fancy that."

"You've been slacking, I can see." Paddy laughed. "You've

got some catching up to do." Then he held up a finger. "Wait a minute. I know where you'd find a vehicle. I saw your uncle Dooley the other day and he was being driven by their old butler and he said they had to give the motorcar an airing occasionally as they hardly got out anymore."

"Uncle Dooley. Brilliant. Why didn't I think of that! I suppose we could walk to their place but the weather is not exactly inviting at the moment."

"I can take you over there myself if you don't mind waiting while I complete my errands," Paddy said. "I need to pick up a sack of chicken feed and some fence wire, then I'm going past Mountjoy."

"That would be marvelous," Darcy said and I noticed his voice had started to have an Irish lilt to it. "You live out that way yourself now, do you?"

"I do. I've taken over the small holding my grandfather used to have. Nothing much but we've a few cows and chickens and we grow barley."

"But weren't you working at the stables before?"

"I was until it was taken over. When I questioned the way something was being done, Mr. Roach told me to get out. Can't say I was sorry to leave either. I didn't like the feel of things there anymore."

Darcy looked at him sharply. "You didn't like the way things were being done?" he said. "Do you think Mr. Roach knew about the horse doping?"

"I wouldn't be surprised if he didn't order it himself," Paddy said. "Where would your father know how to get his hands on the latest drugs? And your father cared about those horses. You know he did. He'd never have risked one of them dying just to win a race."

"Interesting." Darcy nodded. "And you're right. The only thing my father has shown affection for in recent years has been his horses. And yet Roach publicly blamed him for that dead horse at the racetrack. And sacked him from being a trainer at what used to be his own stable. The ultimate insult and injury, wouldn't you say? Unfortunately it only provides another nail in his coffin, doesn't it?"

Paddy looked confused then said, "Oh, you mean another reason to want to kill Roach? Yes, I have to confess, it doesn't look good for him. Well, we're behind him here, no matter what." He touched Darcy's arm. "The van is parked outside the butcher's. If you and the young lady want to get in, we'll drive over to the farm shop."

"Georgie needs to pick up her suitcase from your mother first," Darcy said. "You drive over and we'll catch up with you."

"Go ahead of me just in case that woman reporter is lurking inside," I whispered to Darcy. He nodded. I hung back in the shadows. But before we reached the door Mrs. Murphy herself came out. She beamed when she saw Darcy. "Well, this is a treat, I must say. You're looking fine, Mr. Darcy. And you must have bumped into our Paddy. They are expecting their third this week."

"So we heard," Darcy said. "We've come to pick up this young lady's suitcase you were kind enough to look after."

"Oh, right you are, Mr. Darcy. I'll just fetch it."

Mrs. Murphy eyed me inquiringly as she came out with the suitcase. "I didn't realize this young lady was a friend of yours, Mr. Darcy."

"Yes, I'm part of his London set," I said, again in my best "bright young thing" voice. "I was in Dublin and heard he was here so I had to stop by to say hello."

Mrs. Murphy looked down at the suitcase as if trying to work out why I'd be lugging a suitcase from Dublin if saying hello was all I wanted to do.

"We should be going," Darcy said. "Your Paddy is giving us a lift."

"We're really sorry about your father, Mr. Darcy," she said. "It must be awful hard on you."

Darcy nodded. Tried to find something to say, but couldn't. Then he picked up my suitcase and turned away.

As we walked down the village street I said, "You have an uncle and aunt living nearby?"

"Great-uncle and great-aunt," he said. "Uncle Dooley and Aunt Oona. She's my father's aunt. She lives in the old family manor house on the other side of the village. They're both completely batty, of course. And they haven't spoken to my father for years."

"Why not?"

"There was a falling-out ages ago because my father killed their dog."

"He killed their dog?" My voice must have sounded shrill. I couldn't help thinking that Darcy's father had a history of killing things.

"Not on purpose, you understand. The stupid dog used to like to lie on the driveway at night. It was a black dog and my father simply didn't see it. He was actually quite upset about it but my father is not good at saying what he feels. When he wants to hide emotion he makes a joke of it. So he made some kind of flippant remark about the dog being old and smelly and saving them the trouble of putting it down. But Oona adored that animal and has never spoken to him since."

"How sad."

"Irish families tend to make this kind of drama," he said. "Be forewarned."

I felt a small jolt of happiness at that remark because it indicated he was still thinking of a possible future for us together.

"So, Darcy," I said, voicing something that had always confused me, "you're Irish and yet you seem to work for the English government from time to time. How is that possible?"

He smiled. "As you know, my mother was English. I was educated in England. I saw myself as British. And when Ireland became a republic I opted to retain my English passport, much to my father's annoyance. So we've been on opposite sides for some time now."

"At least I won't be marrying a foreigner as well as a Catholic," I said, half jokingly.

He gave me a warning frown. "We can't talk of marriage, Georgie. Not here. Not at all. We can't afford to forget for a minute why we're here."

Then he set off, walking briskly ahead of me with the suitcase.

Chapter 14

I'm feeling a little better. In spite of the chaos, I think I might feel safe here.

It took a while to reach Great-Aunt Oona and Great-Uncle Dooley's house. I was squashed between Paddy and Darcy into the middle of the front seat of Paddy's rickety van while Paddy completed his errands, then we bumped and lurched along the road out of the village until I began to feel quite sick. I realized then that I had spent the night being tossed around on the high seas and had hardly slept at all. And here I was, being tossed about in another vehicle. Darcy and Paddy chatted across me about old times, pranks they had played, gossip about fellow villagers.

"Well, it was quite obvious she was in the family way," Paddy said and Darcy laughed.

"And did he do the right thing?" Darcy asked his old friend.

I sneaked a glance at him. This was a side of Darcy I hadn't seen before. Not the sophisticated member of high society, but the local boy, coming home to his roots. They seemed to have forgotten I was in the car with them and I stared ahead as the last of the houses gave way to rolling countryside. The lane had high banks on either side, topped with hedgerows, and we dropped down a steep hill to a bridge over a stream. With all this rain the water was frothing and tumbling over rocks. I was more than glad when we turned into a long straight driveway, just wide enough for the vehicle with ditches on either side.

"Not the sort of place you'd want to drive back to after a night at the pub," Paddy commented.

"I think Dooley had to be towed out often enough in his younger days," Darcy said.

Ahead of us a large ramshackle stone building came into view. It looked as if it had been added to over the centuries in various periods and various styles—a gabled roof here, an octagonal turret there.

"There it is: Mountjoy," Darcy said.

To me it seemed oddly named, neither on a mountain nor particularly joyful. In fact the land around it was flat and on this day the house itself presented a gloomy picture with its narrow windows and rain-slicked roof tiles. Chickens scattered as we drove onto the forecourt. A pack of dogs rushed out barking and started jumping up around the van. Then an enormous woman appeared in the doorway, staring at us, hands on hips.

"Get down, get away, you dreadful curs," she shouted in a booming voice to match her bulk. "Come over here, do you hear?"

The dogs were still jumping up, barking, but I noticed the tails were wagging.

"You're all hopeless, hopeless," she went on, clapping her hands now. "One word from me and they do exactly as they please. No discipline at all."

Paddy opened the driver's side door and the dogs surrounded him as he stepped down.

"Oh, it's you, Paddy," she said. "And what brings you here, I'd like to know—not just coming on a friendly call to see if the old folks have snuffed it yet? You're not delivering something, are you? I don't remember ordering anything and we've certainly no money to pay you."

"Delivering somebody, Lady Whyte," Paddy said as Darcy opened the door and stepped out.

I hadn't been sure if this was Aunt Oona or maybe her housekeeper, but the moment she saw Darcy she opened her arms. "Jesus, Mary and Joseph! Would you look here," she exclaimed. "What a nice surprise. I began to think you'd completely forgotten about your old aunt and uncle. Or were you staying away out of loyalty to that fatheaded father of yours?"

"How are you, Aunt Oona?" Darcy said, stepping forward to be smothered in a giant embrace. "I haven't deliberately stayed away. I've just had things to do that kept me occupied in England. I'm glad to see you looking so well."

"I'm surviving, thank you. Could be worse," she said. "Dooley gets the odd twinge of rheumatics, but all in all I'd say we'll stick around for a while yet. Especially since you're to inherit this property someday. I'm not leaving this earth without a darned good fight, you know." And she gave a deep-throated laugh.

I had hesitated to climb down behind Darcy, waiting to see how he wanted to introduce me, or even if he wanted to introduce me. But Aunt Oona looked over his shoulder. "And who might this be, Darcy? Not a young bride you've kept secret from your family?"

"Just one of my friends from London. She came out from Dublin to see how I was faring," Darcy said. "Her name is Georgie."

I stepped forward to shake hands. "How do you do?" I said.

"Well, Miss Georgie with no apparent last name, you're very welcome at this house of horrors," she said, pumping my hand and laughing. Her hair was iron gray and drawn back into a bun at the back of her head, but her face was unlined and her eyes were bright blue. It was hard to tell how old she was. I noticed now that she was wearing a coarse apron over various bright and mismatched layers of clothing and she had a beaded jet scarf draped at her neck. Although she was large she was certainly not flabby. Statuesque might be a better description.

"Well, don't just stand there," she said. "Come in, do. And don't mind the dogs. They're completely untrained and untrainable but they don't have a mean bone in their bodies. If a burglar ever came they might lick him to death. Not that a burglar would ever bother with us. What have we got worth stealing?"

She had released my hand and started toward the house.

"I should be getting along," Paddy said. "I have things to do at home and I don't like leaving Maureen for too long."

"Of course. Thank you for the ride," Darcy said.

"You'll be all right if I leave you here, then?"

"We'll sort something out," Darcy said as Paddy unloaded my suitcase from the back of the van. "Let's try and meet up at the Harp sometime and do some real catching up."

"We'll do that. Grand idea," Paddy said. "Glad to see you're hale and hearty, Lady Whyte. My best to Sir Dooley."

"And my best wishes to your wife for a successful delivery," she called as he went around to the driver's door. "And make sure you have her sewn up after this. Three children is quite enough these days. None of this nine or ten nonsense and I don't care what the parish priest says. There will soon be so many people on this planet that it will be standing room only."

Paddy gave her a nervous smile as he shut the door behind him.

"Well, don't just stand there," Oona repeated. "I expect we've got something to feed you, if you don't mind catch as catch can." She looked at Darcy, carrying my suitcase. "Or are you planning something much longer than a meal?"

"Oh no," Darcy said. "Georgie brought her suitcase with her because she thought she might stay in the area for a few days. But of course she can't stay as every nook and cranny is full."

"Why would that be?" Oona looked back as she led us into a dark hallway. The hall stand had vanished under a mountain of coats, hats, mufflers and rain gear. Around it, strewn across the floor, were wellies and boots of various sorts, making stepping across them a dangerous business. The dogs pushed past us and ran ahead down the hall.

"The trial, of course," Darcy said. "I know you live cut off from the world but you have heard about my father, I take it?"

"Oh, that? Yes, we heard something. Silly fool getting himself into trouble again. Probably said the wrong thing at the wrong time."

"He's been arrested for murder, Aunt Oona. He could well hang."

"He killed the American who bought Kilhenny, did he?"

"So they say."

She sniffed indignantly. "The rotten man probably deserved it. We drove over there once, soon after he had moved in. Dooley was writing a book on Irish peat bogs at the time and we knew there were some old family photos of peat cutting, up on the Bog of Allen. But do you know, that insufferable person wouldn't let us in, let alone have access to our own family photographs. Not let me into Kilhenny Castle where I was born and raised! He said he'd paid good money for the castle and its contents and we should get lost before his manservant came after us with a shotgun." She had been talking all the way down the passage, her voice booming up the stairwell to our right. Then she spun to face us, her face a picture of indignation. "Can you imagine the nerve? No wonder your father killed him. I'd have done so myself if I'd had a weapon handy at that moment."

Darcy shot me a glance. I didn't know whether to grin or be shocked. Aunt Oona opened a door and we stepped into a sitting room. At least it would have been a sitting room if there had been anywhere to sit. The sofa was buried under piles of books. A cat was asleep in one of the armchairs.

The other had a large canvas lying over it, and the smell of fresh paint permeated the room. There was a bucket of potatoes, a fancy-looking hat and a pair of kid gloves on the low table.

"Move some of that stuff and sit down," she said. "But mind the wet paint. I've been working on that one. My latest opus, and I have to say I'm rather proud of it."

Darcy picked up the painting by its edges. To me it was horribly bright daubs, but Oona went on, "Recognize him, Darcy? Oh, come on. The likeness is quite visible. It's Dooley, standing on his head when he does his yoga exercises. I had to rush to finish it. He complained about posing too long in that position."

Darcy winked at me as he leaned the picture against a wall. I have to say that wink felt wonderful. We were a unit, connected, inseparable, whatever happened.

"And mind Mr. Gladstone," Oona boomed at us. "He scratches. Horrible creature. He's even more bad tempered than your stupid father, Darcy."

I sat where the painting had been, and almost coughed as dust rose from the cushions. Darcy tried to remove the cat from the other chair but it hissed and lashed out, making him opt for perching on the arm of my chair instead.

"That will never work with him," Aunt Oona said. "You need to show him who is master." She grabbed the animal by the scruff of its neck, hoisted it in the air and held it up in front of her face. "Remember who feeds you and show gratitude," she said before putting it down quite gently. The cat turned its back on her and licked itself as if it hadn't a care in the world. The dogs settled around our feet, wisely ignoring the cat.

"Tea or coffee?" Oona asked. "Or would you prefer something stronger? Whiskey? Sherry?" She went over and tugged on a bellpull. Somewhere far off a bell jangled. "I don't know where he's got to," she said. "Probably out digging up carrots."

"Your gardener serves the drinks around here?"

"No, you silly boy. The butler digs up the carrots. You have to be a jack-of-all-trades in this establishment. We're down to a skeleton crew here, you know. Can't afford a proper staff anymore. Treadwell does most of it and we muck in."

"Treadwell? You have Treadwell working for you? I didn't know that."

"Well, you haven't been to see us for ages, have you?" she replied. "Your father didn't need him and the new American didn't want him so we invited him to come to Mountjoy. It's not exactly what he's used to but it's better than the workhouse."

Darcy looked down to me. "Treadwell was our butler at Kilhenny. He was old even when I was a child. Frightfully old-school and correct."

"Yes, well, he's had to learn to turn a blind eye to a lot of things here," Oona said. "When he first came he thought he could whip us into shape, but now I rather think he's given up." She rang the bell again. "I suppose I'd better go and make the coffee myself," she said. "I've become quite a dab hand at domestic chores since we had to let Cook go."

Darcy and I exchanged a look of amusement as she swept out of the room.

"I told you they were quite batty," Darcy whispered to me.

However, she had only been gone for an instant when she returned.

"I met Treadwell coming in with the carrots and he'll bring us coffee right away. But knowing Treadwell, he'll have to go and put on his frock coat first. So silly in a place like this."

She sat where the cat had been. "So the young lady needs a place to stay, does she? Well, why not stay here? We've got more empty rooms than I can count. And you too, Darcy. You're welcome here as well. Make a change for us dreary old folk to have some bright young people around."

Darcy's eyes met mine, then he said, "You're very kind, Aunt Oona, and I think Georgie would be happy to accept, but I'm afraid I have to keep an eye on my father. He's in a deep state of depression. He already threatened to blow his brains out last night."

"Always was one for high drama," Oona sniffed. "Used

to make a fuss as a child if he so much as got a splinter in his finger."

"This is rather more serious than a splinter, Aunt Oona," Darcy reminded her. "He's accused of murder, and it very much looks as if he's guilty."

"Rubbish," Oona said. "Your father couldn't kill anyone. He killed our poor dog, of course, but I know that was an accident. But as for doing it deliberately, with malice aforethought, no. Not possible. You should have seen him after his first hunt. They bloodied him, the way one does, and when they threw the fox to the hounds he was sick all over the master's boots. He never did like killing anything." She shook her head. "Oh, I know he's all bark. Fly off the handle at the least little thing. But there's no bite. He might have swung a punch at that American, but he wouldn't have killed him. How did he die?"

"Hit on the head with one of the old weapons hanging on the wall."

She thought about this for a moment. "Yes, I suppose he could have done that. Grabbed something in the spur of the moment and whacked the bloke. Ah, Treadwell. Coffee. Jolly good."

The ancient butler came in, wearing, as she had predicted, his frock coat.

"Your coffee, Lady Whyte." He waited while she removed the hat and gloves from the low table, then he put the tray down and picked up the potatoes. "Should I pour the coffee or take these back to the kitchen? Or were you planning to do something with them in here?"

Oona stared at them. "I've no idea how they got here, Treadwell. I remember digging them up yesterday but then I suppose I got distracted. Probably had the urge to finish that new painting. So please do take them to the kitchen."

"Very good, your ladyship. And may I be permitted to say that it's good to see you, Mr. Darcy, although in such tragic circumstances. Will you please convey my respects to your father and tell him that I am willing to testify to his character, if that would be of help."

"Very good of you, Treadwell," Darcy said. "Yes, I will tell him."

Treadwell gave a little bow and left.

"For heaven's sake don't let Treadwell testify in court," Oona said. "He's too scrupulously honest. The prosecution would make mincemeat of him and get him to tell about every occasion on which your father lost his temper, starting with his two-year-old tantrums in the nursery."

"I agree," Darcy said. "But I rather fear that will all be brought up at the trial, Treadwell or not."

"Does he have a good lawyer?" Oona asked.

"Only Leach and Leach so far. No barrister has been engaged."

"You should let Dooley help you," she said, waving her arms with great enthusiasm.

"Uncle Dooley?"

"Oh yes. He studied law, you know. Even practiced it for a while. He was a second son, you see. Didn't expect to inherit anything. But he gave a brilliant oration—had a young man sent to prison; but afterward Dooley doubted the man's guilt. He gave up the profession after that. Said he hadn't the stomach for the court but didn't want to sit in a solicitor's office all day. Then my father gave us Mountjoy when we married, and it came with enough money to live on in those days."

"What happened to the money?" Darcy asked.

"Well, there were the death duties when Father died. And then when your grandfather died we had to sell off more of the land, and your father was put in bad financial straits. Never recovered, did he? But Dooley's brain is razor sharp. He may come up with a defense you've never even thought of."

"I thought I heard voices," said a small voice in the doorway and we turned to see a tiny skinny man standing there. He had a shock of white hair that stood up in all directions and he was wearing a bright red waistcoat and a red bow tie. Like Oona's his face was unlined and his eyes bright. "Visitors. How lovely. We don't often get visitors these days. Please tell me they are not Jehovah's Witnesses."

"It's our great-nephew Darcy and his friend, Dooley," Oona boomed. "What's wrong with your eyes?"

"How are you, Uncle Dooley?" Darcy said, standing to shake the man's hand. "This is my friend Georgie, visiting from London."

The small man blinked and gave us a beaming smile. The vision of Jack Sprat leaped into my mind. Jack Sprat who could eat no fat, and his wife who could eat no lean.

"I've been concentrating too long up there," he said. "But you'll be pleased to know that Wellington is finally winning the day."

"Wellington?" Darcy asked.

"Battle of Waterloo, my boy!" Dooley exclaimed with great enthusiasm.

I was beginning to think that Darcy's description of "quite batty" wasn't an exaggeration. I also questioned whether I wanted to stay in this crazy household, however much I wanted to be close to Darcy.

"He's reenacting the battle of Waterloo with his toy soldiers," Oona said.

"Miniatures, Oona. Not toy soldiers. I've built the whole battlefield to scale and painted every one of the regiments in their correct uniforms. I even have tiny cannons that fire ball bearings. You must come up and see, if you have time. We've reached quite a dramatic part of the battle. A turning point. Napoleon thinks he has us, but he's made a tactical error."

And he waved a finger triumphantly. Oona reached across and poured coffee into exquisitely thin china cups. I wondered how those cups had survived in this household.

"If you are here for a few days, you'll be able to see the glorious victory," he said. "Are you planning to stay for a while?"

"The young lady will, I think," Oona said.

"Jolly good show!" Dooley beamed at me. "Never say no to a pretty face."

Oona gave him a warning frown and went on, "Darcy, on the other hand, thinks he needs to be with his father. You must help them, Dooley. You must put the battle of Waterloo aside and use your legal skills to prove Thaddy's innocence."

There was a flicker of alarm in Darcy's eyes. He drained his coffee cup and stood up.

"I should be getting back to my father right away," he said. "I'm afraid he'll be pestered by newspaper reporters and he'll say something stupid and harm his cause even further."

"He's at home?" Dooley asked. "Not locked up in a Dublin prison?"

"They released him on bail yesterday," Darcy said. "We managed to sneak him home without anyone noticing."

"And why haven't the police provided a guard for him?" Oona demanded angrily.

"They are guarding the castle grounds, but they don't seem concerned that he is unprotected and unguarded at the gamekeeper's lodge. So I'm afraid I have a favor to ask. Do you have a vehicle of some sort that I could borrow? My father's estate car is locked away in the garage at the castle and everything is potential evidence at the moment. But I may need to go into Dublin to see the police there and I'll need to come and get Georgie, if she's to stay here."

"Well, of course, dear boy," Dooley said. "There's no reason he can't have the Rolls, is there, Oona? We hardly ever use it. I don't see well enough to drive anymore. Oona never could drive in a straight line. And Treadwell only goes into Kildare once in a while to do some shopping. We have most of what we need here. Quite self-sufficient, aren't we, Oona?"

"Yes, we are, my dear. Quite self-sufficient. And quite content."

They nodded to each other while the dogs stood around them, tails wagging. Darcy looked across at me and grinned. It felt wonderful.

Chapter 15

Dooley and Oona both escorted Darcy to the stables where an ancient Rolls was parked. He managed to get it started and waved as it inched forward, avoiding dogs, ducks and chickens.

"I've a splendid idea," Oona said, running up to him and putting a hand on the door handle. "Why don't you bring your father over to dinner? It's time we let bygones be bygones. Time for family to stick together. Tell him that. And tell him we'll have Branson kill a duck."

"Who's Branson?"

"One of our farmworkers. We've had to dispense with most of the household staff but we still have a couple of chaps working the land for us. They live in rent-free cottages and get their share of the produce so we don't have to pay them much. And they do the dirty work like killing animals."

Darcy nodded.

"So you'll bring your father tonight?"

"I'll tell him," Darcy said. "I can't guarantee that he'll

come." He turned to me. "I'll be back later." I watched the Rolls disappear down the long driveway.

Oona put an arm around my shoulder. "Come on inside, my dear. It's unpleasantly cold today. Let's go and see which of the bedrooms might be suitable for visitors."

"I'll take her up, if you like," Uncle Dooley said.

Oona shook her head. "Oh no, Dooley. I'm not having you taking her anywhere near a bedroom. I know your wicked ways." She looked at me. "You have to watch him, I'm afraid. He's always been rather a lad where ladies are concerned. Wandering hands and evil intentions." But she smiled as she said it. "He's been quite out of practice since the last of the maids left, haven't you, old thing?"

Dooley grinned sheepishly. "You do exaggerate, Oona. I might pinch the odd bottom, but I'm not exactly dangerous."

"All the same, I'll take Miss Georgie's case up for her. You go back to the Duke of Wellington. On second thoughts, you go to your study and start thinking up a possible defense for your nephew-in-law."

She picked up the suitcase Darcy had left in the front hall and started up the stairs with it. I followed, picking my way past a basket of knitting, a bowl of withered apples, and the cat, who had now taken up position on the top step. Oona headed straight toward the front of the house and opened the door to a small room over the front porch. It felt horribly cold and damp and was rather spartan with a single bed and small chest of drawers.

"This might be our best bet right now," she said. "At least I know the mice haven't got at this bed. But it's haunted. I hope you don't mind that. A young female ghost. Tends to yank the covers off the bed of people she doesn't like. She's fine with family members." She looked up at me then. "Or almost family members, I expect."

Then she laughed at my stricken face. "I didn't buy that 'just one of my friends from London' speech for a minute. Casual friends don't trek out to the middle of Ireland to be with a pal. So it's more than that, isn't it?" She gave me a long, quizzical stare, then added, "I saw how he looked at you."

"He didn't want me to come," I said. "He was afraid the newspapers would pick up on it. In fact he tried to break off with me altogether, because he didn't want to put me through the unpleasantness."

"But you showed you are made of sterner stuff. Good for you." Oona nodded with satisfaction. "I can see he's chosen the right girl. But why would the newspapers care?"

"Because I'm the king's cousin," I said, wincing.

Oona clapped her hands together. "Now I know why you looked familiar. One of the Rannochs. Of course. I was lady-in-waiting to your grandmother for a while before I married Dooley. You have the look of her."

She had once been described as the least attractive of Queen Victoria's daughters so I didn't exactly find this flattering.

"And now I see Darcy's point," she said. "It might well have been wiser not to come."

"But I couldn't leave Darcy to face this alone, could I? Not when his father is being so beastly and unhelpful."

"Of course you couldn't. I would have acted in the same way if it had been Dooley. Leave your suitcase for now. We'll get Branson to bring up some peat for a fire when he brings in the duck. This room will be warm as toast in no time at all."

She led me downstairs again, moving with surprising agility for one so large. We ate a good lunch at the kitchen table and by midafternoon my room was indeed warm and toasty. I unpacked my clothes, asking myself what I was doing here and whether I could be any use at all to Darcy. When I went through everything I had heard of the crime I'm afraid I was inclined to believe, as Darcy clearly did, that his father was guilty. The big question was: who else might have wanted Mr. Roach dead, had been able to get into the castle to kill him and was clever enough to frame Lord Kilhenny? I decided that one thing I could do would be to ask around in the village if they had noticed any strangers. Inhabitants of villages notice anyone who doesn't belong. Snooping is a major sport in rural locations. I could also ask Barney whether he had driven anybody out to the castle recently, apart from the stream of newspapermen. And then I realized that there had been strangers in the vicinity. That archeological dig, right across the lane from the castle gates. I'd need to find out more about them if it ever stopped raining and they resumed their work. They were in a perfect position to spy on what went on at the castle. But again the question returned—why would anyone want to kill a reclusive American who apparently was devoted to horses and books?

I came up with an answer to that one pretty quickly. He was rich. Rich enough to buy a castle and a racing stable. He had inherited a fortune. He was supposedly the last surviving member of a family. But what if there was another claimant? Someone who would inherit if he was dead? In which case why not kill him in a more subtle manner? A quick bullet from behind a bush would have worked well. Bludgeoning someone to death with a club was bound to attract attention, and if the police discovered that another member of the Roach family was in Ireland, surely that gave someone apart from Darcy's father a good motive.

This made me feel a little more hopeful. It's always good to have something positive to work on. I wondered if the detective here had been in touch with the police in America and had checked into Mr. Roach's family circumstances. That might be something we could suggest to them. Or to Darcy's father's lawyer.

The afternoon seemed to drag on. Now that I was here I was itching to do something useful. I sat with a notebook on my knee and jotted down all the thoughts that were going through my mind. *Inherit fortune? Next of kin? Visitors to the castle? Who might have seen? Question valet?* It didn't seem to be much but at least it would be a start, and I've always found that one small clue or fact often leads to another.

We all waited expectantly that evening for the sound of a motorcar. At last it came but only Darcy got out. He ran to the front door, as it was now raining heavily again.

"He wouldn't come," Darcy said. "Absolutely refused, whatever I said to him."

"How annoying," Oona said. "What a waste of a good duck."

"Georgie and I are here," Darcy replied. "I hope you don't think it's a waste to feed us."

"Of course not. But I was hoping . . . Oh, never mind. The man is his own worst enemy. How does he expect help if he rejects every olive branch extended to him?"

"That's the point," Darcy said, taking off his wet raincoat. "He doesn't expect help. He doesn't want help. He seems to me quite resigned to his fate. He babbled some nonsense about joining his dear Mary."

"Well, that's a good sign, isn't it?" Oona said. "He must think that that sweet soul is in heaven, so he must expect to be headed in that direction himself. If he'd actually committed murder he would be going to t'other place."

We went through into a vast dining room. Places had been laid at one end of a long mahogany table that would easily seat thirty. Only that one end had been dusted, and candlelight twinkled on the polished wood. Treadwell came in with a tureen of thick vegetable soup, then served the roast duck, accompanied by roast potatoes and tiny Brussels sprouts.

"Did you actually cook this, Treadwell?" Darcy asked as he was served.

"Lady Whyte does most of the cooking these days," Treadwell replied. "She has become rather proficient at it."

"Well, there's a rare compliment," Oona commented as the butler left us. "Usually he lets us know how inferior this household is to his usual standards."

The meal was rounded off with an apple pie and custard. Then a good cheddar and biscuits.

"I'm sorry we're down to so few courses these days," Oona said. "We're living the life of peasants."

"It was all quite delicious, Lady Whyte," I said.

"Please, call me Aunt Oona. Everyone else does." She gave Darcy a knowing look.

"So what are we going to do about this father of yours?" she asked as we went through to the sitting room and Treadwell brought in coffee and brandy. "Have you had your thinking cap on yet, Dooley? What might be his best line of defense? Insanity? Runs in the family, you know."

"Oh, not insanity," Dooley said hastily. "They'll lock him away for life in a mental institution. We wouldn't want that for him."

"I've been thinking," I said. "Two things, actually. Has anyone checked into this man's inheritance? Might there be other claimants who would get the fortune if and when Mr. Roach died?"

"The Garda must have notified the authorities in Chicago by now," Darcy said. "His next of kin would have to be told."

"So they should know if any of them had recently traveled to Ireland, shouldn't they?"

"Good point," Oona said. "In my experience money and greed are behind a good many murders."

Darcy laughed. "And how many murders have you experienced, Aunt Oona?"

"One reads newspapers," she said haughtily. "But Miss Georgie was going to add a second thought when we interrupted her. One thing she should know about this family is that we never shut up. Go on, Georgie. Tell us what you were going to say."

"I was told that he was killed by a blow to the back of the head, and yet the manservant said there had been signs of a struggle. Those two don't seem compatible, do they?" I looked around at those faces in the candlelight. "If you are struggling with somebody, you can't very well hit him in the back of the head—even if one of you falls over, it would usually be faceup. A blow to the back of the head to me implies creeping up behind someone and catching him unawares."

"The girl has a good head on her shoulders," Oona exclaimed.

Darcy nodded agreement. "That did cross my mind too," he said, "but unfortunately it wouldn't exactly help my father to suggest that he'd crept up behind Roach and bashed him to death, rather than struggling with him and maybe killing him accidentally."

"Yes, I see your point," Oona said. "If the death was accidental during a struggle, it would be manslaughter, not murder. And if your father's lawyer could prove that the American instigated the struggle, maybe attacked first, then your father was defending his own life." She turned to her husband. "You're awfully quiet, Dooley. What has that sharp little mind of yours been thinking?"

"I've been thinking about the club," Dooley said. "So was it really a shillelagh, a walking stick, or a weapon we are talking about here?"

"They said it was one of the weapons that was hanging on the walls," Darcy replied.

Dooley wagged a finger excitedly. "In that case it was the Burda club. I wondered about that."

"The Burda club?"

"A rare artifact," Dooley said. "A Celtic weapon of great antiquity, owned by the O'Mara clan from time immemorial. Did your father never show it to you? It was dug from the bog and miraculously preserved. I wrote all about it in my book on bogs of Ireland. I was surprised to see it hanging carelessly on a wall in Kilhenny Castle rather than being in the museum in Dublin."

"So it's a valuable object, is it?" I asked.

"Priceless. Absolutely priceless," Dooley said. "Do you know how many wooden artifacts have survived from Celtic times? Almost none."

"Worth killing for, would you say?" Oona asked.

"If anyone actually knew of its value," Dooley said. "Not your everyday burglar."

"But that doesn't add up, Aunt Oona," Darcy said. "If

you came to steal it, you'd kill and take the club with you, not leave it lying beside the body."

"That's true." Oona sighed. "Dooley always did say I could never think or drive straight. Never mind. We have three good brains here. You'll figure it out between you."

Chapter 16

Feeling a little better now that I'm with Darcy again.

After that meal I slept surprisingly well. The room was warm and if any ghost came to visit during the night she did not disturb me. I awoke to find the sun shining on me, a brilliant blue sky dotted with puffy white clouds. When I looked out of the window there was Oona down below feeding chickens. It was all very rural and pleasant, hard to remember for a moment that a man's life was at stake. From Dooley's babbling on about ancient clubs the previous night it was clear that he probably wouldn't be much use to us. It was up to Darcy and me to find a way to save his father. I got up, bathed and was on my way back to my bedroom when I found Dooley loitering on the landing.

"Well, hello there," he said. "You slept well, I trust?"

"Very, thank you."

"Jolly good," he said. "So no mysterious visits during the night?"

"Not that I know of."

As I headed for my room I noticed that he was following. This was awkward. One cannot slug one's host, even if he did try anything improper. I could almost feel his breath down my neck and wondered if I could slam the bedroom door on him in time, or even if the bedroom door had a lock. Luckily I never had to find out if his intentions were dishonorable. Help came in the form of a booming voice, yelling, "Dooley, what are you doing? Are you annoying that young woman? Leave her to get dressed in peace." And Oona appeared at the top of the stairs as Dooley gave an embarrassed little smile.

Oona beamed at me. "It's wonderful. Absolutely wonderful, you know. Old Dooley is feeling his oats again. Hasn't been as perky as this for years. Well done, you."

I wasn't sure how I felt about helping Old Dooley to be perky but decided he was probably quite harmless. I finished dressing and had eaten a most satisfying breakfast of eggs, bacon and sausage by the time Darcy arrived. Darcy joined me at the breakfast table and tucked into a breakfast himself.

"So what do you think we should do first?" I asked as we found ourselves alone.

He frowned. "Thinking about this in the cold light of day, Georgie, I'm still not at all sure I want to involve you. Now that the word has got out that my father is home at Kilhenny the village is already crawling with reporters. I think it might be wiser if you stayed safely here with Oona and Dooley and you three used your thinking caps from afar."

"But I want to help, Darcy," I said. "Nobody will recognize me, I'm sure. If asked I'll say I'm reporting for the *Horse and Hound*."

This made Darcy and Oona chuckle.

"And I'll hide as we go through the village, if you like."

"Let her go with you, Darcy," Oona said. "The girl has a good brain. Your stupid father needs all the help he can get at the moment. Did he appreciate the portion of duck I sent back with you?"

"He pretended not to, but I noticed by this morning that he'd eaten it," Darcy said.

"You see, stubborn as ever, but we'll win him round, won't we, Dooley?" she asked as Dooley poked his head in through the door.

"A splendid day for Wellington today," he said. "Don't you want to come up to the attic and see it for yourselves? It's not every day you can witness an epic battle."

"They've a battle of their own, Dooley," Oona said. "And frankly you should leave Waterloo until my nephew is exonerated, and put that brilliant mind of yours to saving him."

Dooley sighed. "Very well, my dear. If you say so. Do you think I should come over with you and talk to him myself? I'd like to hear his side of the story."

"At the moment I don't think he'd talk to you, Uncle Dooley. And the problem is that he half believes he is guilty. He went on a bender, you see. Blind drunk. Can't remember a thing."

"Dear me, that's too worrying," Dooley said. "Even I couldn't come up with a good defense for a man who thinks he has done the deed. Perhaps he did."

"Of course he didn't," Oona said hotly. "You know Thaddy too well for that, Dooley. When has he ever shown signs of violence?"

"He has always lost his temper with monotonous regularity," Dooley said. "He hates to lose at cards. He hates to be laughed at."

"But did he ever try to throttle you for any of those things? As I told the young'uns, he's all bark and no bite."

"All the same I would like to talk to him myself," Dooley said. "Perhaps he needs a sympathetic ear at this moment."

"He wouldn't talk to me," Darcy said. "But then, he hasn't wanted me around since my mother died."

"So put it to him," Oona said. "Remind him that Dooley used to be in the legal profession and could have had a brilliant career if he hadn't been so softhearted. See if he'll agree to talk to Dooley. You never know. Something might just come out of it."

"I'll try." Darcy gave her a halfhearted grin.

I put on my overcoat and jammed my hat low onto my forehead, so that I shouldn't be recognized, then I climbed into the Rolls beside Darcy.

"I suppose it's out of the question to see the scene of the crime for ourselves?" I asked.

He shook his head. "There are still police guarding the house," he said. "And the inspector from Dublin wouldn't take it kindly if we were poking our noses in."

"Is the manservant still living there?"

"I believe so."

"Then they must have cleared him of suspicion or he could have disposed of any potential evidence."

"Why would a manservant want to kill his master? He had a damned good job and I'm sure he was paid well. Americans always do overpay, don't they? Now he'll have to go back to a country still mired in a depression. And if you were a servant and wanted to kill your employer . . ." He paused.

"You'd poison him slowly," I said. "Or at the very least make it look like an accident."

Darcy laughed. "You have a criminal mind, do you know that?"

"That's just it," I said. "This whole murder scene. Leaving Mr. Roach lying on the floor with the weapon nearby. If you'd just killed, wouldn't you try to dispose of the weapon, or at least wipe it clean and put it back on the wall with the other weapons so that nobody would notice it?"

Darcy nodded thoughtfully. "If my father was blind drunk at the time, he might not have been thinking clearly. Or he might have just wanted to get back to the lodge as quickly as possible before the manservant heard the commotion and came to investigate."

"In which case, being blind drunk, he would have staggered back, probably knocked something over, touched a tree with a bloody finger. We should try to retrace his route. And surely if this man guarded his privacy as they say he did, wouldn't the manservant have had to let your father in? Served them drinks?"

"Unfortunately, not necessarily. He says the servants' entrance was rarely locked and anyway he believed my father still had a key. He had come into the house unannounced before."

"Are those big gates always kept locked?" I asked. "Is there a gatekeeper?"

"No gatekeeper, these days," Darcy said, "but I understand the new gates are always locked and anyone who comes to visit has to communicate with the castle by telephone before they are let in. At this moment there is a constable on guard just inside."

"I saw him when I arrived in my taxi," I said. "So how did your father even get onto the grounds?"

"Ah, that's simple," Darcy said. "There is a small side gate in the wall behind the lodge. And a path that leads up to the house."

"And that is not kept locked?"

"You'd have to know about it to find it," Darcy said. "It's more or less hidden under the ivy. When we were young it was always open. But then so was the main gateway. No gates across it at all."

"So anyone could get in if they found out about the secret little gate?"

"I suppose so. If anyone was determined enough he could climb over the wall. There are places where trees grow close enough to make it possible."

We reached the bottom of the driveway and turned out into the lane. How different it looked on a sunny day—the fields an unbelievably bright green, almost glowing. The whitewashed cottages sparkled and even the sheep looked like bright little dots against the green of the fields. It was the sort of day when one simply had to feel more cheerful.

"I wonder why Roach felt the need to put up such impressive gates and to lock them," I said. "One would think he had something to hide, or he believed items in the castle were worth stealing."

"Or he was one of these strange people who are paranoid about being pursued. Maybe that was why he chose to flee to an out-of-the-way place like this. Maybe we can find out whether he has been seeing a doctor while he has been in Ireland."

"Your father should know whether he showed any signs of insanity or persecution. After all, they worked together for quite a while before that horrid incident at the stables." I glanced across at Darcy. "Speaking of which, we should go to the stables and try to find the truth about what happened with that horse doping. Someone there may know."

"And if we find out?" Darcy asked. The bleakness had now returned to his face. "I can't see how it would help prove my father's innocence. I'm sure my father wouldn't have doped one of his horses, but enough people believe that he did. And it only gives him another motive for murder if he felt he was wrongly sacked from his job. The prosecution will make hay with it."

I touched his hand on the steering wheel. "I know it all looks awful and hopeless, but maybe we'll find a glimmer of hope soon. Actually we've already got one. That club that Dooley was talking about. If it really is as priceless as he says then maybe someone did sneak in to steal it. Roach confronted him and he swung the club."

"But then the club would have had someone else's fingerprints on it, not just my father's."

"Doesn't that strike you as odd?" I asked. "Just your father's prints? Think how many other people must have handled that club."

"Maybe they mean recent and clear prints, as opposed to old and smudged ones."

"If you think we can get onto the grounds we should trace your father's route. If he was as drunk as he says, he would have bumped into things, maybe left a bloody fingerprint somewhere."

"You forget it's been raining for several days. Wouldn't any traces have been washed away?"

I slapped his hand now. "You're being negative, Darcy. This isn't like you. The Darcy I know is game for anything, takes on the hardest challenge. Anything I suggest, you shoot down. I came over here to help you, you know."

He managed a weak smile. "I'm sorry. Yes, I am being negative, I know. I just can't seem to find much hope."

"I'm here. I'm beside you no matter what. Doesn't that make you feel a tiny bit better?"

"It should do, but all I can think is that I don't want you to go through this. I really wish you were miles and miles away."

I sat beside him in silence. Was I being selfish to give him additional worry? Should I admit defeat and go back to London, let him wallow in his own misery and face things by himself?

"All right," I said at last. "If that's what you really want. I'll collect my things from Aunt Oona's and go home. But I would like to point out to you that I do have some experience with this sort of thing. And I am prepared to believe that your father is innocent until someone hands me irrefutable proof that he's guilty."

Again there was a silence, then he said, with emotion in his voice, "You're a grand girl, Georgie. And I don't know what I want. I want you safe and far from scandal. I don't want your life blighted. . . ."

"So there will be some scandal," I said. "But I really don't see how our lives will be blighted. Our behavior has been beyond reproach. Or at least mine has. Yours might have been questionable at times—" I watched him grin. "There might be gossip, but then people will accept us for who we are. It's not your fault, Darcy. You are not to blame for anything. Now, let's forget all this nonsense and get on with proving your father's innocence."

He reached across and grabbed my hand. "I'm glad you're here," he said. "I'm really glad." And the motorcar almost swerved into a ditch as he kissed me.

Chapter 17

As we approached Kilhenny Darcy turned to me. "There seems to be activity in the high street. Maybe you should duck down out of sight."

I did as he suggested, curling up into a little ball. We hadn't gone far before Darcy muttered, "Damn."

"What is it?" I asked from beneath the dashboard.

"Mrs. McNalley has spotted me."

"Mrs. McNalley? The one who works at the castle?"

"She used to be our cook and she stayed on to cook for the new owner. But she also keeps the place tidy for my father and makes meals for him as well. Oh no, she's heading straight for us."

I heard him roll down the window and say, "Good morning, Mrs. McNalley. Lovely day, isn't it?"

"You're just the person I wanted to see," she said. "I've got these two bags of shopping and my rheumatics are playing up something terrible, so if you don't mind I'll just hop in"—she opened the back door of the Rolls—"and let you drive me to the lodge in style."

I heard her grunting as she hauled herself into the backseat.

Now I wasn't sure what to do. Stay curled up or reveal my presence? I decided that of course she'd see me and think me very odd for sitting with my head between my knees. So I sat up again, giving her a start. "I've found it," I said, waving a triumphant hand. "Oh, hello. I was looking for my missing earring. I'm Georgie, one of Darcy's friends from London."

"Pleased to meet you, miss," she said. "You're not coming to stay at the lodge, I take it? I don't think the accommodation there is suitable for a young lady like yourself these days."

"Oh, good heavens no," I said, with my "bright young London society girl" laugh. "I'm staying with friends nearby. I just popped over to show my support to Darcy as soon as I heard the dreadful news. I know this whole thing must be absolutely beastly for him."

"It surely is," she said. "For all of us. I've been with his lordship's family for nearly forty years. Started out as kitchen maid and then took over as cook. And I can't say I enjoyed the way things had become, however much that American man paid me. You wouldn't actually call it cooking, what he wanted to eat: simple and plain, that's what he liked. A good rump steak. I'd no problem with that. But bangers and mash. Pork chop and mash. No good pies or puddings or fancy sauces at all. Nursery food. That's what I called it. And then Mr. Darcy's poor father, hardly eating a thing at all. I've been bringing him leftovers from the big house to save me from cooking twice. I never exactly asked for permission but as my old father used to say, what the eye don't see the heart don't grieve after."

It was clear that she liked to talk. She delivered this monologue without stopping for breath.

"I don't know what will happen to the castle now," she said. "Have you any idea, Mr. Darcy?"

"I expect it will go to Mr. Roach's next of kin. Whoever he has left it to in his will," Darcy replied, stony faced.

"Did he ever have any relatives to visit him?" I asked.

"He never had visitors at all that I knew of," she said. "No post. No cards. Never heard him speak of relatives either. Not that he was a great one for conversation. Sometimes I'd ask him questions about home, trying to be friendly and make him feel welcome in a new country, but he'd bite my head off and tell me to mind my own business."

"Did he chat with his manservant at all?"

"I wouldn't say I ever heard them chatting, but at least he tolerated him. I understand he hired this man through an advertisement when he came here. Never had a manservant before, so I gather. I don't know what he was before he inherited money, but I can tell you it wasn't high-class. His manners were terrible. Do you know he blew his nose on the table napkin? And you should see how he used his knife and fork. Oh, I know they do it differently in America, but he used to cut up his pork chop and then stab it with his fork and cram it into his mouth. No wonder he had no guests. I can tell you I'm glad to be out of there. I'll miss the money, of course, but I'm glad all the same. Between you and me there's been a bad feeling about the place since he moved in. In fact I think it's haunted."

"Haunted?" Darcy said.

"I always heard that there was a ghost or two in the castle, so the servants used to tell me in the old days. I never paid much attention because my work was always down in the kitchen and high-born ghosts would never come down there. Did you ever see one yourself, Mr. Darcy?"

"I can't say I did," Darcy replied. "As children we used to sit up at night in the long gallery to see if we could spot a ghost, but none of us did. Although we used to scare each other silly in the process." And he laughed, for a moment forgetting the weight that lay on him.

"Well, I think I've seen one recently," she said. "Under the American gentleman I turned into a cook general—a general dogsbody if you ask me, doing a bit of cleaning and polishing as well as cooking. Not that it was exactly strenuous work. He didn't use most of the rooms and kept them shut under dust sheets. Sent out all the laundry. Had the food delivered. And there wasn't even much cooking to do. But a couple of times recently I thought I saw a light glowing or a shadow moving in a strange part of the castle that wasn't currently occupied."

"How recently was this?" I asked and saw Darcy turn to look at me. "Before Mr. Roach died?"

"Oh yes. Several times in the last weeks I could have sworn I saw a movement or a shadow. But then it might just be my imagination. And you know what us Irish people are like. We tend to take things like ghosts and omens very seriously, don't we, Mr. Darcy?"

"Uh, yes. I'm sure we do," Darcy replied and I could tell he'd been thinking about something else.

"So I'm glad I'm no longer wanted at the castle," she said. "Except I expect they'll call me in to do a final cleanup after the Garda have finished their investigation."

"Were you there when the American man's body was found?" I asked. "Did you actually see it?"

"I didn't," she said. "There were Garda at the gate when I arrived first thing next morning and they didn't want to let me in, but wouldn't tell me why. Then they said the inspector would want to question me. Mickey, the man who worked for Mr. Roach, met me as I was coming up the stairs. He looked terrible—white-faced and his eyes just sort of staring. I said to him, 'What's the matter? You look as if you've seen a ghost yourself,' and he said, 'No ghost. But it was horrible. I found Mr. Roach lying on the library floor with his head bashed in last night.'"

"He seemed really upset by this, did he?" I asked.

"Upset? He looked as if he might pass out at any minute. And I'm thankful that he discovered the body, not me, or I might have gone in there to dust and stumbled upon it myself."

While we had been talking we had left the village and the castle wall appeared before us.

"So you want me to take you to the lodge and not the castle, Mrs. McNalley?" Darcy asked. "Is that shopping you have there for my father?"

"It is, Mr. Darcy. You see, I had no idea he'd been allowed to come back home. And with you staying there too, I thought you'd want some proper food, not the odd bits and pieces your father has been living on."

"It's very kind of you to think of us."

"Oh, I'd do anything in the world for your family, Mr. Darcy," she said. "I know your father hasn't been the easiest man in recent years, but I can understand what he's been through and that would have broken most of us. And your family is the only family I have, so to speak."

Darcy pulled up on the lane outside the lodge, stopped the car and came around to open her door. "Let me carry the bags for you, Mrs. McNalley." He looked back at me. "I won't be a minute."

As they started to walk away I heard her voice, loud and clear. "You can't fool me, Mr. Darcy. I know who that young lady is."

Oh crikey, I thought. Now it really will be all over the village. I waited for Darcy to return, expecting him to be upset and angry, but instead he came back with a big smile on his face.

"What?" I asked. "What did she say?"

"He said that it was quite clear to her that you were one of those lady newspaper reporters and she warned me that I should be careful what I tell you."

For once we both laughed.

"That's wonderful," I said. "Now I really have been given carte blanche to poke my nose around the village. But what she said was interesting, wasn't it?"

"About the ghost? Absolutely. It might hint that someone has been creeping around for some time now."

"And doing what? Stealing the odd piece to sell? In which case the whole murder could have quite a different complexion. A petty criminal, helping himself to the odd item he could sell in London or Dublin, is caught off guard by Mr. Roach. The American is strong, maybe. Threatens to overpower him and have him arrested. The burglar grabs the nearest weapon and hits out, accidentally killing Mr. Roach."

"Interesting," Darcy said. "I wonder if they would allow my father and me to look around and see if anything obvious is missing. Then we can put forward that theory and they can start looking for known criminals in the area and checking with fences."

"And removing suspicion from your father," I added.

"We'll have to see about that."

He went to climb back into the motorcar.

"So where to now?" I asked. "The stables, do you think?"

"If you like." Darcy didn't seem too enthusiastic.

"Well, what do you propose that we do? We must come up with a line of defense for him."

"Your suggestion of an interrupted burglary was a good one," he said. "I'd like to find out a bit more about this Roach fellow. Until we know more about him and his previous life we don't know who might have a motive for wanting him dead."

"And how do you plan to do that?"

"I could visit the American embassy in Dublin, I suppose. They must have had to find out about his next of kin."

"It seems silly to rush into Dublin now we are here," I said. "Why don't you drive into that clearing among the trees over there and then you can show me the secret gate and we can look for clues up to the castle. We might even be able to get inside."

"Breaking and entering during broad daylight?" Darcy said. "Yes, that will certainly help my father's case."

"All right. We won't go into the house until the police guard is removed. But we can see if there is any evidence that your father returned drunk from killing Mr. Roach."

Darcy nodded. I gave him a quick glance. Ever since I had known him he had been daring, dashing, full of energy. He had seemed to me like a person who enjoyed living on the edge, laughing in the face of danger. Now he appeared like a shadow of his former self, a deflated balloon, and all that wonderful enthusiasm quite missing. And I realized once again that he feared that any evidence we found would only point all the more strongly to his father's guilt. Nevertheless he did as I had asked and edged the Rolls among the trees. We got out, closing the doors quietly. I followed Darcy as we skirted the lodge, watching warily for signs that someone might spot us from a window. But the curtains were drawn and the building had a blank, unlived-in feel to it. On the other side was a small kitchen garden, more or less bare at this time of year. We moved among rhododendron bushes until we came to the wall. Here it was overgrown with ivy and Darcy had to search for a while before he found the place where the ivy had been disturbed. He lifted a luxuriant branch and under it was the iron handle of a small door. It turned easily and we were through into the park surrounding Kilhenny Castle. The stillness was overpowering, as if every bird and creature that lived there was watchful. My first thought was of the Secret Garden, that we had blundered into a place where nobody went these days. But of course that wasn't true, as I saw almost immediately a large footprint in a muddy patch close to the wall. I pointed it out to Darcy.

"Your father's?" I asked.

He shrugged. "I've no idea what kind of footwear he favors, but this is a shoe, as opposed to a workman's boot, so it could be his."

"The print looks to be quite recent."

"But there is no way of knowing when it was made."

"We can see if subsequent prints move in a straight line or if they weave."

"Well, they'd have to weave a bit because the path twists and turns." He sounded testy now and I realized that he was scared we'd confirm his deepest fears.

"We don't have to do this, Darcy," I said, touching his hand. He flinched at my touch, showing how tense he was.

"Now we're here we might as well see it through," he whispered. "Come on, this way."

We stepped forward, searching like bloodhounds but finding nothing, not even a second footprint. No scraps of cloth conveniently caught on brambles, nor bloody thumbprints on smooth bark. Of course, it was possible that the Garda had done a thorough job and removed anything that might count as evidence. As we passed through a thick stand of bushes something moved in the underbrush, quite close to us. At first I thought it might be a rabbit or a bird, but I heard something pushing through bushes—something large. I grabbed Darcy's arm.

"What could that be?" I hissed.

"There used to be deer in the park," Darcy whispered back. "Maybe some of the herd has survived."

All the same he moved closer to me. We stood there, alert and hearts beating rather fast, but there was no more sound. In fact the woodland had fallen remarkably quiet again. Through the bare branches of the trees we could now see the vast shape of the castle emerging. A true keep from the Middle Ages, designed to keep out intruders with a great stone bastion around it and small slits of windows on the lower floors. It made Castle Rannoch look positively inviting.

"I'm surprised there's not a moat," I whispered to Darcy.

"There used to be. They filled it in a couple of hundred years ago." He grinned at me. "Actually it's nicer inside than it looks. It was added to in the eighteenth century and the other side has bigger windows and a nice view."

A little farther and the woodland ended in a large kitchen garden and outbuildings.

"We probably shouldn't go any closer," Darcy said. "This has been an exercise in futility, hasn't it? Apart from that one footprint, there is no indication that my father came back this way in a drunken stagger."

"What are all those outbuildings?" I asked.

"Gardener's cottage, sheds, stables. All that sort of stuff."

"Plenty of places for someone to hide," I said.

"Why do you say that?"

"Just an observation. If someone did want to get in unobserved and kill Roach, he could easily have done so. We know that Mrs. McNalley saw a ghost."

"He could just as easily have walked back to the road, let himself out of the main gate and not really have risked being observed," Darcy said. "In our day there would have been a pack of servants. Gardeners and grooms would have been around, and of course we had dogs."

"Dogs, of course," I said. "Everyone has dogs, don't they? Except this American. He couldn't have, or they would have sounded the alarm at a stranger. Does your father no longer have any dogs either?"

"He does. We're down to one very old Labrador, Blackie. But unfortunately we can't ask the dog if my father staggered out drunk that night and came back with blood on his clothes."

"You could check his clothes yourself," I said. "It's hard to get bloodstains completely out."

"He wouldn't necessarily have got any blood on his clothing," Darcy said. "One clean blow. The skull is stove in and the man pitches forward. He drops the club and flees."

"Why?" I asked.

"Maybe because he hears someone coming. Maybe because he is horrified with what he has just done."

"Then why not take the club with you when you flee? Bury it. Throw it in a pond. Burn it."

"I agree," he said. "It makes little sense. We should go back."

"It's a pity we can't get into the castle, now we're here." I stared up at the great gray shape looming above us. "I'd dearly like to see the scene of the crime for myself."

"We can't while that man's valet is still in residence." Darcy shook his head.

"We could keep watch to see if he ever goes out."

"And we don't know there aren't any Garda stationed in the castle still," Darcy said.

"It's your house. You should know how to creep around

without being seen," I said. "I bet you did as a child." Now that we were this close, I was itching to see for myself. "Why don't we give it a try?"

Darcy looked wary. "All right," he said.

We had taken two steps out of the woods and across the kitchen garden when a voice yelled, "Hey, you. What are you doing here?"

Chapter 18

TUESDAY, DECEMBER 4
A FRIGHT AT KILHENNY CASTLE.

I wasn't sure whether to run or to freeze. If it was a policeman I certainly didn't want to look guilty, and running away would certainly convey that impression. Then a man stepped out from behind the nearest outbuilding. He was youngish, skinny, pale and wearing a dark suit. He had black hair slicked down and parted in the middle and a neat little line of a mustache.

"It's him," Darcy whispered. "The manservant. Great chance to question him."

The man strode toward us, waving a fist in a menacing manner. "What are you doing? This is private property." This speech was marred only by his tripping over a clod of earth and almost pitching forward onto his face. He regained his feet, flushing angrily. "If you're reporters, you'd better beat it before I call the cops. There's one stationed at the front door, you know."

We pretended not to have noticed his undignified stumble.

"We're not reporters," Darcy said. "I'm Darcy O'Mara. This used to be my family home until recently. I only wanted to show it to my friend from London."

"O'Mara?" The man turned up his lip. "The killer's kid? I'm surprised you have the nerve to be hanging around here."

"Do you happen to be Mr. Roach's valet?" I asked, because I could sense that Darcy might explode. "Mickey, is it?"

"That's right. Mickey Riley."

"Well, Mr. Riley, we are here because Mr. O'Mara believes in his father's innocence and is naturally doing everything he can to exonerate him," I said.

The American frowned and it flashed into my head that the word "exonerate" was outside the scope of his vocabulary.

"You're wasting your time, fella," he said. "Your old man is as guilty as hell. Like I told the cops. Couldn't have been anyone else, could it? He was the only one who knew how to sneak into the castle without knocking at the front door. He and Mr. Roach had had a doozy of a run-in that afternoon. He was hopping mad. He went home, drank enough to get up his courage and then came back to finish off my boss. That's the only way it could have happened."

"Do you know what this row was about?" Darcy asked.

"Your dad and Mr. Roach had been mad at each other ever since that business with the horse dropping dead. My boss blamed your pa for killing one of his best horses. Your pa held a grudge for being fired. Thought he'd been wrongly dismissed and kept saying he had nothing to do with the doping. But again the question was, if he didn't do it, who did? Who else had the opportunity to get close to the horse right before the race, huh? And why was the syringe found in your father's drawer?"

"And on that particular afternoon before Mr. Roach died, did you overhear anything of what they were fighting about?" Darcy pressed the subject.

"I stayed well away. My boss wasn't the easiest guy at the best of times. When he was mad, it was best to make myself scarce."

"So you heard nothing at all? Nothing to give me a clue?"

"Ask your old man yourself," he said insolently.

"On the night of the murder you told the police that you heard nothing," I said. "You didn't hear any signs of a struggle?"

He glared at me. "Who are you, a reporter?"

"No, I'm an investigator, working for a top-notch firm in London," I said, trying to sound brisk, efficient and top-notch. "Lord Kilhenny has many friends in high places who are rallying to his aid."

Did I detect a flicker of alarm on his face?

"So would you like to answer my question? Why did you hear nothing? You were still up and awake."

He smirked then. I had taken rather a dislike to him from the first. This was now confirmed. "Because I was down in the kitchen. I went into the library where he was working to see if he wanted anything before I went to bed, and I found him lying there."

"That must have been a shock for you," Darcy said.

"Sure was. All that blood. I thought the killer might still be in the building and I'd be next."

"You didn't hear any footsteps running or a door slamming, as you would have done if someone had to get away in a hurry?" I asked.

He shook his head. "How many times do I have to tell you that I heard nothing?"

"If you heard nothing of a struggle, presumably you would not have heard anyone coming into the castle, or even knocking at the front door and being admitted by Mr. Roach," I suggested.

"That's ridiculous," he snapped. "Mr. Roach never answered the front door himself. And visitors had to telephone the house from the front gate before they were admitted. And for that matter, he had no visitors. He was a private kind of guy. Kept himself to himself and no one from the States knew he was over here."

We didn't seem to be getting anywhere.

"So what will you do now?" I asked. "Were you Mr. Roach's valet for long?"

"He hired me when he was coming to Ireland," he said. "I guess I'll have to find myself another job. I might just stay on in Ireland. There seem to be more high-class people with money and big houses than there are in the States these days."

I thought he'd need to refine his speech and manners somewhat if he wanted to be hired by Irish aristocrats, but I kept this opinion to myself. Instead I asked, "So how long are you expected to stay on at the castle? Until the end of the investigation?"

"Nobody's actually told me," he said. "That inspector guy said I should stick around for now, just to make sure the place is secure and nothing gets touched. Then I'll have to give evidence at the trial. But I hope they get this thing over in a hurry. Staying in this place alone gives me the creeps."

"Of course, there could be another reason why you've been asked to stay on," I said.

"What's that?"

"That you are also a suspect," I said.

I really did notice the alarm in his eyes this time. "Me? How can I be a suspect? I found the guy lying there."

"So you say," I said. His eyes were darting nervously now. I was rather enjoying this. "But it's only your word, isn't it? You could easily have killed Mr. Roach yourself and then tried to put the blame on Lord Kilhenny. To frame Lord Kilhenny."

"Why would I want to kill the guy?" he demanded.

"I don't know. Why would you?" I asked sweetly. "Maybe something will emerge when the police in America check into your background."

"They can't pin nothing on me," he said hastily. "I've led a blameless life, kid."

"Then you've nothing to worry about, have you?" I said.

"You'd better beat it before I yell for the cops," he said, giving me a hate-filled stare.

"Come on, Darcy," I said. "I think we've learned all we need to for now." I gave Mickey Riley a curt little nod, then turned on my heel and headed back for the forest.

"You were brilliant," Darcy said when we were out of the man's hearing. "You should have been a lawyer."

"Sometimes I manage to channel my great-grandmother," I said, giving him a pleased little grin. "But it was interesting, wasn't it? I had him truly rattled. And the way he speaks, he'd certainly not find it easy to get a job in service with a family in Ireland. Can you imagine my sister-in-law, Fig, hiring someone like him? She becomes hysterical over Queenie. Do you really think that valets in America are so uncouth?"

"He may be a good actor and able to adopt the correctly subservient attitude when needed," Darcy said. "We're seeing him as he really is. Perhaps Mr. Roach never did."

"I'd love to know if he was employed before this as a valet." I turned back to Darcy as we pushed between tall bushes. "Can you see the Rockefellers hiring him? How can we find out whether the police in America are checking into his background?"

"I have my connections," Darcy said. "When we go to Dublin there is usually someone at the embassy who is secretly placed there by the FBI. And if not, I can pass that request along through a chap that I know in London." He paused, looking back. "But presumably the detectives here will have ruled him out as a suspect before they arrested my father."

"Because his prints aren't on the club and they could find no motive," I said with a sigh.

"And because my father more or less confessed," Darcy said.

"We need to talk to your father," I said. "Find out about that row in the afternoon."

"Do you think I haven't tried talking to him?" Darcy snapped. "He either shuts up like a clam or flies off the handle. One can't have a normal conversation with him."

We had been walking fast and reached the little gate in

the wall. I looked across at the brilliant green fields as we emerged. In the distance I spotted horses, unsaddled now, but running on their own, just for the joy of it. The stables next, I thought. The strong sunlight made me blink. I held up my hand to shield my eyes and another thought came to me. "Darcy, do you know if it was raining on the day that Mr. Roach was killed, or the days before it?"

Darcy frowned. "Why would I know that? And why is it important? Are you suggesting muddy prints in the house?"

"No, I'm thinking about that archeological dig in the field across from the gate. If they were working, they might have noticed whether there were any visitors at the castle that day or the days before."

"But Roach was killed late at night," Darcy said. "They'd have gone home long before that hour, even if they were working."

"But it would be good to know if Mr. Roach had visitors, wouldn't it? His man claimed he had none. And who knows, there might have been someone loitering around the gate, snooping to find a way in . . . casing the joint, as the Americans would say."

This made Darcy grin. "I never thought I would hear the words 'casing the joint' coming from your lips," he said. "And speaking of your lips. They look particularly inviting this morning." And he kissed me.

Chapter 19

An unexpected drop-in visit.

So we decided to check the dig next and see if anyone was working. We turned toward the castle's front gate and sure enough there was activity in the field opposite. There was also a Garda constable standing outside the castle gate, watching everything that was going on. Darcy turned the Rolls onto the track leading to the field gate and brought it to a halt.

"Is this one of your fields?" I asked, as the thought had just occurred to me.

"All the fields around here used to be Kilhenny land. I believe this is part of the home farm, which is rented out to tenants these days."

"So any treasure found in this dig would still belong to your family?"

"Belong to the dead American now, I suppose," he said. "I'm not sure what the conditions of the sale were and whether he bought all Kilhenny property or just the castle and stables."

The young Garda constable was now walking toward us.

"No reporters, please," he said. "No stopping here. Please move along." Then his face changed. "Oh, it's you, Mr. Darcy. It's a long time since we've seen you around here. Sorry it has to be in such tragic circumstances now."

"How are you, Kevin?" Darcy said. "Or do I have to say Constable Byrne these days?"

The constable grinned, looking ridiculously schoolboy-ish. "I bet you never thought I'd be on the right side of the law one day, did you?"

"Not after the number of times we caught you poaching rabbits on the estate." Darcy was smiling too. "Look, Kevin." He leaned out of the motor window. "I'd like a word with the archeologists. Your inspector from Dublin seems convinced that my father is guilty. So it's up to me to try and prove his innocence. All I want to find out is whether these people saw anyone going to the castle in the days before Mr. Roach was killed."

"I don't know, Mr. Darcy." Kevin looked worried. "I'd like to help but my orders are—"

"The dig is not part of a crime scene," Darcy said. "I'm sure your inspector can't prevent people from speaking to each other in an open field."

"I suppose not," the young Garda replied, his forehead still wrinkled. "All right, then, but don't be long. I don't want to get that inspector breathing down my neck."

Darcy helped me from the motorcar and we plowed through mud to the field. Tarps had now been removed and a large trench was revealed. Two women were down in this hole and a man was standing at a trestle table on which sat what looked like some lumps of mud. He glanced up as we approached him.

"Sorry, this place is off-limits," he said, coming around the table to fend us off. He was thin, bald and worried look-ing and had that distinctive academic air to him—the worn tweed jacket and baggy trousers.

"I'm Darcy O'Mara, heir to the Kilhenny title, and this land has been in my family for at least a thousand years,"

Darcy said. "Any antiquities you find represent my family's history."

"I'm sorry, Mr. O'Mara—or is it 'Lord' something?" he asked.

"Just 'mister.' So can you tell me what made you excavate here and what you hope to find?"

"We're excavating here because Pamela, down there in the trench, is doing her PhD thesis on burial chambers, and from aerial photographs she is convinced that she has found an ancient settlement here. Based on the present lay of the land she thinks the burial chamber must be close to this position. And of course the historic Burda club was found nearby, wasn't it? That's what really inspired the dig and gives us hope."

"What have you found so far?" I asked.

He turned to look at me with interest and I could see him sizing up who I might be. "Only the usual, such as one finds in almost any field in Ireland. Pottery shards. Old farming implements. A couple of nice spearheads. Would you like to see the latest?" And he led us to the table on which the brown lumps now revealed themselves to be muddy shards.

"Are you Pamela's professor?" Darcy asked, looking down at the girl in the trench who had now stopped work and was watching us.

"That's right. Alex Harmon, professor of archeology, Trinity College." The man held out his hand.

"And just the three of you working here? All from Trinity?" Darcy continued.

"Not just the three of us. The numbers fluctuate depending on who has time to come and help, and the weather conditions. Sometimes we've had as many as ten . . . but that's a bit of overkill, actually. We get in each other's way."

"But they are all your students?"

"Students and faculty. Some of my fellow teachers enjoy getting down and dirty sometimes." And he smiled, making the worried expression vanish from his face.

"But no outsiders?"

"We've had a couple of visiting academics as well as a reporter or two from Dublin."

"How recently?"

The man sighed, thinking. "It's been raining a lot so we haven't been able to get out here much." He looked down at the trench. "Pamela, Carol, do you remember when we last had a visitor?"

Pamela shook her head. "Not for a couple of weeks. The weather has been beastly."

"These visiting academics," Darcy said. "All from Ireland, were they? People you knew?"

Pamela looked at Carol and grinned. "There was that American professor, remember? He was really funny."

"Amusing? Witty?"

Pamela shook her head. "Strange. He didn't really seem interested in what we've found. He seemed awfully keen on gold, didn't he, Carol? I told him the likelihood of gold in a burial chamber is not very high, but he didn't seem to have much clue about Irish burial customs. I suppose old in America is two hundred years, not two thousand."

"Do you remember where he was from?"

"University of Southern Nebraska, was it?" Pamela asked.

"Did he join in the dig?"

"We invited him, but he said he was in his traveling clothes and didn't want to get dirty."

"Who invited him to come?" I asked.

"Nobody. He just showed up one day and said he was touring Ireland and had heard about us and had to come and see for himself," the professor answered.

"Do you remember his name?"

"Peabody. Professor Peabody," Pamela said. "We had a bit of a giggle about it because he was quite large and Carol whispered that she had never seen a pea that size."

"Thank you," Darcy said. "Good luck with your dig. Does a portion of any gold found go to the O'Maras?"

"If it's valuable it's all treasure trove and the government has first pick," the professor said with a smile. "Naturally we hope that any significant find will be donated to Trinity. But we'll obviously let your family know exactly what has been found. We plan to have an exhibition at Trinity if the site eventually warrants it."

"Why start now? At this time of year?" I asked Pamela. "Wouldn't the summer be more pleasant?"

"Definitely." She smiled at me. "But I wanted to get started on the research part of this PhD, so as soon as I identified the site in the photographs, I asked if we could start work right away." She paused and grinned at Carol. "I've regretted it several times already when we've been up to our ankles in mud and freezing our fingers off. I can't think what January will be like."

"Good luck," I said. "I hope you find something worthwhile."

We exchanged a smile.

"Before you go back to work," Darcy said, squatting to be closer to them, "have you noticed anybody going into the castle in the last week or so?"

"There are deliveries from time to time," Carol said. "A grocer and butcher from Dublin about once a week."

"But no visitors?"

The girls checked with each other. "I don't think so. We're concentrating quite hard when we work, so we might not have noticed anybody on foot. But we would have heard a motorcar."

"There was that priest," Carol commented. "A young man wearing heavy specs. He asked if Lord Kilhenny was still at the castle and we said he wasn't. Then he asked if the American was Catholic and we said we didn't know. And he said it was his duty to visit everyone in the parish and he'd give it a try."

"Did he get in?" I asked.

Carol shook her head. "I don't know. We went back to work. He was on foot."

"And then there was the newspaper reporter that time," Pamela said. "I don't think she got in, did she? She tried asking us questions but of course we knew nothing. She's been around a few times since, but never got in."

"I suppose you've had quite a few reporters since . . . since the American died?" I said.

"Oodles of them. It's too bad we can't dish the dirt, as they say, but of course there's nothing we can tell them. We didn't know the man. We never saw him, except once or twice coming out in the backseat of a big black car."

There really seemed nothing more to ask. I looked at Darcy. He nodded to the three of them. "Sorry to have taken up your time. Do let us know if you dig up the O'Mara hoard."

He gave them a good-natured wave, then took my arm and steered me across the muddy clumps in the field.

"Well, that all seems aboveboard, doesn't it?" I said. "I mean, I thought it was interesting at first that they had started a dig right across the road from the castle so recently. And I began to wonder whether they might actually be digging a tunnel to get into the grounds or something."

"It would have to be a long tunnel," Darcy said. "But I have to think they are what they claim to be. And so easy to check with Trinity as to who is out here."

"So strike one line of inquiry," I said and he nodded.

The policeman was still standing beside our motorcar.

"Thank you, Kevin," Darcy said. "We'll be off now."

"Did you learn anything?" Kevin asked.

"There was a visiting American professor," I said. "And a young priest. They seem to have been the only visitors."

"Young priest?" The constable looked thoughtful. "Now, I wonder who that would have been? Father Flannery is over seventy and I can't think of a parish around here that has a young curate."

Darcy looked at me. "Interesting," he said. "Two people who could have been checking on Mr. Roach. Now I'm really interested to find out more about him." He turned to me. "Let's head for Dublin right away."

"What about the stables?" I asked as we climbed back into the vehicle. "Didn't we say we'd find out what we could there first?"

"Don't we know all there is to know?" Darcy said shortly. "Either my father doped that horse and was found out and fired, or Mr. Roach had someone else dope the horse and let my father take the blame when the horse dropped dead. Either way he has a strong motive for revenge, doesn't he?"

"It certainly seems that way," I agreed.

"And his anger could have been festering all this time, so that when they had that final blowup the afternoon of the murder it was the last straw. He went home, got drunk and then decided to kill Roach."

We looked at each other for a long moment. It seemed all too plausible, but one of us had to stay positive.

"We need to find out what that final argument was about," I said.

He nodded. "If we can get the stubborn old fool to tell us." He sighed. "All right. We'll visit the stables first since they are right here." And we drove down that little lane, past the lodge, until we came to a handsome whitewashed building with a weather vane of a galloping horse on top of a red tiled roof. At the center of that building was an arch leading through to a stable yard beyond, and as we watched, a horse was led across that archway, walking with the easy graceful strides of the Thoroughbred. Darcy stared, went to say something, then turned away, and I saw now why he was not anxious to visit the stables. It was too painful for him to visit a place he had loved that no longer belonged to him.

"If you don't want to do this, it's all right with me," I said. "I know it must be hard for you."

"I got over it long ago," he said. "When my father first sold up it was very hard. I'd always imagined myself taking over the stables from him one day, training a Gold Cup winner. Now who knows what will happen. It's all lost, everything."

I touched his hand gently. "We're going to have a good life together somewhere," I said.

He nodded, still staring in front of him. I got out of the motorcar and started to walk toward the archway. I heard

Darcy slam his door and his footsteps clattered on the cobbles as he came after me.

"Hey, you," a voice shouted, and a young man came striding toward us. He was redheaded, red faced and scowling. "What do you want? Not more reporters, are you? You're the third lot this morning and we've work to do."

"Who are you?" Darcy asked him.

"Ted Benson, stable manager," the man said, eyeing Darcy with dislike, "and for that matter who might you be?"

"Darcy O'Mara, Lord Kilhenny's son and heir."

The man sneered. "I'm surprised you dare show your face around here after what your old man did."

"My old man, as you so crudely put it, is innocent until proven guilty," Darcy said. "And what happened to Harry?"

"You mean the old man who looked after the horses when your father ran the stable? Mr. Roach got rid of him. Too old to do the job anymore. He needed a younger man, with more modern ideas."

Darcy was looking around the stables where a horse's head looked out of each open door. "You've still got Sultan, I see," he said, and went over to stroke the nose of a big dark bay. The horse whickered and rubbed up against Darcy.

"He seems to like you," Ted Benson commented, sounding surprised. "He doesn't get on with anyone else here and he's a devil to ride. Pity because he's strong over the jumps."

Darcy gave the big horse a final pat and came back to me.

"So you weren't here when there was the doping incident?" he asked.

"I was not. Mr. Roach hired me after he got rid of your father. He tried running the place himself for a while but that was a disaster. He knew nothing about horses, did he? Not a thing."

"So what is going to happen to the stables now?" Darcy asked.

"Search me," Benson said. "I don't even know if my wages are going to be paid. And we certainly can't go ahead and enter any of the races in the upcoming meetings. I'm not paying jockeys out of my pocket and the Garda have said nothing. Looking for a will and the next of kin, I suppose. Probably put the whole bally lot up for auction. Some good horses here."

Darcy was looking around as if he couldn't wait to be off again. "We won't trouble you any longer," he said, and he escorted me back under the archway. I could feel Ted Benson watching us all the way back to the Rolls.

"He was an unpleasant sort of chap, wasn't he?" I said.

"I don't know why Mr. Roach fired old Harry," Darcy said. "He knew everything there was to know about horses, and he had a way with them too. Almost as if he knew what they were thinking. He taught me to ride and to jump. I wonder if he still lives around here."

"Interesting that he was sacked right after that horse doping, wasn't it?" I said.

"You mean that he might have been responsible?" Darcy asked sharply.

"Quite the opposite. I mean that he might have deduced what really happened, or seen something he shouldn't."

"So what do you think happened?"

"I'm just surmising, but what if Mr. Roach himself had the horse doped to make it run faster, only it died before it reached the finish line. Perhaps Harry witnessed someone injecting the horse, or suspected what had happened."

"Possible. I wonder if he got another job. Not easy at his age. But we can ask at Punchestown Racecourse when we drive into Dublin. Someone there should know what happened to him. And someone there might even be able to shed some light on the horse doping."

So it looked as if we had a busy day ahead of us!

We were just reversing out of the stable forecourt when there was a loud noise above our heads.

"What the devil . . ." Darcy began.

A small aeroplane dropped from the sky and skimmed over us, just missing the treetops, then landed in the field, bouncing over the turf and sending the horses racing off in panic.

Darcy was out of the motorcar in a second, running toward

the five-bar gate and vaulting nimbly over it. "The bloody fool," he shouted. "What does he think he's doing?"

The plane was now taxiing toward us and came to a halt. The pilot climbed down and headed toward Darcy.

"Are you mad? You're on private property," Darcy shouted. "And you have frightened the horses. You should leave immediately."

The pilot now removed goggles and helmet and shook out luxurious dark hair. "Is that any way to greet an old friend who has come all this way to help you?" said the Princess Zamanska.

Chapter 20

STILL TUESDAY, DECEMBER 4

The princess has arrived. I can't say I'm thrilled with this new complication! Too fond of Darcy, for one thing. But I can't ask Darcy to make her leave without seeming jealous—which I am, of course.

"Zou Zou, what are you doing?" Darcy exclaimed. "Have you lost your senses?"

Princess Zamanska advanced on Darcy, her arms open. "I couldn't stop worrying about you so I decided I had to come in person to rescue you and offer my help. And I did want to see if my new toy could make it over the Irish Sea—which it did beautifully, I have to tell you. So stop looking so cross and give me a kiss."

And she threw her arms around his neck and was kissing him in a most unsisterly manner. I felt a stab of jealousy and had to force myself to stay put and not leap out shouting, "He's mine. Hands off."

"It was kind of you to come, but there's really nothing you can do to help me, Zou Zou." Darcy's voice was unsteady. She was still draped around his neck, her body pressed against his.

"But of course there is. I was just speaking to my dear pal Sir Roderick Altringham. Do you know him? He's a QC, you can't do any better than that. And he'd do anything for me."

"Zou Zou, an English QC is of no use to us here. We're in Ireland. Different legal system. Different judges."

"I am aware of that, darling. I'm not a complete idiot." She stroked his cheek. "But Roddy knows everybody who is anybody. He says he'll choose the very best barrister that Ireland has to offer for your father."

"Zou Zou, again it's kind of you, but I have to point out that we can't afford to pay the very best barrister in Ireland. My father is bankrupt. That's the whole reason he had to sell the estate in the beginning."

"Silly, silly." She patted his cheek now. "I'm happy to pay, of course. Anything to take that worried frown from your darling face and make you smile again. I might even know the odd Irish judge or two if I go through my little black book. . . . Wouldn't that be helpful?"

Darcy gave a nervous chuckle. "And I certainly can't allow you to blackmail a judge for me."

"What a nasty word." The princess released Darcy from her octopus-like grip. "I would merely suggest that they do a favor for an old friend. Someone has to help you, dear boy. Your dear little lady friend was quite distraught when she came to visit me."

I could see that Darcy had just remembered I was sitting in the Rolls. I suppose people like Princess Zamanska have that effect on men.

"My dear little lady friend is actually in the motorcar now."

"She is? She came to you after all? I thought you had forbidden her to come."

"I had," Darcy said with the hint of a bitter smile. "But she didn't listen."

"Good for her. She has spunk. I like that."

"We've been interviewing people who might have seen something," Darcy said as they started to walk across the field. "Come and say hello."

"Interviewing people? Don't the police do that over here?"

"Not very well, it would seem. They are convinced my father is guilty and not looking beyond him."

"Your father claims he is innocent, does he? I rather thought it was a foregone conclusion that he did it, from what I've read in the papers. I could quite understand it myself. There have been several Americans I've wanted to kill, especially the rich ones who think that their money can buy anything. I even met a chap once who wanted to marry me and it turned out that he thought he would become a prince by marrying a princess. I ask you!" She paused, then added, "Well, I suppose there is a certain lady we know who rather thinks she will become queen one day."

"To get back to my father," Darcy said. "Whether he's guilty or not, we have to do our best for him. We have to come up with the best defense possible, because he's doing nothing to help himself."

Darcy had opened the gate and they came toward the motor. I decided the right thing would be to get out to say hello to Zou Zou. I stepped down and managed a bright smile.

"That was quite an entrance, Your Highness," I said.

She beamed. "My new toy. I adore it. Is it all right to leave it here for the moment, do you think? This field doesn't belong to you, by any chance?"

"Used to," Darcy said. "Now it belongs to a dead man. And I don't see any harm in leaving it here for now. You can't stay, of course. There's nowhere to put you up nearby. Even the pubs are full. I'm camping out with my father at the lodge and there are no hotel beds for miles. The place is buzzing with reporters. In fact the wisest thing would be for you to take off again before anyone in the village comes to have a look at the plane."

"But I want to be useful," the princess said. "Tell me

what you need doing and I'll do it. And as soon as Roddy has found the best barrister in Ireland, we'll snap him up."

I could see that Darcy was in an agony of indecision. He didn't want the princess here, that was clear. He didn't want her dramatic arrival alerting the press to our presence. But he did want the best barrister in Ireland. "Then I suppose you had better find a hotel in Dublin, at least for tonight," Darcy said. "We were on our way there now. You can come with us."

"Why don't we all go in my aeroplane?" Princess Zamanska said, waving her hands excitedly. "I'm sure we can just fit in three, if we hold our breath."

"You can't fly an aeroplane to Dublin." Darcy shook his head. "The airfield is miles outside the city and then we'd have no transportation."

"Are there no taxies to be had in Dublin? I always found it a most civilized city."

"We'll drive," Darcy said. "The object at the moment is to attract the least amount of attention, and zooming over the city in a plane piloted by an exotic foreign princess is hardly what I call going about unnoticed."

She laughed and patted his cheek again. "So sweet," she said.

"Do you have a bag you want to bring with you?" Darcy said, opening the back door for her.

She sighed. "I suppose so. This all seems so silly with a hulking great castle sitting right here. How many bedrooms does it have? Surely a corner for tiny *moi*?"

"Forty-seven," Darcy said. "But it's currently in the hands of the Garda and even if it weren't, it no longer belongs to my family."

He went back into the field to retrieve a small suitcase from her aircraft. As soon as he was gone, she turned to me. "This is not good for him, you know. All those frown lines. They are spoiling his handsome face. We must bring this thing to a swift conclusion."

"That's not going to be easy," I said.

"So Georgie tells me you've started your investigation.

What have you found out so far? Any likely suspects apart from your father?" she asked as Darcy returned, and then helped her into the backseat of the Rolls.

"Not much," Darcy said. "Almost nothing, in fact. We've talked to his valet, to the people at the archeological dig, to the man who runs the stables, but I don't know if we've learned anything significant so far."

The princess clapped her hands. "Isn't this exciting? I feel just like Hercule Poirot. We'll track down the real killer and make him confess. We'll summon everyone and sit them in a circle and say, 'I've called you all here to name the murderer.'"

"This isn't a game, Zou Zou," Darcy said, his voice taut with emotion. "It's my father's life at stake. It's the reputation of my family."

She reached forward and caressed the back of his neck. "I know that, darling boy. I was just trying to cheer you up. So tell me, what do you hope to achieve in Dublin?"

"We are trying to find out more about this Mr. Roach. Nobody seems to know anything. He was a recluse. No friends or family came to visit him. He was interested in horses but apparently knew little about them. So we're trying to find if anyone else had a motive for wanting him dead."

"I see," the princess said. "And who might know this in Dublin?"

"We're going to the American embassy," I said, not wanting this to turn into a dialogue between Darcy and the princess. "They must have tried to contact his next of kin by now."

"Good point. So how was he murdered, exactly?"

"Hit over the head with a club."

"Darlings, how terribly primitive. Is your father a violent man?"

"Not usually," Darcy said. "And it wasn't just any club. It was a prehistoric club of great rarity that has been in my family forever."

"Ah, so it could have been symbolic of reclaiming the family honor. Perhaps this man insulted your father one time too many. Perhaps he was planning to do something awful with the castle—turn it into a tourist attraction or something."

"But that's just giving another reason to make him guilty," I said. "We did wonder whether Mr. Roach had surprised a burglar trying to take this valuable club and they struggled over it."

"Splendid," she exclaimed. "I like that one. The unknown burglar. Nothing to do with any of the parties involved. Yes, I can see the defense counsel could do well with that. I suppose your father has no alibi that night? Did the servants not see him?"

"He has no servants any longer," Darcy said, "apart from Mrs. McNalley, who comes in to clean and bring him food. And she's only there in the daytime. She was long gone."

"And I suppose nobody passed his house and noticed him through the window or something?"

"He lives in the lodge, which we are about to pass on your right. See, there, through the trees?"

"Oh mon Dieu," she said. "How utterly dreary. No wonder your father's thoughts turned to murder. It couldn't be more out of the way, could it? Should we just pop in and let me introduce myself to your pa and tell him my plans for his barrister?"

"I think not," Darcy said hastily. "My father is not exactly welcoming callers at the moment."

"Don't be silly, he'd love to see me," the princess said. "I'm sure we have oodles of friends in common. And I'm good at putting anyone at their ease. You know that. I can make monsters eat out of my hand. Do you know that Mussolini actually kissed my cheek once?"

I turned to look at her. I was sure she really did have the power of melting even the hardest of hearts. But Darcy said shortly, "Absolutely not, Zou Zou. At least not until we have something positive to tell him."

"I'll telephone Roddy when we get to Dublin and chivvy him along with his barrister search," she said. "Knowing he has the best chap in Ireland on his side will certainly cheer your father up, surely?"

"You'd think so, wouldn't you?" Darcy said. "But he has sunk into such a depression that I'm not sure what would cheer him right now."

"Then it's up to us," Princess Zamanska said. "If anyone can do it, we can."

I admired her confidence. I wasn't at all sure myself.

Chapter 21

TUESDAY, DECEMBER 4
A SURPRISE IN DUBLIN.

We drove through open countryside and then met the main road in Kildare. After the town of Newbridge, Darcy drove off the main road into the countryside again.

"Didn't you say we were going to Dublin?" the princess asked. "This doesn't look very citylike."

"We have to stop on the way at the Punchestown Racecourse. We are looking for an old man who managed the stables in my father's time."

"How lovely. I adore racehorses," Zou Zou said. "I keep meaning to buy myself a couple. I rather fancy standing in the winner's circle in my best hat. You must advise me, Darcy, and you can train them and we'll win the Derby or the Grand National or both."

"Different horses, Zou Zou," Darcy said. "Flat racers are no good for steeplechases. We have the latter. Strong horses needed for jumps."

"You see, I know nothing. I need you to advise me," she said.

It passed through my mind again that Mr. Roach had known nothing about racehorses. What had made him buy a racing stable in Ireland? Had it always been a secret dream of his, which he had made a reality when he inherited the family fortune?

We approached the racecourse with the grandstand rising above outbuildings and the white picket fence outlining the curve of the track. The car park was empty and at first the place had a deserted air to it.

"Obviously no meeting today," Darcy said. "I wonder if this is a waste of time."

We bumped over ruts and mud into the stable area to the left. As we approached the first of the stable buildings a man came toward us, leading a horse. Darcy wound down the motorcar window. "Excuse me," he called out, "you wouldn't happen to know where I might find Harry Paine?"

"Old Harry? I think he's around today. He works for the Sullivan stables these days and I know they've got horses running in the novice stakes tomorrow."

"Thank you." Darcy switched off the motor then came around to help us from the vehicle. "It's a bit muddy. Are you sure you'd not rather stay in the motorcar? I won't be long."

"We don't want to miss out on the fun," Zou Zou said. "Of course we're not staying put. Come on, Georgie." And she set off bravely slithering through the mud. I followed. There was plenty of activity in this stable area. Horse boxes were arriving and their passengers led carefully down ramps to waiting stalls. Other horses were standing outside, while stable hands brushed them or attended to their hooves. Nobody stopped us or even asked us what we wanted as we walked down the lines of stalls. Perhaps they were used to owners paying a surprise visit. We were almost at the end when Darcy exclaimed, "There he is. That's Harry." And he hurried forward as an old man came out of the end stall, a cigarette dangling from the corner of his mouth. He was small and wiry and I wondered if he had started life as a jockey. He was scowling, but his face broke into a grin as he saw Darcy and took the cigarette from his mouth, throwing it down into the mud.

"Well, well. This is a surprise. What are you doing here, Mr. Darcy?"

"Come to see you, Harry." Darcy shook the man's hand. "I'm glad to see you're working."

"No thanks to that devil Roach," he said. "Dismissed me just like that, for no reason at all. Me, who had given the best years of my life to that stable. And in my place I hear he's brought in a nobody with no experience at all. A flat racing man. Never trained for the jumps."

Darcy nodded with understanding. Harry pushed his cap back on his head.

"Look, I'm awfully sorry to hear about your father. He was a good man. Knew his horses. Treated them like his children."

"Better than his children," Darcy said and they laughed.

"That may be true. I won't say he was always an easy man but he was fair, and he knew his stuff. And I can't say I blame him for killing that man. Such rudeness and ignorance. You've never seen the likes of it."

"That's what I heard," Darcy said. "Apparently his loves were horses and books but this new man, Ted Benson, told me he actually knew precious little about horses."

"Didn't know a thing," Harry said, "except how to bet on them." He moved closer to Darcy, looking around before he spoke. "It's my belief that's why he was so angry when Gladiator died. Not that he'd lost his best horse, but that he'd bet heavily on it and he lost a lot of money."

"He bet on the horse?"

Harry nodded. "Oh, he didn't put the money on himself but he got someone to do it for him. At least that's what I heard from a bookmaker pal of mine."

"You were there that day, Harry," Darcy said. "What do you think happened?"

"What happened?" Harry asked angrily. "Someone injected the horse with a powerful stimulant and it was too much for the poor creature's heart."

"And do you think the person who did that was my father?"

"Of course I don't," he said. "Like I told you, your father treated those horses like his children. He'd never have risked a horse's life to make him run faster and win races. Never."

"So do you have any idea who did dope the horse? Roach himself?"

"I'd give you ten to one that it was him. Right before the race I saw him coming out of the stall and he spotted me and he looked startled and said he'd just wanted to check Gladiator's girth. Well, I think he'd just drugged the horse himself then and he thought that I'd seen him do it. That's why he got rid of me. Not because I was too old or not good enough at my job, but because I knew the truth."

"Very interesting," Darcy said. "And he put the syringe into my father's drawer to place the blame on him."

Harry nodded. "That's what he did. And made an almighty fuss and dismissed your father on the spot. No wonder your father finally gave him what he deserved."

"You think my father killed him?"

"Didn't he? And if he didn't, then who did?" Harry asked.

"That's what we aim to find out," Darcy said. "So tell me, all the time you worked at Kilhenny stables, did Roach have any visitors? Did he ever talk about friends or family in America?"

Harry made a disparaging grunt. "Hardly ever showed his face at the stables and certainly didn't chat with the likes of us."

Standing well back while Darcy and Harry chatted, I had just had a brilliant thought. I couldn't wait to share this insight. I watched while Darcy shook hands with the old man, then came back to join us. "I suppose you heard everything, didn't you?"

"We did," I said. "And it confirmed what you suspected, didn't it?"

Darcy nodded. "Interesting that Roach had bet heavily on his horse."

"That's what I wanted to tell you," I said. "Remember we were told that Roach was a reclusive gentleman whose interests were horses and books? Well, someone was having a laugh at our expense. His interests were horses and books—but only in the sense of betting on them."

"Bookmakers, you mean?" Darcy's eyes lit up. "That's clever, Georgie. So much for our impression of a reclusive gentleman in the old sense. He might have been reclusive, but not a gentleman."

"How do you know that?" Zou Zou demanded.

"From what we've been told of his behavior. From my impression of the valet he hired, and from the fact that he knew nothing about horses. How many gentlemen do you know who have not grown up with horses as a part of their lives?"

"You're talking about the word 'gentlemen' as it applies to the English and Irish," Zou Zou said. "It may be different in America."

"And he might have started life quite humbly," I said. "He might have been a bank clerk or something until he inherited a fortune as the last surviving relative of a rich family. Remember when you were sent to Australia to locate the heir to the Duke of Eynsford and he turned out to be a boy from the Outback?"

"I do remember," he agreed. "I suppose that's perfectly plausible. But if you inherit money, why shut yourself away in Ireland? Why not enjoy it in America? With the depression still lingering on over there I'd imagine one could snap up some good pieces of property for a song."

"He was a shy and retiring sort of chap and he'd always had a dream of living as his Irish ancestors had done?" I suggested.

"Delusions of grandeur," the princess chimed in. "Pictured himself as an aristocrat."

"In which case why not act the part?" I countered. "Why not show yourself as the benevolent new landowner, not shut yourself away."

"I find it all most perplexing," Darcy said. "I'm dying to hear what the American embassy has to say. Someone must know something about him."

We were approaching the outskirts of Dublin, streets of humble houses and factories such as one finds on the outskirts of any big town.

"Where is the American embassy?" I asked.

"In Phoenix Park," Darcy said. "Lovely old house. Have you never been in Phoenix Park?"

"I've never been to Dublin before," I answered.

"Have you not? Then your education is sadly lacking, my lady," Darcy said. "Unfortunately this is not the time for a guided tour, but you'll see a bit of the park as we drive through."

We passed old brick buildings, an old jail, a barracks—not the most attractive of areas. I was keeping quiet about what I thought of Dublin until we came out to the River Liffey. As we crossed the water on a bridge I caught a glimpse of the city center with its spires and domes off to our right. We followed a rough stone wall for quite a while before we came to a gateway. Darcy swung the motorcar and we entered an area of parkland. I was expecting a city park to be an ordered affair with rose gardens, flower beds, arbors, but this was wild enough to make one feel one was out in the country. We drove across a vast expanse of trees and grass. In the distance we spotted deer. Then we came upon a large gray building that Darcy said was the headquarters of the Garda. It certainly was in a nice setting for a police station. Then as we drove on, Darcy pointed out the entrance to the zoo, off to our right among the trees.

"A zoo!" the princess exclaimed with delight. "I adore animals, don't you? When this is all over and settled we must come back and feed the giraffes. They have the longest tongues you've ever seen. So impressive! You have no idea what they can do with them." She somehow managed to make this remark sound sexy and she followed it up with a glance at Darcy, making me wonder again exactly what those two had been up to and how long ago. Still, it didn't do to torture myself with questions like this about Darcy. He loved me now, I reminded myself. That was all that mattered.

"Ah, here we are." Darcy slowed the motorcar as we approached a white gate, manned by two American soldiers, or maybe Marines. An American flag fluttered above it. Darcy wound down the window and before he could say anything, one of the uniformed men saluted and opened the gate to let us through.

"We must not look too disreputable." Darcy turned to us with a grin.

"I've always found that arriving in a Rolls does somehow dispel the notion that one is disreputable," Zou Zou said dryly.

As we came up a driveway and the bushes opened up, we got our first glimpse of the house, a handsome white Georgian building, surrounded by lawns. Darcy parked the Rolls in the forecourt then came around to open doors for us. "I think that maybe I should do the talking. We need to tread carefully here," he said in a low voice. "And of course they may not tell us anything since we're not official. Oh well. Here goes." And he led us up to the front door.

We were greeted by a tall serious young man who listened to Darcy and then bade us sit until someone had time to speak with us. We took leather armchairs in a pleasantly warm foyer and waited. After a few minutes we heard a door opening, the sound of deep voices and two men coming down the hall toward us.

"So where do we go from here?" an Irish voice asked.

"I can't tell you that yet. Naturally we'll alert the police in Illinois and have them follow up on this matter. I presume this will put your whole investigation on hold for the moment."

Darcy was on his feet as they approached. One of the men reacted with surprise as he saw Darcy.

"What are you doing here, O'Mara?" he demanded.

"Chief Inspector Callahan. What a surprise," Darcy said. "I'm here for the same reason as you, I would guess. Wanting to know more about Mr. Timothy Roach."

"Who is this young man?" the other man asked. He had a distinctly American look to him and a rumbling transatlantic voice.

The inspector started to say, "He is the son of—" but Darcy broke in at the same time. "Darcy O'Mara, sir," he said. "Son of Lord Kilhenny and currently working on my father's defense. Do I understand you've found some details for us about Mr. Timothy Roach?"

"I see no reason to share any information with a member of the public," Inspector Callahan said stiffly before the American could respond.

"I'm not exactly a random member of the public," Darcy said. "My father is on trial for his life, for the murder of Timothy Roach. I think we're entitled to all facts pertaining to this case."

The American nodded. "I think he has a right to know. We have just learned from the Illinois state authorities that the only Timothy Roach with that date and place of birth is shown as having died in 1920 of the Spanish flu."

Chapter 22

TUESDAY, DECEMBER 4
IN DUBLIN, AT THE AMERICAN EMBASSY.

**We learn an interesting piece of news. There may be a
light for us at the end of this tunnel.**

There was complete silence in the foyer while we digested this. From the other end of the hallway came the clatter of a typewriter. Darcy exchanged a glance with me, then turned back to the American. "So you are telling us that this man was not Timothy Roach?"

"So it would appear," the American said.

"He was traveling with a dead man's credentials?" Darcy asked. "Are you currently looking into what his real name was and what he was doing in Ireland?"

Inspector Callahan still looked as if he were fighting to control his annoyance. "I must object, Mr. Wexler. This is a criminal investigation. Whatever this man's real name was does not alter the fact that he was murdered in Ireland and all evidence points to Mr. O'Mara's father."

"I disagree." Darcy turned to face Callahan. "It might

have everything to do with the man's murder. Since my father's guilt has not yet been proven, then surely the case now opens up to a whole lot of motives and a whole lot of different suspects. If he wasn't Timothy Roach, then who was he? And how did he come by his money, and who might have wanted to murder him?"

"You have a point there, son," the American said. "You can rest assured we will be asking the authorities in Illinois to follow up on this. Can you supply me with photographs of the dead man, Chief Inspector Callahan? We'll need to circulate them to the appropriate people."

"And fingerprints," I said. I had forgotten that Darcy had told us he wanted to do all the talking, and I was conscious that everyone was now looking at me. "It makes sense to check his fingerprints, surely," I went on. "If he is not the man he claimed to be on his passport then he had to be hiding his true identity for a reason. You might find that his fingerprints are on file."

"And who might you be, young lady?" Chief Inspector Callahan asked.

I decided this was not a time for concealment. It was a time to pull rank. "Lady Georgiana Rannoch, cousin to His Majesty, King George," I said. "And this is the Princess Zamanska. We are both old friends of Mr. O'Mara and we are over here to show our support for the O'Mara family, and to do a little preliminary work while a barrister is being chosen for the defense."

I think that Inspector Callahan swallowed hard. "It's good to know that O'Mara has friends in such high places," he said. "Not that it will do much good. Unfortunately we are no longer part of Great Britain here. You can have no influence on the outcome of Irish justice, however royal you are."

"Of course not," Princess Zamanska said in a sweet, gentle tone. "But that doesn't prevent us from helping a chum in need, does it? Especially now that the whole matter appears to have taken on a very different twist. I think your investigation should now focus on why this man was here and who might have paid him a visit recently, don't you, Chief Inspector?"

The chief inspector had now gone very red in the face. "I work with facts, madam," he said, either not knowing that she should be addressed as "Your Highness" or choosing to ignore it. "The facts are that there was no sign of forced entry into the castle. There were no visitors that day. Lord Kilhenny's fingerprints were the only ones found on the club *and* he admits that he was so drunk he remembers nothing of the evening in question. Those are facts and good enough for me to come to the conclusion that Lord Kilhenny struck Timothy Roach, or whoever he is now, over the head with the club during an argument and killed him. Now if you will excuse me, I need to get back to work. I will have the photographs sent over to you, Mr. Wexler, and please keep me informed of any further developments." He nodded to the American, then turned back to us. "And may I suggest to you ladies that you confine yourselves to more suitable pursuits like dances and dressmakers. A little knowledge is a very dangerous thing and you could end up only making things worse for the man you are trying to help."

"Odious man," Princess Zamanska muttered as he stalked out. "Even if I did not care so passionately about Darcy I should now feel compelled to throw myself into the fray on behalf of his father."

Darcy had retrieved a calling card from his pocket. "I am currently staying at the lodge with my father," he said, handing it to the American, who looked rather uncomfortable following the heated scene he had just witnessed. "I would appreciate it if you would contact me as soon as you have any pertinent information."

"I certainly will, Mr. O'Mara." The American held out a big hand and shook Darcy's. "We could well find that someone is sent over from the States to assist in this investigation. And until I am advised how my government wishes to proceed, you can rest assured I will not allow any criminal trial to go forward."

"Thank you," Darcy said.

As we came out of the building the princess turned to Darcy. "Maybe one of us should go over and dig into this ourselves," she said. "I've just been wondering whether my little aeroplane would make it across the Atlantic. It takes so horribly long by sea. Two weeks wasted in the crossings, and then trains and things. By then that boorish policeman will have your father convicted and hanged."

Darcy shook his head. "Zou Zou, there is no way you can fly across the Atlantic Ocean. Don't be ridiculous. You're not Lindbergh."

She shrugged. "I only wanted to do something useful, you know. I could buy a bigger plane. One that carries more fuel."

Darcy put a hand on her shoulder. "It's a kind gesture, but I don't think anyone needs to go over there. I'm going to telephone a certain chap in London and I think he'll know who to contact in the States so that we have someone on our side over there."

"You're such a spoilsport, Darcy," the princess said. "I was looking forward to braving the elements and flying in to the rescue and earning your undying gratitude."

"You're a hopeless romantic, Zou Zou," Darcy said.

"Just doing my bit to help a chum, as I told the horrid policeman," she said. "So what do you propose doing next? We can't just sit back and leave it to other people. If this man was here under an assumed name, then he had to be up to no good. He was probably hiding from someone, and that person found him, crept into the castle and finished him off."

"I don't think you've taken a good look at the castle yet," Darcy said. "It's not that easy to gain entry. The gates are locked. There's a high wall. Besides, the manservant was there."

"And claimed he heard nothing. And he has already said that your father came in and out without being noticed," I pointed out.

"That's a fact that hardly helps my father's case," Darcy said dryly.

"What I am saying is that if anyone was keeping an eye

on the castle and observed your father, they could see how he got into the castle and emulate it."

"I presume my father still had a key to the servants' entrance or the wine cellar."

"Which someone could have taken and borrowed or copied if your father fell into a drunken sleep," I went on. I saw him wince at the word "drunken" and wished I had been more tactful.

"This implies that someone was in the neighborhood long enough to have studied my father's comings and goings, to have had a key cut. Kilhenny is a small community. A stranger who lingered would be noticed."

"We should consider the strangers we know about," I said. "The American professor who didn't seem to know much about archeology. And the young priest who Kevin the Garda didn't know." I waved my hands. "And the ghost. Don't forget Mrs. McNalley saw a ghost."

"A ghost? How divine," Zou Zou said. "I adore haunted houses."

"I was suggesting that this ghost might have been an intruder she observed," I said.

"Ah. I see." She nodded.

"We could make use of the embassy while we're here," I said to Darcy. "Could they not check up for us on a Professor Peabody from the University of . . . Southern Nebraska, wasn't it?"

"That's right," Darcy said. "Wait here. I'll go back inside and ask."

We waited. It was not unpleasant in the sunny forecourt. A robin flew down and landed a few feet from us, looking up hopefully. It flew off again as a door slammed and Darcy emerged from the building with a determined look on his face.

"We might be onto something here," he said as he approached us. His eyes were finally bright again, with hope in them. "I asked the young chap at the reception desk and he looked it up for me. There is no University of Southern Nebraska."

"Aha. An imposter." Zou Zou clapped her hands in delight. "The plot thickens. He was here to case the joint."

I had to smile at these words coming from her lips.

"Of course, the graduate students we spoke to might have got the name wrong," Darcy said. "One doesn't always take in such things, especially if they were concentrating on their task."

"But it's a starting point," I said. "And we have a description. A big man. Big enough that the girls giggled when he said his name was Peabody. Now, there can't be too many large Americans in this part of Ireland. It's not the time of year for tourists. Someone will have spoken to him at the station, or given him directions, or driven him in a taxicab."

"And if they did, what is any of this going to prove?" Darcy demanded. I could tell his temper was wearing thin. "We have no way of knowing who this Peabody really is or why he might have wanted to visit Timothy Roach. We can really do nothing until someone in America identifies Roach from his photograph and finds out why he came to Ireland."

"You don't seem keen on doing anything, Darcy," I said.

"I agree," Zou Zou added. "A complete wet blanket, which isn't at all like you. The Darcy I know and love is a man of action. He wouldn't give up so easily."

Darcy shrugged. "I can't get over the fact that there were no other prints on that club. Or that my father will say nothing in his own defense. He must believe that he is guilty. In which case, what hope do I have of proving his innocence?"

"We must get cracking on finding that barrister," Zou Zou said. "Why don't you drive me to a suitable hotel first, since it appears there is nowhere closer to put me up. Where do people stay in Dublin, Darcy? I mean, people like us?"

"That would be the Shelbourne," Darcy said. "But are you sure you want to stay, Zou Zou?"

"Wouldn't miss it for the world, darling boy. I haven't had this much excitement since I had to flee from Poland with just the clothes on my back." She put her hand on his arm. "So come on. Buck up. Drive me to this hotel then I'll telephone Roddy and tell him to get a move on and find us the best barrister in Ireland."

"Zou Zou, we'll have to find out first whether my father's solicitor has already engaged the services of a barrister."

"Oh, so there already is a legal team working for your father? Why didn't you tell me that?"

Darcy grimaced. "Because it is Leach and Leach, the family solicitors, and I don't expect they are much use. They are fine with wills and conveyances, but I'd like to bet that they have never tackled a murder case before."

"Then let's go and visit them and tell them not to bother, that we have everything under control and have the top barrister in Ireland representing your father."

He had to smile at this. "Zou Zou, you make it all sound so simple, don't you? Everything under control. I wish it were."

Chapter 23

TUESDAY, DECEMBER 4
IN DUBLIN.

**So relieved to find Darcy thinks the princess is an added
complication too!**

My opinion of Dublin as a city rose considerably as we followed the Liffey to the city center where elegant sandstone
buildings replaced brick factories and row houses, and spires
and domes replaced factory chimneys. Darcy had been right.
It was an attractive city and one that he would be proud to
show me someday. We passed the lovely yellow stone buildings of Trinity College where students swarmed across the
lawns, looking like flocks of bats in their gowns. The Shelbourne Hotel, facing a garden called St. Stephen's Green,
looked as elegant as any of the public buildings, with its
glass portico and sculptures. I was just thinking that it
looked horribly expensive when Zou Zou exclaimed, "Oh,
I think this will do nicely." How lovely to have money!

She was welcomed with suitable decorum. A room was

found for her and she was escorted up to it, leaving Darcy and me standing in the lobby.

"Oh God, Georgie," he said, leaning closer to me. "I really wish she hadn't come. I mean, she's absolutely adorable and so generous and all that, but life is a big game to her. I rather fear she'll be an infernal nuisance. And draw unwanted attention to us."

"I don't think you'll manage to get rid of her that easily," I said. "Not unless you can find her something to do that will require flying around in her aeroplane, or something that has to be done back in London."

He had to laugh at this. "Flying around in her aeroplane. Maybe we should have her fly low looking for Peabody."

I laughed too. It was a wonderful feeling that we were coconspirators, two of us against the world.

"How long will she be, do you think?" I asked. "Is there something else we should be doing while we wait?"

Darcy stared at the lift into which she had disappeared. "I don't see what else we can do until we know who the dead man really was. That was a turnup for the books, wasn't it? He comes to Ireland with enough money to buy a castle. . . ."

"And enough know-how to get a passport in the name of a dead man. That must indicate he's a criminal, don't you think?"

"Either that or a very rich man who needs to escape for some reason."

"Like what?"

"He's murdered his wife? He was involved in a scandal and he's faking his own death?"

"Oh yes. Good point. And anyone rich enough can pay for most things. But if he was rich wouldn't he be well-known? Wouldn't he worry about being recognized and having somebody say, 'You're not Timothy Roach, you are . . .'"

"Which is why he acted the recluse," Darcy finished for me.

"But he went to race meetings. We know that."

"Maybe just to the stable area, though. Maybe he never

appeared in the grandstand or the paddock where he might
have been recognized."

"So . . ." I was warming to this subject now. "We need
to know of any scandals among the rich in the last few years.
Any millionaires who disappeared and were presumed dead.
That shouldn't be too hard to find out. And Chief Inspector
Callahan has photographs he's going to give to the American
embassy. There's a good chance someone will recognize
him."

"But none of this alters the fact that my father's prints
were the only ones on the club," Darcy said. He stared past
me, out to the front door where a lively party had just entered, laughing as if they hadn't a care in the world.

"There may be an explanation for that too," I said.

"Such as?"

"What if the club was not the weapon? What if it was left
beside the corpse and the real weapon was destroyed or
hidden? Surely your father would have handled the club
sometime. Maybe he showed it to somebody. Took it down
from the wall and it has his prints on it."

"Then how would the real killer know to plant that particular weapon, chosen from all of them, on the wall? A
little far-fetched, I'm afraid."

"What about an interrupted burglary?" I said. "That's
not far-fetched. It's all too plausible. Drat. We should have
brought up the possibility of burglary when we were speaking to the detective inspector. He should let you look around
the castle to see if anything has been taken."

"I suggested that to my father," Darcy said. "There would
be no point in looking around without him. I haven't been
home for several years. I've no way of knowing if my father
sold off family heirlooms when he was short of money, or
if the dead man sold them off since."

This, of course, was true. "But it would introduce an element of doubt to a trial, wouldn't it? You could testify that
there used to be a valuable painting on the wall and now it's
missing." I waved a hand at him. "We could get Mickey
Whatever-his-name-is to testify."

Darcy snorted. "Hardly. If something's missing there's a chance he took it himself. He doesn't seem like the most trustworthy of chaps to me. Certainly not my view of an old retainer. Which shoots down our suggestion that Roach was a millionaire gone into hiding. If you were a rich man you'd hire a servant with more class, wouldn't you?"

"We've never seen Mickey in action. As we said before, perhaps he's a brilliant actor and plays the part of the valet to perfection when he's working. But I agree there is something about him I don't trust. When you come to think of it, so much of the damning evidence against your father comes from him. He says nobody else came to the castle that day. He says he overheard an argument in the afternoon but heard nothing when there was a scuffle that evening and he says he found his master dead. But what if he were lying? What if he killed the man himself?"

"What reason would he have to kill his employer? Jobs are hard to come by these days, and the depression is even worse in America, so I hear. I should think this job was a plum—not much work and only one man to look after."

"But if he also wasn't who he claimed to be? If he was on the run and Roach found out about it?" I touched Darcy's arm as another thought struck me. "We should take a photograph of him and give that to the embassy too. You never know, someone might recognize him. And his fingerprints. We could get those."

"And how do you propose doing that?" Darcy looked almost amused now.

"We'll have him touch something. We'll say, 'Here, look at this.'"

"'Here, look at this?'" Darcy actually laughed.

"Yes, you know. We'll show him a photograph and say, 'Do you recognize this man as having come to the castle?' and he'll take the photograph from us and we'll have his prints on it."

Darcy looked at me, long and hard. "God, Georgie, I love you," he said. "The eternal optimist. In spite of everything, I'm very glad you came."

"Am I interrupting something?" said a voice behind us, and Princess Zamanska came toward us, having changed out of the leather jacket and trousers of her flying gear into a mink coat and a scarlet pillbox hat and matching scarf. I wondered how she had managed to get so many things into such a small suitcase.

"It looked like such a touching and intimate little scene," she said. I realized I had been standing with my hand on Darcy's arm and withdrew it.

"We were strategizing," I said. "Trying to think what we should do next."

"And I have been doing the same," she said. "I had them put through a telephone call to London for me. Roddy promised me faithfully that he is working hard on our behalf and should have news any moment now. I told him he can leave messages for me at the hotel. So it's lucky I'm staying here, isn't it? More chance of getting messages than at the pub in your village."

"Do you want to remain here now, or come back to Kilhenny with us?" Darcy asked.

"With you, naturally," she said. "Unless you can think of anything useful I could do in Dublin. But I have to visit my dear little aeroplane and make sure it's taken care of. I can't just leave it in a field full of horses, exposed to the elements. Is there an airfield nearby, a proper one with hangars, do you know? I don't think they'd let me land it on St. Stephen's Green. Too many people and trees." She glanced out of the windows as if to confirm this. "I should have bought a seaplane. Then I could have landed it on the Liffey."

"Zou Zou, you are something else," Darcy said.

"What do you mean? I'm a perfectly ordinary woman. So what are we going to do next? I'm game for anything."

"You say you just put through a telephone call to England," Darcy said. "Do you think I could use the telephone in your room and also make a call to London? I think there's a chap there who might be useful and has connections in the States."

"Of course, darling. It's 217." She held out the key. "Tell them to put the call on my bill."

Darcy went off, leaving the princess and me standing together.

"So what do you think?" she asked. "Darcy believes his father is guilty, doesn't he? He's not trying very hard."

"I know," I said. "But I'm more optimistic now than I was. Now that we know the man was using a false identity, it opens up all kinds of possibilities. I'm hoping the American embassy will recognize him and come up with good reasons why other people might want him dead. And I told Darcy that we should take photographs of his manservant, and maybe try to get his fingerprints. Because most of the damning evidence against Lord Kilhenny comes from him."

"Good idea," Zou Zou said. "You and I will do the donkey work. If Darcy's not going to bat for himself, then it's up to us. Women to the rescue." And she waved her arms, almost knocking over an elderly couple who were crossing the foyer.

In spite of everything I had to laugh.

Darcy returned from his telephone call looking relieved, I thought. When Zou Zou pressed him about who he had called, he would say nothing, making me sure that it was somebody in the spy business with whom he was somehow associated.

"Well, that's settled at least," he said. "Should we head back to Kilhenny or is there anything more that we can do here?"

"We can't do any more here until the embassy finds out Mr. Roach's real name," I said. "And we wanted to take a photograph of Mickey the manservant, and try to get his fingerprints."

"We can't go anywhere before luncheon," the princess said. "I don't know about you, but I'm starving, and I'm fairly sure there will be nowhere decent to stop for a meal in your village. It will be cottage pie or something equally ghastly. And I'm sure the Shelbourne can provide a passable lunch. Come on, this way."

Darcy looked at me again and raised an eyebrow as she set off ahead of us. I could see why he thought she'd be a complication for us. Long and expensive meals would take valuable time away from our main objective. But I did have to admit that I was hungry, and it was lovely to be seated at a table in the window overlooking the green while Zou Zou ordered what seemed like an elaborate meal.

"Zou Zou, we are in the middle of a murder investigation," Darcy pointed out. "You said you'd come over to help, but we'll be here all afternoon if you order so many courses. Besides, Georgie and I are on a tight budget."

"Silly, silly," she said, reaching across to slap his hand. But she did cut her order to a clear consommé, pheasant and a sweet soufflé, all of which were utterly delicious. And the bottle of rosé certainly revived our spirits so that we were in a good mood as Darcy drove us back to Kilhenny. The bright morning had turned to cloudy afternoon and I couldn't help thinking that Darcy would have to make this trip again later to return the princess to her hotel. She definitely was proving a complication.

"I think we should stop off and visit your solicitors on the way back to the castle," Princess Zamanska said as we left the city behind us. "Find out exactly what they have been doing so far and let them know our thoughts."

"I spoke to them when I arrived," Darcy said. "Frankly I'm not too hopeful. Old Mr. Leach even suggested pleading insanity. He said there were some quite pleasant institutions these days."

"Good heavens," Zou Zou exclaimed. "Then we definitely need to go and set them straight. Where are they, Darcy? In Dublin?"

"No, in Kildare."

"Oh dear. Country solicitors. They are always hopeless. The sooner the case is taken away from them, the better."

"That's up to my father, not me," Darcy said. "He hired them."

"Don't worry, as soon as we have my brilliant barrister chappie, all will be well," Zou Zou said. "And we really must sit down and speak to this father of yours. I'd like to hear what he's got to say for himself."

"He won't even talk to me, Zou Zou. Any attempts at conversation have been met with a curt 'mind your own business.'"

"Ah, but I'm awfully good at getting people to talk," Zou Zou said. "I should have been a spy in the Great War. I'd have winkled all kinds of secrets out of the Germans."

Darcy exchanged a quick look with me. We arrived in Kildare.

"Solicitors?" Zou Zou said.

"I don't think that's the wisest idea at the moment. Not with three of us."

"But we have new information for them. The mysterious identity of Mr. Roach."

"Let's wait until we find out who he really was, and until we have the name of your barrister, Zou Zou," Darcy said.

I could understand his reluctance. Introducing Princess Zou Zou in a country solicitor's office would be rather like bringing a peacock into a henhouse.

"Very well, then what shall we do next?"

"You wanted to take care of your aeroplane, didn't you?" I suggested.

"Of course. And I want to see your castle, Darcy. I grew up in a medieval castle too. Such fun, but drafty."

So we continued on toward Kilhenny.

"Where are you staying, Georgiana darling?" she asked from the backseat. "Also in Dublin? Or are you being naughty and sharing a place with Darcy?" Before either of us could answer, she went on. "I'm concerned about Darcy having to drive me back and forth all that way into Dublin. Such a time waster. If I can't use my little plane, then I'll have to beg, borrow or steal a motorcar. Your father doesn't have one to spare, does he?"

"He had the use of an estate car, but they are all locked away in the castle garage at the moment. It's still being treated as a crime scene."

"So where did you get your hands on this ancient Rolls?"

"Ah, that came from the great-aunt Georgie is staying with."

"A great-aunt? Nearby?"

"Yes, we'll be passing the house shortly."

"Then why didn't you say so before I checked into the Shelbourne? I could stay there too, couldn't I?" Zou Zou said.

Oh crikey, I thought, trying to picture the glamorous princess among the dust and chaos of Oona's house. Darcy must have had the same thoughts.

"It's not up to your standards, Zou Zou," Darcy said. "The place has gone to wrack and ruin and they are living with almost no servants. She's an eccentric old biddy. He's as queer as a coot."

"But I could rough it. I'm a lot tougher than I seem. I've climbed the Matterhorn, you know. And I've been marooned in a snowdrift in Bulgaria—surrounded by wolves. I'm sure I could cope with a batty great-aunt. Is it only a tiny cottage, then?"

I was about to say that yes, it was a tiny cottage. Unfortunately, at that moment we were passing the entrance to Oona's driveway. The rambling old house could be seen and I had found that Darcy wasn't good at telling lies. Subterfuge, yes. Withholding information, definitely, but there was something in his upbringing that made lying impossible. I'm the same. It's that duty and integrity that are rammed down the throat of every upper-class child by nannies and governesses.

"Actually that's the house, through the trees back there," he said, "but really, it isn't fit for guests, and I think it would embarrass Great-Aunt Oona to have a guest of your quality pressed upon her."

"Georgiana is of my quality," she said. "And the house looks charming. Certainly enough bedrooms to find a spot for little *moi*."

She really did see things through rose-tinted spectacles, I thought. The house looked old, rambling and almost derelict, but could not, by any stretch of the imagination, be described as charming.

"And this is all their land?" she went on. "Perfect. I can park my plane in one of their barns. Why don't we go and pay a call on them now and get everything settled? I'm sure a local peasant boy can tow my plane over on his tractor, or I could even fly it over. That might be more fun."

"Zou Zou, I really think you'd be happier at the Shelbourne," Darcy said. "I really don't mind driving over to pick you up. And we'll want to go back to Dublin anyway to meet your barrister."

"Anyone would think you didn't want me to meet your relatives, Darcy," she said in a peeved voice. "If we were in Poland I'd be happy to take you to see my batty relatives. Including Great-Uncle Zygmund, who thinks he is Napoleon but is quite harmless."

Darcy had to laugh at this. "And my great-uncle Dooley is currently playing at the battle of Waterloo. They'd get on well together."

"Only Dooley would want to capture Napoleon," I pointed out. "He was about to do so when I left today."

"They sound absolutely delightful. Much more fun than the staff at the stuffy Shelbourne and 'Yes, Your Highness, no, Your Highness.' And Georgie can lend me her maid. I had to leave mine behind in London because she gets horribly airsick."

"I didn't bring my maid, I'm afraid," I said. "I left her in London too."

"Then we'll both rough it together. Jolly good fun." She tapped Darcy on the shoulder. "Don't you dare try to drive past."

Poor Darcy. He glanced at me, then at Oona's driveway. "But you've left all your things at the Shelbourne," he said, "and I don't feel like driving all the way back there to retrieve them. Why don't you go back to the Shelbourne tonight and I'll broach the subject carefully with my aunt," Darcy said. "And if she is up to another guest we can fetch your suitcase tomorrow."

"Oh, all right," she said, miffed at not getting her own way, I suspected.

I heaved a sigh of relief. By tomorrow all sorts of things might have happened. She might be called back to London. The clouds had now thickened and hung low and heavy over the distant mountains.

"It's going to rain again," I said.

"Then we must hurry back to my poor little plane and find a tarpaulin or somewhere to put it," she said. "We can't have the cockpit filling with water."

At least this had stopped her from wanting to meet Great-Aunt Oona. We drove through the village. Several men who were clearly from the press were standing together outside the pub. They looked up at us with interest as we drove past.

"Oh Lord, that's torn it," Darcy said. "What's the betting they follow us?"

"Then I shall tell them that I am the Princess Zamanska and I am thinking of buying this racing stable now that its owner is deceased," she said. "You two are my faithful retainers."

"I rather fear they'd recognize both of your faithful retainers," Darcy said.

"No matter. Lady Georgiana has simply come with me as my companion."

This did seem like a good solution and one that didn't make suspicious people tie me in any way to Darcy.

As we turned in to the lane raindrops started to spatter on the windscreen. The clouds looked as if they might open at any moment.

"Does your father have a tarpaulin or anything that might cover the aeroplane?" she asked. "Or could we push it into an outbuilding?"

"The outbuildings are all on the estate, currently watched by a Garda," Darcy said. "My father merely has a garden shed, not big enough for an aeroplane. But they should have something to cover a cockpit at the stables. Let's go and ask."

We did, this time not seeing Ted Benson but a stable boy who knew Darcy and who found us a piece of oilcloth that would do the trick. It was now raining hard and the princess sat in the backseat of the motor as we returned to the field with the aeroplane in it. Darcy and I, dressed more sensibly for inclement weather, got out and managed to cover the cockpit. The rest of the plane would just have to get wet for now. We had just finished our task and were returning to the motorcar when we heard the sound of an approaching vehicle.

"Those bloody reporters," Darcy muttered, and sure enough the motorcar stopped and out climbed three men wearing trilby hats and raincoats.

"Excuse me, could we have a word?" One of them came toward us with a notebook at the ready. "Are you connected to Lord Kilhenny? Coming to visit him?"

Zou Zou wound down her window. "These kind people were just helping me with my dear little aeroplane," she said in a strong foreign accent, quite unlike her normal voice. "I had to make an emergency landing in this field and now I must find a way to have it towed. So annoying."

"And your name, madam?"

"I am not a madam," she said, her hand at her throat in a dramatic gesture. "I am a princess. Princess Alexandra Maria Zamanska."

I think we might have fooled them and they might have left us alone except at that moment a voice bellowed out, "What the hell is that aeroplane doing in the field? Are you reporters coming in from the sky now? Go on, be off with you. I've told you you're wasting your time. I've nothing to say to you. Now beat it before I get my shotgun."

Chapter 24

Lord Kilhenny stood there, his hair wild and windswept, and wearing a black smoking jacket. He reminded me of an aging Heathcliff or even a Lord Byron. In fact he looked so formidable that the reporters actually headed back to their motorcar and drove off.

As the motorcar backed away he turned on us. "And that means you too. I don't know who the hell you are, but you are not welcome here."

"Father, this is my good friend Princess Alexandra Zamanska." Darcy stepped in to intercept his father as he advanced on the Rolls. "And she was good enough to fly her aeroplane over to Ireland because she wanted to help you. At this very moment a barrister friend of hers is searching out the best defense counsel in Ireland on your behalf."

Lord Kilhenny took in the glamorous woman in the backseat of the Rolls. "Why on earth would you go to that amount of trouble for me, Your Highness?" he demanded. "You don't know me from Adam."

"Because I adore your son and I can see that this silly business could ruin his life."

"I don't want charity. I don't need charity. So thank you very much but please leave." He stood there with his arms folded across his chest, glaring at her defiantly.

"Silly stubborn man," Princess Zamanska said. "You should at least listen to what we have to say. We want to help you. Don't you understand that?"

"But don't *you* understand, it's no good." He turned his head away. "Even if I could afford the best barrister in Ireland, there's nothing he or you can do. There's nothing anyone can do, as I keep telling this son of mine. That brainless inspector has decided I'm guilty and that's that."

Princess Zamanska opened the door of the Rolls and stepped down. The wind swept at her dark mink coat and she drew it around her. She looked like a figure from a tragic Russian novel. "The whole question comes down to this," she said, walking toward him. "Do you think you are guilty?"

"I don't know!" he shouted at her over the wind. "I don't goddamn well know. I can't remember a damned thing. And what does it matter anyway?"

"Because if you don't let people help you, if you aren't prepared to help yourself, you will hang," she said.

"I really don't care," he said. "I've lost everything that matters to me."

While this exchange had been going on, I stood next to the motorcar, unnoticed in the background as the scene played out. I knew it would be wiser to stay silent, but when I heard him say those words, something inside me snapped. I stalked up to him. "That is a cruel and wicked thing to say. You have a son who loves you, who has done nothing to warrant the way you have treated him. He came rushing to your side the moment he heard of your predicament, and what's more, he had to leave something that was really important to him. But he didn't hesitate for a second, even though he said you wouldn't welcome him."

Lord Kilhenny's gaze moved from me to Darcy and back

again. "A friend from London, eh?" There was almost the hint of a smile. "Didn't fool me for a second. *You* were the thing that was important to him, weren't you?"

Darcy stepped to my side. "That's right, Father. Before this we were actually on our way to be married. Afterward I realized we could no longer marry; I didn't want her to suffer through being associated with me. I tried to end all contact with her. But she wouldn't listen. She came here anyway. That's what people do when they care about each other."

There was a long silence, then Lord Kilhenny said gruffly, "You'd better come inside. We're all getting soaked standing here."

He led the way back to the lodge. It was a gloomy little place, dark with low ceilings and heavy dark furniture. I could easily see how a person could become depressed living alone there.

"I'll make us some tea," Darcy said. "Unless Mrs. Mc-Nalley is around?"

"I sent her home and told her to stay away from here for the time being," Lord Kilhenny said. "I don't want her bothered by those bloody pressmen every time she sets foot outside the door."

"I can make the tea," I said. "I'm good at it."

"A young lady of many talents," Lord Kilhenny said. "I suppose you'd better introduce us properly, Darcy."

"Father, this is Georgiana Rannoch," Darcy said. "Georgie, may I present my father, Lord Kilhenny."

If the situation hadn't been so deadly serious I think we would have laughed. Being presented with great formality to a man I hoped would be my future father-in-law in a poky little living room with a smoky fire was just too absurd.

"Rannoch?" he said. "Daughter of the duke?"

I nodded.

"You and Darcy make a good pair. Your father was as useless as I have been."

I could see what Darcy had told me about his father not being an easy man. I didn't reply to this but went through to the kitchen. There was evidence here of a woman's touch. Mrs. McNalley had left everything spotless and neat. I put the kettle on and found the pot and tea caddy. Then I put cups and saucers on a tray and added a milk jug and a sugar bowl. When I brought the tray back out, they were sitting in armchairs around the fire, not saying much by the look of it. I handed each of them a cup.

"Now, this is a novelty," Lord Kilhenny said. "It's not every day I sit next to a princess and I'm waited on by the daughter of a royal duke."

"Then you should take that as a sign that you have help in high places," Zou Zou said. "We are here. We came to Ireland for one reason. To save you from the hangman's noose. So let's get started. Darcy?"

She turned to Darcy, who was staring into the flickering flames of the fire. Wind puffed smoke down the chimney, making it swirl out across the room. Darcy cleared his throat then spoke. "You say you remember nothing about that evening. Have no details come back to you? You don't remember going over to the castle?"

"In the afternoon, I did," Lord Kilhenny said. "But as to the evening, it's all a blank. I remember sitting down and pouring myself a glass of Jameson and turning on the wireless to listen to the news. The next thing I knew it was daylight and the police were pounding on the door."

"When you went up to the castle in the afternoon, apparently you had an argument with Mr. Roach. The valet overheard you shouting."

Lord Kilhenny nodded. "That is correct. I was furious. I got a copy of an auction catalog and I learned that he planned to sell several of our family treasures, including the Burda club. I went up to the castle to tell him he couldn't do that. They belonged in the castle—they were part of the O'Mara family heritage."

"Why did you let him have those things in the first place?" Darcy demanded. "Surely they could have been kept out of the sale."

"Should have," Lord Kilhenny said angrily. "Naturally I assumed that I would be able to keep items that were important to me. But his damned lawyer had things written in such a way that I couldn't touch anything on the estate the moment the document was signed. I was lucky to come away with my clothes. I also thought, naïvely as it turned out, that if Roach and I worked together, if the stables flourished, we'd develop an understanding between us and I could ask for the return of items that meant a lot to me but not to him. That never happened. The man kept his distance and only spoke to me when absolutely necessary. He treated me like a hired hand, and what's more, he enjoyed it. I think it gave him great pleasure to lord it over a real lord. He was a sadistic bastard. He deserved to be wiped from the face of the earth."

"None of this looks good for you, Father," Darcy said. "It gives you a strong motive to want him dead."

"I agree," Lord Kilhenny said, "and if the prosecution asks me if I wanted him dead, I'd have to answer honestly that I would have rejoiced at that news."

Darcy sighed. "So you saw he was about to put certain items up for auction and went to confront him."

"That's right. He had the club lying on the table. I picked it up and tried to tell him how important it had been to the history of our family. I told him I would buy it from him if he'd give me time to raise the money. And do you know what? He laughed at me. He said he knew a couple of museums that would be willing to pay more money for the club than I'd ever raise in my lifetime. Then he taunted me and said I should have hired myself a sharper lawyer when the deeds were drawn up."

"What did you do then?" Darcy asked in a quiet voice.

"I put down the club. I told him that one day he'd push me too far and then I stalked out. I walked around the grounds for a while to calm down. Then I went home."

We sat there, all of us staring into the fire, wrapped in our own thoughts. Then Darcy said, "It seems to me, Father, that the evidence against you is centered on your fingerprints on that club. Yours and only yours."

"That struck me as strange too," I said. "You say the club was on the table. Someone must have lifted it from the wall and left their own fingerprints on it. Come to that, it must have been handled millions of times. So why just your fingerprints? It makes me think that someone deliberately set you up to look like the murderer."

"Who would do that?" Lord Kilhenny asked. "And why?"

"There's something we found out in Dublin today that may change everything," Darcy said. "The murder victim was not really Timothy Roach. He was using a dead man's passport."

Lord Kilhenny looked up with interest for the first time. "Then who was he?"

"That's what we hope the American embassy will find out," Darcy said. "They'll be sending pictures of him back to Chicago in hopes that someone there may recognize him. Also his fingerprints, just in case they're on file."

"Really?"

I could see a flicker of hope in his eyes.

"It shouldn't be that hard to trace him," I said. "How many millionaires can there be in America these days who can afford to pay cash for a castle and a racing stable? The depression hit them harder than us over there, didn't it?"

"So the question is, who might have wanted him dead and come over here to kill him?" Princess Zamanska leaned forward, waving a red-nailed finger at us. I don't think she liked being left out of the conversation.

"Do you remember anyone coming from America to visit him recently?" Darcy asked. "Anyone he met who made him uneasy?"

Lord Kilhenny stared into the fire again. A log had just dropped into place, sending up a shower of sparks. "I wasn't exactly part of his inner circle, you know. He and I hardly exchanged a word. And from my situation here, I couldn't see anyone coming to the main gate. He might have had any number of visitors, except that his manservant claimed that he had none. And he certainly seldom went out, only in the motorcar or to the race meetings."

"And he didn't talk to anybody there?" Darcy asked. "You didn't see any interactions where he was confrontational or wary?"

Lord Kilhenny shook his head. "He stayed well away from the other owners. Answered in one-syllable words if they approached him. Of course, from what we suspect now, he was betting on his own horses. Now I look back on it, I wonder if he was betting on them to lose sometimes. There were occasions when I could have sworn a horse should have won and it didn't seem to me that the jockey was urging it on in the final stretch."

"This shows he had a devious mentality," Princess Zamanska said, "but it doesn't seem relevant to his murder. Apart from people who put money on losing horses, there is not one person who would have been angry enough to seek his death."

"Apart from me," Lord Kilhenny said. "After the way he treated me, the way he tarnished my reputation like that, I could easily have killed him."

"But you didn't," I said. "And I don't believe you did this time either. Somebody has cleverly worked to make you look guilty."

"So nobody came to visit that you know of. He never went out." Darcy shook his head. "This is a ridiculous puzzle."

I had been trying to collect my thoughts, to make the most of this opportunity to talk with Darcy's father, just in case it was never repeated. "Do you know if a professor from an American university came to visit him?" I asked. "Or a priest? Because they were both seen near the main gate."

Lord Kilhenny nodded. "That's right. There was an American professor. He said he had come to visit the dig and asked if there were any rooms for rent in the castle. I laughed and told him what I knew about Roach. He thanked me and went on his way."

"That was all he asked you?"

"I didn't exactly invite him in for a cup of tea," he said. "He said something about the front gate being locked and I told him there was a telephone to the castle if he wanted to be admitted. And he asked if that was the only way in."

"You didn't tell him about the little door in the wall, did you?" Darcy asked.

"Of course not. Do you think I'm stupid?" he snapped, then seemed to collect himself. "No. I saw no reason to disclose that."

"And the priest?" I asked. "A young priest asked about him. Did he come here?"

Lord Kilhenny shook his head, then he said, "Wait. There was someone. Not a priest, a doctor. About a month ago Roach wasn't feeling well. A doctor was summoned, but not the local quack. In fact I rather think he was American. Mickey, his valet, told me that he was going to fetch the doctor. I asked if it was serious and Mickey said no, probably just a bad cold, but Mr. Roach wanted to be sure. Then, later that day, I was coming from the garage, having just parked the estate wagon, when I overheard an exchange at the front of the house. Roach sounded rather put out. He said something like, 'How do you think they discovered?' and there was some kind of answer in a deep voice that I didn't quite catch. Then he said, 'What now? I can't go through an operation like that again. Once was bad enough.' And then another reply and I came around the corner to see the doctor getting into the motorcar and Roach said, 'Thanks for telling me, although I've no doubt you'll want to be well paid for coming to see me.' And Mickey drove him off."

"That's interesting." Darcy looked at us for confirmation. "It sounds as if he had some kind of medical condition that had reappeared. He'd had an operation and now he needed a second one. Maybe that's why he came over to Ireland, because he knew he was dying and he wanted to be alone."

Chapter 25

STILL DECEMBER 4

A lot has happened today but we seem to be getting somewhere at last.

Zou Zou and I are brilliant! I think I might actually like her.

We stared at each other, digesting this news. It was Darcy who voiced the conclusion we had all come to. "But if he was terminally ill, why might this doctor—if indeed he was the murderer—bother to kill him?"

"Perhaps he had decided to change his will and one of his relatives in the States decided to kill him before he could do so," Zou Zou suggested.

"That's one thing we haven't done," I said. "Asked the local postman if any letters had come from America recently. It's my experience of village postmen that they are terribly nosy and he might well remember where the letters came from."

"Good idea," Darcy said. "We should follow up on that.

Of course, we have no way of knowing what telephone calls he received."

"The exchange would know," I said. "I wonder if the local police followed up on that, or if we'd be allowed to do so."

"Now that they know Roach was traveling on a false passport, I think they will have to start a proper investigation," Darcy said. "We can make suggestions as to the directions that investigation should take."

"Tactfully, of course," Zou Zou said and we smiled.

"I still think the most important figure in this is Mickey, the manservant," I said. "The whole case against Lord Kilhenny hinges on his testimony. He claimed nobody else visited the castle. But now we know that a doctor visited recently. He claimed he overheard the argument that afternoon and then a scuffle that evening. But what if there was no scuffle? What if he is actually the murderer? What if he made sure Lord Kilhenny's fingerprints were on the club?"

"But what possible motive could he have?" Lord Kilhenny asked. "He has just lost a well-paid job. Jobs are not easy to find these days."

"If he really was a manservant," I said. "What if he really had some other connection to Mr. Roach and came over here to murder him?"

"What kind of connection?" Darcy's father asked. "He was a low-class kind of chap. Roach wasn't exactly top-drawer himself but he had money."

"Precisely," I said. "What if Mickey felt that the fortune Roach inherited should have gone to him?"

"The only fly in that ointment is, why did he wait so long?" Darcy said. "How many years was Roach here, Father? Four, was it?"

"Almost," Lord Kilhenny said.

"So you want to murder someone but you wait four years?"

"I know," I said as the idea crystallized in my head. "He knew that Mr. Roach was terminally ill. He didn't expect him to live long. But when he lingered on for four years he decided to take matters into his own hands, just in case Roach recovered. The doctor came, didn't he? Perhaps he told Roach another operation might cure him."

"Possible." Lord Kilhenny looked at me. He had dark blue eyes like his son. He was still a very handsome man in spite of his wild, unshaven appearance.

I found his glance slightly unnerving, but went on. "So what we have to do is to make the American embassy check into Mickey's background as well as Roach's. Perhaps he's here under an assumed name too. What we have to do is take a photograph of him and get his fingerprints to send to America."

"He's an unpleasant little weasel," Lord Kilhenny said. "Do you think he'll let you take his photograph and get his fingerprints?"

"We'll do it by subterfuge," Princess Zamanska said. "Georgie has a brilliant plan. Such a clever girl. We'll go up to the castle and I will show him a photograph and ask him if he recognizes the person. He'll take it and look at it, thus leaving us with lovely fingerprints. And while he's looking, Georgie will take a photograph of him. Couldn't be simpler."

Lord Kilhenny scowled at her. "How can you be so bloody optimistic, Your Highness?" he demanded.

"Because it's better than wallowing in self-pity," she said. "I find that looking ahead and making a plan of action is the only way to cope with devastating circumstances. That's how I managed to survive when I had to flee for my life after my beloved Peter was hacked to pieces by peasants. And your language is atrocious. I'm sure Georgie has never heard so many swearwords in her life."

The ghost of a smile crossed his face. "You're right. It has become atrocious. I apologize."

"Apology accepted. And please call me Zou Zou. Everyone else does."

"I hardly think I know you well enough for pet names," he said.

"Alexandra, then. But none of this stuffy 'highness' business."

"Very well," he said gruffly. "In which case you'd better call me Thaddy."

"Thaddy. Nice name." She nodded. "Now we're making progress, aren't we? Splendid. So do you have a camera and film we could borrow? And a photograph? A nice big one?"

"I have a camera in my bag, as it happens. I'll go and get it," Darcy said. I realized he had brought a camera along to record a happier event that was supposed to have taken place. At least now it was going to be useful.

As Darcy left the room, Lord Kilhenny looked at the two of us. "Are you sure this is a sensible course of action? If this man really has just murdered his employer, I certainly don't want you and Georgiana confronting him. And Darcy and I couldn't go, because he'd be suspicious and not want to talk to us."

"We won't be confronting him," Zou Zou said. "We'll be asking for his help. A possible line of inquiry we are following. He doesn't know me. I can say with complete truth that I'm doing preliminary investigations on behalf of the barrister in Dublin. That is absolutely true and may unnerve him a little. And if he did kill his employer he'll be secretly laughing at us for barking up the wrong tree, as the English would say. What's more, we are not stupid. If he says, 'Come down to the dungeons with me and I'll look at the photograph,' we won't go." And she gave that delightful tinkling laugh.

Lord Kilhenny got to his feet as Darcy came back, triumphantly waving the camera. "Very well," he said. "I'm not sure what photographs I have that would fit the bill."

"You have some newspaper photographs taken at race meetings, don't you?" Darcy said. "Standing in the winner's circle. That kind of thing."

"Yes, but you can't show him a photograph of me," Lord Kilhenny said testily.

"One of the other people in the photograph—that's who they'll ask about," Darcy said. "You must have pictures of being presented with a cup, or talking with officials. This Mickey creature won't know who they are."

Lord Kilhenny nodded and we heard the heavy tread of

his feet going up stairs. We sat looking at each other. "Well done, Zou Zou," Darcy said. "I don't think we'd ever have got him to talk without you. Now at least we're onto something with the doctor."

"And proof that Mickey lied about one thing," I said.

We looked up as Lord Kilhenny returned. I noticed that he had combed his hair. "This one might do," he said and handed Zou Zou a photograph. It was a press picture showing him shaking hands with another man while several others looked on.

"Perfect," Zou Zou said. "Now we need to wipe it completely clean to get rid of all fingerprints." She took out a white lace handkerchief, picked up the photograph and began to rub diligently. "There, that should do it," she said after a while. "If there are still fingerprints on it they will be smudged while Mickey's will be nice and fresh over the top of them. Well, let's get on with it. It will be dark soon and even I don't like the thought of creeping around the estate in the dark with a murderer on the loose." She stood up, holding the photograph by the handkerchief. "Coming, Georgie? You have to show me the way. Camera, Darcy, please?"

Darcy reacted sharply. "You two ladies are not going alone without me."

"You can't come with us," I said. "He knows you."

"He saw you before too."

"But he didn't know who I really was. I told him I was working for an investigator in London, remember. And when he hears that Alexandra is working on behalf of the barrister, he may be seriously rattled."

"He might also find another weapon and club you both to death," Darcy said.

"Don't be silly, darling," Zou Zou said. "This will all be conducted on the doorstep. I understand there is still a policeman on guard at the main gate. He'll be within shouting distance. Nothing to worry about. You would be of more use going into the village and finding out at the post office whether any letters have arrived from America recently."

"I don't like this," Darcy said, but his father nodded.

"Let them go. I'll stand and keep watch in the trees where I can't be seen."

Darcy sighed. "Very well. I suppose it has to be done. The sooner we have help from the American embassy, the better. But I don't think you should let it be known that we've found out Roach was not his real name. He may already know that. He may not. Either way this isn't the right time to divulge."

We nodded.

"Ready?" Zou Zou looked at me. I stood up, taking the camera from Darcy. "Don't worry. We'll be fine." I gave him what I hoped was a reassuring smile.

The rain had stopped as we left the lodge and the sky to our west was streaked blood red, dramatically outlining the bare bones of the trees. We crossed the kitchen garden and found the little door in the wall beneath the ivy. Then we made our way to the castle through the woodland. Again I experienced that feeling of extreme watchfulness, as if every creature on the estate was alert. I marveled at Zou Zou's sangfroid until there was a rustle in the undergrowth nearby and she grabbed my arm.

"What was that?" she whispered.

"There are deer on the estate, so I'm told," I said, glad that for once I was the brave one.

When we set off again I noticed that she kept closer to me. The castle loomed over us, its stone glowing pink in the rays of the setting sun. We followed the path around the castle wall to the front where the driveway ended in a circle of gravel with a fountain playing in the middle. I glanced back along the drive to the main gate but could not catch a glimpse of the Garda who was stationed there. Maybe this was a good thing, I decided, or he might have come to stop us. But I would have found it more reassuring to know he was close by.

The front door was up a flight of stone steps.

"You stay at the bottom where he can't see you and you can take a good picture of his face," Zou Zou said.

She went up the steps and waited until I had found a position where I could focus the camera on the front door. Then she gave me a thumbs-up sign and tugged on a bellpull. We heard a jangle echoing inside and waited. And waited. Zou Zou had almost decided to turn away and give up when the front door opened with an ominous creaking sound, such as one hears in horror films. Mickey stood there and reacted with surprise.

"Who are you? How did you get in here past the constable at the gate? If you're a reporter . . ."

"Of course I am not a reporter," Zou Zou said in her most autocratic voice. "I am here on behalf of the barrister in Dublin who is to represent Lord Kilhenny. He wanted me to ask you a few questions. You are Mr. Roach's manservant, are you not?"

"Would I be living in this dump if I wasn't?" he said cockily, but his eyes darted nervously and I could tell he was rattled.

"Naturally you will be called to testify," Zou Zou continued. "That should be no problem as long as you tell the truth. Now if you could just answer a couple of questions, please."

"You'd better come inside," he said.

"No, thank you. Here will do perfectly," she said. "I have to show you a photograph and I want you to see it in good light." She held it out to him. "Please take a look at this. You see the man standing behind Lord Kilhenny. Do you recognize him?"

He took the photograph. I focused the camera lens on him and as he looked up, I took the picture. Then wound on the film and took a couple more for good measure. I tried to make sure that my hand wasn't shaking, which wasn't easy. After one brief glance he handed the photograph back to Zou Zou.

"Never saw him before in my life," he said. "Is he the guy you suspect of killing my boss?"

"Let's just say he is a person of interest," she said.

This time I did see a flicker of amusement cross his face.

It was fleeting but definitely there. He does know more, I thought.

"Thank you. I'll report back that you have never met him," she said. "And I also wanted to check something else you said. I am told that you said Mr. Roach had no visitors."

"That's right."

"But it seems that his doctor came to see him."

The surprise on his face was obvious. "His doctor? Well, yes. But that's not a visitor, is it? He had tradesmen arriving all the time, delivering groceries and meat. He had a barber come to cut his hair. But that's not proper visitors. Yeah, a doctor came when he wasn't feeling well."

"An American doctor?"

"That's right. His doctor from back in the States was making a trip to Ireland so he stopped by to check on the boss's health."

"And where is he now? Would he be available to testify?"

"To what?" Mickey's voice rose. "He was here and back in the States long before Mr. Roach was killed. So please tell your barrister guy that he's wasting his time and energy. It's just as I told the Garda. Nobody came to the house that I knew of. The only person was Lord Kilhenny, and he and Mr. Roach got into a fight that very afternoon. The guy is as guilty as hell. What more can he possibly need to know?"

"I'm not privy to the direction the investigation will be taking," she said haughtily. "But we will be checking on some other people who were seen near the castle recently, as well as Mr. Roach's telephone logs."

"What does any of this matter when Kilhenny's prints were the only ones on the club?" he demanded.

He stepped toward her and I took the opportunity to snap another picture as the setting sun highlighted his face.

"Interesting, that, don't you think?" she said, standing her ground and eyeing him calmly. "A club that has been in existence for several thousand years and yet has acquired only one set of fingerprints during that whole time?"

"That's obvious, isn't it?" he said. "Mr. Roach was getting ready to send it to an auction. He had me take it down and polish it so it looked good." This time there was a definite smirk.

"Ah, I see," she said. "Well, thank you, you've been most helpful. I won't trouble you any longer. So I presume you'll go back to America when this is all over?"

"Maybe."

"Well, please don't think of going anywhere in the near future," she said, holding the photograph carefully with the handkerchief around it. "You will be needed as a witness at the trial."

"I know that. It would be much better if the lord guy pleaded guilty right now and we didn't have to go through all the nonsense of a trial."

"Fortunately for Lord Kilhenny, he has many important friends who are going to make sure that justice is done for him," she said, giving him a brisk nod. "Good afternoon to you, Mr. Riley."

Twilight fell swiftly as we walked back through the woods. The rooks were cawing as they came to roost in the big oak trees and their raucous noise drowned out any stirrings in the undergrowth. But even though I could hear no human voices, I had a horrible feeling of eyes on me. I glanced over my shoulder but saw nothing. No branches moved in the undergrowth. But I was still completely sure that someone was watching me.

Chapter 26

We made it back to the door in the wall without incident. Darcy and his father greeted us with obvious relief, and a touch of respect as I recounted Zou Zou's brilliant performance.

"You should have gone on the stage," Darcy said. "You and Georgie's mother. You'd have made a fine pair."

She laughed. "I've often found a few acting skills to be useful in life," she said. "Fortunately I've never needed to live by the sweat of my brow."

"Lucky for you," Lord Kilhenny said. "Some of us have had to struggle to keep our heads above water and haven't always succeeded."

"But life is not always fair, is it?" she said. "I did not know where I should go or how I should live when they killed my husband and burned my home. But I learned to make a new life for myself. That is what one has to do. Pull oneself up by the bootstraps and start over."

"Of course, it helps if you have a nice large Swiss bank account," Darcy pointed out.

She laughed then. "Yes, that does help." She looked at Darcy. "What did you find at the post office?"

"Nothing. The postmistress said that no letters had come for Mr. Roach from America."

"It's quite possible that he had a postbox in Kildare or Dublin and his man picked up letters there," Lord Kilhenny pointed out.

"Of course. Another thing for the Garda to check on," I said. "If they are willing to do so."

"It's getting dark," Darcy said. "I should drive you back to Dublin."

"I have a wonderful idea," Zou Zou said brightly. "Why don't we all pile into the Rolls and I'll treat us to a slap-up dinner at the Shelbourne. The food at luncheon really was rather good, wouldn't you say?" She looked directly at Lord Kilhenny. "You need cheering up."

"I'm afraid you'll have to count me out," he said. "I'm not allowed to leave the immediate area without permission. You go and enjoy yourselves. Mrs. McNalley has brought in some food for me. I'll muddle through."

"Absolutely not," Zou Zou said. "Then we'll all stay. The shops won't have closed yet. We can pop into the village and rummage up something passable to eat, I'm sure. Although I doubt if we can find a decent champagne."

"No," Lord Kilhenny said firmly. "If you don't mind I'd rather be alone. It's not easy being sociable at the moment and I am completely devoid of small talk. I can manage."

"If that's what you really want," Zou Zou said.

"It's for the best at the moment," he said, and I wondered if he was trying to be kind and didn't want us to be associated with him.

"I'll be back later, Father," Darcy said. "Then we can eat together."

"No, you have a good meal with Her Highness," Lord Kilhenny said. "Really, I'd rather be alone."

"I wonder if he means it," Zou Zou said as we drove off in the Rolls, "or if he's just being thoughtful, realizing he's not good company at the moment."

"I don't ever remember my father being the thoughtful type," Darcy said.

"Oh, I'm sure that under that gruff exterior there beats a warm and generous heart," she said, making Darcy laugh.

"You really do see the silver lining in every situation, don't you?" he asked.

"It's easier than being swallowed up in the dark clouds," she said.

"Darcy's father was invited to Great-Aunt Oona's last night and refused to come," I said.

"Great-Aunt Oona. What a delicious name. I have to meet her, Darcy. Why don't we drop off Georgie on our way to Dublin and I can stop in and say hello. Then we can broach the subject of my staying there as well."

"I've been thinking about that and I really don't think you'd be comfortable, Alexandra," he said. I noticed he was using her formal name to emphasize the point. "You might think you can take simplicity, but this is taking something close to chaos. And I also think they'd feel embarrassed at having such a distinguished guest when they no longer have servants or the lifestyle to make you comfortable. Frankly I'd be happier if you went back to London."

"You don't think I'm of any use to you? After my brilliant performance with Mickey today?" She sounded shocked and hurt. "I can't believe you'd say that, Darcy."

"I think you're wonderful, Zou Zou. But I'm asking myself if there's anything you could do that we can't. I don't want to keep you here, wasting your time and spending your money."

"But I'm enjoying myself. It's thrilling. And I won't rest until we've proved your father innocent and given him back his castle."

"I don't see how that is going to happen," Darcy said. "Even if he is proven innocent, the property will pass to Mr. Roach's heirs. He was the rightful owner, whoever he really was."

"You never know," Zou Zou said. "That's one of the enjoyable things about life. You never know what will happen next. That's why I feel so sorry for those poor people who go to an office or a bank on the eight thirty train every morning. They know exactly what will happen for the next twenty years, apart from a holiday in Folkestone or Margate. God, I'd shoot myself."

We were driving through the village. I spotted my American reporter, talking and smoking with two men outside the Harp, and I wondered how long they'd be prepared to stay here if the time dragged on before the trial. As we left the village behind I thought I saw someone running after us. These reporters were certainly keen, but so far so good. As yet they hadn't twigged to who I was. It was quite dark now and lights twinkled here and there in the blackness of the countryside.

"Come on, Darcy. Don't be such a spoilsport. You can at least introduce me to your aunt and uncle," Zou Zou said. "I'm dying to meet your relatives, even if they are batty."

Darcy sighed. "Very well. But please don't suggest that you stay with them."

"Of course not. We'll only pop in to say hello when you deliver Georgie."

I was beginning to feel uncomfortable about this. Zou Zou was a lovely person. She was fun; she was generous. But why was she so keen to drop me off with Darcy's great-aunt and then have Darcy drive her on to Dublin without me? Old insecurities resurfaced. I was quite sure that she and Darcy had been . . . well, more than friends . . . at one stage. I've noticed that one can tell from the way two people look at each other whether they've shared a bed or not. Did she want him back? Did she see me as a challenge? And would he bother to drive all the way back to Kilhenny at night when it would be so much easier to stay with her rather than pick her up in the morning?

I glanced across at him, thinking how handsome he was and how unbelievable it was that he'd chosen someone like me. I suppose I still couldn't quite believe it. I knew I should trust him. I reminded myself firmly that he had asked me to marry him, out of all the women in his life. But his manner of living had been so different from mine. I knew bed hopping was a favorite sport of my class, but I didn't want to share him. I didn't want to worry when he didn't come home. That was no way to live.

We turned off the road and bumped up the driveway to Mountjoy.

"Good God—you know, it is rather a monstrosity." Zou Zou gave a delighted chuckle. "You're living in a house of horrors, Georgie. Great-Aunt Oona is not a witch in her spare time, is she, Darcy?"

"Who knows? I wouldn't be at all surprised." Darcy opened the car door for her, then led her up to the house. As I followed him into the hallway we were greeted by the pack of dogs, jumping up, tails wagging. Oona appeared from the kitchen, wearing an apron.

"I wondered when we'd see you again," she said. "I hope you haven't come to dinner tonight, Darcy, because we've just curried the remains of the duck and there is only enough for three." She broke off as Zou Zou stepped into the light. "Hello, what's this? Another one? Who are you?" she demanded.

Darcy took Zou Zou's arm. "Aunt Oona, this is another friend from London. Her Highness Princess Zamanska. Zou Zou, may I present my great-aunt Oona."

Zou Zou came forward, avoiding dogs and holding out her hand. "How do you do? I popped over from London as soon as I heard to see if I could be of any help to Darcy's father. Forgive the intrusion, but I simply had to meet you."

Oona looked startled, not sure how to respond to this.

"Another friend from London? Are you planning a harem, Darcy?" she demanded.

"This one really is a friend from London, I assure you," Darcy said. "Old chums. We were just on our way back to Dublin. She's staying at the Shelbourne."

"Where else?" Oona said. "Well, I suppose you had better come through and have a glass of sherry. If I'd known you were coming I'd have had Treadwell bake some cheese straws. He's become a dab hand at baking."

"Aunt Oona, I really think we should be getting along. I have to drive into Dublin and back tonight," Darcy said.

"Don't be such a fuddy-duddy, Darcy," Zou Zou said. "I remember many times when you went home at three in the morning and thought nothing of it. And I think a glass of sherry is exactly what is needed. Buck us all up."

"Jolly good. Come on, then. This way," Oona said. "Clear off, dogs. Go on. Out of the way." She tried to clear a dog-free path down the hallway, not too successfully.

"Treadwell is your cook?" Zou Zou asked as she picked her way over boots and past dogs to follow Oona into the sitting room. This time there was no cat on a chair but several new piles of books, the *Times*, with a crossword half done, and a dozen eggs in a basket.

"Treadwell used to be the family butler at Kilhenny," Oona said. "When the castle was sold, we took him in. He's become a marvelous cook among other things, although he still likes to behave as if he's superior to us." She gave the bellpull a firm jerk. Neat footsteps tapped down the hall and Treadwell appeared, hastily taking off an apron. "You rang, Lady Whyte?" he asked.

"We have guests, Treadwell," she said. "We shall need sherry glasses, and we don't happen to have any nibbles, do we?"

"No nibbles, I regret, Lady Whyte. If you had given me advance notice I could have provided cheese straws." He gave her a critical stare.

Oona laughed and slapped her hand on her side. "Exactly what I said, wasn't it? I told them you were a dab hand at cheese straws."

"Is your husband at home?" Zou Zou asked as Treadwell made a dignified exit.

"Dooley? Oh yes, he's bound to be around somewhere. Still busy with the battle of Waterloo, I'm afraid. I told him to put his considerable brainpower to saving poor Thaddy, but he can't leave the Duke of Wellington in the lurch." She looked up as Treadwell returned with sherry glasses and a decanter on a silver tray. He removed the basket of eggs without a change in expression, put the tray down, then began to pour.

"Treadwell, when you're finished, please tell Sir Dooley that we have guests, so perhaps he should comb his hair before he comes down."

Zou Zou gave a happy little smile. We sipped our sherry and soon Dooley appeared, his hair neatly parted and slicked down. But this effect was spoiled because he was still wearing a moth-eaten cardigan over a shirt with egg down the front. Dooley was properly presented to Zou Zou.

"I hear you are re-creating the battle of Waterloo," she said. "How terribly exciting."

"You're interested in history, are you?" he asked.

"In that battle, oh yes," she said. "I have an uncle who thinks he is Napoleon."

"Then would you like to see it? It's all laid out in the attic. Absolute faithful re-creation."

"Dooley, she doesn't want to see your toy soldiers," Oona began but Zou Zou cut in, saying, "I'd absolutely love to."

"Come on, then." Dooley headed for the door. "But be careful not to let the dogs in or they'll spoil everything."

"We'd better come with you or he's likely to pinch your bottom," Oona said.

"Really, Oona. I don't go around pinching princess's bottoms," Dooley said.

"I know you. You can't resist a pretty woman." And she ushered us all into the hall. Up one flight we went, then up a second. Then Dooley opened a door and I gasped. There was no furniture in the room and the floor was covered with literally thousands of lead soldiers as well as horses, cannons and even miniature trees and houses.

"Good heavens, it's quite spectacular," Zou Zou exclaimed. "What a brilliant man you are. So tell me, who is winning at the moment?"

Dooley was beaming. He squatted on his haunches, pointing to an area of the battlefield. "We are," he said. "See there? That's Wellington. Now, what he's about to do . . ."

"Oh, Dooley, please," Oona said in her booming voice. "Once you get started there will be no stopping you."

"And I should be driving Princess Zamanska back to Dublin before it gets too late," Darcy said.

"Pity she doesn't have her belongings or she could bunk down here," Dooley said. "It's not often we have the chance to have two pretty women stay at the same time."

"But I would love to stay," Zou Zou said, getting a warning frown from Darcy. "If it's really not too much trouble?"

"I really don't think that Aunt Oona . . ." Darcy began but Oona cut him off.

"Not a problem, if she doesn't mind mucking in. But I can tell you right now that it's not the Ritz or the Shelbourne, and she'll have to help feed the chickens."

"Of course. I'd love to," Zou Zou said. "See, Darcy, I told you." She shot Darcy a triumphant smile. I realized that she was quite formidable when she wanted to be, and used to getting her own way. "I could even fly over here and park my aeroplane in one of your barns, if that's all right with you."

"Aeroplane?" Oona and Dooley asked in unison.

"Oh yes, didn't we tell you?" Darcy said. "She flew over in her aeroplane and landed in the paddock across from the lodge."

"Good God," Oona said. "You're full of surprises, Your Highness."

"Please don't be so formal," Zou Zou said. "My name is Alexandra—Zou Zou to my friends—and I am definitely going to call you Great-Aunt Oona. You'll be a sort of adoptive aunt because my relatives are all far away in Poland and Russia, where I can no longer visit them." She put a hand on Dooley's shoulder. "And if you don't mind you can be my adoptive uncle. So I look forward to seeing where the battle will take us tomorrow, Uncle Dooley. This will be ripping fun." She took Darcy's arm. "Come on, then, Darcy. I know you're fretting about driving me back to Dublin. Let's get going, then." And she dragged him down the stairs.

Oona turned to me. "You'd better watch that one," she said. "She's got designs on your man."

Chapter 27

LATE EVENING, DECEMBER 4

A good dinner and a not-so-good surprise!

After they had gone the three of us ate the curried duck, which was absolutely delicious, followed it with a delicate orange mousse, then retired to the drawing room for coffee. I turned down the brandy I was offered. My head was already a little woozy from the sherry and wine with dinner. Oona and Dooley both wanted to know exactly what had happened during the day and how we were getting on with the investigation. I suppose the alcohol had loosened my tongue and I found myself telling them everything, including the discovery of the false passport.

"So there we are then!" Oona slapped her thigh, startling the dogs who were lying draped around her feet. "Now we know that he was on the run or hiding out, there are all sorts of people who might have wanted to kill him. That thickheaded inspector from Dublin will have to drop all charges against Thaddy. I'll go and tell him myself if nobody else does."

"It's not quite as easy as that," I said. "There are a couple of stumbling blocks. The manservant says that nobody came to the castle that day apart from Darcy's father. And the only prints on the club were those of Lord Kilhenny. Rather damning evidence, I'm afraid."

"Does Thaddy have any idea how his prints came to be on the club?"

"Oh yes," I said. "He went up to the castle that afternoon. He had just learned that the American planned to auction some of the O'Mara treasures, including the Burda club. He was furious and told Mr. Roach, or whoever he really was, that he couldn't do that. The club was on the table and he picked it up then."

"Setup," Sir Dooley said, suddenly sitting up straight in his armchair. "Quite obvious now. The whole thing was planned. Someone was planning to kill Roach and pin the blame on Thaddy. That's why the club was conveniently on the table. And you say that Thaddy can't remember a thing about that evening except that he got very drunk? I'd wager he was drugged. What if a sleeping draft was put in his whiskey?"

"Well done, Dooley," Oona said, beaming at him. "I knew your superior brain would figure it out."

"Then who could it have been?" I asked. "Apart from the manservant himself?"

"Why not the manservant?" Oona demanded.

"What motive could he have had?" I said. "If he had wanted to rob his master he would not have reported the death and would have been long gone by the time Mr. Roach's body was found. And now he is without a job."

"Then someone paid him to be party to the murder," Dooley said. "Paid him well enough to keep quiet, or even to help with it."

I thought of Mickey's face when Zou Zou confronted him. He definitely had been wary.

"Maybe someone threatened him and frightened him into helping," I suggested.

"Exactly. So all the police have to do is to find a way to

make him talk," Oona said. "And what's the plan for you next?"

"I'm not really sure. We should try to locate this American professor, don't you think? And the young priest? They were both seen close to the castle. Maybe one of them was not who he claimed to be. We suspect the professor invented a nonexistent university. And we understand that none of the neighboring parishes has a young priest."

"Jolly good plan," she said.

"But apart from that, we have to wait and see if anyone in America recognizes the man who called himself Timothy Roach, or if his fingerprints can be identified," I went on.

"That could take weeks, couldn't it?" Oona said. "Ship across the Atlantic, trains across the continent. It could drag on and on, and all the time poor Thaddy is hounded by the press and deemed a criminal."

"Don't they have ways of sending photographs by cable these days?" Dooley said. "I'm pretty sure I read that in the newspaper. That should speed things up."

As I sat there, still feeling the effects of the wine I'd drunk at dinner, and the heat of the crackling fire, I was suddenly overcome with tiredness.

"I hope you don't think it rude of me," I said, "but I'm feeling awfully tired. Would you mind if I went up to bed? We can resume this discussion with Darcy in the morning. Maybe by then Sir Dooley will have come up with more brilliant ideas."

"Off you go, then, my dear," Oona said. "Should I have Treadwell send you up a hot drink?"

"Oh no, thank you. I don't need anything." I turned from one to the other. "Thank you for everything. You've been most kind."

"Delighted to have company," Oona said. "It livens up our boring lives, doesn't it, Dooley?"

"Oh rather!" he replied.

I went up to bed, undressed and climbed in quickly as the room was chilly. No sooner had my head touched the pillow than I was out like a light.

I awoke suddenly, not knowing what had disturbed me. It was pitch-dark in the room, but somehow I was conscious that I wasn't alone. Someone was standing at the foot of my bed. My first thought was that Sir Dooley had crept in, hoping for a bit of nighttime hanky-panky. But he was a frail-looking little man and the vague outline I could make out in the darkness was bigger than him.

So I moved on to my next thought: that my visitor was the ghost that haunted this room. I listened for the sound of breathing but heard nothing. Having grown up in a Scottish castle reputedly haunted by several ghosts, I wasn't as terrified as some people might have been. All the same, I wasn't exactly easy with a ghost standing at the foot of my bed. What did one do to make a ghost go away? Hold up a cross? No, that wouldn't work, because plenty of ghosts were nuns and monks. My brain was refusing to work. Garlic? No, that was vampires, and besides, I didn't happen to have any garlic among my possessions. I tried to remember what I might have read about exorcisms. Begone, foul fiend, and all that sort of stuff. Maybe this was a harmless ghost, just curious about me. Maybe it wasn't. Unfortunately it was standing between me and the door.

I decided on the element of surprise. If I sat up suddenly and shouted at it, it might decide to leave. And at the very least, the dogs would hear and bring Oona or Dooley. I took a deep breath and sat up. "Begone, foul fiend!" I said in my most dramatic voice. "Go back to the netherworld from which you came and leave me in peace!"

The speech didn't exactly have the effect I wanted, as the ghost gave a little shriek and promptly burst into tears. What was more, the accent was decidedly not Irish. "Bloody hell, miss," she said between heaving sobs. "You scared the living daylights out of me. And after I came all this way too."

I reached for the bedside lamp and the room was bathed in a soft pink glow.

"Queenie?" I exclaimed.

She was standing there in that hideous moth-eaten fur coat she had that made her look like a half-drowned hedgehog. Her hands were to her face and she was shaking with sobs. I got out of bed. "Queenie, I'm sorry. I had no idea," I said, helping her to sit down on the bed. "What on earth are you doing here?"

"My family told me to come," she said. "They scolded me for leaving you in the lurch. They said my place was with you, especially when you needed someone to take care of you at a time like this. So they had a whip round and came up with my ticket to Ireland." She was still sobbing, her large body heaving as she spoke so she wasn't easy to understand.

"I didn't quite know how to find you. All I knew was that it was Lord Kilhenny you'd gone to. So I hitched a lift to the village and I went to the castle but there was a policeman at the gate and he said nobody was living there and I wasn't allowed in. Then I spotted you, miss. You was walking through the grounds with another lady. I called out and waved to you but you didn't hear."

"That's right," I said. "I sensed that someone was looking at me, but I couldn't see anyone."

"And by the time I'd walked around the wall to try and find you, you'd gone. So I went back into the village and saw you drive past. I chased after you but you didn't see me."

"I did notice someone running after the motorcar," I said, "but I thought it was another of those newspaper reporters who are camping out in the village."

"I know, miss," she said. "There was a lady reporter who spoke to me and took me into the pub and bought me a couple of pints of Guinness. Really nice she was, and quite delighted to find out who you were."

Oh crikey. Now the beans really were spilled.

"But she didn't know where you were staying, so I wasn't sure what to do next, when who should come into the pub but Mr. Darcy himself. He nearly fell over in surprise when he saw me sitting there. Then he was kind enough to drive me out to you, and the lady what owns this place said I should go up and see if you were already asleep and if there was anything I could do for you. So I crept in, real quiet like, to see if you was still awake."

"Oh, Queenie," I said, not knowing whether to laugh or cry. One had to admire her resiliency. She had managed to travel all the way to Kilhenny when she had never been outside the East End before she met me. I suppose I should have admired her devotion too, but I rather suspected that her family was desperate to do anything to get rid of her again. It would only have taken a day or so before she blew up the kitchen or set fire to the curtains. And now, in all innocence, she had revealed my true identity to the world. I could no longer go anywhere without being besieged by newspaper reporters. Darcy would be furious.

I managed to channel my royal ancestors and be gracious. "It was very brave and enterprising of you to come so far by yourself," I said. "Has Lady Whyte shown you where you can sleep tonight?"

"Oh yes, miss. I'm up one floor from you. Little room in the attic. It's not easy to get to the bed, because there's so much stuff piled on the floor, but it will do. It don't really matter now that I've found you, and I expect I can tidy it up in the morning."

"Then you'd better go up to bed now," I said. "I expect you're very tired."

"Oh yes, miss. Right knackered, I am."

"And hungry, I expect."

"No, I'm all right there. Some nice gentlemen bought me a meat pie and peas at the pub. Ever so friendly they all were. Good night, then. I'll see you in the morning."

And off she went, leaving me staring at the ceiling in horror. Not only was Queenie back in my life, but she had apparently told the entire press community that I was in the vicinity. Oh crikey, I muttered again.

Chapter 28

Queenie is back. Oh crikey. More things to worry about.
 Please let her behave well and not disgrace me.

In the morning there was no sign of Queenie as I got up,
washed and dressed. I came downstairs to find Oona bustling about, laying a table for breakfast.

"Ah, there you are. Did you know that your maid arrived
last night? I told her not to wake you if you were already
asleep."

"She didn't wake me," I said. "In fact she stood silently
at the foot of my bed and I mistook her for the ghost."

Oona gave a big fruity laugh. "A little too solid for a
ghost, wouldn't you say?"

"I'm sorry," I said. "I had no idea she would follow me
to Ireland. I sent her home to her family but they managed
to convince her that her place was here with me."

"Now, there's devotion for you," Oona said. "One doesn't
see that often these days. I thought Treadwell was the last
of the devoted servants."

I gave an embarrassed grin. "I think it was more likely that her family couldn't stand her any longer. She tends to be a little disaster-prone."

Absolutely on cue there came a great primeval roar of rage from upstairs. I couldn't imagine what creature had uttered it. A bull elephant in full charge, maybe, but other than that . . .

Oona and I sprinted upward, one flight, then two. We found Dooley, still in his striped dressing gown, standing at the doorway to his attic room.

"Nooooo!" he yelled.

"Dooley, what on earth is it?" Oona asked, going to put an arm around his shoulder.

"Some bloody fool was here, or let the dogs in," he lamented.

I peered past him and could see that a good part of the battle of Waterloo now lay in complete disarray, soldiers strewn willy-nilly over the floor.

My heart sank. I knew only one person who was able to create chaos in such a short space of time. Before I could answer, the next door opened and a bleary-eyed Queenie came out, wearing a voluminous nightgown, her hair standing up in spikes. "Sorry about that," she said, pointing at the room. "I had to go to the lav and when I came back I wasn't sure which door was mine. I knew right away when my foot kicked something, but then I couldn't find the bloody door again. Don't worry. I'll pick them all up for you as soon as I'm dressed."

"You can't pick them up for me," Dooley said, his voice heavy with despair. "You won't know which regiment they belong to and exactly where the regiments should be. Look, you've got Frenchmen here among the Black Watch."

"We'll all help," I said. "You direct and we'll put the soldiers where you want them. We'll have it back as right as rain, I promise."

Dooley managed the ghost of a smile. "You're a good, kind girl, Georgiana," he said. "And I'm sorry. I'm afraid I flew off the handle. I realize it must have been easy for this young lady to mistake one door for another in the darkness."

"Queenie, go back to your room and don't come out until you are properly dressed," I said, wanting to give the impression of a mistress who is in control of her servants. "And make sure this never happens again."

"Don't worry, I'll put a chair or something across my door so that nobody can make the same mistake again," Dooley said. He had already squatted down and was busily picking up lead soldiers.

"Leave that until you're dressed and have got a good breakfast inside you," Oona said. "Then we'll do as Georgiana says and all help you. It will go quickly. You'll see."

Dooley nodded and shuffled away. I felt terrible for him. We went down to breakfast and, fortified by smoked haddock and poached eggs, returned to tackle the battle of Waterloo disaster. I instructed Queenie to go to my bedroom and stay there until given permission to move. I wasn't about to let her anywhere near the battle. We had managed to rearrange several battalions (not so easy for one who is only slightly less clumsy than Queenie) when we heard the dogs barking and a shout echoing up the stairwell, "Anyone home?"

"Up here, Darcy!" Oona shouted back. "Only don't let the dogs come—"

She didn't finish that sentence as there was the patter of doggie feet on the bare treads and several dogs came into view. Dooley uttered another cry of despair and flung himself at the door, managing to shut it in the nick of time. He then opened it cautiously, a few inches, to see Darcy's surprised face staring at him.

"Well, that's not exactly what I call a warm welcome," Darcy said.

"Not you, dear boy. The blasted dogs," Dooley said. "We have just spent the last hour rearranging the disaster at Waterloo."

"Disaster? I thought we were winning." Darcy looked amused.

"We were, until a certain young person who shall be nameless blundered in upon my battle and wreaked havoc," Dooley said. He stood at the doorway, allowing Darcy to enter while dismissing the dogs. Darcy squeezed into the room.

"You did this?" he asked me.

"Not me. Queenie," I said. "She came back from the loo during the night and opened the wrong door. I rather wish you'd sent her back to England on the first boat, Darcy. You know what a walking disaster she is."

"Sorry," he said, smiling at me. "I knew you wouldn't be thrilled, but there she was, having found Kilhenny all by herself and stuck with nowhere to go for the night, so of course I had to bring her here."

"I know." I gave a big sigh. "She really is the world's worst maid, but she's like an old dog that one can't find it in one's heart to put down. And she has a good heart."

"At least now you have your maid and she can also take care of the princess when she comes here," Oona said. "I don't suppose she usually travels anywhere without her maid."

"Oh golly," I muttered. Queenie and princesses should never be uttered in the same sentence. At least this one had a good sense of humor. I suspected she'd need it.

"So are you ready to head back to Dublin?" Darcy asked me.

"We should stay and help Uncle Dooley put his battlefield to rights first," I said.

"Oh, don't worry about me, dear lady," Dooley said. "It's more important that you do everything you can for young Thaddy. I'm convinced that once they've got the goods on the manservant, all will become clear."

"Got the goods?" Oona boomed. "Dooley, you must stop watching American films. Your language is becoming abysmal."

Dooley shrugged. "I just thought, since we were talking about shady Americans, that I should use appropriate terminology," he said.

I turned to Darcy. "Great-Uncle Dooley thinks that some-one might have paid or threatened Mickey to help with the killing of Mr. Roach. Or at the very least paid him to keep quiet. He did seem most uneasy when Zou Zou spoke with him yesterday."

"Well, we have his fingerprints now, and his photograph, as soon as it can be developed. So let's see what the embassy can make of them. By now my friend in London will have been in touch with Washington and we may be offered a little more help. We'll find out when we go there today."

I collected my overcoat, hat and gloves, instructed Queenie not to open any doors, and to behave herself until I returned, and off we went in the Rolls. It was a bitterly cold day and I was glad of the travel rug over my knees. Threatening gray clouds were building in the western sky, promising rain or even snow. The sort of day when roaring fires and hot chocolate are more inviting than driving around the countryside.

"You must have got back to Kilhenny quite early last night," I said. "I'm surprised Zou Zou didn't ask you to stay—for dinner, I mean," I added, making him smile.

"She did invite me—for dinner, I mean—but I wanted to come straight back to have dinner with my father. He seemed to have perked up quite a bit, actually. I think it was Zou Zou's doing. She had quite an effect on him. Did you notice he had combed his hair?"

I laughed. "I did. And frankly I'm sure she has that kind of effect on any male." I shot him a challenging look. He grinned. "I'm surprised she hasn't married again by now."

"I think she enjoys her freedom too much. What husband would allow her to buy an aeroplane and fly around in it?"

"I hope my husband will let me do anything I want to," I said. "Not that I want to fly around in aeroplanes."

"Glad to hear it," he said. There was a moment's silence. Then he added, "Georgie, I hope you realize that we are not out of the woods yet. My father's fingerprints. His claim that he remembers nothing. A jury could well find him guilty if they choose to go ahead with this case."

"Then we have to make sure they don't," I said. "Once the dead man has been correctly identified they will have new motives and new suspects."

"Yes." He nodded emphatically, clearly trying to convince himself.

I reached across and stroked his cheek. He grabbed my hand and kissed it, then looked at me, my fingers still on his lips. "Oh, Georgie," he said, "I'm so glad you're here."

"Me too." Then I yelled, "Watch it!" as he leaned across to kiss me and we headed for a ditch beside the road.

We drove into the hustle and bustle of Dublin and found Zou Zou sitting in the foyer, getting admiring looks from all who passed. Today, along with the dark mink, she was wearing an emerald green hat perched to one side with a feather curling down her cheek. She stood up as we approached. "There you both are. Would you like a drink or a late breakfast or should we get going?"

"We've eaten, thank you," Darcy said. He picked up the suitcase that lay at her feet. "Is this your luggage? You've checked out of the Shelbourne, then?" He looked around at the elegant foyer. "You're sure you want to exchange this for lodging with my aunt Oona? It's not too late to change your mind and it's no problem to pick you up here, you know."

"Darling, I'm positively dying to stay with your aunt Oona. There are so few true eccentrics in the world any longer. It will be an adventure."

"I hope you'll feel the same way in a few days," Darcy said. "Actually I was thinking that you might want to fly your little aeroplane home while you can. There is supposed to be a spate of bad weather coming in. You might find yourself stuck here for a while."

"I really am getting the distinct impression that you don't want me anymore," she said, making me read an incredible amount of double meaning into those words.

Darcy looked embarrassed. "Zou Zou, I'm delighted to have you around. It's just that . . . well, I know you have an incredibly busy social life and Christmas is rapidly approaching and you'd be missing all kinds of parties."

She laughed. "I don't think it's that at all. You'd rather not have me around playing gooseberry when you want to be alone with your lady love."

"This is hardly a time for being alone with my lady love," Darcy replied. "We're all here for one purpose and that is to prove my father's innocence."

"Speaking of which," Zou Zou said, reaching into her purse and bringing out a piece of paper. "There was a telegram waiting for me from my friend in London last night. He's given me the name of the man he says is the best barrister in Dublin. Sir Grenville Hobbes. That sounds distinguished enough, don't you think? We should go and see him right away."

"Do you think we should do that before we go to the embassy and drop off the reel of film and the fingerprints?" Darcy asked. "He may not be there."

"He will be there," Zou Zou said with conviction, "because I telephoned him and told him that my friend Roddy was sending me to him on a matter of great urgency." She checked her wristwatch. "So you see we have time to do both. Embassy first. The sooner we have those fingerprints sent to America, the better."

And she strode ahead of us toward the front entrance where several bellboys fought for the privilege of opening the door for her.

Chapter 29

WEDNESDAY, DECEMBER 5
IN DUBLIN AND HOPE AT LAST.

We meet a splendid barrister.

"I can't wait to hear what they've been doing at the embassy," Zou Zou said as we stepped out of the warmth of the Shelbourne into the blustery cold of St. Stephen's Green. "Perhaps they'll already have identified our Mr. Roach." She raised a hand to clamp her adorable little hat to her head in the strong wind and with the other clasped her mink around her. "How exciting. This really is positively thrilling, Darcy. Thank you for drawing me away from dreary London."

"I hardly arranged this for your enjoyment, Alexandra," Darcy shouted back over the wind.

She hurried to catch up with him. "I know that, my darling. But I can't help finding it thrilling. I feel just like Hercule Poirot. Do you ever read mystery novels? So clever."

We retrieved the Rolls and drove along the river back to Phoenix Park and the embassy. The promised rain had not yet reached us but the wind was buffeting the bare trees and tossing around the seagulls as they flew overhead. We parked the car close to the door and made a dash inside without getting blown away. The same lanky young man was at the reception desk. He rose this time as we came in.

"Good morning," Darcy said. "My name is O'Mara. We were here yesterday, about the Timothy Roach murder, and we have brought more pertinent information. Was it the ambassador himself we were speaking with yesterday?"

"It was." The young man came around the desk. "However, the ambassador is otherwise occupied today and I'd be pleased to help you."

"Oh, I really don't think . . ." Darcy began. "Maybe we should come back at another time?"

"If I could just have a word, Mr. O'Mara?" the man said. "If you'd care to step this way."

He took Darcy's arm and ushered him off down a side hallway. I sensed we were being given what the Americans would call the brush-off. Our matter was not important enough for the ambassador himself, or somebody didn't want us getting involved. Perhaps the inspector from the Garda had warned the Americans not to include us in any more details. We waited, and a minute or two later the men returned, both looking grave.

"If you'd care to follow me to a reception room," the man said. At least we were not being shown the door. Perhaps we would be waiting for the ambassador to be free. We were shown into a pleasant room overlooking the gardens. The view would have been lovely in summer, I thought. Now the rhododendron bushes were dancing crazily and sleet was already peppering the windows. We took our places on the sofa and armchairs around the fire. The lanky American pulled up a straight-backed chair and sat facing us. This was unexpected. I shot Darcy a glance.

"This is Mr. Lennox," Darcy said. "He has been notified about us and I think he's just the person we need to help us."

He didn't say it but now I realized that this was the man planted at the embassy from the FBI, the man who could get things moving. Darcy introduced us and told Mr. Lennox about our escapade the afternoon before. "So we now have photographs of the man's employee, as well as his fingerprints."

"Well done." Lennox nodded appreciation to Zou Zou and me. "That was smart thinking."

"I hope the prints are clear enough," Zou Zou said. "I made sure the photograph was wiped clean before I handed it to him."

"I'm sure we'll be able to glean some good prints from it," Lennox said. "And get them off to Washington for a match."

"Won't that take an awfully long time?" Zou Zou asked.

"Not at all. We now have the facility to send photographs via the cable, just as one would a message. Brilliant technology, developed by RCA a few years ago. Now AT and T has a facsimile service that can send a picture in six minutes. Speeds things up no end. If this man has a criminal record of any kind, we should know in a day or two."

"How absolutely clever of you." Zou Zou gave him her dazzling smile, which made him blush bright red. I was rather glad I didn't have that effect on men.

"And speaking of fingerprints," Lennox went on, "I have some news to share with you. I went to the morgue yesterday to take the victim's fingerprints, and . . . he doesn't appear to have any."

"Oh, do fingerprints fade after death?" Zou Zou asked.

Lennox shook his head. "No. The tissue shrinks and wrinkles, of course, but it is normally possible to get fingerprints for quite some time. This man has no fingerprints for one of two reasons: either he worked with acids, in a profession such as a printer, etcher, photography developer, and his prints were burned away over time, or"—and he paused, looking at each of us in turn—"or his prints were deliberately removed. Filed smooth, or even replaced with a skin graft. We're inclined to suspect the latter. We suspect he has had some quite sophisticated surgery done to his face. There is a slight scar along his left cheek and another at his hairline. So either he is a Germanic type who was involved in duels or an attempt was made to change his appearance."

"Golly," I said, swallowing back the word too late. I really didn't want Princess Alexandra to think that I used such childish expressions. "Can they really do that?"

"It would take a highly skilled doctor, but yes, it can be done and we know it has been done."

"Then that must have been the doctor who came to see him," I exclaimed. I turned to Lennox. "Lord Kilhenny overheard a conversation between Roach and an American doctor. It was implied that he might have to undergo another operation and Roach seemed unwilling. But the doctor told him it might be necessary."

"Meaning that someone had found out where he was and who he was," Lennox said. "I wonder if Lord Kilhenny can describe this doctor for us. We know of a couple of medical men who have made a good living altering the facial features of criminals."

"So if this man has no fingerprints and his facial features have been altered, it will be impossible to know who he was, won't it?" I asked.

Lennox nodded. "It will certainly make it tough."

"So our photographs and fingerprints of the manservant might be crucial," Zou Zou said with a grin of satisfaction. "How super if you and I solved the case, Georgie."

"You did the interviewing and got the fingerprints. I just took the pictures, and I hope they came out all right," I replied.

"I'm sure they could be helpful," Mr. Lennox said. "But if the prints don't show up on any of the FBI's lists of wanted criminals, it might take a while as our operatives show them to local law enforcement. In the meantime . . ." He left the rest of the sentence hanging.

"So you've already sent the dead man's picture to Washington, have you?" Darcy asked.

Lennox nodded. "Yesterday. And he didn't show up on the FBI's wanted lists or we'd have heard by now. The only possibility seems to be a millionaire who vanished from his yacht a few years ago. The yacht was found off Florida with nobody on board. His wife's body was later found washed ashore but he was never found and was presumed drowned. However, if he chose to fake his own death, he would have had the funds to do what this Mr. Roach did. And he is about the right build and coloring."

"And perhaps his doctor came to warn him that someone was on his trail," I suggested.

"Yes, it would certainly help to find out if a doctor who is known to us has been in Dublin. It's too bad that there is no passport control between Ireland and England. He could have gone back to London or taken a ship out of Liverpool or Southampton by now. I'll check with the shipping companies to see if any names come up."

"And also see if Professor Peabody has left Ireland," I said, making Lennox look up in surprise.

"Peabody? Who is he?"

"Someone calling himself Professor Peabody came to the archeological dig right outside the castle gates," I said. "He claimed he was from the University of Southern Nebraska."

Lennox frowned. "Oh right. You asked me about this yesterday. And I told you there was no such university. Peabody. We can see if anyone traveled under that name, or stayed under that name in Dublin." He looked from Darcy to Zou Zou to me. "So that's about all we can do for now. It's a case of wait and see."

"But you will give this information to the inspector, won't you?" I said. "You will tell him that the man was almost definitely some kind of fugitive and the most likely reason he was killed was that somebody caught up with him. And that his death had nothing at all to do with Lord Kilhenny."

Lennox made a face. "I'm afraid it's not up to me to tell the police in a foreign country how to conduct their investigations. I have already reported to him the lack of fingerprints and the suspicion that he has had facial surgery, but it's up to him what he concludes from that."

I turned to Darcy. "We should go and see him ourselves.

We have to tell him how your father's fingerprints came to be on the club and suggest that he was framed."

Darcy grimaced. "I don't think he'd take kindly to a visit from us, telling him what he should be doing. It might have the opposite effect. You never know, he might decide to rush through my father's trial before any information has time to come from America."

"But a good barrister wouldn't let him do that," Zou Zou said triumphantly. "And we'll have the best. I agree with Georgie. If Mr. Lennox is going to check with shipping companies to see if Professor Peabody has left the country, then the local police should be looking into whether he's still in the neighborhood. And that's something we could take on ourselves. I'd be happy to drive around asking at hotels and train stations within a radius of Kilhenny to see if anyone of his description has been seen."

Mr. Lennox couldn't stifle a grin. "I see you've assembled a keen team, Mr. O'Mara," he said. "But I think you will find there are an awful lot of hotels and boardinghouses in Dublin alone. Impossible for one or two people to check them all out."

"Then the police have to do it," Zou Zou said. "We must go and see my barrister immediately and if he agrees to take the case, then we can use the weight of his name to get things moving. Come on." She stood up. "Thank you, Mr. Lennox. I'm so glad we now have you as part of our team." She gave him another beaming smile and he blushed yet again.

"Delighted to be of help, ma'am," he said and scrambled to open the door for her.

"Well, that was an interesting development, wasn't it?" I said as we climbed into the Rolls and attempted to wrestle the doors from the wind. "I hope your father can give them a good description of the doctor. And we'll get a good description of Professor Peabody from the girls at the dig."

"And the young priest," Darcy added. "Don't forget about him. What better way to move around the Irish countryside than disguised as a priest."

"I'm dying to know if Mickey the manservant really is a valet hired from an agency or whether he has any connection to the murder," Zou Zou said. "I thought he had a frightfully suspicious face, didn't you? I would never have hired a man who looked like that. Too shifty eyed."

"I certainly would never have hired a man who spoke and behaved like that," Darcy agreed. "But perhaps things are different in America. And perhaps, as we've said, he acted quite differently when he was doing his job. I've known plenty of servants who put on a frightfully posh accent when speaking with their masters, but are actually quite rough in speech among themselves."

I laughed. "I must have the only servant who never attempts to put on any airs and graces for me."

"But then she's a hopeless case, we all admit that," Darcy said.

"Then why don't you dismiss her and get someone better?" Zou Zou looked puzzled.

"For two reasons," I said. "Firstly I have no money to hire a top-quality maid, and secondly I feel obligated to keep her because I know that nobody else would hire her."

"Then you must educate her," Zou Zou said.

"Believe me, I've tried. She is either extremely thick or stubborn. I'm never sure which."

"Where can this barrister be found?" Darcy asked, interrupting the treatise on Queenie. Zou Zou pulled the telegram from her purse and read out an address on Merrion Street.

We drove back into the center of Georgian Dublin with its elegant weathered sandstone buildings. When we found the right one, we were admitted by a severe and efficient young woman.

"Sir Grenville has a luncheon appointment, so I hope you won't keep him long," she said. "Please wait while I tell him you're here."

We waited and then were shown into a well-appointed room—every item of furniture shouted good taste and luxury. Sir Grenville lived up to the impression his name had given me. Perfectly attired. Old-school tie, longish steel gray hair and a distinguished profile. He came forward and held out his hand to the princess. "Princess Zamanska? I've had strict instructions from old Roddy Altringham that I'm to take good care of your friend. As it happens, I already know Lord Kilhenny. I believe we played cricket together in our youth. I've been following the case with interest." He released Zou Zou's hand and shook Darcy's. "And you must be young O'Mara. My boy was at school with you."

Darcy smiled. "Oh yes. I remember there was a Hobbes in Smythe House. That was your son? He was a good bit younger than I. A third former when I was in the sixth."

"He told me you were a damn fine rugby player," Sir Grenville said. "Wing forward, wasn't it?"

I followed the conversation, thinking that I was observing that things worked pretty much the same way in Ireland as they did in England. You went to the right schools. You played sports together and then it was decided that you were the right sort of chap. Our kind. Our class. And if you were, then all went smoothly and you helped each other.

We were offered chairs and coffee. We told Sir Grenville everything we knew. He listened, took notes, asked questions. Then he looked up and said, "The problem here is that you cannot engage my services to take on your case. It is the solicitor who engages me. Who is he?"

"It is a 'they,'" Darcy said. "Leach and Leach in Kildare. Family solicitor for generations, I'm afraid."

"So I suggest you talk to whichever Mr. Leach is running the business at the moment and ask him to get in touch with me. He may not think I'm the right man for the job, of course. And I warn you that my services are not exactly cheap."

"That's of no consequence," Zou Zou said. "Money is no object in this case. We want the best and we want Lord Kilhenny freed."

"I also warn you that while I am damned good at what I do, I cannot work miracles," Sir Grenville added. "A jury may be swayed by the fingerprints. The alcoholic stupor and lack of memory may well make them react negatively. It really all comes down to what transpires in America. If and when this man is identified, then other motives, other suspects may come to light. In the meantime I look forward to hearing from Mr. Leach of Leach and Leach."

It was all so civilized. I had to remind myself that it was a man's life we were dealing with.

Chapter 30

WEDNESDAY, DECEMBER 5
BACK TO KILHENNY.

I could tell that Darcy was really reluctant to visit the Garda headquarters and meet with Chief Inspector Callahan, but Zou Zou could be quite persuasive when she wanted something.

"I'm sure he'll listen to me," she said.

"I have to remind you that the man is an ardent republican," Darcy said. "He is probably also a rabid socialist and wishes to abolish all aristocracy."

"Silly boy." Zou Zou chuckled. "It is not my pedigree that interests men, as you very well know." She gave him one of those looks that felt like a dagger in my heart.

So we returned to the park and the Garda headquarters only to find that the inspector was out, working on a case. Darcy heaved a sigh of relief. Zou Zou was all for doing the rounds of Dublin hotels, asking about American doctors and Professor Peabody, but Darcy thought the next step should be to visit Leach and Leach. "We have to tell them about Sir Grenville. And my father, of course," he added.

"After all, it is his case. If he doesn't agree to the barrister, then we certainly can't engage him."

"Who could possibly turn down the best barrister in Ireland?" Zou Zou asked. "Especially when he looks the part so well. He'd have the jurors believing every word he said."

"All the same, it will be my father's decision."

"I'm sure I can persuade him," Zou Zou said. "I usually can. And I think our next mission should not be to boring old solicitors but to somewhere we can have luncheon. I'm positively starving."

"I'd like to catch the solicitors now, before they go to lunch," Darcy said. "We'll grab a bite to eat in Kildare."

"If I'm not dead of starvation by then," she said. "Very well. Put your foot down, Darcy."

He did, and we were soon back in Kildare, which was bustling with people trying to finish their shopping before the weather deteriorated. Indeed the rain had already turned to sleet and the wind had picked up.

"It looks as if it might snow later. It's certainly cold enough," Darcy said as he drew up the Rolls outside a row of Victorian houses. "I think, given the weather, it would be better if I went in to see Mr. Leach," he said. "I don't want you two ladies to end up looking like drowned rats."

"He doesn't want us trying our womanly charms on Mr. Leach," Zou Zou said as he left us in the Rolls and sprinted toward the front door. "Typical man. Wants to handle everything himself. You must make sure he doesn't boss you around when you are married, Georgie. Be your own woman from day one."

"I just hope we do get married," I said. "If his father is convicted, he has sworn he won't marry me."

"Then we'll just have to ensure that a mere trifle like a hanging doesn't stand in the way of true love, won't we?" she said, with that delightful laugh. Then her face became serious. "I'm sure it will all turn out well, Georgie. They'll find out the truth about Mr. Roach and then they'll know who would have wanted to kill him."

"But if Inspector Callahan can't get past the prints on that club, then maybe a jury won't either," I said.

"Moving on to more practical matters," she said, waving this aside, "we should not arrive at the aunt and uncle's house empty-handed. I can see they are not exactly flush with funds, so I suggest we pop into a few local shops and have some items delivered . . . just so that we are not a burden, you understand."

"All right," I said.

"And since my mink really does hate getting wet and you are wearing a good stout Harris Tweed, may I possibly ask you to do the job for me? There seems to be a butcher across the road, and a wine merchant too. What luck."

"What would you like me to buy?" I asked.

"Just some basics," she said. "A case of champagne, of course. And several bottles of a good Bordeaux. Then a brace of pheasant . . . a leg of lamb, do you think, or is that too mundane?"

"I think a leg of lamb is always lovely," I said. "And one can make shepherd's pie with the leftovers."

She laughed at this. "Leftovers. What a quaint idea." She opened her purse and produced several five-pound notes. "This should cover it," she said. "Oh, and maybe they should throw in some sausages and kidneys for breakfast, and a few rump steaks in case we feel like something more solid."

"How long are you expecting to stay with them?" I couldn't help asking. It seemed to me like enough food for weeks.

"I'm only ordering enough to tide us over for a day or so," she said. "I wonder if there is a fishmonger nearby. I could do with some oysters and I adore caviar."

"I don't know whether you'd find caviar in the wilds of Ireland," I said. "And are we close enough to the sea for oysters?"

"Very well," she said. "I'll have them sent out from Dublin next time we're there. Oh, and tell both the merchants to deliver, won't you? Off you go, then."

I braved the elements and dashed across to the two shops.

When they heard my order they were most accommodating and of course they would be happy to deliver. I returned to the car, thinking again how different and simple life is for the rich. I reached the Rolls at the same time as Darcy and explained I'd been on a food mission for Zou Zou.

He nodded. "That was a kind thought of hers. I must confess I was a little worried about Aunt Oona providing enough food."

"So was Mr. Leach overjoyed at the news?" I asked as we both climbed back into the motor.

"Not at all. Quite the opposite, in fact. He considers Sir Grenville rather flash and vulgar, in spite of his successes, and feels his obviously aristocratic bearing may adversely influence a jury of common people."

"Oh dear. So what happens now?" I asked.

"The silly man must be made to see sense," Zou Zou said firmly.

"He did say he would abide by the wishes of his client. If my father instructs him to hire Sir Grenville then he is obligated to do so." He glanced across at us as he let out the clutch and the motorcar moved away smoothly, its lovely engine still purring in spite of its age. "I've never liked him much. Always came across as very narrow and cautious to me. So it's up to my father now."

"And I'm sure he'll be delighted," Zou Zou said. I wasn't so sure myself.

"Now I positively insist that we find somewhere to eat," Zou Zou continued. "I don't know about you but I need regular meals and it is already almost two o'clock."

I had to say I was feeling a little peckish myself and glad when Darcy found a café in the square, where we had a simple but acceptable meal of meat pie and peas, followed by a baked jam roll. Zou Zou declared it to be quaint and interesting, as if she was eating a native delicacy in darkest Africa. You'd have thought that the meal would have put the thought of food from the princess's mind, but when we reached the village of Kilhenny she spotted a bakery and decided she needed to add some biscuits and cakes to the food she was taking to Oona, and some treats for Darcy's father too. "Poor man. He doesn't look as if he's had a decent meal in months."

"Oona did invite him to dinner a couple of nights ago, but he wouldn't come," Darcy said. "I suppose I can understand how he feels. If you're worried about your very life, the last thing you want is small talk."

"Look, there's Mrs. McNalley," I said, as I spotted a group of women standing under an awning, deep in gossip. "We need to talk to her. We should ask her whether she took food down to your father that evening. I still suspect he might have been drugged, and what better way than putting the substance in his food."

"Good idea." Darcy came around to help us out of the motorcar. The rain had indeed turned into a light snow and flakes fluttered down around us as Zou Zou headed for the bakery and we made our way across to Mrs. McNalley.

"Well now, Mr. Darcy," she said. "And how is your poor father doing? Are you sure he doesn't want me to come in and do some cooking and cleaning for him? I don't like the thought of him trying to look after himself."

"Not at the moment, Mrs. McNalley," Darcy said. "I'm with him and I'll make sure he eats. But speaking of food, I wanted to ask you a question."

"Oh yes?" She moved away from the other women.

"On the evening that Mr. Roach was killed, did you take my father down some food from the castle?"

"I did," she said. "I made a big pot of stew and left it in the oven, keeping warm, for when Mr. Roach wanted to eat. And I put some in a bowl to take down to his lordship when I went home."

"So that bowl was left on a counter for a while?" Darcy asked. "Could it have been tampered with?"

"Tampered with? What on earth are you suggesting?"

"That someone might have drugged his lordship's food," I said.

"Jesus, Mary and Joseph," she said. "Drugged his food? What for?"

"So that he fell asleep and didn't remember anything of that night and was convinced that he'd drunk himself into a stupor, thus having no alibi for the murder."

"Mercy me," she said and crossed herself. "Now I think of it the bowl of stew was sitting on the counter for quite a while. That Mickey person told me that Mr. Roach didn't want to eat in the dining room but would have a tray by the fire in the study, so I could clear away the place I'd set for him. So I went in there and I polished the table a little as it was looking dusty. Then when I came back Mickey said I could go home. I don't know why he thought he could give me orders, but he always did."

"And did he know that bowl of stew was going to Lord Kilhenny?" I asked.

She thought then nodded. "He did. In fact he made some snide remark about it. Something about getting the scraps from the master's table. I replied that I didn't like to see good food going to waste and it was clear Mr. Roach wouldn't eat the whole thing."

"So you took the stew down to his lordship," I continued.

"I did, and left it beside the stove for him to heat up when he felt like it. He was sitting in his chair with a glass of whiskey beside him and was not in the best of moods, I can tell you. He didn't even thank me but told me to go away. So I did."

"Then the whiskey and the drugs would have knocked him out for the night," I said as we left Mrs. McNalley. "Only everything has been washed up long since and we've no way of proving anything. But it does suggest that Mickey was part of the plan, sending Mrs. McNalley into the dining room to get her out of the way."

"Again we've no way of proving it," Darcy said. "Oh no. I can see that Zou Zou has been shopping!"

Zou Zou emerged from the bakery while a boy followed her, his arms piled high with boxes. Darcy ran across the street to open the back door for her. I was about to follow when a voice behind me said, "Well, if it isn't the young lady. What perfect timing. I've been dying to have a little chat with you." And it was the female American reporter I had met at the Harp. She was wearing a raincoat and had a scarf tied over her blond curls. And she was giving me a big friendly smile. "I'd just love to have a little chat, honey. Do you have a minute? I believe the pub is shut, with your stupid licensing laws, but we could go into the tearoom. They do cream buns. Much better than we can get at home."

"I'm afraid I'm with friends and I can't just desert them," I said.

"With a special friend, so I gather." She gave me a knowing look. I was noticing that in spite of the blond hair her eyes were dark. Not a natural hair color, I suspected. But then neither was my mother's. She moved closer and touched my arm. "So tell me, he's the son of the lord, isn't he? I don't suppose you could use your charms to get me an interview with his lordship? The police have set up a barrier now that everyone has realized the lord has been released and is at home. We can't get anywhere near the place. So frustrating."

"I can assure you that the last thing his lordship wants is to talk to any reporters," I said. "Please respect his privacy. You can understand what a difficult time it must be for him."

"So tell me," she went on, lowering her voice. "Do you think he did it? Is he going to plead guilty when it comes to trial?"

"I'm sure he's not, and I'm sure he didn't do it," I replied. "Now if you'll excuse me . . ." I broke away from her and was returning to the Rolls, where boxes were still being loaded onto the backseat, when I spotted a familiar figure parked outside the Harp pub. It was Barney the taxi driver. He waved when he saw me.

"Still here, then? So you found yourself a place to stay?"

"I did, thank you," I said.

"Well, that's good, isn't it? And I notice she's still here," he said, nodding across the street to where my American lady lingered, watching me.

"Was she the one who gave you the pound tip?" I asked, remembering.

He grinned. "That's the one. Of course, after her there

have been other daft Americans who don't know our money and hand out big tips. Not that I'm complaining, mind you. It's been like early Christmas with all the comings and goings. I just brought in another Yank now. From Chicago, of all places." He paused, frowning. "Now, that's interesting, isn't it?" he said. "The lady was from Chicago too."

"Well, that's where Mr. Roach was from," I said, "so I suppose it would be big news there."

He laughed. "In Chicago? That's where the gangsters are, isn't it? Killing each other left and right every day."

Then a thought crossed my mind. I went closer to the taxi. "Barney, are you the only taxi that comes out from Kildare?"

"For the most part, yes," he said.

"Do you remember driving an American professor—a big man—called Professor Peabody?"

He screwed up his face in concentration. "I remember a big chap once," he said. "That's right. Had me drive him out here and then back again. He wanted to look at the digging that was going on. But that was a while ago now."

"So you drove him back to Kildare and he hasn't come back since?"

"Not to my knowledge," he said.

"And you haven't seen him around Kildare?"

"Oh, I'd have heard if a strange American was hanging around in Kildare," he said.

So that put a damper on our theory that Professor Peabody was somehow involved in the murder, unless he hadn't come through Kildare on a second occasion, which was quite possible. I thanked Barney and was hurrying back to the others in the Rolls when I saw a figure slink past me, heading for the pub. It was Mickey Riley.

Chapter 31

WEDNESDAY, DECEMBER 5

A tragedy in Kilhenny. Or was it?

"Of course, Professor Peabody could have hired himself a car in Dublin," Darcy said when I related the conversation as we drove off again. "And who was that blond woman you were talking to?"

"The American reporter I met when I first arrived," I said. "She was trying to sweet-talk me into arranging an interview with your father. I gather the police have finally stopped reporters from bothering him."

"Thank heavens for that," Darcy said. "At least the Garda have done something useful."

Zou Zou was now peering anxiously out of the car window. "Oh dear. My poor little aeroplane. Do you think we can find someone to move it before it gets too cold and wet?"

"I think planes are made to fly through the elements, aren't they?" Darcy said. "And we did cover the cockpit."

"But the wings . . . they are so delicate. They are not

made to be buried in snowdrifts. We have to find some nice boys to move it into a barn or a stable."

"We can try the stables," Darcy said. "Someone might still be working there. Or we can see who we can find in the village."

We rounded the corner before the castle and a constable stepped out from behind the hedge, holding up a hand for us to stop.

"I'm sorry, sir, but nobody is allowed this way at the moment. Can you please go around?"

"I happen to live here," Darcy said. "I'm Lord Kilhenny's son and these are my friends."

The constable frowned, considering this. "I was told nobody was to pass," he said.

"No newspaper reporters or gawkers or onlookers," Darcy said. "But I am actually living at the lodge and we're bringing back food for my father. You can't stop me."

The constable was looking clearly uncomfortable now. "We'll have to get an okay from one of my superiors, sir," he said, rolling his *r*'s with the strongest Irish brogue. "I'm just obeying orders as they were put to me."

"And where would we find one of your superiors?" Darcy snapped, his patience wearing thin, I could tell. "Back in Dublin?"

"Oh no, sir. Chief Inspector Callahan is up at the castle right now."

"Then may we drive up to the castle to find him?"

Again the wrinkled brow. "I'm not sure about that, sir. It's my belief that nobody is allowed onto the castle grounds. It's a crime scene, isn't it? A murder scene." He sounded very excited to be saying this.

"Constable, I'm not going to sit in this motorcar while we freeze to death and get buried under feet of snow," Darcy said. "And I need to speak with Chief Inspector Callahan anyway. I'll take my chances." And he drove right past the worried-looking constable and up to the castle gate.

I noticed that nobody was working at the dig. It was

covered in tarpaulins on which puddles had collected. The gates, for once, were open and a black police vehicle was parked just inside. A driver stood beside this, looking miserable in the freezing conditions.

"We need a word with the inspector," Darcy said. "Is he up at the castle?"

"Yes, sir," the man replied. "But you're not allowed to—"

Darcy had already driven past him, up the driveway, and drew up at the front entrance. Another Garda constable was stationed there and came rushing down to intercept us.

"What are you doing here?" he demanded.

"I'm Darcy O'Mara. This is my family home and I want a word with the inspector," Darcy said. "Please go and fetch him if you won't let us in."

"Very good, sir." The young man looked scared. "Can you tell me what this is about?"

"I should have thought that was obvious," Darcy snapped. "It is about my father's wrongful arrest and recent developments. And also about the fact that I am not being allowed to drive to my own home."

The man swallowed hard. "I'll go and see if he's available."

Darcy got out of the car. We waited inside. The snow was now falling quite heavily and snowflakes lingered on Darcy's dark curls. But in spite of the cold, the princess and I had both wound down our windows to be able to hear better. After a few minutes Chief Inspector Callahan appeared. "You wanted to see me, O'Mara?" he asked.

"I did, sir. First, there's the small matter that your constable won't let me drive down the lane to my father's house where I'm currently staying. I'll be grateful if you'll pass along a message that I'm allowed to my own home."

"Oh yes. Of course," he said. "The men tend to take their jobs too literally at times. Not always the brightest buttons in the box, if you get my meaning."

"Thank you." Darcy nodded. "I appreciate it. And as to the other matter: We've been to the American embassy again, so we're fully up to date with developments in this case. Now that we know this man was clearly a fugitive, possibly a criminal, may we conclude that you are finally looking beyond my father as a possible suspect?"

"We are making our inquiries," the inspector said, with a guarded expression on his face. "In fact the reason my men are here at the moment is to try to find any evidence of the man's real identity."

"Any luck?" Darcy asked.

"Not a trace, so far," the inspector said. "The one thing that is evident is the lack of personal papers. No correspondence, nothing."

"He was a man in hiding," Darcy agreed. "Not wanting to be found. But somebody found him and killed him."

"Hold on a moment. You can't escape the fact that only your father's fingerprints are on that club," Callahan said.

"Rather strange that, wouldn't you say?" Darcy said. "A club that's thousands of years old and has only one set of fingerprints on it. And by the way, my father can tell you why his prints were on it. He went to see Roach that afternoon and the club was lying on the table. He found out that Roach was planning to sell it. He told him he couldn't do that. It was a family heirloom of great value. While he was talking he picked up the club."

"And came back that evening to do the deed," Callahan said.

"Oh come now, Chief Inspector," Darcy said. "My father is not a stupid man. If you were going to kill somebody, would you leave the weapon, with your fingerprints on it, lying beside the body? You'd take it and burn it or bury it."

"Unless he was surprised by someone or something and had to drop it and flee," the inspector said smugly.

"It's my belief that my father was set up for this crime. It was planned to make him look like the murderer," Darcy said. "And I'm also beginning to suspect that Mickey Riley either knew about it or was part of it. The American embassy is investigating him too, so it will be interesting to hear what they discover."

"Mr. Riley already told us he found this job through an employment agency," Inspector Callahan said.

"Have you confirmed that with the agency?" Darcy asked.

A frown crossed the inspector's face. "I would appreciate it if you left the investigation to those who are trained to do it. I can understand your desire to help your father, but frankly you're not doing so by poking your nose where it's not wanted. So go home and leave us to get on with our work."

"I'll be happy to go home if I'm allowed to pass by your constable," Darcy said sweetly.

"Of course. Tell him you have my permission."

Darcy started to walk away, then turned back. "I don't suppose you'd like me to take a look around the castle to see if I notice anything suspicious? Or anywhere Roach might have hidden documents? I used to have several secret hiding places here when I was a child."

I could see that Chief Inspector Callahan was in an agony of indecision. Then to my surprise he finally nodded. "That might not be a bad idea, given the circumstances. Do you want to come in right now?"

Darcy looked back at us. "I have my two friends in the motorcar," he said. "I can hardly leave them outside on a day like this."

"Then I suppose they can wait inside the castle. It shouldn't take long."

"Shouldn't take long?" I muttered to Zou Zou. "Darcy told me the castle had forty-seven bedrooms."

Darcy came down the steps and opened the doors for us. "The inspector will let me take a look around," he said. "He suggests you wait inside rather than in the Rolls."

"How kind of him." Zou Zou flashed the chief inspector one of her dazzling smiles. I thought I saw him blush a little. We mounted the flight of worn steps and entered the castle. My first impression reminded me a lot of Castle Rannoch. We were in a towering entrance hall with a broad flight of stairs ascending to a gallery. The ceiling was vaulted oak and the chandelier that hung down hardly managed to make the room any lighter. The only windows were pencil-thin slots, dating from the Middle Ages. And it was freezing cold, hardly any warmer than the motorcar had been. What was more, I had left my traveling rug on the seat. We stood with a Garda constable watching us as the inspector and Darcy disappeared up the stairs. I tried desperately to think of an excuse to follow him because I'd have loved to see the scene of the murder for myself, and for once I knew that Mickey was out of the way, but I couldn't come up with anything plausible. We heard their voices echoing faintly as they made their way from room to room. Then silence for quite a while.

"My God, it's dreary in here, isn't it?" Zou Zou said. "No wonder Lord Kilhenny sank into bleak depression. I would have thrown myself from the battlements by now."

"Darcy said there is a later addition with more modern rooms at the back of the castle," I said, "and it would be a lot more cheerful with a fire in the grate."

"Now who is looking on the bright side?" she asked with a wicked smile. "But then you have a vested interest in the place, don't you? You could well wind up living here one day."

That made me stop and think. Golly. Did I really want to live here one day? In a cold castle in an Irish backwater? It was something I hadn't really considered before. The thought of being married to Darcy had been so delicious that I hadn't stopped to think what being Lady Kilhenny one day might mean. Then I decided there were too many things to worry about right now without thinking of the future. I had just come to this conclusion when I heard the voices again and Darcy came back down the stairs with the inspector.

"No luck, I'm afraid," he said. "But I did find a slingshot and two conkers in one of my hiding places."

"Thank you for looking, anyway," the inspector said. He sounded quite pally after the frosty reception he'd given Darcy earlier. Perhaps he was preparing himself to admit that he was wrong and that Lord Kilhenny did not kill Mr. Roach.

"There is something else, Chief Inspector," I said, wondering as I uttered the words whether I should have kept quiet.

"If we now think an outsider came here to kill Mr. Roach, we have been told of two strangers seen near the castle who might be of interest. One was a big man who claimed to be Professor Peabody of the University of Southern Nebraska. He visited the archeological site across the lane, but the students who were working there got the impression that he didn't know much about Irish archeology. What's more, there is no University of Southern Nebraska, apparently. And then there was a young priest who inquired about Mr. Roach. One of your constables—Constable Byrne, wasn't it?—said that he didn't know of any young priests in this area. So either of them could have come looking for Roach."

The inspector was watching me intently. "The young lady with royal connections, I remember. But this still doesn't answer the question of how any of them could have gotten into the castle. Riley says nobody came and he would have had to let them in."

"It is possible to scale the wall in places if one puts one's mind to it," Darcy said.

"But it's not exactly easy to get into the building itself, is it?" Callahan said.

"Riley said the servants' entrance wasn't always locked," Darcy said.

The inspector's face remained passive. "I shall take what you've said under advisement. In the meantime I suggest we all wait and see what the Americans turn up. Perhaps the man wasn't even American. Perhaps we'll never know."

And with those encouraging words he turned to the constable who was hovering by the door. "Please show these people out, Harris."

"Well?" I asked as we drove back to the gates. "Did you see anything of interest? Did he let you look at the scene of the crime?"

"To be frank it was so dark everywhere that I couldn't see much," he said. "I didn't notice anything obvious missing from the walls. Of course, I hadn't been home here for many years now. It's funny, but things always seemed so much bigger as a child. The library was smaller than I remembered it, but then, we were not encouraged to go into the library. It was my father's realm."

"Goodness, the snow is really coming down now, isn't it?" Zou Zou said. "Reminds me of Poland. I can't tell you how dreary our winters were there."

The constable guarding the lane leading to the lodge was looking decidedly miserable now and a coating of snow had formed on his helmet. We relayed permission from Callahan and were allowed to pass. Night was falling fast and no lights shone out from the lodge. Zou Zou had to go and see her aeroplane, which already had a coating of snow. At her bidding, we drove past and down to the stables but they were deserted. So the three of us maneuvered the plane under the trees, where it would at least be more protected.

We were starting to look like three snowmen by the time we made for Darcy's father's front door. Lord Kilhenny had fallen asleep in front of the fire. A glass of whiskey, half empty, stood on the table beside him. He looked older than his years and I felt an intense wave of pity for him. Then I reminded myself that his loneliness was of his own doing. He had kept his remaining children away and condemned himself to this life.

Darcy turned on the electric light and his father sat up, blinking. "What the devil?" he demanded.

"We've come back with news, Father," Darcy said. "And Alexandra has been kind enough to bring you a treat for your tea."

"Oh, thank you, but I don't feel much like eating these days," Lord Kilhenny said. "Take them over to Oona."

"You have to eat," Zou Zou said firmly. "And speaking of Aunt Oona, we have some lovely things being delivered to her house. Steaks and lamb and pheasant. You must come over to dinner and eat properly for once. I know she has invited you and you turned her down."

"And I'll turn her down again," he said. "I don't want to be the recipient of charity or pity."

"You're a stubborn man," Zou Zou said. "Well, you don't have to eat, but we want to. And these look delicious enough to tempt anybody. Besides, I think we could all do with a cup of tea. We're frozen to the marrow . . . what funny expressions there are in the English language."

"I'll go and put the kettle on," I said. I went through to the kitchen and heard snatches of their conversation as Darcy told his father about the events of the day—the discoveries about the dead man's fingerprints and face, and our suspicion that he had been drugged that night.

"It's odd you should say that," Lord Kilhenny said. "I felt terrible when I woke up in the morning. Oh, I realize I'd had a drink or two, but my brain was in a complete fog. I couldn't even think clearly when those Garda chaps showed up on my doorstep. So it had to have been the Mickey creature who put something in the stew, didn't it? I'd wondered about him all along. Never liked the fellow."

The kettle boiled and I poured the water onto the tea leaves, then carried through the tray.

"So we might learn more about him when they've had a chance to examine his fingerprints," Darcy was saying. "At least we have the American government working on our behalf now. So that's good, isn't it?"

His father grunted. I couldn't tell if he was agreeing or not.

"And we've all been busy on your behalf today," Darcy continued. "Alexandra has been in touch with a QC friend of hers in London and he recommended a barrister to us. We went to see him today. A splendid chap. The best in Dublin, they say. Sir Grenville Hobbes. Of course, Leach is dead against him, but it's up to you. You're the client. So can we suggest he come to see you tomorrow and you two can talk? You'll get along well. He's one of us. His son went to school with me. And he used to play cricket with you."

Darcy's father had been staring at him. Then he said, "You seem to forget one thing, my boy. I am living in this hovel because I have no money. And I'm sure barristers of the quality of Grenville Hobbes don't work for charity. I can't pay him. You've wasted your time."

"Lord Kilhenny—Thaddy—" Zou Zou said. "Please don't worry about the money side of it. The important thing is that you meet this man and you trust him to represent you. I think you'll be happy to put your life in his hands."

Lord Kilhenny was frowning now. "Don't worry about the money side of things? I don't think you grasp the situation. I cannot pay a barrister."

"Then you must rely on kind friends who will take care of matters for you," Zou Zou said.

"What kind friends? I have no friends any longer."

"You have us," Zou Zou said.

"No, no, a thousand times no," Lord Kilhenny roared. "I most certainly will not allow you or anybody to pay for me. Do you hear that? I absolutely forbid it. I do not want your charity."

Zou Zou's face had gone very pink. "You really are a most stubborn man," she said. "And a stupid one too. You should realize that there are people who care about you and want to help you. But fine. If that's the way you want it, reject our help, just like you have rejected your son all these years. Come on, Darcy, let's go. We'll have tea at your great-aunt's house where we are welcome."

She made a magnificent exit. Darcy and I hesitated for a moment, both feeling upset and embarrassed.

"We do want to help you, Father," Darcy said. "But you have to want to help yourself." He took my arm. "Come, Georgie." And he led me outside.

We drove through the village, which now looked deserted, everyone having gone inside at the onset of the snow. Night was falling fast and snow now stuck to the windscreen, mounting up as it was pushed aside by the wipers. Darcy muttered a swearword under his breath. "I won't be staying at Oona's after I deposit you," he said. "I'm not looking forward to going back to my father's, but I think I'll soon be trapped if I don't get home quickly. And I don't want to leave him alone on a night like this."

"You're a good son," Zou Zou said. "He doesn't deserve you, the way he behaves."

We left the last lights of the village and were now in darkness with white flakes driving toward us in the headlights' beams. As we were driving down the hill to the little stone bridge, Darcy saw headlights facing us and suddenly put on the brake. We felt the motorcar sliding on the soft snow. He pumped the brakes but we kept on sliding. Then he turned the wheel into the hedge, we heard the scraping of twigs against the side and luckily we came to a halt.

"What is some fool doing? Is he stuck on the bridge?" he asked. He sounded a little shaken. He got out of the Rolls and walked forward. There appeared to be more than one vehicle ahead of us, although they were just indistinct outlines through the snow.

"What's going on?" Darcy shouted.

"There's a car gone off the road into the stream," someone called back. "We've sent for the police and the breakdown lorry from the garage."

I got out in a hurry and slithered after Darcy, my heart beating very fast. It was an eerie scene with headlights sending narrow shafts of light and snow swirling. Below us we could hear the water rushing. Where it had tripped merrily over rocks before, it was now a raging torrent, and in the blackness we could make out the shape of a vehicle. What was more, I recognized that distinct shape. It was a taxi. And inside the cab I could make out a white hand up against the window.

Chapter 32

Not much joy tonight.

We were a somber group as we drove up to Mountjoy. We had stayed until help arrived. Of course Barney was quite dead, having pitched forward and hit his head against the windscreen.

"He must have taken that sharp bend too fast and skidded over the side," Darcy said in a shaken voice. "Poor man. You saw how easily something like that could happen."

I did see. In fact I was still shivering. But a whisper was nagging at the back of my mind. I had asked Barney about Professor Peabody, and he had died. And Mickey had observed us on his way to the pub. Had he waited until we drove off, then asked Barney to drive him, and then orchestrated his death? Hit him on the head and then taken off the brake and headed him for the river, maybe? It was now clear to me that this whole business was much more than a burglary gone wrong, a simple feud. It was well thought-out and I suspected that Mickey was at the heart of it. I prayed that our finger-prints would reveal something of importance.

"You were brilliant to save us, Darcy," Zou Zou said. "I hope they delivered my goodies before the weather set in. I am in desperate need of a glass of champagne, aren't you?"

"I thought you wanted tea and cakes," I said.

"That was before the tragedy," she said. "One needs something stronger to bolster the nerves."

Oona met us at the front door. "Beastly night. Glad you made it safely. Dooley was getting worried," she said. "Are you staying for dinner, Darcy? I've cooked the pheasant that Her Highness so kindly had delivered. I hope that was all right?"

"All right? It was splendid," Zou Zou said. "And I hope the champagne was delivered too?"

"Out in the washhouse, keeping cold," Oona said.

"I'm afraid I can't stay, Aunt Oona," Darcy said. "I should get back to my father before the snow gets too thick."

"It's a damned blizzard out there. We hardly ever see snow, at least not like this. I wonder if it will be a white Christmas."

It was funny but I had completely forgotten that Christmas was approaching. It was as if time had stood still since Darcy and I had driven north that night.

"You have to stay and have a drink first, Darcy," Zou Zou said. "Steady your nerves."

"Steady his nerves?" Oona asked. "What for?"

"There was a nasty accident at the bridge," Darcy said.

"I thought I heard the bell of a police car," she said. "What happened?"

"It was the taxi from Kildare."

"Poor old Barney? We've used him a few times when Dooley didn't feel like driving. Nice chap. A bit too friendly. Or should one say nosy. Is he all right?"

"He's dead," I heard myself saying. "His car went into the water."

"How terribly sad. What a shock for you to come upon

that. A cup of tea, do you think, or something stronger? Brandy?"

"I think we should open a champagne," Zou Zou said. "Not that we've anything to celebrate, but I find it always goes down well at moments of stress."

"Good show. Brilliant idea," Oona said. "I'll tell Treadwell. He's making apple dumplings with the help of your girl, Georgie. I must say she's a good little cook."

"Queenie?" I asked. "She's a good cook?"

"Yes. And so willing. She was obviously so upset by what she did last night that she's been trying desperately to be helpful."

This did not sound like Queenie at all. I was almost tempted to tiptoe into the kitchen and see if her body had been taken over by one of the family ghosts, when the girl herself appeared, carrying a tray.

"Mr. Treadwell told me to bring these through to the sitting room," she said. "They're cheese straws. Just came out of the oven."

She looked around for somewhere to put them. As usual there was no clear surface. But Oona stepped up and took the tray from her. "I'll pass them around, my dear. Will you make sure the table is laid in the dining room? We'll be four for dinner. Mr. O'Mara will not be staying, I regret to say."

I waited for her to say "Bob's yer uncle" but to my astonishment she said, "Very good, Lady Whyte."

Champagne was poured. Cheese straws were handed around as we related the events of the day.

"I knew young Thaddy couldn't have done it," Dooley said. "Now the truth will come out. Well done."

"We're not home free yet, Uncle Dooley," Darcy said. "Chief Inspector Callahan will take some convincing. But at least he'll be held up from going ahead with the trial until all the facts are in, and that could take a while."

On that somber note Darcy bade us farewell. I followed him to the front door, where he gave me a chaste but tender kiss.

"Take care of yourself, won't you?" I whispered.

He gave me a questioning look.

"I'm wondering whether Barney's death was an accident, and I'm beginning to believe that Mickey is at the bottom of this whole thing. He watched me talking to Barney earlier when I asked him about Professor Peabody. And a little while later Barney is dead. You and your father should take extra care."

Darcy nodded. "But if he is behind all this, then why wait this long to kill Roach? He's been with him—what— four years? Plenty of opportunity to kill him before then and plenty of chances to make it look like an accident too. Kilhenny is an old castle. There are crooked steps, dark corners, lots of opportunities to give someone a push."

I had to grin. "If we ever live there and I come into money, then I'll watch my back."

"Are you likely to come into money?" he asked. There was the slightest hint of a smile on that worried face.

"I am the only heir to Sir Hubert Anstruther, remember. But he's hale and hearty and not even fifty yet, so I'll be ancient by the time he dies."

Darcy wrapped me in his arms. "We'll manage somehow. We'll survive on our own, if we can just get through this." He kissed me again, this time with real passion, leaving me breathless as he ran out into the swirling snow.

Dinner was a masterpiece. The pheasant was tender enough to eat with a spoon, the gravy rich and the apple dumplings perfect. I was relieved that Treadwell served at table and didn't ask Queenie to help. I was dreading the thought of custard spilled over the princess's dress. In fact I didn't see Queenie until I went up to bed.

"I've brought up a hot water bottle, my lady," Queenie said. "I thought you'd like a warm bed."

"Queenie?" I looked at her. "I've had glowing reports on you today. What happened?"

"Well, miss," she said, looking down at her hands, "after what I did last night, I saw that I was a right bloomin' failure, and what's more, I was a discredit to you, who's been so kind to me. So I decided I'd try really hard and make myself a credit to you."

I felt a lump come into my throat. "Why, Queenie, I'm impressed and pleased. And I hear that you are a good cook too. I never knew that."

She made a face. "Not really, miss. I just know how to make a couple of things and custard is one of them. And I did knock over a jug of milk, but luckily the cat lapped it up before Mr. Treadwell saw."

As she spoke, she helped me out of my dress and hung it in the wardrobe. Then she helped me on with my night-dress. "Anything else, my lady?" she asked.

"No, thank you, Queenie. You can go to bed now," I said. I felt a great bubble of happiness inside. Queenie was going to turn into a real lady's maid and Fig was going to have to approve, and I would never have to worry. . . . I slid under the covers and recoiled as my foot touched warm wetness. I turned back the sheets.

"Queenie!" I called as she was disappearing down the hall. She came running back.

"Yes, my lady?" she asked sweetly.

"My bed has turned into a lake. You didn't put the stopper on the hot water bottle properly," I said.

"Nobody's perfect," she replied.

We spent the next hour drying the sheets in front of the fire. Luckily the moisture hadn't been there long enough to soak into the mattress but I was cold, tired and crotchety by the time I finally went to bed. Would she ever cease to be a liability, I wondered. How could I keep her as my maid if and when I married Darcy?

Chapter 33

The next morning we woke to a Christmas card scene with a sparkling snowy landscape and smoke curling from cottage chimneys. Darcy came over around ten, announcing that the snow was already starting to melt and it should be safe to drive where we wanted to go. We debated what we could possibly do until we got more news from Mr. Lennox at the embassy. Zou Zou was all for driving around and trying to locate Professor Peabody or the young priest. Darcy looked doubtful. "They could be anywhere by now and we don't know when all the roads will be clear. I'm afraid we'll just have to sit and wait."

"At least we can go and check on my poor little aeroplane," Zou Zou said. "I want to know if it's still in one piece."

"Are planes not supposed to withstand the elements?" Darcy asked, looking amused.

"A little rain maybe, but not mountains of snow."

We drove toward the village. Men were still working at

the site of the accident. A winch had now been attached to the taxi and they were attempting to haul it out as rushing water splashed over it. We skirted them and drove cautiously up the hill. As we passed through the village I spotted Mrs. Murphy standing outside the Harp, chatting with some women.

"Wait," I said, touching Darcy's arm. "I've just thought of something that might shed some light on poor Barney's death. I won't be a minute." I got out of the car and hurried over to the pub. Mrs. Murphy was about to go in at the side door when I caught up with her.

She turned back as I called her name. "I was wondering whether the American man's servant, Mickey Riley, often comes into your pub in the evening."

She nodded. "He's been coming here for all his meals since the tragedy. Never says a word, though, or talks with the local men. Keeps himself to himself. Eats in a corner and then goes again. Unfriendly type, I'd say."

"I think I saw him going into your pub yesterday evening," I said. "Do you happen to remember what time he left?" I asked.

She shook her head. "It was a busy night, my dear. We're always run off our feet these days, what with all the visitors from out of town. I remember seeing him, but that's about it."

So I was none the wiser when I returned to Darcy and Zou Zou. Then Zou Zou insisted she had to visit her aeroplane to make sure it was all right. This time the constable on duty waved us past. Apart from a coating of snow on the tarpaulin, the plane seemed to have weathered the storm quite well.

"As soon as the snow melts I'm going to fly around looking for this Professor Peabody," she said. "I could cover so much more ground than we could in the motorcar."

Darcy had to laugh. "You can't buzz every village, Zou Zou. And I feel you'd be rather conspicuous. We don't want the whole world knowing what we're doing. It would make more sense to ask at the train station and the harbor to see whether he has already left Ireland."

"You spoil all the fun," she said.

Lord Kilhenny opened the door warily, peered around it and scowled. "Oh, it's you," he said. "What do you want?"

"What a charming greeting," Zou Zou said. "Did you really mean to say, 'Oh, how wonderful to see my son and his friends'?"

I thought I saw a smile twitch at the corners of his mouth and realized I had rarely seen him smile once. "I suppose you want to come in," he said, "but I can tell you, you won't make me change my mind about accepting charity and this barrister I can't afford to pay."

"You'd rather hang, would you?" Zou Zou said. "Your choice, of course. If it were me, I'd choose life."

"Because you have plenty to live for," he said.

"Recently, yes, but only because I came through incredible darkness, just like you. I saw my husband hacked to pieces. I had to flee for my life with just the clothes on my back. I had to rely on the charity of others to get me out of Poland, across Europe and to England, where I was made welcome by people who didn't know me. I spoke good French but little English. I had to start from square one with my life, and look at me now."

He was looking at her. He nodded. "You've turned out quite well."

"I should bloody well say so," she replied and he actually laughed.

"But we won't talk of barristers or crime today," she said." And we come with a special request. Your aunt Oona wants you to join us for luncheon. It's leg of lamb. The Rolls is waiting outside, but we'll wait for you to dress more suitably."

"Is this Aunt Oona's idea or yours?" he asked.

"The request came from your aunt originally but I added mine to it." She looked at him long and hard. "Will you come?"

"Very well," he said gruffly. "I am fond of roast lamb."

Zou Zou shot a look of triumph at Darcy and me. We

were waiting in the sitting room when there was a knock at the door. Darcy went to answer it.

"Good morning, sir," said a very Irish voice. "Are you the owner of the house?"

"I am not," Darcy said. "What do you want with him?"

Curiosity got the better of me. I tiptoed to the door, followed in hot pursuit by Zou Zou, and peeked around it. A young priest was standing there.

"It's the annual collection for the children in the slums," he said. "We try to provide some Christmas cheer for those in need."

"Were you here once before?" Darcy asked. "A week or so ago?"

"No, that would have been Father Brendan. But he marked that there was nobody at this house at the time, so I've been sent out to do the follow-up, so to speak."

"Did Father Brendan try to go to the castle?" Darcy asked.

"He did. He thought that there might be a generous donation because he'd heard that a rich American had moved in, and Americans are known to be free with their money. But he never got past the gate, I'm afraid."

Zou Zou pushed past me. "A donation you're wanting?" she said and pushed a pound note into the tin that he carried.

Like other men we had encountered while with Zou Zou, the priest actually blushed. "You're most generous," he said. "God bless you."

"Well." Darcy turned to me as he shut the door behind our visitor. "So the priest was genuine."

"Makes one wonder whether Professor Peabody will also turn out to be who he said he was," I said.

"What about the University of Southern Nebraska?" Darcy asked.

"I suppose the girls at the dig could have got the name of the university wrong," I suggested. "Which means either that an unknown person was responsible for the murder or Mickey acted alone."

"I'm coming to believe the latter," Darcy said. "Maybe he was waiting for orders from America before he did the deed."

I shook my head. "I still wonder why he went to all that trouble when you could so easily make a death look like an accident in an old castle."

"We'll find out more when—" He broke off as his father came down the stairs. Lord Kilhenny had changed into a dark suit and looked remarkably handsome. And quite young too.

Zou Zou went over to him. "Well, that's more like it," she said. And to my astonishment she slipped her arm through his and escorted him out to the motorcar.

Oona was equally impressed when we arrived with him. "I never thought I'd live to see the day," she said, her round face alight with joy. "Come in. Come in." She pushed the dogs aside. "Dooley, look who has come to eat with us. Such a celebration."

"Not exactly a celebration, dear Aunt," Darcy's father said. "I'm still out on bail with a charge of murder hanging over me. But I thought I should make peace if I'm about to meet my maker."

"Don't say that," Oona said. "You've got a good team on your side now. And you have the truth too."

With that we went into a splendid luncheon. Queenie helped to serve and didn't spill anything. All in all, a day of miracles.

Chapter 34

FRIDAY, DECEMBER 7, AND LATER THE FOLLOWING WEEKEND

After so much frantic activity, we sit and wait. This is hard.

By the next morning the snow had turned to rain and the last traces of snow were rapidly being washed away. A gloomy dark day when a roaring fire and a hot cup of tea seemed like the best idea. Darcy came over after breakfast, saying that he had been into the village to telephone Sir Grenville and suggested that no meeting with my father should be arranged until we had more information from America. Zou Zou acknowledged that this was a smart move, giving us time to make him see sense. Nobody apart from her felt like scouring the countryside looking for Professor Peabody, but she made us agree that it was something we could do while we waited. I suggested that we might try Trinity College itself to see if he had presented his credentials there, which any visiting academic would surely do. That way we'd know if he was a fake.

So we bundled into the car and drove through the rain. We ascertained that nobody of that name had visited the history or archeology departments. In fact we ran into our two graduate students who had been kept from their dig by the weather. From them we got a little more detailed description with which we then tackled the Dublin train station. A ticket collector did remember a large American gentleman asking for the train to Kilhenny, but then he added that the destination seemed popular with Americans these days. So not a definitive identification.

We were tempted to go to the embassy but realized that it was still too early in the day for any results from Chicago. We'd just have to wait and be patient. We went back to Kildare and asked at the local pubs to see if Professor Peabody had stayed there, but drew a blank. So we returned to Mountjoy. It was hard to be patient and do nothing, but everything now hinged on the results from America.

"I don't suppose anything will happen over the weekend," Darcy said.

Aunt Oona frowned at him. "What a horrid Americanism, Darcy. Where did you learn such a word?"

Darcy was amused. "You mean 'weekend'?"

"Absolutely."

"Well, it does nicely define the two days when not much is going to happen and we'll be stuck here."

"You make it sound like a penance," Aunt Oona said. "Speaking of which, you can all come to church with us on Sunday."

Darcy shot me a look. "We have Georgie with us," he said. "She won't want to—"

"I'll come too," I said. "Will your father want to join us?"

Darcy shook his head. "He rejected the church long ago."

"Stupid man," Zou Zou said. "Rejecting everything and everyone who could give him comfort and solace. Someone needs to make him see sense."

So on Sunday morning we all piled into the Rolls and joined the villagers of Kilhenny in the little church. It was strange to hear the Latin chanted and to watch the smoke of incense curling up and hovering in the cold air. Strange, but somehow special in a way that church services had never seemed when I was growing up. We got plenty of inquisitive stares and after mass the villagers came up to Darcy, shaking his hand and wishing him well. It was quite moving to see how well liked he was and how the inhabitants of Kilhenny village still felt an attachment and obligation to the O'Mara family.

After mass Oona insisted on visiting Darcy's father, but he had sunk back into a black mood and didn't want our company. We drove home feeling subdued and spent a rainy afternoon with each of us wrapped up in our own thoughts.

When we heard nothing on Monday, I began to worry that they would find no information on the true identity of Timothy Roach or that the background of Mickey Riley raised no red flags. In that case Chief Inspector Callahan would be anxious to push ahead with the trial. We were a gloomy lot at dinner that night. Oona hadn't dared to invite her nephew to join us again, and Darcy had chosen to eat with his father.

Thus we were most surprised when at nine o'clock, as we were sitting by the fire, enjoying a cup of coffee after dinner, there came a thunderous knocking at the front door that set the dogs barking furiously.

"What in heaven's name?" Oona demanded.

"I'll go," Dooley said, getting up hurriedly.

"You? You couldn't deter a mouse, my darling," she said. "I present a much more formidable figure." And she strode toward the door. We waited, holding our breath, for bad news. Then we heard Oona's deep, booming voice. "Ye gods, Darcy, you scared the pants off us, banging on the door like that."

"I came as soon as I got the news," he said breathlessly. "Mr. Lennox just sent me a telegram. He's heard from Chicago. And he's driving out to meet with us in the morning."

It was hard to sleep that night. Tomorrow we would perhaps learn the truth and maybe exonerate Lord Kilhenny for good. I was up early, put on my coat and walked around the property to try to tame that excess energy. It was a typical old-fashioned estate with a large kitchen garden growing rows of cabbages and cauliflower, a few sheep, a couple of cows and chickens and ducks all over the place. The thought crossed my mind that I could be happy in such a place as this. I met Oona herself coming back from the henhouse with the day's eggs.

"Not laying well in the winter, I'm afraid," she said. "Can't say that I blame them." She gave me an inquiring stare. "You're out early. Excited about what the day will bring, or worried?"

"Hopeful," I said.

She nodded as if she understood. "Any idiot could tell that Thaddy didn't kill anyone," she said. "Unfortunately some juries have their fair share of idiots."

We walked back to the house together and breakfasted on fried eggs and bacon. The princess joined us just as we were on the toast and marmalade. She looked composed, elegant and serene, as if her biggest task today would be shopping at Harrods. I waited impatiently until Darcy arrived at ten, and we all drove back to the lodge. On our way down the drive we passed Queenie, walking with a shopping basket over her arm.

"Should we give her a ride?" Darcy asked. He slowed the car. "Where are you off to, Queenie?" he asked.

"Lady Whyte was out of some things we needed for baking," Queenie said, "so I said I'd go into the village for her."

"Jump in, we'll give you a lift," Darcy said.

"Oh, thank you, sir. Most kind," she said, blushing scarlet, and climbed in beside the princess. Again I waited for something disastrous to happen, like snagging her basket on Zou Zou's silk stockings, but miraculously we dropped Queenie off in the village with no ill effects. A new leaf was definitely turning.

Lord Kilhenny was looking tense and drawn, staring into the crackling flames as we sat around the fire at the lodge waiting for Mr. Lennox to arrive. None of us spoke much, each wrapped in our own thoughts and worries. Mr. Lennox came before eleven. He still had that serious look on his face, like an anxious schoolboy, and we couldn't tell if he brought good news or bad.

"Okay, this is what we know so far," he said, stretching out his long legs as he sat across from us. "Still no identification on the dead man. Naturally his face matches no pictures we have on our wanted files, so I think we can confirm that he had facial surgery done. And we have no real fingerprints. However . . ." And he paused for effect. "We have a match on Mickey Riley."

"I knew it!" I gave Darcy an excited smile.

"He's a small-time gangster called Mickey 'the Weasel' McHenry. Small potatoes, as I said. On the fringes of big crime. Acts as driver, lookout, that kind of thing. Has done time for receiving stolen goods, participating in a robbery."

"So a criminal element is involved in this," Darcy said.

"Almost certainly. So the question is still, who was the dead man, and who wanted to kill him?"

"As I mentioned before, the only suspicious person who was seen near the castle recently is the one who called himself Professor Peabody," Darcy said. "We checked with Trinity College and he was not known there. And we have a better description of him now: about six foot two, not fat but stocky, large head, sagging jowls and a bulldog look to him."

Lennox was actually smiling. "I knew it! That's a good description of Lofty Schultz," he said.

We looked at him expectantly.

"Lofty Schultz, member of the Lake Shore Gang. They had been a powerful force in Chicago crime since the twenties. Made their first money in bootlegging rackets. Then, when liquor was made legal again, they set their sights on bigger things." He paused, taking a deep breath. "In 1929, before the crash, they pulled off the heist of a US mail truck containing cash, bonds and jewelry. Two million dollars' worth of assets."

Darcy whistled.

"Which was never recovered," Lennox went on. "They

took off in a getaway van, leaving Lofty Schultz behind. He was arrested. There wasn't enough evidence to pin that crime on him and he was sent to Leavenworth federal prison in Kansas for five years on a lesser charge of tax evasion. He was released after four years for good behavior."

"So what happened to the money and the rest of the gang?" Zou Zou asked. She had seemed composed at first, but now she was sitting on the edge of her seat.

"The gang split up. We think Weasel McHenry was the driver but again it was never proved. We think the gang leader's girlfriend, Lola Martinez, was the one who made sweet with a contact at the US post office and got the information on when the shipment was going to be sent. Neither of them was caught or prosecuted and both seemed to have vanished off the face of the earth. However, two of the big players were caught. Skeets Kelly—we reckon he pulled the trigger that shot the mail truck driver—and Bugsy Barker. Bugsy was the gang leader. He masterminded the whole thing. They were both sentenced to life and later moved to the federal prison on Alcatraz. That's an island prison in San Francisco Bay. No one has ever escaped from it. The freezing water and the currents make swimming impossible for more than a few minutes."

"So they are still there?" I asked.

Lennox shook his head. "A few months after they were sentenced they managed to escape. They cut their way into a ventilation shaft, went down a wall on a rope and swam for it. Through the grapevine we believed they had arranged a boat to be waiting for them, but there was a high wind that night, and the water was quite rough. We found Skeets Kelly's body washed up on the San Francisco shoreline. Bugsy was never found, presumed drowned."

"And the contents of the mail truck?" Darcy asked.

"Never found, either."

He looked around us with satisfaction.

"So you think that the man who called himself Timothy Roach was really Bugsy Barker?" Darcy said, his voice sounding unsteady. "He didn't drown, but was rescued by the boat?"

Lennox nodded. "We're beginning to consider that possibility."

"Of course," I exclaimed as something struck me, then flushed as all eyes turned to me. "Bugsy, and he chooses the name Roach. Isn't it funny how often people give themselves away in their choice of names?"

"Well done." Mr. Lennox looked at me with new appreciation. "Quite astute."

"Then if Professor Peabody was really this Lofty person," Zou Zou chimed in, "he discovered who Roach was and came to seek revenge for being left behind and for leaving their fellow gang member to drown."

Lennox nodded again. "But I think it's more likely that Lofty came to find out where the rest of the loot was hidden. Obviously Bugsy/Roach used some of the cash to buy the property. But none of the bonds or jewels have turned up yet."

"You think Bugsy brought them with him to Ireland and has hidden them in the castle?" I asked. "Do you think Mickey was sent to find them? Or do you think that Bugsy was doing him a favor by hiding him over here?"

"The latter, probably," Mr. Lennox said.

"Until Lofty showed up, posing as Professor Peabody, and persuaded him to help find the bonds and jewels." Zou Zou clapped her hands like a delighted child.

"Or threatened to go to the police and expose him," I added.

"So he had to have let Lofty in, planted evidence against my father, and got Lofty away again after they killed Bugsy," Darcy said.

All this time Lord Kilhenny had sat silent and brooding, staring into the fire as if he was in his own world. Now he looked up. "Let me get this straight," he said. "The man who called himself Timothy Roach was really Bugsy Something, leader of a gang. And Mickey and this professor chap are really former gang members?"

"That's correct," Lennox said.

Darcy's father continued to stare into the flames. "Can any of this be proven?" he asked.

"I've already asked the Garda to arrest Mickey Riley, alias Mickey Weasel McHenry," Lennox said. "I think he's the kind of small-time crook who will squeal."

"Crook and squeal? Don't you love the terminology? It's like living in an American film," Zou Zou said happily. "I am glad I decided to fly over to join you. I wouldn't have missed this for the world."

Chapter 35

News at last and hope that this may soon be all over.

Mr. Lennox rose to his feet. "I'll keep you informed as soon as we learn more," he said. "We need to take a closer look at the corpse. It's possible there are dental records or small scars on the body that would positively identify him. And in the meantime I'll ask the local police to put their best effort into locating Professor Peabody, and I'll certainly want to be present when they question Weasel McHenry."

Lord Kilhenny also stood up. "Thank you. I'm most grateful," he said gruffly.

"My pleasure, sir."

Lord Kilhenny was escorting him to the front door when there was a knocking.

"What now?" we heard him bark as he opened the door.

"Lord Kilhenny?" the voice said. "I've been asked by Chief Inspector Callahan to bring you to Dublin."

"What for this time, may one ask?" Darcy's father's voice was tense.

"I can't exactly say, sir. I was only told to bring in Lord Kilhenny. The chief inspector wishes to ask some further questions."

"We have been over this again and again," Lord Kilhenny said angrily. "I have told the Garda everything that I know."

Darcy was out of his seat and joined his father in the front hall. "I'll come with you, Father."

"I'm afraid that won't be possible, sir," the Garda constable said.

"Father, you are to say nothing more without a lawyer present," Darcy said. "You've already done yourself enough damage."

Lord Kilhenny hesitated. Mr. Lennox now also stepped behind Darcy. "I'm from the US embassy, and I thought we agreed that we would wait until we had more evidence from the States before we proceeded in this case. Why don't I drive Lord Kilhenny to your headquarters and I can be present at any questioning, since it concerns my country."

"I'm sorry, sir." The constable's voice came again. "But I was told to fetch Lord Kilhenny and I have to do just that."

"Then I'll come in a separate motorcar with you, Mr. Lennox," Darcy said.

The princess jumped up and ran out to them. "I have a better idea, Darcy. Why don't I go with Mr. Lennox, and we can swing by to pick up Sir Grenville if we feel it's necessary? You stay with Georgie. It will only annoy that inspector if too many of us are there."

"Oh no, Alexandra," Darcy said, "I think it's my place—"

But Lord Kilhenny cut in, saying, "No, she's right, my boy. You stay here with Georgie. If anyone can make that inspector behave like a civilized human being, it will be Alexandra."

Darcy turned to give me a quizzical look. "Very well, Father, if that's what you want," he said. We watched them go.

"I do believe he's sweet on her," he said as he closed the door. "I hope it won't lead to disappointment. She's quite out of his league."

"I don't know," I said. "I rather suspect she has developed a soft spot for him."

"Only in the way that one does when one rescues a drowning kitten, I fear. She has a big heart."

I nodded and said nothing more.

"So we were right about Mickey Riley," Darcy said. "I knew that he'd never make a manservant. I hope they are able to pin the murder on him—" He broke off as there were footsteps outside and a loud rap on the knocker.

"Now what?" Darcy said. "They've probably come back because Zou Zou has forgotten her powder compact." He strode back to the door and opened it. Yet another Garda officer was standing there, and there were two police vehicles in the lane.

"I wonder if you can help us, sir," the Garda constable said. "We were sent to bring in a man called Mickey Riley who was working at the castle. But the gate is locked and we can't raise anyone inside to open it. So we wondered, is there perhaps another way in?"

"Of course," Darcy said. "Follow me."

I came too. I wasn't about to be left out of the fun. Darcy led them to the little door in the wall.

"Presumably you'll need to get into the castle, won't you?" he asked. "It doesn't exactly have the sort of doors you can kick down."

"Can you help us with that, sir?"

"I believe my father still has a key to the servants' quarters," Darcy said. "Let me go and see if I can find it."

"Much appreciated, sir. We'll wait."

Darcy went back to the lodge. He wasn't gone long and came out bearing a large key on a ring. As he passed me he said, "You wait inside, Georgie. This man may well be armed. I don't want you in danger."

Then he led the Garda officers through the estate to the castle. Of course I followed behind. The grounds were soggy underfoot and we squelched through mud. Patches of snow still lingered under big Scotch pine trees. A bitter wind swept through the trees, rattling bare branches. Darcy led the way to the back of the castle, then went down a narrow flight of steps. They were moss covered and quite slippery. Water dripped down from above. He put the key in a weathered door and it opened with an ominous creak.

"This leads through the cellars and up to the kitchen," he said in a low voice. "You should go cautiously from here on. This man may be armed."

I saw the constables look at each other with concern. Darcy went into the dark interior with them. I was reluctant to follow but also too curious to stay behind outside. The passageway smelled damp and musty and very old. We passed rooms that looked more like dungeons than cellars. I suppose that was what they were once. Then up a winding stone stair and we were all at once in a mammoth kitchen with a flagstone floor and a row of copper pots hanging over an old-fashioned stove. There was no sign of food having been prepared recently. I remembered that Mickey had taken his meals at the pub. Maybe he was on his way there for his lunch now. I decided I should mention this and touched the nearest constable on the shoulder, making him yell out and leap as if burned. The others all reacted with fear. Darcy frowned when he saw me. "I told you to stay behind."

"I didn't want to miss out on the fun," I said. "And I wanted to mention that Mickey Riley has been taking all his meals at the pub recently. Have you asked about him there?"

"We did," one of them said. "The landlady says she hasn't seen him since Wednesday night."

When Barney's taxi went into the river. So my hunch was right. Or maybe he met up with Lofty and they killed Barney together. That gave them five whole days to be well clear of here. We went from the kitchen past the butler's pantry, the laundry room, various storerooms.

"He's not down here," one of Garda constables said. "Where would his bedroom be?"

"Presumably on the third or fourth floor," Darcy said and led us up a flight of stairs and through a baize door to the main part of the castle. Here we were in tall vaulted hallways. Banners and tapestries hung from the walls. It was bitterly cold. Clearly no fire had been lit for a long while, and the space had that abandoned feeling. I realized how hard it must be for Darcy to come back to his family home like this. The dining room, sitting room, several other reception rooms all lay cold and unoccupied. There was a pretty morning room at the back of the castle that had bigger windows and a view over the grounds to the distant hills. We went up a broad curved staircase to the next floor. Here was a gallery with a fireplace big enough to roast an ox at its center. The walls were decorated with displays of weapons—swords, spears, battle-axes and shields. Beyond it was the library where Bugsy's body had been found.

We went up again to bedrooms. At the back of the house was a nursery with an old-fashioned rocking horse and a big dollhouse. I pictured Darcy riding that horse, a happy, adventurous little boy until tragedy struck his family. Up a narrow stair this time and we were in a plain corridor of simple rooms. This dated back to the time when there were plenty of servants to make this vast place run smoothly. But none of the rooms showed any sign that they had been occupied recently. We all came to the same conclusion. Mickey Riley had fled.

As the Garda vehicles drove away, Darcy and I looked at each other, each thinking the same thing: the castle was unoccupied.

"Now might be a good time to search for anything Mickey might have left behind, oh and the missing bonds and jewels."

"I thought you'd searched the place with Chief Inspector Callahan," I said.

"Another look can't hurt," Darcy said. "Are you game?"

We went back inside and I followed him as he checked every known hiding place in the lower level, then the ground floor. We found nothing and ascended the staircase to the first floor.

"I wonder if there was a reason he was killed in the library," Darcy said, going into that room and switching on the electric light.

"The club was lying on the table in there," I said. "Remember your father picked it up that afternoon."

"I wonder why he was planning to sell it." Darcy stared at the table as if willing the club to appear.

"Maybe he was short of cash," I suggested, making Darcy laugh.

"With two million dollars in his pocket?" he asked me.

"Maybe the majority of that heist wasn't in the form of cash. Maybe he used the cash to buy the castle and racing stable. But we know he gambled on horse racing. Perhaps he had actually used up his money but couldn't do anything with the bonds or jewelry for fear of giving himself away."

Darcy nodded. "That's possible." He looked around at the library walls. "Do you think we should check all the books to see if any of them have been hollowed out? They'd make good hiding places, wouldn't they?"

I stared around the book-lined walls in dismay. "That would take forever."

"I'm going to start on it anyway," he said. "Some of these big tomes here." He lifted down a large leather-bound book.

"I don't think he'd go to all that trouble in his own house," I said. "There must be easier places."

I walked back out into the long gallery, staring up at the weapons on the walls. Then my eye moved to the great fireplace. If I wanted to hide something, might I not shove it up a chimney? As I walked toward it I saw something shining ahead of me as a shaft of slanted sunlight suddenly shone in through a window. It was one of the knobs of the big brass fender. The strange thing was that the other knob was dull and dusty. Which made no sense, unless . . .

"Darcy!" I called. "Look at this!"

Darcy came to join me.

"This knob has been polished, but the one at the other end hasn't. Why do you think that is?"

"Someone had reason to wipe it clean," he said slowly. I nodded.

"What if he wasn't killed with the club at all? What if he was pushed or fell backward and hit his head on the fender?"

"But that could be classed as an accident," Darcy said. "Why turn it into a crime?"

"Because someone wanted to make it look as if your father was guilty, because he had the good motive. Everyone here knew he was sacked after the doping scandal. It would be a local crime and nobody would look into American connections too deeply."

"Perhaps they hadn't meant to kill Roach at all," Darcy went on. "Perhaps there was a struggle when this Lofty fellow showed up and wanted a share of the profits and threatened to expose Roach." He got down on his knees and examined the Persian rug on the floor. Then he lifted it and gave a small cry of glee. "We're right, Georgie. Look, some blood has seeped through to the other side. He did die here. And was dragged or carried through to the library, where blood from the wound was transferred onto the club."

"Unfortunately that doesn't prove that your father didn't do it," I said. "He could easily have shoved Bugsy. We have to just pray that they find the other two gang members."

"And that they talk," Darcy said grimly. Then he added, "You know, I'm sure the library used to be bigger. Not just because I remember it as a child. My sister and I used to build forts with books when my father wasn't around and we would both lie on the floor over there. Now there isn't enough room." He stopped, thinking. Then he went to the far wall, pulled out some books and rapped on the back of the bookcase. It made a hollow sort of sound.

"Look at this, Georgie," Darcy exclaimed. "These shelves are newly made—not from good old oak like the rest, but ordinary pine."

I ran over to join him. We pulled out more books and in the corner there was a lever. Darcy pulled on it and books fell to the floor as a section of bookshelf swung open. Behind it was a narrow space stacked with boxes.

"What's the betting these are the bonds?" Darcy said. "I wonder if there are any jewels in here too."

"Be careful," I said as he squeezed himself into the space. "It's awfully dark in there."

"Bring the table lamp over," he said. "It has a long cord. That will give me more light."

I picked it up and held it as close as I could to the narrow opening.

"They are bonds all right," he said. He opened a suitcase and whistled. "And US dollar bills as well. Look at these. Hundred-dollar bills! Of course, he couldn't change US currency over here. But I don't see any jewels, unless . . ."

"How convenient," said a voice behind us. "So good of you to do the spadework for me."

I almost dropped the lamp I was holding as I spun around. A woman was standing a few feet away from me, holding a gun that was pointed directly at me. I blinked as I recognized her. The American reporter who had shown such an interest in me.

"You really have made it easy for me," she said. "Showing me the way into the castle. Trust me, I've tried to get in ever since I arrived in Ireland. Just hand me that suitcase with the cash in it, honey. I don't think I'll bother with the bonds. Too messy. And I expect I'll find the jewels if I look long enough. There was a bag of cut diamonds and another one of rubies. Small enough to hide almost anywhere."

"I know who you are," I blurted out. "You must be Lola Martinez, Bugsy's girlfriend." So that was why the blond hair had looked wrong on her. She didn't have the skin tone for it.

"Ex-girlfriend, honey," she said. "I set the whole thing up for him, then the rat disappeared and left me without a bean. I thought he'd drowned. I couldn't believe it when I heard from Dr. Meyer that he was alive and in Ireland."

"So you came and killed him."

"Me? Hey, I didn't kill him," she said. "I might have, if I'd found a way to get into this place. But Lofty must have got to him first." She frowned. "But I don't have time to hang around chatting with you. Give me the suitcase."

She was waving the gun at me impatiently. Darcy passed it to me and I to her. I was trying desperately to think of anything I could do to stop her, but Darcy was trapped behind me in the narrow space and I was holding a lamp in one hand. What was more, my brain was refusing to cooperate. It seemed the only safe thing to do was comply. I held out the suitcase. She snatched the case from me. "Put down that lamp," she commanded. I put it down. "Get in there."

Then without warning she shoved me backward. As I lost my footing and staggered she pulled on the lever. The section of wall swung shut and we were in total darkness.

Chapter 36

Darcy flung himself at the section of wall but it was too late. It had snapped shut. We felt around desperately trying to find a latch on our side but the wood appeared to be smooth. If there was a secret way to open the door from the inside, we couldn't find it.

"I wonder how thick that wood is and whether we can kick our way out," he said. He tried, then muttered a curse. "There's not enough room to exert any force. And I can't straighten my leg."

"We'll be all right, won't we?" I tried to sound more confident than I felt. "Your father and the princess will be back and come looking for us."

"How would they ever think of looking for us here?" I heard the tension in his voice. "And if they were in this room, would they necessarily find the lever that opened the wall?"

"We'd hear them coming and shout," I said.

"If we haven't passed out from lack of oxygen by then," Darcy said. That hadn't occurred to me before. We were essentially sealed into a small space. We'd use up the air supply quickly.

"Could we climb on those boxes and see if we can punch our way out through the ceiling?" I asked.

"Good idea."

We fumbled around in total darkness and I heard Darcy's ragged breath as he hauled himself up. Then he said, "It's no use. I can't reach the ceiling. It was pretty high in this room."

He slithered down again.

"There must be some way . . ." I began but I couldn't think of one. "I love you, Darcy," I whispered. "If I've got to die, I'm glad it's with you."

He slipped an arm around me. "I wonder why I don't find that a comforting thought," he whispered. I rested my head against him, feeling his cheek against mine, and the realization struck me that I might now never know what it was like to be made love to by him. Such a waste. All those times I'd stopped him. And now . . .

"We'll think of something," he said. Even through the thickness of the wall we heard an almighty crash. And a scream. Then as we waited, alert and ready, the wall swung open and we blinked in the light. Queenie stood before us, her eyes as wide as saucers, her face a mask of terror. "Blimey, miss, I thought you was a goner," she said.

I staggered out, breathing hard. "Queenie, what on earth are you doing here?" I demanded. "How did you know?"

"Well, miss, I saw that lady again in the village and she asked me more funny questions about you and Mr. Darcy. Then I saw her heading off in the direction of the castle and I thought I should warn you she was coming so I followed her. And I watched her go after you and sneak into the castle. I didn't think there was any real danger, mind you, until I saw her take out that gun. And I wasn't quite sure what to do then, because I ain't had no real dealings with guns and I didn't want to get shot. So I stayed well hidden, but I was standing behind one of them suits of armor, and when she locked you up and was going to escape I thought I might take out the pike the man in armor was carrying and bash her on the bonce."

"What?" I asked.

"'It her on the 'ead," she clarified. "But the bloody thing wouldn't come loose and then when I yanked it hard, the whole ruddy thing toppled over. And the helmet came flying off and bashed that woman on the head as she was going past. She went out like a light."

We went around the corner and there, in the long gallery, Lola Martinez was lying sprawled on the floor. The gun lay a few feet away from her. Darcy leaped to retrieve it.

"We need something to tie her up with," he said.

"The cord from the lamp will do for now." I ran to retrieve it, yanking it from the socket. As I drew her arms together she suddenly came back to life and turned on me like a wild thing, clawing and scratching, going for my throat. Darcy tried to grab her as we rolled over together. Queenie ran to the weapons on the wall and took down a shield. As Lola tried to choke me, Queenie brought the shield crashing down on Lola's head. For the second time Lola slumped forward, unconscious. And around me on the floor I heard a tinkling sound, like the pattering of rain. Darcy dragged Lola off me and helped me to my feet. Queenie stood there, still looking scared and amazed. And the floor sparkled with hundreds of cut diamonds.

LATER THAT DAY we assembled together at Mountjoy with Mr. Lennox and Chief Inspector Callahan. Mr. Lennox informed us that a team was being sent over from Washington and Chicago to take charge of the stolen goods found at the castle. Lola Martinez had been taken into custody but was not talking. Mr. Lennox suggested that if she was charged with the murder of Bugsy Barker she might well want to confess to lesser charges, like attempted murder or being an accessory to a robbery. I now suspected it was she who'd killed the taxi driver, Barney. He had obviously remembered that she came to the area before Bugsy/Roach was killed and was foolish enough to mention this to her. But that crime, I'm afraid, could never be proven when it was all too easy to skid off an icy road in the dead of night. It seemed that Mickey and Lofty had been seen crossing into Northern Ireland and had taken the ferry from Belfast to Liverpool two days back. Since they couldn't leave England without taking a boat or an aeroplane, Lennox was confident that they would soon be caught.

Princess Zamanska turned to Inspector Callahan. "In the light of all this evidence, Chief Inspector, I think that you have to agree that Lord Kilhenny did not commit the crime with which you charged him."

Callahan coughed. I could tell it pained him to say what he had to. "It would appear so," he said. "Of course, I personally need to speak with the purported gang members and with the law enforcement officers who can identify them before I can make a final decision."

"So my father is free to come and go as he pleases?" Darcy asked.

"He will need to stay in touch as he is certain to be called to give evidence at a trial," Callahan said.

When the Garda had departed, Oona invited Mr. Lennox to stay to dinner. "We're all very grateful," she said.

"It wasn't me, ma'am. It was your family and friends here who did the hard work," he said. "You should be thanking them."

"So what will happen to the castle and stables now?" Dooley asked. "Surely they won't pass to his next of kin if they were purchased with stolen money?"

"I believe they will become the property of the United States government," Lennox said. "And the government will put the property up for auction, to recoup some of the money."

"Then you must bid on it, Thaddy," Oona said. "Buy back the family home."

Darcy's father gave a sharp laugh. "With what?" he said. "I'm still as poor as a church mouse, Aunt Oona."

"I could ride Sultan in the Boxing Day stakes—it has a

handsome purse for the winner, doesn't it?" Darcy said, his face lighting up with enthusiasm.

"Don't be ridiculous," Lord Kilhenny said, making Darcy flush with embarrassed anger.

"I'm one of the few people who can ride Sultan," he said.

"You might ride well, my boy, but you're an amateur," Lord Kilhenny said, "and you weigh more than a jockey. Besides, the stables and horses do not belong to us. And the purse may be handsome but nothing like enough to buy back the castle."

"Such defeatist talk," Zou Zou said. "I know. You could do what Bugsy was going to, and sell off the Burda club and some other family treasures."

"The club doesn't belong to me," Lord Kilhenny replied gruffly. "It went to that despicable man as part of the estate. Something I would never have agreed to."

Mr. Lennox gave a little cough. "I think we can say that there was never an intention to make personal items part of the estate. We'll agree the club is yours."

"Thank you, but in that case I could never sell it. Something that has been in the family since the dawn of time?"

"Father, wouldn't you want the chance to get our old home back? Isn't that more important than a stupid war club?" Darcy said. "Do you want to live your life in that lodge?"

"He's right, Thaddy," Oona said. "It's nice to have family heirlooms, but how many times have you looked at it in the past twenty years? And isn't a home the most important thing? Where will your children live and raise their families one day?" And she looked at Darcy and me.

"I suppose you're right," Lord Kilhenny admitted grudgingly, "but surely those odd things are not going to make enough money to buy back the property."

Mr. Lennox coughed, making us realize that he was still part of the group. "I think the US government would be only too delighted to get the property off our hands as soon as possible," he said. "And I think I could arrange it that the auction wasn't well publicized—say on a cold January day?"

Oona burst out laughing. "Mr. Lennox, you must have Irish roots. You're as devious as any of us."

"This calls for a toast. Let's open the champagne," Zou Zou said. "Thaddy is free and has a chance to get his home back. How wonderful."

"I suppose you should fly your contraption back to London while the weather is holding," Lord Kilhenny said.

"Why is everyone so keen to get rid of me!" she demanded. "Anyone would think you didn't enjoy my company."

To my amusement Lord Kilhenny blushed. "It's not that, but I'm sure you have a busy social life waiting for you at home."

"Most of the people at home are absolute bores," she said. "I find it much more fascinating here."

"You're studying us as specimens, are you? Going to write a treatise on the strange habits of the Irish?" Dooley asked with a twinkle in his eye.

"I might." They exchanged a grin.

"I think you should all stay for Christmas," Oona said. "We haven't had a jolly Christmas in years, have we, Dooley?"

"We haven't," he agreed. "Jolly good idea. So what about it? Will you stay?"

Darcy's father looked at the princess.

"I don't see why not," she said.

THE NEXT DAYS were caught up in trips to Dublin, answering more police questions, giving evidence against Lola Martinez and hoping that Mickey and Lofty would be caught. And against this background the Christmas preparations were begun. The pudding was stirred for good luck and silver charms were dropped into the batter. Queenie turned out to be a whiz with pastry and made the best mince pies and sausage rolls.

"That girl is a treasure," Oona said. "I don't suppose you'd let her stay on with me here? Treadwell is as old as I am and I could certainly do with more help around the house."

Those words should have been music to my ears. Life without Queenie. No more dresses ruined. No more lost shoes or beds soaked as a result of unscrewed hot water bottles. No more scathing remarks by Fig. But I found myself saying, "I think it would be up to her, Lady Whyte."

Queenie was called into the room and Oona asked her if she'd like to stay on as cook general. Queenie looked at me. I tried to prevent emotion from showing on my face. Then she shook her head firmly. "I'm sorry, Lady Whyte, but I can't desert Lady Georgiana after she's been so good to me and put up with me making a right cock-up of things. My place is with her."

"Queenie, I don't want to stand in your way," I said. "If you want to get more experience of cooking and running a house, I think you should stay on with Sir Dooley and Lady Whyte. I don't even know where I'll be going after Christmas. I can always call for you if I need you, can't I?"

She looked at Oona and then at me and gave a beaming smile. "Bob's yer uncle, my lady," she said.

THEN ON A sunny day, a week before Christmas, Zou Zou had her little aeroplane wheeled out of the barn and took off for London, but not before she had given Dooley a taste of flight. He came back so excited that he quite forgot about the Duke of Wellington. I wondered if Zou Zou had decided that Christmas would be too boring with us in this backwater after all. And a day later Darcy came to tell me that he had to go away too on an important errand, but promised he'd be back in good time for Christmas. I just prayed he hadn't gone off to Argentina or Mongolia on one of those suspicious errands for the British government. But he returned two days later, looking rather pleased with himself.

"Where did you go to?" I asked. "Or is one not supposed to know?"

He grinned. "I went to London, saw the king's private

secretary and asked him to put the machinery in motion to
have you officially removed from the line of succession. I
gave him a letter to be delivered to Their Majesties, announcing my intention of asking for your hand. So no more
Gretna Green. We're going to do this properly."

I said nothing but simply nodded. He took my hand.
"Georgie, I want you to have a proper wedding. Long white
dress. Bridesmaids. All those things that matter to women."

I had to smile at this statement. "All right," I said. "But
for now we have to wait and see what Their Majesties say.
They could refuse . . ."

"Refuse a splendid chap like me?" he asked. "After I
saved their lives once?"

"They might find another Prince Siegfried for me."

"If another Prince Siegfried shows up, I'll challenge him
to a duel for your hand."

I flung my arms around his neck, laughing. "Oh, Darcy,
you're wonderful."

"You're not so bad yourself," he whispered, nuzzling at
my ear. "You saved my father's life. You wouldn't let go
when I tried to break up with you. You believed in him. You
believed in us."

"Of course I did. You can't just stop loving somebody."
I looked up into those alarming dark blue eyes and then for
a while nothing more was said.

※

MICKEY THE WEASEL was caught trying to board the boat
train to Dover and was more than happy to put the blame
for everything on his former gang members. He claimed
that Lofty had shown up one day in the village, met Mickey
and made Mickey let him into the castle to look for the hidden stash. They had waited until Mrs. McNalley went home
then Mickey had sneaked him in. When he couldn't find any
of the loot, he had confronted Bugsy and threatened to disclose him to the police if he didn't reveal the hiding place
of the stolen goods. A scuffle had ensued. Bugsy had fallen
and hit his head. Lofty had decided that he didn't want the

police looking too closely into their past and that it would be better to pin the crime on someone else. Lord Kilhenny was the obvious suspect.

On Christmas Eve, Zou Zou came back, this time more conventionally in a taxi laden with a Fortnum's hamper, crackers and lots of champagne. We all went to midnight mass and welcomed the holiday with hot buttered rum and Queenie's mince pies. Christmas was the merriest one I remembered. We ate, drank, laughed and played silly parlor games.

"This is what it will be like," I found myself thinking. My family. My new family. We hadn't yet heard back from the king's secretary, but we had been assured it was only a matter of formality. We started talking about a summer wedding, but timed not to interfere with the upcoming royal Silver Jubilee, of course. And after Belinda's baby.

On Christmas Day, Darcy took me aside and gave me a little leather box. Inside was a ruby and diamond ring. "It was my mother's," Darcy said. "My father wants you to have it."

It fitted perfectly. And actually now that we were getting married Darcy treated me with the greatest of respect, although we had plenty of opportunities. It must have been the result of going to confession before Christmas.

And as promised, the auction for the castle was held on a bleak rainy day in January. There was only one bidder—Mr. Leach on behalf of Lord Kilhenny. So the castle went back to its rightful owner. There was just one small fly in the ointment. The stables were not part of the sale. They had been sold off to a private bidder at a fair market value before the auction. Lord Kilhenny was lamenting this fact as we sat together in the castle celebrating his return.

"The blighter better know something about horses," Darcy's father said. "I wonder if he'll let me give him a hand and show him the ropes. I hope it's not some foreigner."

"Oh, but it is," Zou Zou said. "How will you stand it?"

"A damned foreigner? How do you know that?" he snapped.

She gave a delighted laugh. "Because it's me, you silly man. I bought the stables. I told you I'd always wanted to get involved with horse racing, and I knew the stables wouldn't be part of that auction and that there were several parties interested in acquiring them. So I made a little deal with Mr. Lennox, paid a fair price and they were never put up to auction. And I have a favor to ask, dear Thaddy. I know nothing about horses or racing stables. Will you take over and run it for me?"

I saw the conflicting emotions on Lord Kilhenny's face. His wounded pride that someone else had had the money to buy his stables and his relief that Zou Zou had made it safe for him and essentially handed it back to him. He struggled for a moment until Zou Zou said, "How about saying thank you, darling Alexandra, and how happy you are that I'll be part of your life, annoying you for years and years to come?"

He got to his feet and took her hands in his. "You, madam, are a remarkable woman and I am extremely happy that you'll be part of my life, annoying me for years and years to come."

Darcy shot me a glance. It seemed as if there might be more than one wedding in the summer. I couldn't have been happier.

Historical Note

Southern Ireland broke away from the United Kingdom to become the Irish Free State in 1921. Its police force is known as the Garda (guards).

Darcy, having been born a British citizen, has opted to retain loyalty to the UK while his father has opted to become an Irish citizen. In spite of conflicts the two are still closely linked. You do not need to show a passport to travel from England to Ireland and can cross freely between the republic and Northern Ireland.

The American gangster story is based on a real heist of a mail truck in which the gang got away with two million dollars in money, bonds and jewels. They were never recovered. And I have to confess to tweaking history just a little for this story:

Alcatraz did not actually become a federal prison until a year or two after I sent Bugsy there. Sorry if you're a history buff. But after all, it is fiction!

KILHENNY CASTLE, IRELAND
MONDAY. APRIL 8, 1935

Darcy has gone. Not sure what to do next.

I should have known it was too good to last.

I had spent the last two months at Kilhenny Castle, Darcy's ancestral home. I had experienced the merriest Christmas I had ever known, with Darcy, his eccentric family and the Polish princess Zou Zou Zamanska. We had fought hard to prove Lord Kilhenny's innocence when he was wrongly accused of a crime and had managed to gain back his castle. The next month was spent making it habitable again. It had been a wonderful, almost miraculous time to be close to the man I loved, to actually be planning our wedding in the summer. Darcy had also been helping his father to restore the racing stable, now owned by the princess, to its former glory and they had succeeded in winning the gold cup at the races.

But all good things must come to an end. Darcy had never been the sort to stay in one place for long. Neither had the princess. She had flitted between Ireland and London in her little aeroplane as casually as if she was going down to the corner shop for a loaf of bread. Then one day in March she announced that she was leaving to enter a round-the-world air race. Darcy's father, usually never one to let his feelings show, had stomped around miserably for days after she had gone. They were clearly fond of each other, but as far as I knew he hadn't declared his love for her. Perhaps his stupid pride made him think that he didn't have enough to offer her, either in rank or in fortune. Not that she would have cared. Zou Zou, as she liked her friends to call her, was one of the most open and generous people I have ever met. And I think she had definitely fallen for the roguish Lord Kilhenny. Who wouldn't? He had the same rugged good looks and wicked twinkle in his eye as his son!

Then shortly after Zou Zou flew off in her tiny plane, Darcy came to me and said he'd have to leave for a while. He had an assignment that he couldn't refuse. Even though we were engaged to be married he had never revealed to me for whom he was actually working, although he had dropped hints that it was the British secret service.

"How long will you be gone, do you think?" I asked, trying to look light and cheerful.

"I have no idea," he said.

"And I suppose you can't tell me where you'll be going or what you'll be doing?"

He grinned then. "You know I can't. And actually I don't know myself yet."

I stood there, looking at him, thinking how incredibly handsome he was with those wild dark curls and alarming blue eyes. I took his hands. "Darcy, will it be like this when we're married?" I asked and heard a little catch in my voice. "Will you always be going off somewhere and leaving me at home to worry about you?"

"You don't need to worry about me," he said. "I'm a big boy. I can take good care of myself. But as to what I do when we're married, we'll just have to play it by ear. Maybe we'll move back here to the castle and raise our children the way I was raised. But I want to make enough money to provide for you. You know that."

"Yes, I know," I said, fighting back an embarrassing tear, "but I'll miss you."

"I'll miss you too, you silly old thing." He stroked back a curl from my cheek. "I'll be in London first," he added. "I'll make an appointment to see the king's private secretary and see how things are progressing."

He was talking about our wedding, of course. In case you don't know, I am the daughter of the Duke of Rannoch, great-granddaughter to Queen Victoria and second cousin to the king. As such I am part of the line of succession—currently thirty-fifth in line to the throne. And members of the royal family are not allowed by law to marry Catholics. Darcy was a Catholic so the only way to be allowed to marry him was to renounce my claim to the throne. This was all rather silly as there was little likelihood that I'd find myself crowned Queen of England (not unless there was a plague or flood of biblical proportions). But the whole thing had to be done properly. Darcy had presented a petition on my behalf. Then it had to be approved by Parliament. The petition had been presented, but we had heard nothing. So the wedding date was in limbo and it was most unsettling. I rather wished we had managed to reach Gretna Green, as Darcy had once tried to do, and been married in secret.

But left alone in the Irish countryside, doubts now crept into my mind. What if Parliament refused to let me renounce my claim? Could we defy them and marry? We'd have to leave England and live abroad if necessary because I was going to marry Darcy. Nothing was going to stop me. But it was an unsettling time, suddenly finding myself alone at Kilhenny Castle with Darcy's father. He had never been the most genial of men. Now he was clearly worried about Zou Zou so he went around with a scowl on his face and became annoyed by the smallest of things—much the way he had been when I first arrived there in December.

I, in turn, was worried about Darcy, about the future of our marriage and to what dangerous part of the globe he might be sent. More than anything I wondered what I should be doing next. I sensed that Lord Kilhenny welcomed my company and would sink into deeper gloom if I left. And yet I felt lonely, unsettled and out of place in Ireland. I enjoyed visits to Darcy's eccentric great-aunt and great-uncle, who lived in a rambling old house nearby, as well as walks through the countryside, where roadside hedges were now blooming with flowers and the air smelled of spring. But I wanted to be gone.

My thoughts often turned to my friend Belinda who had fled to Italy to have a baby that no one should know about. Was she feeling equally lonely? She had suggested when I last saw her that I come and stay with her in Italy, but I had heard nothing since and had no address in Italy to write to. I hoped she was all right. I also worried about my grandfather in London. I had written to him several times, but had heard nothing in return since Christmas, when I had received a rather lurid card and a box of Quality Street chocolates. I knew he wasn't much of a writer, but I was concerned about his health. He had a weak chest and the London fogs were often brutal in winter. I would have gone to London to visit him, but I had nowhere to stay. My brother, the current duke, owned our family home, Rannoch House on Belgrave Square, but he and my dreaded sister-in-law, Fig, had gone to the south of France for the winter and Fig had made it clear to me that I was not to use their house while they were gone.

Zou Zou had also said that I was always welcome to stay with her when I was in London, but she was on a round-the-world race, which might take months. So I stayed on in Ireland, rushing to the post every morning in the hope of news from somebody. And then one morning I went out for an early walk. It was a perfect spring day. Daffodils were blooming all over the castle grounds. Birds were singing madly in the trees, which now sported new buds. The air smelled fresh and fragrant. It was the sort of day to go for a long ride, but the only horses at Kilhenny these days were at the racing stable, and I didn't think Darcy's father would trust me with one of his prized mounts.

I was halfway down the path to the front gate when I met the postman, coming toward me on his bicycle.

"Top of the morning, my lady," he said, coming to a halt beside me. "'Tis a grand day, is it not? And a letter for yourself from London, no less."

He handed it to me. A fat envelope. I looked for Darcy's black, impatient scrawl, but instead I saw my brother's handwriting. So they were home in England again.

"I see there's a crest on the back of that envelope," the postman said, eyeing it curiously. "So it's from some lord or lady, is it? I expect it's important, then."

He was hovering, waiting for me to open it. Although I was dying to know why my brother might be writing to me after such a long silence, I certainly wasn't going to open it with the postman peering over my shoulder, ready to spread the news to the rest of the village.

"Thank you very much," I said. "I'd better go indoors and read it, hadn't I?"

I saw him watching me with disappointment as I went back up the path to the castle. Once inside I went into the dining room and poured myself a cup of coffee. There was no sign of Darcy's father. He went to the stables at the crack of dawn most mornings and I had become used to eating breakfast alone. I had just sat down when the housekeeper, Mrs. McCarthy, came into the room bringing a dish of smoked haddock.

She started when she saw me. "Oh, your ladyship, I didn't know you were already up, and me with no breakfast ready for you."

"Please don't worry, Mrs. McCarthy," I said. "I was going out for a walk and then I met the postman and he had a letter for me, so I wanted to come inside and read it right away."

"Oh, how lovely. A letter for you." She beamed with pleasure. "It's not from Mr. Darcy himself, is it?"

"Unfortunately, no," I said.

"My, but that's a grand crest on the envelope," she said, hovering behind me with the dish of haddock still in her hands.

"It's from my brother, the Duke of Rannoch," I said.

"Oh, your brother. Well, isn't that grand." She showed no sign of moving away. I was beginning to think that curiosity was a local trait. "No doubt he's got some news for you. That looks like it could be a long letter."

"Well, he's just come back from the south of France," I said. "I expect he's giving me a full report on his time there."

"Oh, the Riviera. Now, isn't that grand? I expect they had a lovely time there. All those yachts and things."

It was quite clear she didn't plan to move.

"Don't you think you should put the dish of haddock onto the warming tray or it will get cold?" I said.

She chuckled. "Would you look at me. I'd quite forgotten I'd got the thing in my hands."

As she headed for the sideboard with the various breakfast dishes on it, I opened the envelope. Two more letters fell out as well as one page of writing paper with the Rannoch crest on it. I read that first.

My dear Georgiana,

I hope this finds you in good health. We were not sure where to send the enclosed, but I'm mailing them to O'Mara's address in Ireland in the hope that you might still be there. We did read in the English newspapers about the amazing turn of events concerning Lord Kilhenny and I must say I am very glad for you that he was cleared of any wrongdoing.

We arrived back from Nice to find the enclosed letters waiting on the hall table. It appears they had been posted some time ago, but the house had been shut up with no servants until we returned home. I see one of the letters comes from Buckingham Palace. I do hope it was nothing urgent. I took the liberty of dropping a line to Their Majesties' private secretary to say we had all been out of the country and I was forwarding the letter to you.

We all had a splendid time at Foggy and Ducky's villa—well, not exactly splendid. It was a trifle crowded. The term "villa" is actually somewhat of an overstatement. It's an ordinary small house on a backstreet in Nice, but is within walking distance of the sea. The water was too cold for bathing, but we took some nice walks. Podge was disgusted that the beach was not sandy, but he's a good little chap and amused himself well.

We'll be in London for a couple of weeks before we head back to Scotland and look forward to hearing from you.

Your affectionate brother,
Binky

I looked up. Mrs. McCarthy had now deposited the haddock on its warming tray and had returned to hover behind me.

"All is well, I trust, your ladyship?" she asked.

I folded the letter. "Thank you, Mrs. McCarthy. All is indeed well. And I think I'll leave the other letters until I've enjoyed your delicious smoked haddock."

I think I heard her sigh as she admitted defeat and went back to the kitchen.

When I had finished my breakfast I retreated to my bedroom and opened the other letters. The royal one first, naturally. It was from the queen, not dictated to a secretary but written with her own hand.

My dear Georgiana,

I trust you are well. I understand from the king's secretary that your young man has indicated that you wish to marry him and, given his Catholic faith, have expressed

*yourself willing to abandon your place in the line of
succession.*

*This is indeed a big step, Georgiana, and one not to
be undertaken without a great deal of thought. I would
expect to hear from your lips that this is indeed your
intention and that you are quite sure of the ramifica-
tions. To that end I hope you will come to the palace and
we can discuss your situation over tea. Please let my
secretary know when might be a convenient date for you.*

His Majesty sends you his warmest wishes, as do I,
                                                 Mary R.

(You'll notice that even in an informal letter to a cousin
she was still Mary Regina. One never stops being a queen.)

I stared at the letter for a long time while my stomach
twisted itself into knots. Did this mean that they might not
approve the marriage, nor give me permission to abandon
my claim to the throne? It all seemed so silly. They had four
healthy sons and already two granddaughters, with the
promise of many more grandchildren to come. I should go
to London immediately and sort things out with her. Let her
know that I intended to marry Darcy no matter what. I felt
my stomach give an extra little twist when that thought
popped into my mind. Queen Mary was a rather terrifying
person. I had never crossed her in my life before. I don't
believe many people have dared to do so. The only exception
being her son and heir, the Prince of Wales. She had let him
know quite clearly that she did not approve of his friendship
with the American woman Mrs. Simpson. Not only was that
lady currently married to someone else, but she had already
been divorced once. The Church of England, of which the
king is the head, does not countenance divorce. I don't think
the queen ever believed that her son would contemplate marriage to such a person. She trusted that he would do the right
thing when the time came and make a suitable match, like
his younger brother George, whose wedding to the Greek
princess Marina I had just attended.

I put that letter on my dressing table, then opened the other. It bore Italian stamps and I noticed the date on the postmark. January 21, 1935. Poor Belinda—she had written to me in January and I hadn't replied.

My dear Georgie,

Well, I have done it! I have fled to Italy as I promised and have rented an adorable little cottage on the shore of Lake Maggiore, just outside the town of Stresa. The views are spectacular. I have oranges growing on my back terrace. I have engaged Francesca, who comes in daily to cook and clean. She is determined to fatten me up and cooks the most divine pastas and cakes. So everything is going as smoothly as one could hope at this moment. Except for the loneliness. You know me—I like to be in the middle of things, out dancing, having fun. And here I am shut away from my own kind, reading books and even knitting during the long evenings. I'm not a very good knitter, I have to confess, and the poor child would be naked were it not for Francesca and her sisters, who have knitted little garments with lightning speed for me.

As to the question of the poor child—I am still in an agony of indecision. I cannot be saddled with a baby. How could I? If word got out I should be spoiled goods for life with no hope of ever marrying well. To be honest, with my past I have little hope of securing the son of a duke or earl, but an American millionaire would do quite well! But what to do with the baby? At least I have made inquiries about a clinic where I can give birth. Not in Italy, definitely. All those Francescas fussing around me!

Fortunately, Lake Maggiore lies half in Italy and half in Switzerland. So all I have to do is take the steamer to the top end of the lake and admit myself to a lovely clean, sterile and efficient Swiss clinic in good time for the birth. Golly, when I write that word I feel most apprehensive. One hears such horror stories.

I sit here on my terrace, watching the ships going up and down the lake, and I think of you. I hope you are with your dear Darcy and all is finally well. I did read in an English newspaper that his father was found to be innocent. Jolly good for you and Darcy, finding out the truth. I'm glad one of us is going to be happy. Do let me know when the wedding will be, won't you?

Or better yet, come over to stay for a while, if Darcy can spare you. You'd love my sweet little house and we'd pick oranges and gossip and laugh just like we did when we were in school together. Please say yes, even if it's only for a week or two. I will happily pay your fare. To be completely honest I wish you could be with me around the time of the birth. It's rather frightening to know that I'll be alone with no relative to hold my hand. Of course my family cannot be told under any circumstances. Can you imagine my stepmother crowing with delight over my downfall and shame? She would probably try to stop me from inheriting Grandmama's money if she knew.

So do write back, dear, dear Georgie. I long to get a letter and long even more to see your smiling face.

> *Your lonely friend,*
> *Belinda*

I put that letter to join the queen's on my dressing table and sat staring out of the window. White clouds raced across the sky. Seagulls wheeled in the strong spring breeze. I pictured Belinda's lake with the orange tree on her terrace and poor Belinda sitting all alone, dreading what lay ahead of her, hoping for a letter or a visit from a friend.

I should go to her, I decided. I'd want my friend to come to my aid if such a thing had happened to me. There was nothing to stop me from going out to Italy if Darcy was away. He hadn't told me how long he'd be gone. I don't suppose he knew it himself. In the past he'd been in such far-flung regions as Australia and Argentina. This time it might be China or Antarctica for all I knew. And Belinda had offered to pay my fare. I now had a small savings account so I could afford to buy the ticket, but that money was for my wedding . . . if it was allowed to happen.

I went over to the wall and tugged on the bell pull. Now that I had come to a decision, I wanted to leave on the next boat before I got cold feet about crossing the Continent alone.

RHYS BOWEN

"Wonderful characters . . . A delight."

—Charlaine Harris, #1 *New York Times* bestselling author

For a complete list of titles,
please visit prh.com/rhysbowen